Denise Barne unpacking he countries and she cares to ones include selling lipstick in a Denver department store, catwalk modelling in Atlanta, assistant to the UN Narcotics Director in Geneva, chauffeuring a Swiss multi-millionaire in Zurich, assistant to an internationally-famous film producer based in London, and cooking in a sanatorium in Germany. The latter gave rise to her first book, *from Bad to Wurst: Bavarian Adventures of a Veggie Cook*.

Back home in England, Denise took up Britain's third most reviled profession – estate agent! Juggling the running of her chain of eight offices in Kent and taking an Honours Degree with Open University, Denise had difficulty pursuing her life-long passion for writing.

To give herself the freedom to write seriously, she sold her business in 2005, but unfortunately to the wrong buyers, namely a couple of tricksters, and *Seller Beware: How Not To Sell Your Business* was the result. This was published by Biteback Publishing in 2013. Denise now has time to resume her love of writing fiction and has written a trilogy called *The Voyagers*, a family saga stretching from 1913–2012, under her pen name, Fenella Forster.

Find Denise on her blog: www.denisebarneswriter.com and follow her on Twitter: @denisebarnesuk.

Praise for *Annie's Story*

'Fenella Forster's saga of emigration, struggle against adversity and shocking family secrets in the early years of the twentieth century is vigorous, vibrant and filled with authentic detail. A thoroughly absorbing, page-turning read.'
– Joanne Walsh, Romance Author

'Fenella Forster's debut novel is a moving and beautifully crafted exploration of the hardships of emigration, especially for women, at the beginning of the twentieth century. It left me thinking about my own identity and roots. It was a joy to read from the first word to the last.'
– Nina Milton, Author

For Carol

THE VOYAGERS

Annie's Story

FENELLA FORSTER

With heartfelt thanks,
Fenella Forster

SilverWood

Published in 2015 by SilverWood Books

SilverWood Books Ltd
30 Queen Charlotte Street, Bristol, BS1 4HJ
www.silverwoodbooks.co.uk

ISBN 978-1-78132-308-3 (paperback)
ISBN 978-1-78132-309-0 (ebook)

British Library Cataloguing in Publication Data
A CIP catalogue record for this book is available from
the British Library

Set in Sabon by SilverWood Books
Printed on responsibly sourced paper

For Nana and Pop – their seven years spent in Australia (1913 – 1920), where my father, Harry, was born, was the inspiration for this novel, though the story is entirely fictitious

PART I

The Decision

1

Bonham Place, Norfolk, England

New Year's Eve 1912

Guests had been arriving for the costume ball since first thing that morning, and in the cold windblown afternoon Annie Ring was stealing five minutes to watch the spectacle from the imposing entrance of Bonham Place. Some of the guests had elected to come in their traditional carriages, but Annie's attention was fixed on the motor cars which scattered the gravel as they proceeded up the long tree-lined drive, the more exuberant chauffeurs causing their wheels to spin, to the delight of the waiting staff. They were definitely the coming thing, Annie thought, as she peeped out from behind a tall footman who was standing at the top of the steps to get a better view. Would *she* ever ride in one?

Annie shot her hand up to stop her cap from flying off her head in the bitter wind, which battered everything in its way as it whipped across the open fields that stretched as far as she could see. She gave a rueful smile as she glanced at the threatening clouds, the notion of the beautiful hat she imagined she was holding on to in one of those motor cars fading fast.

It was no use standing there daydreaming.

She was just about to slip back inside before Mr Stanton, the butler, caught sight of her when she spied a lone figure some way off, sauntering in and out of the trees towards the house. She squinted her eyes, then frowned. There was something about the way the man swung his arms. She narrowed her eyes again and fancied he looked familiar. If only she could see his hair, but this man was wearing a white curled wig. He held himself proudly, giving himself extra inches. That was Ferguson all over. Could it really be him? Her heart thumped. Don't be so ridiculous, she told herself. Ferguson would never be so rash as to walk as bold as you please up the front drive of Bonham Place in his full footman's uniform.

But the thought kept nagging at her. If it *were* him...just supposing...then he wouldn't be the person she thought she was marrying. Someone who would take such a risk with Sir Henry. A risk serious enough to get not only himself sacked but Annie too. She bit her lip as her eyes followed him. His strides quickened and he caught up with a lady and gentleman dressed as Ancient Egyptians. They turned their heads to talk to him and although his features were still blurred, she breathed out a long sigh, chiding herself for thinking such disloyal thoughts about the man she loved. Of course it wasn't Ferguson. Her mind had been playing tricks, that's all. The couple obviously recognised him as one of the guests. Irritation bubbled in her throat that this guest, a member of the aristocracy, should think it amusing to dress as a servant for the fancy dress party. As though he was mocking them. She shrugged. It was none of her business. She'd better get back to work.

A dark-blue Rolls-Royce crunched to a standstill. Mr Stanton, who was about to step forward to greet the alighting guests with his stately manner, suddenly turned. She had no time to duck. His icy glare met her as he stood rooted to the ground, his portly, commanding form unnerving her. Heart pounding, Annie flew up the steps. Drat. He was sure to give her a dressing down that she, the head housemaid, had strayed on to the forbidden ground outside the front entrance. Just as well Mr Stanton had more than enough to keep him busy at the moment.

Most of the guests stopped to admire the magnificent Christmas tree as they swept through the Great Hall, but Annie was disappointed that they barely glanced at the display of marble and plaster sculptures. In the evening shadows, whenever there was a party, the figures always deceived her into thinking there were even more people around. The emperors and their wives, and the various gods and goddesses, would probably enjoy being introduced to everyone, she thought, suppressing a smile. Oh, dear, the long day must be making her light-headed.

After Annie had shown the ladies to their rooms she made her way back to the kitchen, pausing in one of the long servants' corridors which led from the back of the ballroom.

She hunched against the wall and closed her eyes, picturing the scene. Footmen in their best livery would be carrying trays crammed with champagne flutes, handing out glasses to the laughing, chattering ladies and gentlemen.

She strained to hear the quartet of violins above the rise and fall of voices. It was always the same when she heard the first notes; everything receded and she was transported by the music. The Strauss waltz, though faint, was one she instantly recognised: 'Morning Papers'. Her mother had often played it at home on her ancient piano, the yellowing keys staunchly carrying the tune, and it had been one of the many waltzes they both loved. Annie hummed almost under her breath as her foot tapped in time, imagining herself as one of the ladies in a beautiful gown, her jewellery sparkling under the Venetian chandeliers, swept along in the arms of her suitor. If only she could catch a glimpse of them all. She glanced down at her plain grey dress, only partly relieved by an equally long white apron. Annie pulled a face as she tucked a strand of chestnut hair back under her cap.

She imagined Mr Stanton thrusting out his chest as he announced the guests in his loud clear tones. What would it feel like to be a real lady attending such a party with Ferguson at her side? She let her mind drift for a few moments, then pulled herself up. At least Eric, the new third footman, had promised to give an

11

account after the ball. She'd have to be content hearing about it second-hand. As the last notes of the second waltz died away she hastened to the end of the corridor and down the steps, arriving in the kitchen where Mrs Jenner was preparing fresh canapés.

'Oh, it's you, Annie,' she grumbled, as she arranged them on an enormous oval plate. 'Where's that girl, Mollie?'

'I've not seen her,' Annie said. Mollie had seemed off-colour this morning. She would check on her later, but in the meantime there was work to do. Mrs Jenner would need help in the kitchen for the rest of the night.

'She didn't clean and black the range this morning,' Mrs Jenner went on, her mottled face reddening with every word. 'She needs a good talking to, that girl. I'm sorry about the leg an' all, but it don't help me none.' She glanced at Annie. 'That apron's not fit for kitchen work. You'd better put this on if you've come to help.'

Mrs Jenner yanked an enormous apron from the back of the kitchen door and tossed it over. Obediently, Annie slipped it over her slim frame and tied the strings at the back into a bow, while smothering a yawn. She'd been up since half-past five supervising the maids to clean the reception rooms and had given Gladys a hand with preparing the bedrooms. Mrs Morgan, the housekeeper, had been admitted to hospital a fortnight ago, and Annie had had to take on some of her duties.

Mrs Jenner was rushing to do the work of three and supper was now priority. Nothing must be overlooked. Mr Stanton had warned them all that the evening must run like clockwork.

One hour later the door burst open and Eric shot in, sweat trickling from his forehead and running down his nose. He slammed a tray of empty glasses on the draining board, pulled a chair out from the kitchen table and flung his stocky figure on to it. Annie, concentrating on slicing a savoury pie, looked round in alarm. Mrs Jenner had just taken out a dish from the range. She turned and glared at the boy.

'Whatever's the matter? You'll give me a heart attack, coming in like that.'

'Funny you should say that, Cook. It's Mr Stanton. They're sending for a doctor. But it's too late. He's gone.'

'What do you mean – gone?' Mrs Jenner plonked the dish on the table, blowing her fingers and giving the lemon meringue pie a critical once-over.

'He's dead!'

Clutching the edge of the kitchen table, the cook swung her hefty body to face the boy. 'I'll box your ears if you're having me on.'

'Honest truth, Mrs Jenner.'

'Poor Mr Stanton,' Annie said, perfectly meaning it, though she couldn't squash an uncharitable thought that he wouldn't be the only one to get some peace. She looked at Eric. 'Are you sure he's really dead?'

'As a doornail.' Eric snatched one of the canapés, and crammed it into his mouth.

'That's quite enough, Eric,' Mrs Jenner said, leaning over the table and slapping his wrist. 'Them's for upstairs.'

'Sorry, Mrs Jenner. I weren't thinking, what with Mr Stanton and all.'

'To think he's left us to do all the work this weekend.' Mrs Jenner's forehead creased in deep folds, her lips tight as she made no obvious attempt to hide her irritation that the butler had been less than considerate.

Annie put a hand to her mouth to hide a smile. There'd never been any love lost between those two.

'I don't suppose Mr Stanton planned to leave us in the lurch,' Eric grinned.

'You need to watch your tongue, lad.' Mrs Jenner sat down heavily. 'Well, what happened?'

'Drunk as a fiddler's bitch, I thought he was.' Eric's eyes bulged

13

with the delivery of such news. 'But it weren't the booze. It were his heart. All of a sudden he grabbed the tablecloth and keeled over, taking Lady Bonham's best lamp with him. It's a wonder the place i'n't up in flames.'

Annie went back to slicing the pie. She must concentrate. They needed it upstairs. Deftly, she arranged the slices on a platter and rinsed the knife, all the while thinking about the butler. Mr Stanton had ruled the house with a heavy hand. He'd been as right as rain that morning and now he was dead. It didn't seem possible. Who would replace him? The next butler might have an even worse temper. Annie bit her lip. She mustn't think like that. Poor Mr Stanton wasn't even cold—

'One of the toffs,' Eric broke into Annie's thoughts, 'dressed like a footman...he went to the rescue, but he were too late. Fair kicked the bucket, he told Sir Henry. Sure as his name were Ferguson Percy Bishop.'

Annie froze. Surely Eric must have misheard the name. Before she could say a word, Mrs Jenner lurched to her feet.

'Did you say *Ferguson Bishop*?' The cook shot Annie a look of triumph.

Annie felt a suffocating heat crawl over her scalp. That figure coming up the drive – she hadn't been seeing things. It *was* him. She laid the knife down on the bread board. Keep calm, she told herself. Don't let Mrs Jenner notice you're upset. She put her hand out to grasp the back of the nearest chair.

'Yes, that were his name,' Eric said. 'Why? Do you know him?'

Mrs Jenner opened her mouth to reply, but Annie said quietly, 'We're engaged to be married.'

'But...' Eric stared at Annie in awe. 'You mean you're engaged to one of *them*?

'Ferguson is first footman from Hatherleigh Hall,' Annie said sharply, though why she should be explaining her personal circumstances to this new young lad, she had no idea.

'Oh, *now* I see.' Eric threw Annie a sly look.

'See what?' Mrs Jenner demanded, clutching the edge of the table.

'Why he had on his full uniform…to look like he was in fancy dress so he could get into the party, sneaky like. He wanted to give me a note for Annie.'

'Saucy young devil!' Mrs Jenner turned to face Annie, who hadn't moved.

'A note from Ferguson?' Annie swallowed.

'Yes,' Eric said. 'I thought it was queer, one of the toffs tangling with a maid.' He winked at Annie. 'There was quite a few of them dressed like servants – it's the nearest they'll ever get to us. He had me well and truly diddled.'

Annie flushed. Eric was far too outspoken. But what was in the note? Why was it so important that Ferguson had pretended he was one of the guests in order to deliver it? Why had he planned this absurd escapade? Her heart missed a beat as a terrible thought struck her. His employers, Lord and Lady Hamilton, were here tonight, she knew, because Mr Stanton had told the staff who would be attending. Surely they would recognise one of their own footmen. He could lose his job for less. Be turned out of Hatherleigh Hall without a reference. And Sir Henry would take for granted that she was part of the deception. She'd get the sack, no doubt about it. There'd be no reference for her either. Tears of dismay pricked the back of her eyes. Her father would never allow her to marry such a man. Oh, to think Ferguson had blurted out his name in front of Sir Henry.

Her head felt like a pin-cushion as she tried to collect her thoughts. Perhaps nothing would come of it. Sir Henry wouldn't connect a Ferguson Percy Bishop with anyone at Bonham Place, would he? Oh, how could Ferguson be so foolish? She tried to stamp down her anger as she held out an unsteady hand.

'Please give me the note, Eric.'

'Here…' Eric shoved his hand up his sleeve, then pulled a face. He tried the other sleeve. Eyes wide with alarm, he patted his arms and fumbled again. He looked away, his face beetroot. 'Sorry, Annie, it must've dropped out in all the excitement.'

Annie's hand fell to her side. Now she'd never know the contents until she saw him again. It was too bad.

'You'd better find it, young man,' Mrs Jenner flashed, as Eric unbuttoned his waistcoat. A piece of paper floated down.

'That's it,' Eric said, grinning with relief as he bent to retrieve it.

Annie seized it from his hand, and doing her best to ignore the cook's glowering expression, tucked the note into her apron pocket. She was not going to be intimidated. Whatever the message contained, at least she would read it in private.

2

New Year's Day 1913

Annie knelt down to open her bedside cupboard and felt for the small velvet box. She sat on the edge of the sagging armchair and pushed the lid of the box up with her thumb. The six tiny garnets in their flower-like setting glowed softly in the dim light. Gently, she pulled the ring from its tight bed and slipped it on, aware of the smooth feel of the metal, and tilted her hand upwards, spreading her fingers to admire the effect. She wished she could wear her ring all the time – show the world – but of course that was impossible while she was at work. Reluctantly, she took it off and put the box back in its hiding place.

Annie shivered. With the fire already gone out, the cold dug deep into her bones. She glanced at the clock on the mantelpiece and sighed. A quarter to ten. She'd arisen even earlier this morning to make sure all traces of last night's party were swept away. What an evening. The butler having a heart attack, then Ferguson's antics. Whatever had got into him? She bit her lip, and careful not to disturb her cap, smoothed her hair at the sides, and pulled out the crumpled note, which she knew off by heart.

Dearest Annie,

I must see you tomorrow morning. I have something important to tell you.

Do not worry until we meet.

I hope to be at B.P. by 10 o'clock.
Yours ever,
Ferguson Percy Bishop

How could he think she wouldn't worry? The note had such a serious tone, completely unlike Ferguson, who was usually so happy-go-lucky. She churned the questions over and over in her mind. Why had he come to the party under false pretences? Was it just a dare? Had he been caught out? Well, it was no use wondering. He'd be here soon enough. Pinching her cheeks and dabbing her wrists with a touch of lavender water from the precious bottle her sister, Ethel, had given her last year on her eighteenth birthday, she rushed out.

She sped down the three flights of dark winding stairs, her boots clattering as she half ran along the narrow inner hall to the kitchen.

Mrs Jenner stood at the huge scrubbed table, her forehead perspiring from the heat. Her fingers, thickened with years of hard work, flew up and down as she rubbed pieces of fat into the flour, the contents of the cream bowl fast becoming like breadcrumbs.

'Shut the door, girl, you're letting all the cold air in.'

Annie's heart beat faster as she closed the door behind her, and turned into the warmth of the kitchen. Thank goodness they were alone. She drew a deep breath and began:

'Mrs Jenner, Ferguson—'

'What's he want now?' Mrs Jenner didn't bother to look up as she added water and forked the mixture together. 'He's in enough trouble, if you ask me.'

By her tone, Annie could tell Mrs Jenner was still peeved she hadn't been told the contents of Ferguson's letter the evening before. There wasn't too much that escaped Mrs Jenner's sharp brown eyes, but Annie had deliberately not read the note in front of her, despite her fingers itching to pull out the sheet of paper and

18

find out what Ferguson thought he was doing. But at least Mrs Jenner hadn't reported her when she had first found out Annie had a follower. That could have been serious, Annie knew. But things were different now she was engaged. Even Lady Bonham had taken the time to say she hoped Annie would be happy, and added that she would be pleased for her head housemaid to stay on. And Annie had agreed to, relieved she wouldn't have to look for a new position.

Now, facing the cook, Annie drew a shaky breath. 'Ferguson says he's got something important to tell me.'

Mrs Jenner's head jerked up and her eyes alighted on Annie's note, which poked out of her apron pocket. 'Probably breaking off the engagement, I shouldn't wonder,' she sniffed, pausing for a sip of water.

'Oh, please don't say that.' Was that what Ferguson was hinting at? Could he have met someone else? Once or twice, especially when they went dancing, she'd noticed other girls giving him the glad eye, and he'd sometimes returned their smiles, but she hadn't imagined he might be going to break the engagement. She swallowed.

'You're too young anyway.' Mrs Jenner briskly rolled out her pastry. 'He's a bit too cheeky for my liking. And you've not known him long and already you've got yourself engaged. It's all too quick, if you ask me.'

'Lots of people get married far younger than me.' Annie hoped she didn't sound rude. 'We've known one another nearly a year and we haven't set a date yet.'

'You don't know 'em till you marry 'em.' Mrs Jenner pressed the pastry into a pie tin with more than her usual firmness.

Annie risked a question. 'How can you ever tell, until you *do* marry one?'

'You can't. And even when you're married they can still surprise you – and it's not usually a very good surprise, neither.' The cook glared at Annie. 'Can they spare you upstairs?' Annie nodded. 'Well, get this apron on then and be quiet so I can think straight. All this talk about men is doing nothing towards putting lunch on the table. I need you to get the pea soup going for downstairs.'

'Yes, of course, Mrs Jenner.' Annie glanced at the kitchen clock as she pulled one of Mrs Jenner's aprons over her dress. The hands were creeping towards ten o'clock. She put the large basin of peas she'd soaked the night before into a copper saucepan and poured a pan of potato and leek stock over them. She placed the pan on the range and looked at the clock again. It was nearly five past. He was bound to be here in another minute or two. She had to say something right now.

'Mrs Jenner,' she tried again, 'Ferguson has written to ask if he can come over this morning to see me. That was what the note was about. Might I see him alone for a few minutes? I promise not to be long. He'll—'

There was a rap at the back door, followed by an insistent ringing.

'That's probably him now,' Annie said, her heart thumping.

'Why didn't you ask me before?' Mrs Jenner grumbled, taking her irritation out on her pastry for the second pie, pounding it without looking up. 'Well, don't just stand there – let him in! And make sure he wipes his boots thoroughly.'

'I will, Mrs Jenner. May we go into the servants' hall?'

'So long as you're no more 'an ten minutes. And don't cry on my shoulder when he tells you it's off.'

Annie opened the back door and Ferguson stood there smiling his crooked smile, making her pulse race, her anger dissolve. How lucky she was to be betrothed to such a fine-looking young man, with his straw-blond hair and dancing blue eyes. She loved the way his cheeks dimpled when he smiled and the tiny laughter lines at the corners of his eyes. But it wasn't just his looks, she reminded herself. She truly loved him. Loved the way he made her laugh, and the fun they had together on their precious days off. Last night had been a prank. She'd have it out with him; warn him never to do anything

20

like it again, and that would be the end of it. He'd settle once they were married. That was, she thought, her stomach suddenly turning over, unless Mrs Jenner was right and he'd come to break off the engagement. She searched his face for a sign that he was no longer interested.

'Is it all right if I come in, Annie?' He stepped towards her and quickly kissed her cheek.

'I can't be long.' Annie's cheek felt warm from his kiss. He must still love her. But the kiss might not mean anything. It might be his way of telling her kindly that he didn't want to marry her after all. She swallowed. 'Mrs Jenner's short in the kitchen,' she said, her voice sounding a little shaky. 'She's only given us ten minutes.'

'It won't take any longer,' he said, closing the door behind him.

No, it wouldn't take longer than ten minutes to break off an engagement. Not even five.

Annie led the way into the servants' hall, praying her legs would stop trembling, and Ferguson made for one of the benches that ran along three sides of the long room. No one was about but in another hour the footmen would be in to lay the table. He sat himself down and looked up at her with a disarming smile and she knew he was unaware of the tumult spreading inside her. Then he straightened up and shifted forward until he perched on the edge. And still he hadn't spoken. She opened her mouth to say something but the words refused to come. She cleared her throat. Ferguson spread out his hands and tapped his fingers on the bench, looking as though he were about to burst. Annie remained standing, her eyes never leaving his face, rubbing her engagement finger. She knew that tapping sign. It meant he was nervous. Or unsure about something. Unsure about how to tell her it was over?

'Come here, Annie.' He beckoned her towards him. 'I can't think with you standing over there looking so stern. Come and sit down with me.' He patted the space beside him. 'Last night was something, wasn't it?'

21

In spite of her fears, Annie frowned. 'You might have got me into serious trouble, Ferguson,' she said, in a tone sharper than she'd ever used with him. He looked up, his eyebrows raised in surprise. 'Why did you take such a risk?' she went on. 'Didn't you know Lord and Lady Hamilton were invited here? They would have spotted you straight away.'

'Yes, but I also knew that it clashed with another engagement they'd already accepted so it wasn't really a risk. And I didn't need no fancy dress for any disguise. I wear one every day.'

'But I still don't understand why you did it.'

'It was a dare. Sidney dared me. And it seemed like a good idea to get the note to you.'

Annie shook her head in disbelief. 'Who's Sidney?'

'Second footman. He owes me a bob.' Ferguson gave a triumphant grin.

'But you went and told Sir Henry your name. I couldn't believe my ears.'

'I know,' Ferguson chuckled. 'It just came out. But they won't remember it. They'll have forgotten all about me by now, what with poor old Stanton.' His smile disappeared. 'Annie, do come and sit down. I don't want to talk about last night... I want to talk about *us*.'

Anxiety clenched her stomach. He was about to tell her what Mrs Jenner had warned her. That was why his face was so red. He was embarrassed to say he couldn't marry her after all. Even though he seemed to be making every effort to act normally, he looked uncomfortable, as though he was wary of her. Ferguson, who always knew all the answers. Well, if this was the reason he was here she'd make it easy for him.

'I understand if you've changed your mind about me—' she began, thinking how dull life would be without Ferguson. She blinked back the tell-tale prickle of tears, determined not to let him see how much he had hurt her.

'Whatever are you talking about?' He grabbed the bench with both hands and looked up at her, his light-blue eyes piercing hers.

'Your note...isn't it to break our engagement?' Now it was out she felt a relief, and unaccountably a flicker of defiance.

Ferguson shot to his feet and caught her slender hands in his own. He looked horrified.

'Whatever gave you that idea? I've no intention of breaking off our engagement. You really are a goose.'

'But the note—'

'I couldn't say more until I saw you but I might as well come straight out with it.'

Annie tensed.

'I've seen a poster up at The Swan,' he explained, 'for people to work in Australia. I'm thinking of applying.'

Australia!

So he was not being dismissed from his job; he was going of his own free will. And not just to another town. No, he was going thousands of miles from her, and people who went to live in foreign countries didn't come back. She tried to snatch her hands away, but Ferguson held them fast.

'What do you think?' He gave her a little shake. 'Annie, are you listening to me?'

Annie nodded, mesmerised by the movement of Ferguson's lips as he spoke words she was finding difficult to take in.

He released one hand and tipped her chin up. 'Don't you think it would be a marvellous opportunity?'

'It doesn't make any difference what I think.' Her voice was small and tight.

'Of *course* it makes a difference. We can clear out of here. Have a better life.'

We? Annie swallowed. She looked into his face, only a few inches away from her own. 'You want me to go with you?'

'Of *course* you're going with me. Did you think I'd go on

my own? Without you? Dearest Annie, don't look so surprised.' He grasped both her hands again, pressing down on her fingers until she winced. 'I didn't want to say anything until I'd found out if we'd get a grant...they don't always give them. It depends on whether you have a job to go to. We don't...but it looks like we might get help. The Australians are doing everything to get the British over...build up their country.' His words tumbled over themselves.

She stared at Ferguson, his face alive with excitement as he pulled her down on to the bench.

'Annie. Say something.'

How could she? Nothing had prepared her for this. She wasn't sure if she could even trust herself to speak.

'Annie?'

'I don't know what to say,' she managed. Ferguson put his arms awkwardly around her as though he understood, but she knew he didn't. Nor could she draw any comfort from his embrace. He remained silent, waiting for her response. He was her fiancé. She had to tell him her true feelings. 'It's a shock,' she said at last. 'I've never thought about leaving Norfolk, let alone moving to Australia. It's on the other side of the world.'

'I know. In the old days it used to take three months on a sailing boat—' Annie blanched, 'but not now,' Ferguson hurriedly continued. 'They're huge ships these days, and it only takes half the time. Oh, Annie, it will be such an adventure!'

He'd made up his mind. She felt sick in the pit of her stomach.

'But why do you want to leave when you have such a good job in a beautiful house, and Lord and Lady Hamilton are so kind? All the extra meat and beer they give you now you're first footman.' She tried to lighten her tone but all she wanted to do was curl up in a corner.

'That's partly the trouble. Everyone likes working there so much they hang on to their jobs and it could take years before I'm promoted again. Even then, old Jackson will put up a fight. He's too comfortable.'

'Can't we wait a bit longer?' Annie begged, knowing it would kill her father if she left her family. 'I'll be nineteen in June. When I'm twenty-one, if you still want to go to Austra—'

'No, I don't want to wait that long,' he interrupted. 'And quite honestly, I don't want to spend the rest of my life – our lives – in service. You've no idea what I've had to put up with since I was fifteen. Stretching as tall as I can with the other footmen to make sure I look the same height. Being called Percy, which I hate, or worse, some other name they decide on. Waiting on others. "Yes, sir; no, sir." Everything to keep the toffs happy. But they never think if *we* are.' His eyes met hers. 'I've had enough.'

Annie was astonished. It was the first time Ferguson had spoken with such bitterness.

'What about my sisters? How would they manage if I went so far away? And Dad.' Her eyes sparked with a sudden thought. 'And *your* ma and pa. You're all they have.'

A shadow passed over Ferguson's face. Annie guessed he was thinking about his younger brother and sister, only six and eight when they'd been taken with diphtheria. Then his face cleared. 'They want the best for me. Not that they'd *want* to see the back of me, mind, but they'd understand. They've been without me for years now...they're used to it.' He paused. 'Your sisters can come out and see us,' he added, sounding more like his usual confident self. 'Stay as long as they want.'

'But Dad relies on me. He went to pieces when Mum died. And my sisters could never save enough money to visit us.'

Ferguson frowned.

'What would you do for work?' Annie persisted. 'What would *I* do?'

'I want to work on a sheep farm. And you could cook.'

'A *sheep* farm?' Annie jumped up. 'And me a cook? I'm not

trained, and anyway that would be back in service.' She looked down at him, her deep blue eyes flashing in triumph. For once Ferguson was silent. 'We don't know anything about sheep,' she continued, praying he would listen, 'or that kind of life. I'd hate to be stuck on a farm away from everyone. And I'd miss my sisters – they're too young to be left.'

'Your sisters are older now.' His voice had an impatient edge. 'Ruby's fifteen. You were her age when you had to look after them.'

'But a sheep farm,' Annie repeated. 'How—'

'We'll learn. And anyway, if we stay here, we can't work together even if there *was* a vacancy for you at Hatherleigh Hall. The Hamiltons are strictly against married couples working in the same house.'

It was pointless to tell him that rule didn't apply at Bonham Place. Ferguson often reminded her that Hatherleigh Hall was by far the grander house.

A steely look came into his eyes she'd never seen before. Subconsciously, she rubbed her bare finger on her left hand. Would Ferguson still want to marry her when she told him she was not prepared to go along with his mad idea?

'So what do you think, Annie?' Ferguson's tone softened. 'You'd love it once we got there.'

Before Annie could ask how he could possibly be so sure, Mrs Jenner appeared at the door. 'Come along, Annie, you've been gone more 'an ten minutes. There's work to be done.' She looked sharply at Annie, who bit her lip. 'As for you, young man,' Mrs Jenner turned to Ferguson, a sly expression in her eyes, 'Sir Henry wants to see you in his library. Double quick.'

Annie thought her heart would stop as Ferguson jumped up, giving her a rueful smile. Sir Henry must have found out the young guest, dressed as a footman, was indeed a servant at Hatherleigh Hall. Why else would Sir Henry call him into his library? She tried to reason. Maybe Sir Henry would regard it as a New Year's prank.

No, even Ferguson would never get away that lightly.

'Don't worry, Annie,' he said, squeezing her hand. 'I can look after myself.'

The door opened and Gladys stood there, a gleeful smile playing over her thin lips

'I've come to take you to Sir Henry's library, sir.' She bobbed her head on the 'sir' and Ferguson grinned. He twisted his neck round and gave Annie a wink.

'Well, I'm sure I don't know what Sir wants with your young man,' Mrs Jenner said, darting a look at Annie after they'd disappeared. 'What's the matter, girl? What did he have to say for hisself?'

Annie took a ragged breath. 'I'm sorry, Mrs Jenner, I feel a bit queer.'

The cook raised both eyebrows and studied Annie. 'Go to your room, girl, but don't be long. There's plenty of work to get done, and what with Mollie off sick, and me short in the kitchen, I don't know as how we'll all manage, I'm sure. Here...' she reached in a cupboard and took down a tiny bottle, 'take these smelling salts with you.'

Annie seized the bottle before Mrs Jenner could say anything more. She wasn't ready to be questioned about the enormity of what Ferguson had just asked her. With a hand pressed to her head as though to stop it from falling off, she stumbled up the stairs to the top of the house, into one of the attic rooms she shared with Gladys.

She opened the bedroom door, and as usual was struck by the meagre furnishings and the musty smell, no matter how often she and Gladys cleaned and dusted. When she'd first been promoted to head housemaid a few weeks ago at such an early age, Annie had been told she'd have her own separate bedroom. Full of excited expectation she'd peered inside the room Mrs Morgan had shown her and immediately said she would prefer to stay where she was. It was not much larger than a box room with a small grubby window looking straight on to the side wall of the kitchen block, destroying any view of the trees and grounds which Annie so loved.

Now, in the shared room, Annie's heart sank. The maids' rooms were such a contrast to the opulence downstairs. Goodness knows what she expected to find. A fire lit for her? Coffee set out on a chiffonier? Annie trembled as she went over to the window, ducking her head under the sloping ceiling. She pulled the curtain as far back as she could and looked out over the courtyard to the coach house. She paused a few moments then turned back into the room. The few inches of extra light from the window did little but show up the cheap bits and pieces, and the worn carpet which she and Gladys constantly tripped over. Sitting on her lumpy bed by the window, she willed her head to stop spinning. She unscrewed the cap off the smelling salts and inhaled. As the ammonia rushed up through her nostrils tears poured down her face and she sneezed and coughed, but at least it seemed to have done the trick. She replaced the cap and dropped the bottle into her apron pocket.

Thank goodness Gladys would be busy preparing the bedrooms for the weekend guests. She knew the maid wasn't very taken with Ferguson. He was ambitious and adventurous and Gladys couldn't abide by all that nonsense. She'd even hinted to Annie that Ferguson seemed a bit above himself since he'd been made first footman, and sometimes Annie found it difficult to defend him.

But, she loved Ferguson and they were to be married. They were both in good situations here in Norfolk but if they went to Australia they might not even *get* jobs.

Her head felt as though the ammonia had disinfected every part of her brain. She got up and paced the room, then picked up the only photograph of her two sisters from the mantelpiece; herself in the middle with her arms linking theirs; the three of them together. One of Dad's mates at the printers had been given a camera. She remembered how she and her two sisters had giggled as the poker-faced amateur had asked them over and over to keep still and stop smiling so he could take the picture. Now, looking intently at the photograph of Ruby and Ethel, it occurred to her that if one of her sisters became ill she would be desperate to get on the first ship back to England. And what would happen if *she* got ill and let any new employer down? With shaking hands she placed the photograph back on the shelf and sat down on the bed again.

Supposing she went. What if her cooking wasn't satisfactory? And Ferguson – would he be some kind of handyman? Working on a sheep farm was all too unknown.

She put her head in her hands.

Seconds later a thought struck her and she sat bolt upright. She would tell him he'd have to go without her. That way, she'd find out whether he really loved her or not. It would prove it once and for all.

She'd never doubted his love before. She wavered again. No, it would be impossible to go with him; to tell Ruby and Ethel that she was going far away and may never return. Not see them grow up into young women, and get married, and have children. And them not see *her* children.

But how could she wave goodbye to Ferguson? Ferguson who made her laugh; who said he loved her and wanted her with him.

She looked at the clock. Drawing in some deep breaths to compose herself she rose to her feet. If she was any longer Mrs Jenner would be cross, not to mention she'd be dying of curiosity.

3

Annie's legs still felt unsteady as she trudged back to the kitchen. She was dreading Mrs Jenner's questioning, but the cook was nowhere to be seen. Mollie stopped in the middle of scrubbing the kitchen table and looked up.

'Mrs Jenner's only gone a minute.'

'Can you tell her I'm just going to check on Gladys? If she needs any help with lunch she can ring for me.'

Annie had always made it as plain as she dared that she would rather be in the kitchen than supervising the housemaids in cleaning rooms and lighting fires. Indeed, when Mrs Jenner was rushed off her feet she would often ask if Annie could lend a hand. Annie was seriously thinking she might have a word with Mrs Morgan when she was out of hospital and back to work, to see whether she might be transferred on an official basis. Mrs Jenner might be a dragon but she could certainly cook. Annie was sure she'd have no better training.

'I'll tell her where you are.' Mollie pushed a damp strand of blonde hair back under her cap.

'Are you feeling better, Mollie?' Annie looked intently at the scullery maid.

'Oh, yes, Annie, thank you. Much better.'

Annie wasn't convinced. Mollie's face was too pale. But there was no time for further talk, and Annie had to leave the girl to rinse off the remaining suds from the table and prepare it for the cook.

Poor little Mollie. Polio as a child had left her with a dragging leg. The doctor said it was a miracle she hadn't died. She was so pretty, too. Prettier than all the other maids put together. But what man would take up with her when he saw her wasted limb? Someone who loved her, that's who. But would Ferguson love her, Annie wondered, if she became ill or was to have an accident that left her an invalid? She pushed away the uncomfortable question. She would have a word with Mollie to make sure she was settling in and wasn't too homesick. There'd been traces of tears more than once.

Thinking about Mollie had made her forget her own predicament, but now it swept over her in a sickening wave. If only she could talk to her father first. But she wouldn't see them all until her day off on Sunday, and she knew Ferguson would be much too impatient to wait that long. Caught up in her thoughts as she hurried along the passage she didn't notice Mrs Jenner's bulk.

'There you are, Annie. I've been looking for you.' Her strident voice made Annie jump. She was aware of Mrs Jenner's penetrating gaze. 'What's the matter, girl? You look like you've seen Old Jimmy.'

Annie smiled in spite of herself. Old Jimmy was Bonham Place's resident ghost whom every new arrival claimed to have seen, but only when they had been told about him. Well, it was no good putting off the moment. Mrs Jenner would never rest until she had extracted every last detail.

'We'll go into the servants' hall, Annie,' said Mrs Jenner firmly. 'There'll be no prying eyes there just yet.'

Reluctantly, Annie followed her up the half-dozen stone steps. Mrs Jenner eased herself down on the same spot Ferguson had chosen only half an hour before, and Annie momentarily closed her eyes at the lingering smell of his spicy cologne. Mrs Jenner tilted her face towards Annie, smiling in encouragement, but her birdlike eyes contained more curiosity than kindness. Annie drew a deep breath.

The cook's spiky grey brows almost disappeared under her white cap as Annie told her about Ferguson's visit, giving a disapproving sniff every so often.

'If he works hard, he'll probably do well for hisself,' Mrs Jenner said, when Annie paused. 'But you'll be goin' into the unknown, and whatever you say, it's different for women. Men like adventure. He'll be all right. But you,' her eyes bored through Annie, 'you'll be miles away. You won't see your family again. It's a terrible risk.'

'I know.' Annie's voice was low. 'But I love him.'

'Like I've always said, what happens to love when the money's tight and you've got a couple of brats to see to? Where will your young man be then? I've seen it over and over.' Mrs Jenner shook her head, making her jowl quiver. 'No, I wouldn't give it much chance.'

Annie blushed at the mention of children, and thought no child of hers would be a 'brat', but was there any truth in Mrs Jenner's words?

Oh, Mum, what would you have me do?

Annie looked at Mrs Jenner – really studied her. She was a big-boned woman with a red face and neck, coarsened from bending over too many hot stoves; her ankles overflowed over the tops of her brogues from standing on a stone floor six days a week, and she had eyes that were inquisitive but joyless. Suddenly, she saw herself ending up like Mrs Jenner – face lined before her time, hands rough and wrinkled, varicose-veined legs, no one of her own to love her, no children, her sisters both married and wrapped up in their own families. Was that *really* what she wanted? Didn't she…wasn't it possible that there was something more in life? Couldn't she have an adventure too? Was she really such a coward? 'Do I dare?' She couldn't be sure if she'd whispered the words. Do I dare?

She looked round the room. The dark-brown lower half of the walls was dingy and the top part, once cream, had now aged to a dull mustard. A row of antlers hung mournfully like a bizarre display of pictures. She shuddered with distaste and looked over Mrs Jenner's heavy shoulder towards the windows on the opposite side. It had begun to rain, and if the dark gloom of the kitchen was anything to go by, it would continue for the rest of the day. A twig had blown across the lawn and lodged itself between one of the sashes, rattling like some ghost in the wind. Probably what people heard when they insisted they'd seen Old Jimmy, Annie thought wryly.

Mollie had lit the range hours ago but the kitchen was vast and the heat hadn't yet seeped into the servants' hall. They weren't even half way through winter. Annie shivered. Although the servants' hall was near the kitchen it didn't ever get really warm until they were all pressed close together on the bench and eating. Ferguson had told her Australia was 'upside down': very hot in what they called their summer, which was from December to May, before it started to cool down. But it never got as raw as Norfolk, he'd added, darting her a sly glance. Her mouth twitched into a half smile, as she knew he hoped that alone might persuade her.

If she didn't go, would she regret it all her life?

She was relieved when a knock at the door interrupted them. Her heart somersaulted as Ferguson stuck his head round.

'Gladys said you were here, Annie.' He turned to the cook and gave her the crooked smile he reserved when he wanted to get his own way. 'Mrs Jenner, might I have just five more minutes with Annie? I promise I won't keep her a second longer.'

Mrs Jenner sniffed. 'Annie's needed for work now, young man. I think you've taken up enough of her time this morning.'

'Please, Mrs Jenner—'

The cook made him wait several long seconds.

'S'long as it's only five minutes.' She rose with difficulty but Ferguson rushed to give her a helping hand.

'Thank you, Cook,' he grinned, and made a face behind her retreating back. He turned to Annie and once again pulled her down on the long seat beside him.

'Oh, Ferguson, what did Sir Henry want? Did he know you weren't one of the guests? Did—'

'Steady on. Yes, he said he knew I was one of the footmen from Hatherleigh Hall. And he also knew me and you were engaged to be married.'

Annie's heart missed a beat. 'How on earth did he find out?' She was puzzled Ferguson didn't seem that concerned. Was he refusing to face up to the fact he was in serious trouble?

'I could hardly ask him that, could I? You know there's always gossip between the big houses. It's no longer a secret. Thing is, he knew all right.' Ferguson grabbed Annie's hand. 'But listen to this. He's only gone and offered me Stanton's job.'

Annie's eyes flew wide. 'To be Sir Henry's butler? After knowing what you did?'

Ferguson gave a smug smile. 'Do you know what he said?' Annie shook her head. Her tongue felt it had deserted her. 'That when he was out in India, I reminded him of some of the officers who used to get up to all kinds of tricks. Said it was the sort of prank he might have done himself. He actually roared with laughter.' Ferguson chuckled at the recollection.

'But you haven't any experience.'

Ferguson's laughter faded and Annie wished she'd bitten her tongue. After all, she'd been praying for something or someone to keep him here with her. And now her prayers had been answered. That was why he'd not seemed worried. He'd been leaving the good news until last. Oh, her dear Ferguson. Everything was going to be all right.

'I must say, you could've knocked me down with a feather, but Sir Henry has even spoken to the Hamiltons, who were good enough to say they'd be sorry to lose me but they couldn't stand in my way with such an opportunity.'

'But aren't you too young?'

Stop it, Annie. Stop coming up with objections.

'Not at twenty-five. It wouldn't take long to learn. I've watched Jackson often enough. It can't be that difficult to iron Sir Henry's

34

newspapers and shoelaces every morning.' Ferguson laughed at Annie's skeptical expression. He laid his hands on her shoulders, gently turning her towards him. 'Why, Annie, don't you think I could do it? Haven't you any faith in me?'

She couldn't quite read the expression in his eyes. 'Of course I have,' she told him.

'Well,' he went on, 'just so you know, Sir Henry said it'd be a breath of fresh air to have someone younger around him. I think I'd be more his valet than a butler anyway.'

It was hard to take it all in. Ferguson wasn't going away. She didn't have to make any decision. Didn't have to test whether he loved her or not. But to her astonishment she felt a stab of disappointment that they would not now be embarking on their adventure. Until this moment, she hadn't realised she wasn't quite so against the idea anymore. She had begun to be a little excited at the thought of sailing away to a new country. She looked at Ferguson, who was carefully watching her; waiting, no doubt, for her to show how pleased she was. He didn't look as disappointed as she would have expected. Maybe he was relieved he wasn't going so far away from his family, after all. Yet he'd told her it was his dream to go to Australia to start a new life. Now they weren't going.

She shook herself, common sense prevailing. She wouldn't have to leave her father and sisters. Ferguson would be more settled knowing he was in charge of the staff, and they could get married next year if her father gave his permission. She wouldn't have to lose her job if Ferguson worked at Bonham Place. And one day, maybe, they'd have a home of their own. And babies. Her heart lifting, she squeezed Ferguson's hand, her face wreathed in smiles.

'I'm so happy, Ferguson. It's wonderful news. Sir Henry might have been really angry. I still wonder how he found out exactly who Ferguson Percy Bishop was.'

'That was a slip, if ever there was.' Ferguson seemed to have regained his humour. 'I think Gladys must have snitched on me.

She never did like me. Don't know why.'

'One of the only girls who hasn't fallen for your charms,' Annie laughed. 'Oh, Ferguson, everything has turned out for the best.'

'I haven't finished,' Ferguson said with a broad grin. '*This* is the best bit.'

Annie waited, her eyes sparkling with pride that Sir Henry Bonham had seen such promise in her fiancé.

'There's more?' she laughed delightedly.

'Yes,' Ferguson said. 'I told him I couldn't accept his offer. That I was going to Australia...and taking you with me. Oh, Annie, you should've seen him. I could hardly keep a straight face. I wish like anything you'd been there.'

Her laughter died. It was as though he'd punched her in the stomach. A feeling of numbness spread through her. She stared at Ferguson's face, his eyes dancing with merriment. She watched him, stony-faced.

'You mean you told him before I had time to even *think* about it? Before I told you my decision?' Her fury rose. 'You've spoken for *me*? I can't even make a decision now. You've cost me my job! You, you...' She swallowed the tears of anger. 'Ferguson, how *could* you be so selfish?'

Ferguson looked shocked. 'Annie, we love each other,' he pleaded. 'I don't want to leave you.'

'But you would if you had to, wouldn't you?'

'I've already explained. I want us to have a new life together... a family one day—'

'You have it all planned,' Annie interrupted, 'and you're going with or without me. And don't deny it because it's true. Well, you can go on your own. And that's *my* decision.'

She stumbled to her feet.

'Annie, come here.' He shot up from the bench and held her arms firmly. 'I'm not going without you. Think what you have here. You like cooking but you don't often get the chance. Your position isn't even in the kitchen. You're really only a housemaid...well, head housemaid,' he added hurriedly, when Annie's face flushed with annoyance, 'and Mrs J will go on for years yet.' Ferguson's blue eyes were bright with persuasion. 'You've said it yourself. Even if you were made under-cook, she's a mean old biddy. Your life would be miserable. Where's the future here? Come with me and you won't regret it.'

4

Bonham

'Sorry I'm late, Annie.' Her father's tall figure blocked the open doorway of the kitchen. Edwin Ring came in and shut the door.

It had to be now, she decided, telling herself the drops of perspiration which she could feel running down her back were merely from the heat of the oven. While they had a few minutes on their own she could tell him her plan. She'd thought and thought about how he'd take it and convinced herself he would give her his blessing when he saw how much it meant to her. She loved her father but had to admit he'd become stricter with the three of them since their mother had died.

There's no time like the present, she heard her mother's voice in her head. If she didn't do this now, she'd have to wait another whole week until her next day off. Another week which might induce her to change her mind again.

Annie turned from the stove and kissed him. 'I was beginning to worry.' Her father's evening stubble scratched her cheek and she caught a whiff of his usual brand of tobacco. His jacket had absorbed the smell of printers' ink long ago, but somehow the familiarity of it was comforting.

'We had to get the last job done. Took longer than expected.' He sniffed the air. 'Something smells good.'

'It's your favourite – mutton and onion suet pudding. And soup that Ethel made yesterday after school.'

'That's my girls. I'm ravenous.'

'Dad, I've got something important to tell you.'

'What's that, love?' His voice sounded weary as he let his coat drop over the back of one of the kitchen chairs.

'It's Ferguson. He wants to—'

The door flew open and Ruby rushed in. 'We've been waiting for you, Pa. Annie wouldn't let us start without you.' She grabbed his hand and marched him into the small dining room.

Annie felt she would burst as she followed them into the room, carrying the saucepan. Her hand trembled as she ladled out the soup and some of it dripped down the side of her father's bowl. He glanced up at her in surprise. She was usually so neat and careful. Annie gulped. There'd never be a perfect time to tell him so she might as well get it over. She served her two sisters and placed a small amount into her own bowl, but she had no appetite.

'Don't slurp, Ruby.' Her father didn't look up from his own soup plate, barely breaking his rhythm except to say, 'It's good soup, Ethel.' His youngest daughter beamed, while Ruby gazed steadily at him as though weighing up her next words.

'Pa,' Ruby leant forward to get her father's attention, 'Mrs Milton says I can help her do some sewing one evening a week at her house. Can I?' She looked across at her father from under her thick black lashes.

'Is she going to pay you?'

'Oh, yes. Half a crown for three hours.'

Her father grunted. 'Well, I suppose it will help with the food.'

'Oh, but...' Ruby looked down at her soup plate, her mouth downturned. 'I was hoping you'd let me keep it for myself.'

'Does your sister keep her money for herself?' their father demanded. 'No. She uses it to help care for all of us.'

'You always take Annie's side in everything.' Ruby's head shot up. 'It's Annie this and Annie that. What about *me*?'

'You're fifteen, Ruby, and you'll do as I say. Now, stop talking and eat.'

Annie's mouth went dry. Even though she felt sorry for Ruby it was imperative that she speak to her father about Ferguson. Ethel helped her clear the dirty crockery and they brought through the suet pudding and cabbage. Annie's heart beat hard. She dished up and watched her father wolf down his meal. He caught her gaze.

'Get on with your supper, my girl. You're too thin as it is.'

Annie swallowed.

'What's the matter, Annie?' Ruby demanded. 'You're like a cat that's lost its tongue.'

Annie drew herself up and blurted, 'Ferguson wants us to go to Australia to live.'

There. It was out. Three pairs of eyes fastened on her in disbelief. Ruby's mouth fell open.

Her father banged his fork down, making Ethel jump. 'Going to *Australia*? What the dickens are you talking about?' His eyes challenged hers.

'He thinks we'll have a better life...he says there's more opportunity over there.' It was easier now she was actually saying the words, though there was a tremor in her voice and she could feel a muffled heartbeat in her ears.

'Australia!' cried Ruby. 'You *are* lucky. When did Fergus ask you? How long will you be gone?'

'Be silent, Ruby,' their father lashed out. 'Your sister's not talking about a trip. Her *fiancé*,' he emphasised the word, 'obviously wants her to go for good. You'll never see her again.'

The only sound was the ticking of the clock on the mantelpiece. Tick, tock, tick, tock. Then a soft whimper broke the silence.

'I don't want Annie to go.' Ethel pressed her eyes with the backs of her hands, trying to stop the tears. 'Annie, don't go to Australia. You can't leave us. You can't love Ferguson more than us.'

A band of pain squeezed Annie's heart. They were words she

dreaded, but she couldn't change her mind again. She'd spent so many sleepless nights trying to make a decision that her work was beginning to suffer. After a week of anguish she realised she must go with him. It was her duty to either be by her husband's side or break off the engagement. As Ferguson said, at least they could give it a try. If it didn't work out they could come home. When she'd finally told him she would go she was rewarded with smiles and hugs.

'And you won't go back on your word?' he'd implored, gripping both her arms and looking deep into her eyes.

'No, Ferguson, I promise.' She'd smiled back at him, keeping her tone light. 'Besides, I'll have to go to Australia now as I won't have a job here anymore.'

He'd laughed and kissed her, his lips warm and tender, and she'd squashed the tiny prick of annoyance that Ferguson had taken it upon himself to make their decision.

Now, facing her father, the honeyed voice of Lady Bonham ran through her mind.

You've been a good worker, Annie, but this is a very disappointing turn of events. Lady Bonham had looked intently at Annie and shaken her head. *Well, I'm afraid your young man has made the decision for you…come what may.*

No, she couldn't mention any of that scene. It would make her father dislike Ferguson and then there'd be no chance at all. He'd already shown his feelings about her engagement, by bluntly saying he thought Ferguson was not the type to settle.

'Have you taken leave of your senses?' Her father's icy tone now broke into her thoughts.

Her throat felt as though it were being strangled.

Don't be a coward.

Ferguson's smiling face danced in front of her. She drew in a breath to gather her courage, and repeated the very words he'd used to finally convince her. 'When a woman marries, it's only right that she goes with her husband.'

'Not to the other side of the world!' Edwin Ring bellowed. 'You're still a child. You don't know what you're talking about.'

Annie had never seen her father so angry. Ethel began to sob again and Ruby slapped her.

'Don't hit your sister,' Annie rounded on Ruby. 'She's upset.'

Their father pushed his plate to one side. 'Stop crying, Ethel.' He looked at Annie. 'There will be no further discussion.'

Even her mother wouldn't have dared say anything more with her father in such a mood.

'I'll be nineteen in June,' Annie said, her insides churning as she defied him. She couldn't let him have the last word or she would never break free to take her place beside Ferguson.

Her father stared at her in disbelief that she should argue with him.

'I said there's to be no further discussion, Annie. I mean it.'

'I'm getting on nineteen,' Annie repeated, her love for Ferguson giving her the strength to override her father's anger, 'and I've been working away from home for nearly four years.'

'Until you're twenty-one you'll not be going anywhere...or, come to that, getting married.' He slammed the flat of his hand on the table. 'As long as you're under my roof you'll do as I say. I'll speak to that young man – tell him it's out of the question.'

'Dad,' she said, with such a crack in her voice that he stopped banging and looked at her in surprise. Ruby and Ethel's eyes never left her face. 'You and Mum got married when you were both young. Mum was only seventeen, and she'd had me by the time she was my age.'

'Not the same thing at all,' her father raised his voice again. 'Your mother had a miserable home life. Did you know that?' He glared at her. 'The first time I came to take your mother out, the door was open and I heard shouting. I went in and there was your grandfather swearing at your grandmother. He had hold of her head and was smashing it against the wall.' Ruby and Ethel's mouths opened in horror. 'When he was drunk, he'd turn on the kids. Your mother was always covered in bruises.' Her father shook his head at the memory.

'Mum told me some of it,' Annie said, feeling wretched. 'But you know Ferguson isn't like that. He loves me and wants me to go with him. If I don't, he'll go anyway. And I couldn't bear it.'

'What do you suppose would happen to your sisters?' her father demanded. 'Have you given *them* any thought? Ethel was only ten when your mother died. And three years later she loses you too? How could you even *think* of going so far away? I never dreamed you were so selfish.'

Annie's face clouded. He'd used the same words she'd thrown at Ferguson.

'I *have* thought about them, Dad. Ferguson and I will get a home out there as soon as we can so they can come and see us, and—'

'How do you suggest they pay for the fare?'

'We're going to save every penny we can so we can rent a little house. That will be the first thing, and then we'll save again for the girls. It will be a wonderful opportunity for them.' She wasn't sure whom she was trying to convince.

'You've lost your senses. You'll never be able to afford to rent any house let alone send for your sisters. Face the fact, girl. You'll never see them again. Or me.' He choked on the last words and pushed his plate away.

'Dad, please don't get so upset. Ferguson and I need to get married as soon as possible—'

Edwin Ring's head shot up. '*Need*? What do you mean, need?' He glowered at her. 'Dear God above. Don't tell me you're in the family way?'

Annie felt herself go hot all over. She couldn't believe what her father was saying. If only her mother were here; had met her dearest Ferguson. She would have understood, would have convinced her father.

'Of course I'm not. How could you think such a thing?' She rose from the table and held his gaze until he lowered his eyes. 'I meant we need to get married soon so we can get things in order before we sail.'

'Well, that's something, I suppose.' He stared at his other daughters as though they too might let him down at any moment. Ethel, plump and placid, at thirteen was still a child. Ruby, two years older, was as high-spirited as a colt. Her father didn't know, as Annie did, that Ruby was desperate to fall in love, but there was no chance of Ruby meeting anyone while she had to stay at home. Annie was more determined than ever to make a new life in the new country and send for Ruby first.

She tried again, her hands tense at her sides. 'Mum would want me to be happy. I hoped you would too.'

'Mum would agree with me,' Edwin barked. 'It's no, and that's the end of it.' Before Annie could open her mouth in protest, he got up from the table saying he'd had a bad day and was going to sit in the parlour and read the paper. He was not to be disturbed.

'Don't take on so, Ethel.' Annie took her sister's hand when her father had disappeared. 'Things will change anyway now I'm engaged to be married. You'll still have Dad and Ruby, and if Ferguson and I go it won't be long before you're grown-up enough to come and visit me – both of you.'

'I shan't come.' Ethel pulled her hand away. 'I'd be too frightened to go all that way on a ship.'

So am I, Annie thought, but I mustn't let on, especially to Dad.

'You're such a baby,' Ruby said, rounding on her younger sister. She turned to Annie. 'Are you really going?'

Her eyes gleamed and Annie wondered what Ruby was thinking. She was so different from Ethel, and not only in appearance. Ruby was impatient with anyone who couldn't make up their mind, or wasn't quick enough to think on their feet. She often opened her mouth before thinking, sounding hard-hearted if you didn't know her, Annie sometimes thought. She gave a wry smile. Ruby was young. She'd learn soon enough how important it was to give and take.

'You haven't answered, Annie.'

'Yes, Ruby, I've made up my mind but it's more difficult than Ferguson thinks. There's a lot of paperwork to do, and the authorities can still say no.' Annie looked at Ethel with a worried frown. Her youngest sister was slumped over the table, and her own eyes stung as she noticed more tears rolling down Ethel's cheeks.

'Don't cry, darling. You'll come and visit, I promise.' She put her arms round the shaking figure. 'Until then, you've got Ruby. She'll look after you and Dad.'

Annie glanced at her sister for reassurance, just in time to catch Ruby pulling a face.

Ethel looked up, her face red and blotchy. 'Ruby doesn't bother about me and Dad,' she said woodenly. 'She's supposed to look after us but she's hardly ever here.'

'It's not true,' Ruby said, her eyes blazing with indignation.

'That's enough, Ruby.' Annie's patience snapped. 'Let's get the kitchen tidied up.'

5

Ruby

Well, stone the crows, to use one of Pa's favourite expressions. Dreary Annie announcing she's going off to Australia. It was bad enough when she got engaged to Fergus. I still don't understand what he sees in her with that nose. And he's so handsome. But going halfway round the world to live – how could she? How could my own sister even *think* of leaving us? Pa says he'll stop her but I know Annie. She's a quiet one but she'll do whatever she decides. Even go against Pa if it suits her.

I'm not stupid. She says she'll send for me and Ethel, but they'd have to live on cabbage water to save up that sort of money. She's only saying it to keep us quiet. But Ethel knows. Ethel knows Annie will never come back. And my precious little sister isn't brave enough to go on such a long journey, even if Annie was able to pay. No, one of us needs to stay with Pa, and it's not going to be me.

Why wasn't I born first? Then it'd be me going off with Fergus to a new exciting country and not Annie. It's not fair. I'll be left to do everything and I *hate* housework.

There's one good thing, though. Pa was talking only the other day about me going into service. He said now I'm fifteen it's high time I earn my own living. He doesn't know going into service is the last thing I intend to do. But he won't send me away now, not if Annie really goes. He'll fall over himself to have me at home to look after him and Ethel. That will change his tune. But it won't suit me.

I'll be so busy playing Mum to the two of them, I won't be able to step foot outside. So how will I ever meet anyone?

I *won't* be stuck here.

6

A week later on Annie's next day off, Ferguson and his father paid Edwin Ring a visit. Luckily it was a Sunday and her father was at home. Annie could hear their loud male voices with long pauses in the front room, though she couldn't make out any of the words. She longed to be there with them, but once she'd brought in a tray of beer, her father had dismissed her.

She dusted the bedrooms, hanging Ruby's dress in the wardrobe and picking up her sister's scattered hair combs and curling rags. No need to do anything with Ethel's side. Her youngest sister was neat as a pin.

Annie's thoughts rushed at her. If her father refused to give his consent they wouldn't be able to get married until she was twenty-one. And now that she was getting used to the idea of starting a new life on the other side of the world she was becoming impatient. It was going to be exciting learning about an almost brand-new country.

But then her mind would play games. How could she leave behind the place that held her heart?

She walked over to the window and looked beyond the back yards where she could see miles of flat green countryside surrounding Bonham village. Two windmills broke through the sky; a sky which came down so low you felt you could reach up and have your very hand disappear in one of the clouds.

Every month she made it a ritual to take a small bunch of

flowers to her mother's grave in the village churchyard. If the grass was dry she would sit down and tilt her head up, trying to work out the weather by those clouds. Then she'd put her hand on the cool headstone for a few minutes and let her mind conjure up the image of her mother: fair hair, cornflower-blue eyes and a wide smiling mouth.

Her mother had been so pretty before she had become ill. But the image which came to Annie's mind this morning was her mother's anxious eyes, her skin so pale it was almost translucent, folding into her cheekbones; her hair turning grey before time. The long, elegant hands – pianist's hands, her father called them – becoming bony, the veins dull. Not long after she was diagnosed with cancer, her mother stopped giving piano lessons, then finally gave up playing altogether. That was the saddest thing of all, as she knew her mother lived for music. Tears stung the back of Annie's eyes. How she still missed those evenings listening to her mother play. Eavesdropping in the corridors at Bonham Place was never a substitute.

At the grave Annie would tell her mother about the daily happenings which made up her life; things she knew her mother would love to hear about. She would tell her about Ruby and Ethel and her father. She told her when she had first met Ferguson at the local dance in Bridgewater. How they'd laughed at themselves in the crazy mirrors at the funfair. How her heart would race when he stole a kiss. And last month when they were walking along one of the dykes Ferguson had made her stop and sit with him on a park bench. He'd taken her hand and asked if she would do him the honour of becoming his wife. Then he'd produced a beautiful garnet ring. It had been such a surprise but she'd said yes immediately, and laughed and cried at the same time. But she still hadn't told her mother her decision to leave her in her cold grave and sail off to Australia.

Annie swallowed hard and gazed out of the window again. If she craned her neck she could see her nearest neighbours who'd been so kind when her mother lay dying. Then there was Bonham Place. How she loved its fine architectural features, its woodland and gardens, and all the beauty of the interior – well, the rooms which were occupied by the family. She gave a wry smile when she thought of the bedroom she shared with Gladys. No, the maids' rooms didn't quite make the mark. But there were compensations. She liked helping in the kitchen and volunteering to go to the market when Mrs Jenner was too busy. Most of the stallholders knew her and wanted to hear any gossip from the big house. Of course she never made any comment, just smiled. But they were all part of everything she was familiar with. She turned away from the window with a helpless sigh. Ferguson was asking her to give up everything.

If only her father had allowed her to stay in the room with the men so she could at least voice her opinion. After all, it was *her* future they were discussing. Why should it always be the men making decisions for women?

Briefly closing her eyes, an image came to her of a poster she'd seen recently in a bus shelter of a girl waving a paper headed 'Votes for Women'. That was why those Suffragettes were so desperate to have the vote – to make their own choices. It was the kind of movement Ruby would join if she heard about it. At first Annie had shuddered at the idea of women smashing windows and going on hunger strikes, but when Sarah, her old school friend, had told her a group of women who didn't believe in using violence had got together in King's Lynn and went on peaceful marches, Annie had become interested. The trouble was, Sarah had added, working women found it almost impossible to get to the meetings. Only last week she'd given Annie a pamphlet announcing the next meeting and invited her to go along, but Annie was working. Now, turning away from the bedroom window, she pictured her father's expression if she told him she was going to join the suffragists. Which she might just do if he refused to grant permission for her to go to Australia.

Oh, well. She supposed she would hear her fate soon enough.

As she went downstairs to the kitchen she heard her father shout, 'No! And that's my final word.'

She squeezed her eyes shut. So that was it. She wouldn't be going anywhere. Wouldn't even be getting married. Ferguson would go on his own and all her dreams would turn to dust. Because the decision had been taken out of her hands, she suddenly wanted to go all the more. How could she ever settle now when she'd come so close to a new life which Ferguson had offered her?

The minutes ticked by.

What was the point of them all still arguing? She knew her father. He would never change his mind once he'd said no. So why didn't Ferguson and his father give up? Now, every minute seemed endless. She felt herself tense, and tried to concentrate on her cooking. Their voices were no longer quite so loud, presumably trying not to end the conversation in an unfriendly manner. Annie sighed as she stirred the cornflour paste into the gravy for the rabbit stew.

Finally, she heard the front room door click and the sound of footsteps. She braced herself and at that moment Ferguson burst into the kitchen. He grabbed the wooden spoon from her hand and threw it down so fiercely drops of gravy splattered over the kitchen table. She looked at him, surprised. He was beaming from ear to ear. He pulled her to him, and with his arms tightly round her waist, he planted a kiss on her lips.

'Your father's given his permission,' he laughed.

Annie's jaw dropped in astonishment.

'It's true, Annie,' Ferguson said, pulling her close. 'We're going.' He looked at her. 'You've got flour on your nose.'

Impatiently, she rubbed her finger on her nose, suddenly aware of her father watching them from the doorway. He wore such a sad expression she was sure he was thinking of Mum. Why had he changed his mind? He'd been adamant the other evening and she'd heard him shouting his refusal not half an hour ago.

But now they were really going. Leaving England. Living in a new country. A frisson of excitement shot down her spine, then left her with an odd feeling of detachment. As if she were stranded. As though she didn't belong anywhere.

Don't be silly. It's just nerves.

How could she leave her father? But it was too late to change her mind. She'd told Ferguson she'd go if her father gave permission, and now he had she must stick to it. She broke from Ferguson's grasp.

'Thank you, Dad,' she said, going up to him and putting a hand on his hard, muscular arm. She studied him and noticed how grey his beautiful thick hair was becoming, and how his whiskers were in desperate need of a trim. 'I'll write to you all the time so you know where I am and what we're doing.'

'Don't thank me.' Edwin Ring's voice was thick. 'It's Mr Bishop you should thank.' He patted her hand absent-mindedly and glanced back towards the open door of the front room where Mr Bishop still stood by the fireplace. 'Said I shouldn't stand in the way of young love, was how I believe he put it.'

It was much later that she learned from Ferguson the real reason why he had given his consent.

'Pa told your dad about how we'd lost little Sam and Lucy. That he'd have given anything to know they'd had a life...even if it meant never setting eyes on them again...just to know they were well and happy. So now all he wants is for me to be happy, wherever I go – and that means with you.'

Annie was the first to arrive at The Swan. So this was where Ferguson had first seen the notice about going to Australia. She looked up at the dormer windows, and the bay windows below. She could just make out some tables and chairs and one or two hazy figures through the leaded panes. Annoyed with herself for feeling uncomfortable, she glanced up and down the road, hoping no one she knew would see her standing outside a public house – something no self-respecting woman would ever do. And if her father caught sight of her…

The minutes ticked by. Was he coming? Had he changed his mind about taking her with him? Then she saw him running towards her, and as he got close she could see he was laughing. Any lingering doubts vanished as he swept her up and twirled her around before setting her down on the ground and kissing her.

'We've heard from Mr Jacobs at last.'

'Mr Jacobs?' she laughed, a little breathless.

'Yes, you know,' Ferguson waved a letter at her, 'the man we spoke to when we filled in all the forms. The Australian government has given us a grant towards our fare. It'll nearly pay for it from what Mr Jacobs says. And, he's found jobs for us.'

Annie's heart skipped a beat. It was really happening.

'Where?'

'In Melbourne. At a house called Amber Bay. You're going to do cooking and I'm going to be a valet.'

It was on the tip of Annie's tongue to remind Ferguson they were supposed to be getting away from being in service. But if it meant he'd given up the idea of working on a sheep farm she would agree to almost anything.

He looked at her, his face now serious, and it seemed to Annie he was hesitating about something. Then he broke into a grin. 'But we have to be married before we can sail, so we must see the vicar in Bridgewater as soon as possible to get the banns read.'

Bridgewater was Ferguson's village.

'Dearest Annie, I know it's all happening fast, and I know you're worried about going such a long way away, but I promise you'll always be safe with me.'

He gave her an affectionate squeeze, but she knew he didn't understand her at all. And he seemed to be taking charge of the arrangements again without first consulting her – though he'd given in when she'd told him she would definitely not work on a sheep farm. But now, looking into his eyes which were sparkling with excitement, she told herself nothing mattered except to be with Ferguson.

Still in a dream, Annie was jolted the next morning when Gladys told her little Mollie had been sacked.

'But why?'

'She's got a bun in the oven,' Gladys said in a self-righteous voice as she thrust a pillow into a clean embroidered pillowcase for Lady Bonham's bed.

Annie looked puzzled.

'She's having a kid.' Gladys took up another pillowcase and looked across the bed at Annie, shaking her head in exasperation. 'Someone didn't tell her the facts of life.'

Annie couldn't bring herself to ask Gladys to explain further, even though she suspected Gladys was bursting to tell her. An image of Mollie came into her mind. Mollie with the withered leg was having a baby. She prayed the boy would marry her and that Mollie would be happy.

The next problem was the wedding dress.

'What about your mother's?' Her father's voice was gruff. 'I think you're about the same size, except you're a tad taller. She keeps...kept,' he corrected himself, 'it in her trunk. Try it on and see what you think.'

Annie threw him a grateful look. 'Are you sure, Dad? It would save a lot of money. I'd love to wear it and I think Mum would approve.'

Her father nodded, then blinked several times before abruptly turning away. Stabs of guilt threatened to choke her. Although he was taking her departure in a better light since he'd spoken to Ferguson's father, he barely mentioned the date of the voyage, let alone discussed what she and Ferguson would do when they arrived.

Annie could hear Ethel crying herself to sleep most nights, her face to the wall. She'd stopped begging Annie to stay, and although Annie tried to comfort her with hugs and reassurances whenever she was home, her sister refused to respond.

To Annie's surprise Ruby had been enthusiastic about her elder sister's proposed emigration right from the start.

'I wish I was going,' she'd said enviously. 'I'll never meet anyone here. I'll be an old maid for the rest of my life.' Her dark eyes were luminous with tears.

'Don't forget I'm three years older than you.' Annie put her arms around her. 'A lot can happen in that time. I didn't even *know* Ferguson then. Of course you'll meet someone. A nice young man who will love you and want to marry you.'

Ruby looked doubtful. She pushed out her lower lip.

'You will send for me, won't you, Annie? Just the minute you can. I'll come on my own. Ethel's too much of a baby and we can't leave Pa by himself. Yes, that's what I'll do… I'll come on my own.'

Ruby sounded so sure of herself. She'd matured without any of the family really noticing, and was becoming a young woman. Annie studied her sister, admiring her curved frame and glowing copper-coloured locks, which she wore pinned up loosely at the sides. She has a prettier nose than me and Ethel, Annie thought, not for the first time. It's short and straight and her pointed chin has a determined set to it. I have a feeling that Ruby will do exactly what Ruby wants to do – when the time comes.

7

Bridgewater, Norfolk

2nd September 1913

Annie spread the dress out on top of her bed, her slender fingers smoothing the material. It was hard to believe that her mother had worn it on her own wedding day and now it was *her* turn. Her eyes brimmed as she pictured her mother, young and pretty and in love, dreaming of her whole future ahead of her.

Although the dress was no longer in the height of fashion, it suited Annie's taste perfectly: cream satin trimmed with lace, and a centre-back skirt panel forming the short train. As she slipped it on, her scalp prickled...imagining she could still smell the rosewater her mother loved among the folds.

The dress felt heavy as she stepped across the creaking floorboards in the back bedroom. She stood in front of the looking-glass. The skirt fell not quite to the floor, but she decided it was not enough for people to notice. The dress emphasised her small waist, and her slender arms looked shapely in the leg of mutton sleeves. Her eyes shone back at her from the glass, and her soft full mouth showed the glimmer of a smile. She ran her middle finger over the bump in her nose. She'd never be a beauty with that, but Ferguson didn't seem to mind, though he sometimes teased her about it.

'Why couldn't you have had a nice straight little nose like Ruby's?' He would then kiss the bump and laugh. Annie would laugh too, knowing he wasn't meaning to be hurtful, but secretly wishing he wouldn't point it out.

She pinned her mother's cameo to the high collar, and was about to try on her veil when Ruby burst into the room.

'Annie, do you need some help?' Her sister stopped in her tracks and gaped at her. 'Oh, you look lovely. I wish *I* was getting married. It's what I want more than anything. And Fergus is so handsome. And you'll be gone and won't even miss me.'

'Of course I will, Ruby.' Annie wondered not for the first time how her sister got away with shortening Ferguson's name. He hated it when anyone called him Fergus – in fact, he would correct them – but he never seemed to mind with Ruby. 'You shall come out and visit us as soon as we can send the fare. It might take a little while but I won't forget.'

'Do you promise, Annie? *Promise?*'

'Of course I promise. Now, see if you can help me with this veil.'

She handed Ruby a two-yard square of muslin and a band of artificial orange-blossom which Ruby, with surprising deftness, pinned into Annie's dark chestnut hair.

'There. Does that feel firm?' Annie nodded. 'You do look a bit pale, though,' Ruby observed. 'Pinch your cheeks. Jane's mother uses colour from a little pot. I wish we had some.'

'Well, we don't,' Annie said. 'And I wouldn't want it if we had.' She picked up the artificial posy Ethel had made.

'It's already coming apart,' Ruby said, taking it from her and trying to tuck in some of the stems. 'She really is hopeless.'

'She means well,' Annie said, her throat constricting with tears. *Dear Ethel. She doesn't have Ruby's talent but she's kinder than either of us.*

There'd been neither time nor money for her sisters to have new dresses, but Ruby had managed to alter her best dress, adding a wide blue satin ribbon at the waist and narrow blue ribbons on the sleeves. She wore her hair loose and curly from last night's rags.

'You look beautiful, Ruby. So grown-up.'

Ruby's lips curved into a smile, as though she was holding back a secret. 'I'll be sixteen soon,' she said. 'You just haven't noticed.'

The door opened and Ethel appeared in her Sunday dress. Her jaw gaped as her eyes alighted on her two sisters. Ruby gave a twirl and laughed.

'Do we look all right?' Ruby asked her dumbstruck sister.

'You look beautiful, Annie,' she said, ignoring Ruby, who pouted.

'That's what I've just told your sister,' Annie laughed. 'You do, too, darling.' She gave Ethel a kiss. 'And thank you for the posy. I love it. I think it's going to bring me luck.' She caught Ruby's eye with a warning look.

Ruby raised her eyes heavenwards.

Ethel smiled for the first time in weeks. 'Dad sent me to see if you're ready,' she said.

Their father was waiting by the front door. He'd dug out his old-fashioned frock coat that he'd worn when he'd married their mother, though he'd been unsuccessful in making the buttons meet. When he saw his daughter he took a step back and gasped.

'What is it, Dad?' Annie asked.

'You look as well as your mother in it,' he answered, in a gruffer tone than usual.

All the villagers, it seemed, had packed into the church, dressed in their Sunday best. The women wore hats decorated with artificial flowers, in memory of the summer that seemed to have come to an abrupt end. The cool breeze played a game with Annie's veil as she and her father entered the church. Inside, it was even cooler.

She noticed Sarah sitting in the back pew, but she couldn't see anyone from Bonham Place. Gladys hadn't come. She'd made an excuse that she couldn't get the time off but Annie knew differently. It was because Gladys didn't approve of her choice of husband.

Annie swallowed and stole a glance up at her father, who kept his gaze fixed firmly ahead. She gripped his arm and he looked down at her.

'It's not too late, you know,' he murmured.

A cold wave swept through her body. For an instant she thought she would turn and run back out of the church. Her fingers loosened their grasp as though they had a will of their own. Was she going mad? But it was too late. Of course it was too late. Several of the women were wearing new hats for the occasion and Mrs Bishop would have spent her meagre savings on a new frock. How could she let them down? Waste their hard-earned money. They were looking forward to the occasion. She wavered again, heart hammering. She'd once heard a friend of her mother say that a young woman she knew had had 'bride's nerves' in the church and it had turned out to be a good marriage. Was that happening to *her*? Had her own mother felt the same?

Slowly, Annie and her father proceeded up the aisle. As they got closer to the altar both sisters' heads twisted round. Ethel sent her a tearful smile, but there was something in Ruby's eyes, almost black in the dim light of the church, that unnerved her. Then Ruby smiled and Annie thought she must have imagined it.

Ferguson had his back to her, but as she reached him he turned round and gave her his crooked smile. If he hadn't smiled at that precise moment she knew she would never have let go of her father's arm. As it was, she felt his strong fingers on her back, gently steering her towards the man who was to be her husband.

How thin and high-pitched her own voice sounded when she repeated her vows; not at all like Ferguson's, which sounded smooth and confident. She didn't dare look at him; instead, she tried to concentrate on what the vicar was saying.

'You may now kiss the bride.'

Ferguson carefully lifted her veil from her face. He kissed her cheek. 'Hello, Mrs Bishop,' he whispered.

'Your mum would have been so proud, Annie. You look a picture,' Mrs Bishop said outside the church as she kissed her new daughter-in-law. The older lady was trying hard to smile, but Annie noticed her mother-in-law's eyes were brimming over. Annie felt her own eyes well up. Mrs Bishop and her husband had suffered such tragedy and now their last child was leaving. It was unlikely they would ever see him again.

'I'll do everything possible to make Ferguson happy,' Annie promised.

'I'm sure you will, dear. I just wish you weren't going so far away to prove it.'

Annie bit her lip. There was no point in reminding Mrs Bishop that this was all her son's idea. 'It doesn't have to be forever,' was all she could answer. Was she trying to comfort Mrs Bishop, letting her think they'd be back one day? Or was she trying to reassure herself that nothing is forever? That she could come home at any time. But if nothing is forever, that would mean Ferguson wouldn't love her forever. A chill ran along her spine but she put it down to the unusually cool September day.

The two families, now united by marriage, had squeezed themselves into Mr and Mrs Bishop's cottage. Mrs Bishop had proudly presented a platter of beef sandwiches, sliced boiled eggs, pickles, scones and jam, beer for the men, and two large pots of tea. In the centre of the table Annie was amazed to see a two-tiered cake with white buttercream icing topped by blue and pink ribbons, intertwined.

'Your Mrs Jenner sent it over from Bonham Place this morning,' Mrs Bishop told Annie with awe. 'Said she'd made it in secret.'

'It looks too lovely to cut,' Annie said. So Mrs Jenner did have a heart after all. Annie smiled at the thought of the cook planning such a treat. She was going to miss her.

As Mr Bishop began to pour the beer, there was a rap at the

door. Ferguson answered it and came back to the room holding two magnums of champagne.

'This is more like it,' he chuckled. 'And there's another box of something on the step.' He disappeared again and came back with a box which turned out to be a dozen champagne glasses.

'Who is it from?' Annie asked. Ferguson handed her a card. 'Lord & Lady Hamilton,' she read out. 'All best wishes on your wedding day. P.S. Please send the glasses back when convenient.' She turned to Ferguson. 'How kind everyone is.'

She took a sip of her first glass of champagne, wondering what all the fuss was about; not at all sure about the slightly acidic taste. The bubbles went up her nose which made her sneeze and Ferguson looked at her with raised eyebrows. She sent him a smile, but the palms of her hands were damp and she could feel her pulse racing. Her first night with Ferguson was getting closer. This time she took a large gulp. Maybe the champagne would give her courage. She'd heard alcohol had that effect.

Her eyes strayed to her father. He didn't seem quite so sure of himself in Mr and Mrs Bishop's cottage. Even when he was chatting with the others he kept clearing his throat and glancing at her when he thought she wasn't looking. She felt her chest tighten.

The rest of the day passed like a dream, as though she wasn't really there but watching events from afar. Voices whispered in her head. *Are you doing the right thing, Annie? Leaving your poor father and sisters to cope on their own.*

She closed her eyes for a few seconds, but her brain was a jumble of worry and doubt. If this was what champagne did to you, she wanted no more of it.

'We should be going, Annie,' Ferguson whispered, several hours later. His face was flushed. Probably from standing too near the open fire, and the unaccustomed champagne, Annie thought.

She gazed over her new husband's shoulder and caught Ruby

watching them, staring at them with her navy-blue eyes. Her sister wore the same expression as she had in the church, and it made Annie feel uncomfortable again, though she couldn't have explained why. Ethel, thank goodness, was sitting with Mrs Bishop and busy stroking one of the kittens that had managed to claw its way on to her lap.

'We can't go yet, in the middle of everything,' Annie protested, hoping to delay the moment a little longer.

'Course we can. Come on.'

'What shall we tell everyone?'

Ferguson grinned. 'No need to explain. They'll understand.'

Annie felt her face grow hot, as though Ferguson had said something off-colour. What was it that everyone understood? She only knew it was something to do with the wedding night that no one would ever talk to her about.

It took another ten minutes to say their goodbyes but finally they were on their own in the pony and trap that Lord Hamilton had lent them for their short journey to the inn Ferguson had booked.

'I'm glad we don't have far to go,' Ferguson confided, as he grasped the reins more firmly. 'We've got to start very early in the morning to get to the ship.' He turned to her. 'How do you like being married, Mrs Bishop?' he chuckled.

Annie smiled. 'So far, I find it most agreeable.' She squeezed his arm. 'Seriously, I *am* happy, but sad, too.'

'I know, dearest. But you're with *me* now.'

He talked about what they would do when they landed in Melbourne. Annie only half listened, hypnotised by the clip-clop of the horses and her own fears. She was about to embark upon something momentous – she was sure of it. What did married couples do that was so mysterious? Why hadn't anyone told her what would happen? She should have asked Gladys that time Mollie was sacked. What had Mollie done to get a baby? And why did the footmen sometimes snigger in the servants' hall when a new maid arrived? Annie desperately tried to recall her mother's words just before she died.

Annie, darling. Her mother had held out her thin hand to clasp her daughter's, the transparent skin veined and lined from the relentless weight loss. *One day you'll meet the right man and fall in love. But always keep yourself pure for him, no matter what he begs you to do. That way, he'll respect you. If you let him have his way there will be no marriage, either with him or anyone else. All men want to be first with their wives.* Her mother had tried to pull herself up in bed, but the effort was too much, and she'd fallen back against the pillows. *Will you promise me?*

Yes, Mum. I promise. But Annie hadn't the least notion what her mother was talking about.

What did 'having his way' mean? Certainly, Ferguson had kissed her several times on her lips when they'd been out walking, and though at first it had seemed daring, she had to admit it was a pleasurable sensation. But surely her mother meant more than kissing.

Standing in the dingy little bedroom on the second floor of The Poachers, half the size of the one she'd shared with Gladys, she couldn't bring herself to meet Ferguson's eyes. Her gaze alighted on the window sill. Hundreds of dead ladybirds, like splatters of blood, lay along the rotting wood.

I'm a married woman. This is my husband. What are we going to do?

'Don't be scared, Annie.' Ferguson lit the single oil lamp. The shadows cast by its light seemed sinister.

Goose pimples travelled up her arms. 'Ferguson...' her voice wavered.

'Come here.' He drew her towards him and held her close.

She was surrounded by the familiar warmth of him, his heart beating next to hers.

'You're trembling,' he said.

'I can't help it.'

He held her away from him and unpinned her hair, then buried his face in the loose waves. 'You're so beautiful.' He looked up. 'Did anyone ever tell you that?'

Annie shook her head.

'I'm going to take your dress off.' Annie's eyes widened. 'It's all right,' he muttered, awkwardly undoing the buttons, then throwing her dress over the chair.

It will get creased.

'Take off your bodice,' Ferguson said, his voice thick.

She drew back. 'Let me put my nightdress on.' She tried to step away.

'You won't need it.' He put his hand on her arm. 'Annie, you must trust me.'

Her face felt hot and damp, as though she were in the grip of fever. Numbly, she stood while he unhooked her bodice and helped her step out of her bloomers. She closed her eyes, desperate not to see him staring at her. Even her own sisters had never seen her completely bare.

And yet, she was curious.

She felt him softly pull her hands away from the space between her thighs where she was trying to cover herself. His hands felt hot.

'It's all right. Everything's all right. We're married now.' He pulled her towards him again and stroked her hair. 'You're allowed to do this.'

She felt a peculiar hardness stir between his thighs as he crushed her to him, kissing her with such an intensity she felt she would never breathe freely again. But she must not let him know she was in any discomfort. Suddenly, he groaned and pulled away. With his back to her he tore off his wedding suit, then the rest of his clothes and shoes, tossing them on to the floor in an untidy heap.

He turned towards her. Her gaze dropped to his sturdy thighs and her face burned with shock. As though sensing her fear, he gathered her in his arms and laid her on the bed without bothering to turn back the coverlet.

'Ferguson,' Annie whispered, her voice sounding far away to her own ears, 'I'm cold.' But she knew it was a feeble excuse. She was desperate to cover herself.

He flung back the quilt and a thin, worn blanket, to expose a grey-white sheet. A whiff of fried onions arose, making her feel sick, but Ferguson seemed oblivious as he lifted her into the bed. Without saying a word he straddled her and she had the full view of him. Caught between shock and disbelief she almost laughed. Instinctively she smothered the urge. He was already lowering himself to her, kissing her neck and eyes and mouth, then down to her breasts.

It was a peculiar sensation. She didn't know what she was sup-posed to do – how she was supposed to feel. Ferguson stopped to look at her, a sheen of sweat over his top lip, a fire in his light-blue eyes.

'I'll try not to hurt you, I promise, dearest Annie,' he murmured, breathing fast, his hands parting her legs which she had pressed tightly together without knowing why.

Just as she was about to answer, though she had no idea what she was going to say, Ferguson pushed himself into her most private part. She bit her lip hard to stop herself from crying out with the pain and the weight of Ferguson's body pressing against her breasts.

'Oh, Annie,' Ferguson grunted in a hoarse voice quite unlike his own. 'My lovely little Annie. My sweet wife.'

Annie tried to imagine what he was doing and thanked God for the dark.

'Do you love me?'

'I do,' Annie gasped, feeling a world away from the first time she'd said those words that day. She tried to ease her cramped leg from under his own.

'Say my name. Say my name.' He began moving rhythmically inside her, each stroke a jolt of agonising pain.

'Ferguson...please...you're hurting me.' She felt his breath heavy on her face. She wanted him to stop. *Please stop the pain.* She gritted her teeth to prevent herself from calling out but he pushed even deeper. 'Ferguson!'

'Annie!' he shouted, but before she could ask him what was wrong, she felt his whole body stiffen; then he reared up, shaking his head, and seconds later flopped down upon her, quivering and sweating and silent. Was he finished? Was that it? That must be what her mother had been trying so hard to tell her. Annie's face burned as she held Ferguson's head to her bare breast, her nipple strangely sore; then he pulled her tightly to him again, and she had to strain to hear him croak, 'It'll be better next time, I promise.' He kissed her cheek and turned over.

She didn't know if she'd be able to bear another time. Her head was numb and she could feel a warm stickiness running down the inside of her thighs. Hardly understanding what had happened to her, she crawled out of bed and tiptoed to the washstand. Awkwardly, her legs apart, she wetted the flannel and wiped the inside of her thighs. Desperately trying to still her racing heart, she noticed streaks of blood on the cloth. He must have torn something in her. But was this how it was supposed to be? She glanced over to the bed. She couldn't have asked him even if she'd wanted to. Ferguson was lightly snoring.

Annie pulled her nightdress on, the cotton making her wince as it touched the tender folds, smarting and throbbing between her legs. She climbed back under the sheet and brushed away the tears. How strange it all was. To think that she was a married woman. That she'd finally learned the secret of what married couples did at night. All of a sudden she felt she'd become a woman. If she put out her hand she could touch this man who was now her husband. Could feel the bones and muscles under his skin. Could smell his spicy cologne.

*

It was still dark the next morning when the landlord shouted up to their window that they had fifteen minutes before they had to leave. Ferguson cursed softly and removed his arm from her waist. He got up and fumbled for his clothes, and Annie could see the pale outline of his bare back as he sat on the bed to hoist up his trousers. She put her hand up to her mouth to smother a yawn and climbed gingerly out of bed, still feeling the imprint of him inside her. Something caught her eye.

'Morning, Mrs Bishop.' He turned to her with his ready smile.

'F-Ferguson…'

'What is it, dearest?'

Flushing, she pointed to a dark red stain on the sheet.

'It's normal. It always happens the first time. Don't worry. It won't be like that next time.'

Annie wondered how he knew so much, but before she could ask him he'd grabbed the quilt that had fallen to the floor, and with one swift movement pulled it over the sheet and blanket. She wondered what the landlord would say when it was discovered, and trembled, wishing she could take the sheet and wash it herself.

'Come on, Annie. We've got to go right away.'

She dressed quickly and pinned up her hair.

'Ready?' Ferguson asked her, straightening up. She nodded and he picked up their bags.

They stole out into the darkness, Annie not giving a backwards glance at the run-down inn. She never wanted to see that dreadful place again.

PART II

The Crossing

8

Tilbury, England

As they stood on the deck, Ferguson waving at the crowd below, Annie gave him a sidelong glance. Although he'd managed to maintain a serious expression when he'd said his farewells to the two families, she could see he was bursting with excitement by the way he kept squeezing her hand and laughing at nothing. She wished she felt the same. Wished the ship would set sail so she could get it over with. Sick with guilt and despair, she'd barely been able to look at her father when she'd said her goodbyes. New lines had appeared across his forehead and around his mouth in the short time since he'd given his permission for her to vanish out of his life forever. All she had to do was tell him she'd changed her mind, that she wasn't going after all, and she knew his face would light up.

St Pancras station at five o'clock in the morning had been pandemonium. Deafening noise and the acrid smell of grease had made Annie's head ache. She had never seen so many people in her life, pushing and shoving and shouting. Terrified her luggage would be swept away in the mêlée she didn't dare move. It was as though life was spinning around her and she could only watch. Harassed mothers clutching babies and trying to hold on to toddlers who were screaming through their dummies; fathers trying to discipline older children; sons and daughters the same age as Ruby and Ethel breaking away from their families, calling to one another and nosing around the platform. Annie glanced at her sisters. Ethel was standing quietly, watching the scene, but Ruby's eyes were darting this way and that, as though she were desperate to take it all in.

Annie caught sight of the labels on the trunks of a family who stood next to hers. R.M.S. *Orsova*. The same ship they were travelling on. For some illogical reason Annie was reassured that she and Ferguson were not embarking on this adventure alone. Others were taking the same risk and she longed to ask them their reasons. Maybe she'd get a chance once they were on board.

A group of men stood not more than ten or twelve feet away, talking and laughing. One of them pointed to a lone woman and Annie couldn't resist following their direction. The woman was older than Annie, maybe as much as ten years. She was a trim, upright figure in a travelling outfit of green and brown checked skirt with short green jacket. A matching hat perched at an angle on her golden curls. As though the woman realised she was being watched she turned, dismissed the group of men with her nose tilted in the air, and looked straight at Annie. The woman smiled, a pillar-box red smile. Annie smiled back hesitantly. She wondered who the woman was; if she was travelling alone; if she too was going to Australia.

Annie turned away, embarrassed to be questioning a stranger, even in her thoughts, and joined her father and Mr Bishop who were talking to a nearby couple, a Mr and Mrs Wells. Ethel was standing close to their father, but Ruby was chatting and throwing her head back and laughing with the couple's son, who was about the same age. This exuberance was unusual for Ruby so early in the morning and for a few seconds Annie looked on, amused. Then her conscience pricked as she thought how difficult it would be for Ruby to meet anyone now she was forced to remain at home to look after Dad and Ethel. But Ruby was strong. She'd manage somehow, Annie was sure.

Mr Wells had discovered there would be a long wait for the train to Tilbury and asked if they would care to join his family for coffee at a nearby hotel. Ferguson shook his head but Ruby immediately said she could think of nothing nicer. Edwin Ring frowned at his daughter, but Ruby pretended not to notice and grabbed Ethel's arm. Ten minutes later they were all sitting in the window of the Temperance Hotel, their luggage surrounding them like a fortress.

'We're going to Sydney,' Mr Wells explained. He looked across at Edwin Ring. 'We'll be pleased to keep an eye on your daughter as far as Melbourne.'

'She has a husband now to do that,' Ferguson unexpectedly broke in. Annie swung her head round in surprise at his rudeness, but Ferguson smiled across the table as though it were only a joke. He said very little more. Instead, he fidgeted with his shirt collar, then twirled his cap round and round between his fingers until Annie felt dizzy. He answered only when spoken to, in short jerky replies, as though he couldn't wait to get on with the next leg of the journey. It was a relief when the waiter brought their tea and coffee and Annie no longer felt obliged to make polite conversation for them both. Her father became almost as quiet, and the sinking feeling in the pit of her stomach refused to go away.

When they arrived at Tilbury docks two hours later it was still barely light and the crowd was even bigger than at St Pancras, but at least there was more room to move and breathe. The salty air filled her head, reminding her of a day she had spent as a child with her family at Hunstanton, the three sisters chasing each other up and down the beach, pulling the sea air into their lungs. She swallowed hard. There'd be no more family outings like that ever again. She shook herself. That was the past and she'd treasure the memories but Melbourne was the future. It would be different, that's all. She'd soon get used to it. Besides, the city was built on the coast; she knew that much from her school atlas. One day she might be taking her own children to the sea.

Her own children. She felt a strange tenderness as she watched a straggly line of other people's children filing by. Most of them

73

were clutching tired adult hands, wailing in protest as their parents led them to a ramshackle building. 'It's to have their eyes examined for infectious diseases,' Annie heard someone remark. Poor little things. They didn't know what was happening to them. She only hoped when she had children that she would never have to put them through such distress.

What had earlier seemed the longest day Annie had ever spent now flew by; suddenly there were only precious minutes left before it was time to leave. Barely registering Mr and Mrs Bishop's kisses on her cheek and wishes for a safe journey, she turned to her own family. Ethel had started crying, and unable to speak she hugged Annie as though she would never let her go. Even Ruby's bottom lip quivered.

'Don't forget your promise,' Ruby said as she kissed her. Then she whispered, 'What was it like, Annie, last night in the bedroom?' and laughed, showing her small white teeth, at her sister's shocked expression.

Nothing had been worse than saying goodbye to her father. Instead of the tall reassuring figure she had always known, he appeared to have lost inches. His shoulders were hunched, and when he looked at her she saw the twinkle had gone from his eyes. She was just about to say her last words when the ship's horn sounded, strident and piercing, startling them. They both stared up at the *Orsova*, which seemed to block out the whole harbour with its bulk. It was a magnificent two-funnelled ship which Ferguson said took over a thousand passengers as well as the crew. She still found it hard to believe a ship carrying that many people wouldn't sink. A blurry image of the *Titanic* suddenly rose in front of her. The unsinkable ship, they'd all said, but the death rate had been terrible. Something like fifteen hundred souls. She imagined the icy water closing over her head, hearing the screams of the drowning, and bit back her own scream. It was only the intensity of her father's expression of love and sorrow that she was able to push the nightmare away.

'Dad...' Her heart was still racing as she rested her hand on his arm, willing him to understand. His face had collapsed into lines of pain, reminding her exactly how he'd looked in the days and weeks and months after her mother died. She swallowed. 'Dad...'

He nodded and patted her hand, then looked away and blew his nose.

People had gathered on several decks to wave goodbye and Annie knew she only had a matter of minutes.

'Will all visitors kindly leave the ship immediately and will all passengers not yet on board make their way up the gangplank now,' boomed a voice through the megaphone.

'Come on, Annie.' Ferguson appeared at her elbow. 'You've said your goodbyes. We must go right away or the ship will leave without us.'

'I haven't said goodbye properly to Dad.'

'You must be quick – it won't wait.'

'Dad...it's time.'

He fumbled in his inside pocket and pressed a brown book into her hands.

'Nearly forgot this,' he said gruffly. 'It's a diary...or journal, I think they call them these days.' Her father's tone was matter-of-fact. 'Morocco leather. I'd like you to keep it so's you can remember things and tell me and your sisters when you write to us. So's we can picture you and what you're doing. See, I've got your new initials printed on the front. AEB.'

Tears threatened to choke her as she ran her gloved hand over the smooth brown hide. She could smell the leather without having to hold it to her nose.

'It's beautiful, Dad, and I'll keep it up,' Annie promised. 'Maybe not every day, but I'll write down the interesting things. And I'll think of you every time I use it.'

Her father nodded. 'Then there's nothing more to say, child, except look after yourself. And make sure that husband of yours does as well.' His voice was thick.

'He will, Dad. And it's not forever. You'll come and see us.' But her father had already turned away.

'We must go *now*.' Ferguson's tone was firm as he took her bag. 'Come on, Annie, come *on*.'

Even if she'd wanted to, it was too late to change anything.

3rd September 1913, on board the *Orsova*

I'm keeping my promise to Dad and starting the journal. It's not the first time I've written things down if they were important, and nothing is more important than today and the future with my dear Ferguson.

I share a cabin with four other girls and a large middle-aged lady. There are two rows of bunks, three tiers high, leaving little room for my belongings. I'm on the top bunk. We are in the bowels of the ship, and are not allowed to mix with first- and second-class passengers. Ferguson is a long way away at the other end of the ship, and he only has to share with three other men. It is a strange way to start married life, and I expect Ferguson feels the same way, though this is all an adventure for him, whereas I...

Annie paused and put down her pen. How did she really feel, besides sad? Her heart had hardly stopped thumping from the moment they'd left the inn that morning, knowing it was to be the last day with her family. She tried to visualise home to calm herself but the image was blurred by tears. She sighed. She must stop thinking of Bonham as home. Amber Bay in Australia, where they were going to work, would be her home from now on. She took up her pen again.

...whereas I am not looking forward to the voyage itself, but in spite of my fears there is a curiosity inside me about seeing something new. Not just new to me but a new country.

We left Tilbury this morning to a lot of cheering and flag-waving and for a few minutes I felt excited and lucky to be starting a new life, but then I remembered I might never see my dear father again, and it may be a long time before Ruby and Ethel will be able to visit. How shall I bear it?

So far the sea is calm but my stomach is churning.

As she put down her pen she heard an announcement: 'Would passengers in third class please make their way to the dining hall.'

Annie didn't think she could face any food. Her mouth tasted stale and dry but she followed the others up some steps, holding a handrail here and touching a panelled wall there as she tried to counter the slight movement of the ship. She was almost the last person to enter the dining hall. Where was Ferguson? Her eyes flicked round the room until she saw him being shepherded into a queue. He looked round at the same time. He smiled and winked and suddenly she felt better. She wasn't alone at all – she was a married woman, married to the best husband in the world.

The women were kept separate from the men but it was no use getting upset. She was glad to see that families with children were together. Other women were rushing around her to find a space. Before she could think where to sit, she was jostled on to a bench in the middle of a long trestle table.

Annie wasn't used to so much chatter and the noise tore through her brain. She instinctively put her hands to her ears, then felt ashamed and pulled them away, but not before she caught the eye of the confident-looking young woman sitting opposite whom she'd glimpsed at St Pancras.

The woman shook her head as if in admonishment. Annie noticed that not only was she wearing lipstick, but her eyebrows looked unnaturally dark and her cheeks were obviously reddened. Annie was fascinated but good manners prevented her from staring. She tried to catch another glimpse from the corner of her eye as she pretended to follow the tureen of soup that was making its way down the table towards her.

The woman smiled. 'Take a good look.'

Annie gave an apologetic smile.

'I shouldn't think powder has ever puffed on that nose of yours,' the woman said, her eyes full of mischief. 'And those pale lips could do with a bit of colour.'

Annie blushed. She hated any attention being drawn to her nose, and she hated being caught staring even more, but she couldn't help admiring the woman's frankness.

'I'm sorry. It was very rude of me. But you look so different.' She could have bitten her tongue as soon as the word was uttered.

'I'm not a floozie, if that's what you're thinking.'

'Oh, no, not at all…' Annie wished she could fall through the floor. 'I meant, you look so glamorous; like an actress.'

Be quiet, Annie. You're making it worse.

The woman smiled.

'Would you pass the soup if you're not partaking yourself?' a sharp voice at Annie's elbow enquired.

'I do beg your pardon.' Goodness, she'd only spoken to two women in as many minutes and already she had apologised to both of them. 'Yes, I would like to try a little but I wish the ship would stay still for a while.'

'This is a baby's bottom compared with what we'll be in for later,' said the woman wearing the make-up. 'By the way, the name's Adele. Adele Frost.'

'I'm Annie Ring…I mean, Annie Bishop.'

'Make up your mind.' The woman's red mouth twitched with amusement.

'I haven't got used to my new name yet,' Annie said defensively.

'Newly married, are we?'

'Yes.' Annie felt her cheeks glow. 'My husband and I are emigrating.'

'I don't think you're alone in that.' Adele's tone was mocking, but Annie was sure she was not being unkind. She wanted to ask Adele why she was travelling to Australia, but decided it was none of her business. She turned to her soup bowl.

Shuddering inwardly at the bubbles of fat swirling on top of the thin brownish liquid, Annie took a spoonful. It tasted of some unrecognisable meat, and parsnips and swedes. She gulped and her stomach heaved. Had she been spoilt by Mrs Jenner's cooking? She glanced along the table and was surprised to see the other passengers tucking in as though it were perfectly to their taste. Everyone, except Adele.

'I bet the rest of the food'll be bloody awful, if the soup's anything to go by.'

Annie winced at the swear word. She had only ever heard her father use the word once, when he'd caught an apprentice at the print shop stealing a florin from someone's apron. 'Bloody little scamp,' she remembered him saying.

'I thought it was me,' Annie ventured, trying another mouthful.

'No, it's disgusting. I've been used to better than this.'

Annie had never encountered anyone quite like Adele, and instinctively knew Ferguson wouldn't approve of her. He hated outspoken women. Maybe because he liked to hold forth himself. She hid a smile at the thought.

'Penny for them,' Adele startled her.

'Oh, I…I was just wondering what life will be like in Australia. If we'll settle in all right.'

'Do you have jobs to go to?'

'Ferguson – that's my husband – found us jobs. We are to work in a beautiful house in Melbourne.'

'And what's the name of this beautiful house?' asked Adele, patting some stray hairs from her forehead, not even attempting a second mouthful of the soup.

'Amber Bay.'

Adele made a strange hissing noise in her throat. 'Amber Bay?' she repeated, her rouge two flames in her white face.

'Adele?' Annie instinctively reached across the table and took her hand. 'Is something wrong? You look as though you've seen a ghost.'

'No...no...it's just stuffy in here, that's all.'

Annie told Ferguson about Adele and Amber Bay when they met on the upper deck later that afternoon.

'I expect you imagined it.'

'I didn't.' Annie was firm. 'She's an unusual woman – not afraid to speak her mind. Yet I'm sure she knew Amber Bay...and she's done this crossing before. I wonder why she went back to England, and is now on her way to Australia again.'

'Probably someone in the family was ill or died.' Ferguson's voice was impatient.

That's what could happen to me, Annie thought. Someone, probably her father, would become ill, and she would have to make the crossing alone. The idea terrified her. She suddenly wished this was all a dream and she could go back to how everything used to be. This was Ferguson's dream, not hers. Her legs began to tremble and she clung on to the rail, desperate to calm herself and not let him suspect her thoughts.

'You've gone very quiet.' Ferguson regarded her curiously.

'Adele didn't say anything about illness or dying.'

'Well, it's none of our business,' was Ferguson's advice. 'She's not the sort of woman you want to bother with.'

'Who do you think is the sort of woman I *would* want to bother with?' Annie's voice was a little sharp. Without waiting for a reply, she added, 'And anyway, I'm not sure you even know what sort of person Adele is.'

'The boys know what she is.'

'What do you mean?'

'She's nothing but a floozie.'

That word again. 'How do you know?'

'I know she leads the boys on. Beds them.'

Annie blushed. Then she felt angry he'd used such crude terms in front of her.

'Has she tried with you?'

Ferguson tapped his fingers on the rail of the deck. 'I'm not interested. Why should I be when I have you?'

'Is she married?'

'I doubt it.'

'Why do you say that?' Annie persisted, sweeping away a tendril which had escaped from her coil of hair.

'She's a bit of a handful for most men, I should think.'

'Just because she knows her own mind?' Annie's intelligent eyes watched him.

'Come on, Annie, I don't want to argue.' Ferguson moved away from the rail and held out his arm.

She wasn't ready to leave the fresh air and the fine sea spray which bathed her face, but she took his arm, suppressing a smile when the first person they bumped into was Adele.

'Hello, Annie.' Adele's smile didn't seem to reach Ferguson.

Not stopping to ask herself why, Annie turned towards Ferguson. 'Adele, this is my husband, Ferguson Bishop.'

'Pleased to meet you, I'm sure.' Adele gave a small bob of her golden head towards Ferguson and swept by.

Annie glanced at her husband, who stood watching until Adele disappeared, his face curiously expressionless. She was right, Ferguson didn't approve. Strangely, that disapproval made Annie all the more determined to make her a friend.

9

Annie lay on her back in the narrow top bunk, her bones pushing through the hard, thin mattress to the metal base. Her head, not much more than a foot from the ceiling, was full of images and events of yesterday. The vibration from the engine below shook her body and the noise was never-ending thunder. She was surprised she'd slept at all. Her eyes were open but unseeing as she listened to the snores of the other women. It was as black as the inside of a coffin. She had no watch but after years of rising at half-past five she felt wide awake and was sure it must be about that time. One of the crew had announced that everyone in third class would be going to the first breakfast sitting at half-past six.

Washing and dressing in the dark would be difficult, let alone being in such close proximity to everyone, but she was determined to have these minutes quietly without switching on the light. As long as they were all asleep, Annie felt she had a modicum of privacy.

She managed to climb down the ladder, carefully stepping past the middle bunk to feel her feet touch the ground. She fumbled her way to a small table at one end where a boy had stood a bowl and a tall enamel jug of water the night before. Washing herself as swiftly as space and her undergarments would allow, she knocked into one of the lower bunks as she tried to dry herself on the mean little towel.

'Is that you, Annie?' a girl called Dorothy grunted from under the blanket, her arm dangling outside. 'Wasser time?'

'Shhh,' Annie whispered, as she did to her sisters. 'We don't want to wake the others up just yet. I don't know what the exact time is. Probably not far off six.'

'I don't know how they can sleep with the row this ship's making.' Dorothy didn't bother to lower the volume as her head briefly emerged. 'I've had a bleedin' shocker of a night. It can't be time yet. They'll ring a bell or something. I'm going back for a doze.' She pulled the blanket over her head.

Annie retrieved her petticoat which had fallen to the floor. But where was her dress? She knew she had folded it carefully and laid it on a stool at the end of her bunk. She edged her way round the other bunks, her eyes gradually becoming used to the dark, and spotted it on Mrs Davey's stool.

'What is it?' came a sleepy voice.

'Just getting my dress, Mrs Davey. It's so crowded in here, our things are all of a muddle.'

'I haven't slept a wink,' Mrs Davey grumbled, 'what with all the noise of the engines.' Annie made the correct sympathetic response, knowing it wasn't true with the amount of snoring that had come from her quarter. 'I might just as well get up. Switch the light on, dear.'

Mrs Davey heaved herself to a sitting position, stopping for a few seconds to pause for breath. Finally, she managed to perch on the edge of her bunk. 'Good thing they put me on the bottom.'

Annie climbed into her dress but couldn't reach the row of hooks. She blinked back the tears. This was the ritual she and her sisters used to carry out every morning – before she worked away from home, that is – helping one another with all the hooks. Gladys's fingers, she recalled, weren't nearly so nimble as Ruby's and Ethel's.

'Mrs Davey, would you mind—?'

'Come here, my girl. Turn around. I'll see if my old fingers can manage them. The light hasn't made much difference.'

The others were yawning and stretching, and two of them

scrambled out of their bunks. Now the whole cabin seemed to tip with the movement of everyone pushing and washing and generally getting in one another's way, trying to complete their toilet. Mrs Davey had dressed quickly and was sitting back on her bunk, fully clothed, lacing her shoes.

In the distance they heard a gong.

'I'll go up to breakfast now,' Annie said. 'It will leave you all a bit more space.'

'I'm ready, so I'll come with you,' said Mrs Davey.

Annie had no idea where she was going. Yesterday's mealtime had been such pandemonium that she hadn't even been aware of what deck the dining room was on; she'd simply followed everyone else. She wondered how Ferguson was getting along. No doubt enjoying the adventure. She smiled to herself, her mind made up that he was not going to be the only one to enjoy the voyage.

'We're early,' she said to Mrs Davey, peering down the empty passage.

They came to a set of stairs with corridors running at either side, and Annie spotted a notice with an arrow pointing upwards to the dining room. They climbed two flights, Mrs Davey puffing and wheezing, and having to stop for several minutes after she'd conquered the first set. More notices directed them along a passage to the far end where they could hear the jabber of voices and smell of toast.

They squeezed together on the dining bench beside two middle-aged women who were engrossed in conversation.

'It was a cockroach and no mistake,' one of the women was telling her companion.

'What did you do?' said the second woman.

'Kill it, o'course. But how many others are there still hiding? It was enough to make you sick.'

If they keep this up, *I'll* be the one being sick, Annie thought, swallowing her tea.

'Now then, dear,' Mrs Davey turned and looked at Annie intently, 'what brings you to Australia?'

Annie gulped. 'My husband wanted to go. He thinks we'll have a better life.'

'Do *you* think so?'

The question was blunt. Annie looked at Mrs Davey, wondering how to answer. She wasn't used to opening her heart to someone she didn't know. She caught a whiff of Mrs Davey's stale breath and musty-smelling clothes, and remembered the older woman hadn't bothered to queue for a wash in cold water this morning. She pushed away the uncharitable thought.

'I didn't want to leave my family,' Annie admitted. 'We only got married the day before we left. It was a difficult decision, but I'm sure I'll soon settle in.'

'I'm sure you will, dear. That husband of yours sounds determined but I know I wouldn't want to leave England for good to face who knows what. I'm going to see my sister who's got to have an operation. But I shall be pleased to get home, I can tell you.'

She sounded like Mrs Jenner and the doubts that Annie had tried so hard to quell raced to the surface. The room tipped.

'Oh.' Annie clutched the table.

'Are you all right, dear?' Mrs Davey's tone was motherly. 'You've gone quite pale.'

'I didn't eat much supper last night. I felt a bit queasy.'

'No wonder you're so thin.' Mrs Davey raked Annie up and down. 'You need fattening—' She interrupted herself as a figure hovered over them. 'Oh, porridge.' Mrs Davey sounded pleased. 'It'll do you good, dear. Coat your stomach.' Her podgy hand took the bowl the young steward handed her, and she immediately began spooning it into her mouth.

'Porridge, miss,' said the boy, setting a bowl down in front of Annie.

'Thank you.' Annie looked at the grey-coloured mass. How

unlike porridge it seemed compared to Mrs Jenner's. She took a wary spoonful. It wasn't quite so bad as it looked. She dipped her spoon in to take a second mouthful when the ship suddenly lurched, and all the bowls slid down the full length of the table, jamming together at the bottom. They were only saved from crashing to the floor by the ledge at the end. Two stewards rushed to set them back in front of the passengers.

Annie stared in dismay at the bowl in front of her, only half full. It wasn't hers. Her stomach turned. She glanced at her companion, but Mrs Davey had taken no notice whatsoever and was busily tucking into her unknown benefactor's full bowl. Annie looked round the table. Everyone was engrossed in eating except Adele, who although several feet away caught Annie's eye and winked, then pulled a face at the porridge.

'Are you all right, miss?'

'Yes, thank you,' Annie answered. Mrs Davey had asked her minutes ago if she was all right, and now the steward was asking her. She suddenly felt ashamed when she thought of the poor children in her village who would have fought each other for the porridge, second-hand or not, in their eagerness for some food. Reluctantly, she took up her spoon and began to eat.

10

Bonham

Ruby, September 1913

Pa says Ethel and I have to write to Annie so she will have a nice surprise when she arrives in Australia. He says it will let her know we are thinking of her and miss her. They've already written, but I don't want to write letters today or any other day. She has left me to look after them. It's so unfair. She has only been gone two weeks but it feels like two years with all the extra work I have to do. I know she was only here once a week, but she used to get through so much – ironing, cleaning, cooking. She would make an extra soup or stew ready for the next day. That's the real reason why I miss her – all the work she did.

Before she left I used to sew and make pretty things. Everyone says I'm clever with my needle. I love altering dresses and hats to make them fashionable. I don't have time anymore since Annie went.

If only I had a job so I could earn money to buy nice things. Not working as a maid in a grand house like Annie. I'd hate that. I want to do something more exciting, like working in a dress shop – or a hat shop. I could start as a milliner's apprentice. Yes, that's it. Then I could use my sewing skills. I'll have to talk to Pa. Make him see how miserable I am, stuck here with nothing to do but housework and no one to talk to. I can't have a proper conversation with Ethel; she's such a baby. All she does is cry over Annie. Pa has always loved Annie best and me last.

I was always last, even with Ma.

Annie has the only thing I want in my life...and sometimes I hate her.

11

On board the Orsova

The days somehow passed. Annie, used to being busy from morning till night, found it hard to adjust to being idle. Ferguson was in the habit of playing deck games and taking part in physical drills, and seemed perfectly happy with his new friends. On one occasion he'd told her to come and join the girls to watch him and some of the lads playing 'chalking the pig's eye', but after quarter of an hour she'd become bored listening to the prattle around her, and had discovered a quiet corner under cover where she could write her journal. If she didn't feel too queasy when she'd finished writing, she would wash her personal pieces in the laundry room and peg them in among the clothes on the already full washing lines strung up on the third-class deck, but there were few other chores to keep her occupied. If only the constant sick feeling would go, she could enjoy the voyage the way Ferguson did.

'You should be used to it by now,' Ferguson remarked more than once.

One morning the captain shouted, 'Whales!' and everyone rushed over to starboard. Annie stood spellbound. The sleek dark silhouettes dived, then broke the surface, spouting bubbles of joy, endlessly repeating their dance. They looked so carefree she was almost envious, and smiled to herself for being childish.

'They're the largest of the sea animals,' Ferguson told her excitedly. 'We're lucky to see them so close.'

Today, she'd gone on deck with the others to admire the

coast of Spain, and had managed to spend snatches of time with Ferguson, mostly walking round the deck, breaking off to watch the games and have afternoon tea. At first, she didn't notice a change in the ship. But then she realised there was no deafening sound of the ship pounding through the waves. The *Orsova* had begun to slide quietly through a sea much calmer, as though the captain had suddenly switched off the engines. Oh, the blessed relief. Her ears and head cleared and praise be, the nausea was fading away.

She climbed up to the next deck where a crowd of third-class passengers gathered, and looked around. No sign of Ferguson. Annie squeezed through some people and leaned over the rail. Without warning, a spray of water shot up and soaked her, causing her to laugh out loud with such joy and relief she felt almost herself again. She was in the middle of an adventure she would never have dreamed of. She sniffed the salty air, savouring the tang, and turned round excitedly to see if Ferguson had appeared. One of the crew smiled back.

'The famous rock of Gibraltar,' he told Annie.

It looked like a huge sloping mountain and was looming closer by the minute. Annie wanted to share the moment with Ferguson. Where on earth was he?

She bumped into him as he emerged from the flight of stairs.

'I was just coming to find you,' he said, his face wreathed in smiles, and gave her a hug. 'Oh, you're all wet.' He held her away. 'The ship is going to stop soon and the lads say there's an opportunity to buy things. I've got a spare bob or two.'

By late morning the *Orsova* came to a standstill in the bay of Gibraltar.

Ferguson grabbed Annie's hand and pulled her up one deck higher, where the local vendors were already swarming up the ladder on to the ship. In a few minutes flat they had set up rudimentary stalls and laid out their handicrafts of beaded necklaces, scarves, bags and combs. Scattered among them were postcards, hats, sandals, and even light clothing to catch those travellers who hadn't bargained for the heat.

This is the best day by far, Annie thought happily, as she meticulously stopped at every stall to see what was on offer, not wishing to offend anyone by walking past, and also wanting to make the day last as long as possible. The thundering of the ship's engines and her nausea had vanished, the sun was shining, Ferguson was by her side, and she could enjoy the laughter and chatter of the stallholders, enticing everyone to buy their goods. It was like going to the market at home, only much more fascinating.

'Things are just as dear as they are in England,' she told Ferguson with disappointment as she put a small bag back on the table.

'That's why you have to get something different,' he told her, picking up a crocheted rose-tinted shawl. He wrapped it around her shoulders. 'You couldn't buy this in King's Lynn.'

Annie adjusted the shawl a little so it fell lower down her arms and across her bosom. 'How does it look?'

'Lovely, but it's *you* who looks lovely,' Ferguson said. 'As pretty a bride as any man could wish for. I just wish we could be a proper husband and wife.'

She blushed, and glanced over her shoulder to see if anyone had heard him.

'Now you've gone the same colour as the shawl,' he teased. 'I'm going to buy it for you. Your wedding present.'

'It'll be too expensive.'.

'Nothing's too good for my wife.' He held the shawl up to the delighted stallholder.

'Ferguson, are you sure—?' Annie began.

'I make it,' the plump lady behind the stall told her proudly. She was wearing a dress the colour of daffodils, and her black oiled hair

91

was held up by a glittering comb. 'Very good price. Four shilling.'

'Four shillings is a lot of money.' Ferguson took it from Annie's shoulders and laid it back on the counter.

Annie was both relieved and disappointed.

'Pretend to walk away,' Ferguson muttered under his breath.

'Why?' Annie raised a puzzled brow.

'Just do as I say.' Ferguson's tone was impatient.

Annie smiled apologetically at the lady before Ferguson took her arm.

'Sir!' the stallholder called. 'How much you give?'

Ferguson stopped. 'I have two shillings. No more.'

'Three shillings? I take three.'

'Two and sixpence. And that's final,' Ferguson said firmly.

The woman thought. In seconds her face changed from disappointment to resignation.

'*Es buen*,' she said, and handed the shawl to Annie.

Ferguson beamed as he handed over the half-crown, but Annie felt uncomfortable. Four shillings was not excessive for such lovely work. She wished Ferguson hadn't made her go through such a mean charade. She was about to say something when she caught his eye. He looked so triumphant and pleased with himself that she bit back the words. After all, he'd spent all he had on her.

'You can only *look* at things now, Annie,' he laughed.

They wandered among the other stalls admiring the wares. Annie looked longingly at a basket of fruit marked one shilling. They had been given very little fruit since they'd sailed.

'Tell her you'll give her ninepence,' Ferguson said in an undertone, barely moving his lips.

All Annie had in her purse were two sixpenny pieces. But the plums and apples and grapes looked so beautiful the way they were arranged in the basket.

'Try one,' said the woman serving. She plucked a purple grape off the bunch and handed it over. As Annie bit into it the juice burst

92

out in her mouth, warm and sweet. Without hesitating, she handed over her two sixpences and the woman gave her a toothy grin.

'Have one, Ferguson,' Annie said. 'They're delicious. Worth the shilling for the grapes alone.'

'No thanks.' He shook his head. 'You should have bargained for them. It's how they do things.'

'I didn't like to. You couldn't get a basket full of fruit like that in England for the same price.'

Ferguson shook his head at her again and sighed.

As they strolled along, the sun began to burn through Annie's new shawl and she longed to remove it but didn't like to in case Ferguson would think she didn't appreciate his gift. Just when she decided she couldn't stand its heat a moment longer she spotted Adele at the stall ahead, trying on sunhats. Before Ferguson could protest, she ran over.

'Hello, Adele.' Annie touched her arm.

Adele lifted off her sunhat and smiled, her green eyes lighting up.

'Hello, young Annie,' she said. 'Oh, is that a new shawl?'

'Yes,' Annie said. 'Ferguson bought it for me just now as a wedding present.'

'It suits you,' Adele said. 'Here, what do you think of this hat?' She twirled around to let Annie see it from all angles.

'It's lovely.'

'Well, I don't know.' Adele pursed her lips, took it off, put it on again. 'I'm not sure.' She set it back on the table and gave Annie a sly grin.

'Lady, you buy?' A man with a face as brown and wrinkled as an unsoaked prune picked up the hat. His birdlike eyes were pleading. 'Hat very pretty for pretty lady.' He tried to hand it back to her.

Adele shrugged.

'Very cheap. One half-crown only.'

Adele shook her head and turned away. 'Half,' she said over her shoulder.

'Lady, what you pay?'

'One shilling and threepence.'

'That no good.'

Annie was aware of the alarm in his voice that he might be losing a customer. She was reminded of Ferguson. Was this really what you were supposed to do? Bargain with people who were trying to make a living? It didn't seem right.

'I'll give you one shilling and sixpence and not a penny more.'

The stallholder looked upset. Then he grinned. 'Okay, lady. You take.'

Adele gave him a wide smile, turned to Annie with triumph, and straight away put the hat back on her head.

'Take that disapproving look off your face, Annie. It's what they expect.' She linked her arm through Annie's. 'I learned it when I was on the ship last time. Oh, good morning, Ferguson.'

'Morning.' Ferguson's voice was terse. 'Come on, Annie, I want to show you something over there.' He pointed vaguely.

His face reminded Annie of one of her old schoolteachers who wore the same expression when he was about to whip one of the boys. *Why does he dislike Adele so much? What gets into him? He was so different a few minutes ago.* She gave Adele an apologetic smile and allowed her husband to march her off, but a spark of resentment flared up in her.

Four days later the captain made an announcement that thrilled Annie: they were going to dock in Naples at half-past eight the following morning. Anyone who wanted to could disembark for six hours. It was the first time the passengers had been allowed off the ship since they'd embarked at Tilbury nearly a fortnight ago, and Annie imagined the joy of feeling dry land under her feet.

After an early breakfast, the passengers went up on deck to

admire and gasp at the view of Vesuvius. Annie thought it looked like a monster beginning to lose its temper, the way it spewed clouds of sparks every few seconds into the misty air. She wished someone could tell her about it but no one seemed to know when it last erupted. Hairs standing up on the back of her neck, she stood watching the volcano, so powerful, so unpredictable. Even Ferguson was silent for a few minutes. Then he began to shuffle his feet.

'Right, Annie, we need to go if we're to have a look at Naples. The boat's ready to take us.'

She gave it another minute.

'Annie?'

With reluctance she dragged herself from the spectacle.

'Are you glad you came?' Ferguson asked her unexpectedly, taking her hand.

'I certainly wouldn't have seen all this if I'd stayed at home,' she smiled at him. 'Though it's easy to be adventurous now I don't feel seasick.'

Not everyone was queuing to go ashore, Annie noticed. Probably most passengers in third couldn't afford the extra cost, but Ferguson had been determined not to miss this city everyone said you had to see. He'd told Annie he'd put some money aside for it. She didn't see Adele anywhere but maybe Adele had seen Naples the first time she'd sailed to Australia.

As soon as Annie's feet touched Italian soil she hugged herself with delight. The sun was already warm, and she was in Naples. Naples, with its famous bay that was the deepest blue she had ever seen. Until she'd come on this voyage she'd never even heard of it.

A bus took them to the town, and when the driver had dropped his passengers off he made a V sign with two fingers to indicate the time the bus would leave to take them back to port. Then he made a stabbing movement towards the bus stop.

'*Si?* You unnerstand?'

Everyone nodded.

'Come on, Annie,' Ferguson said, grabbing her hand.

'Shouldn't we stay with the others?' She noticed they were keeping in a tight group.

'No, I want to explore on our own.'

'But we don't have a map.' Annie felt a jolt of dismay. 'If we miss that two o'clock bus the captain won't wait for us. It's too risky.'

'I'll make sure I note the landmarks,' Ferguson said. 'Don't look so worried, dearest.' He smiled at her. 'You're with your husband now.'

She opened her mouth to argue but thought better of it when she looked at Ferguson's eager expression.

As they wandered along a narrow cobbled street Annie heard loud voices from above. She looked up and the sight made her heart miss a beat. Two women on opposite sides of the street were hanging out of their upper-storey windows. Annie could see a band of plump brown flesh where the top of one woman's flowered skirt had parted company with her white blouse. She was deftly pegging some men's underpants to a washing line and said something which made the other one shriek with laughter. They leaned out even further and managed to touch hands. There was more chuckling and rapid talk.

Annie rubbed her aching neck, but she was hypnotised by the two women. She thought of washing day at home. Whatever would her family say when she told them what happened on washing day in Italy? They probably wouldn't believe her. As though the women felt her presence, one of them glanced down and caught sight of Annie. She waved and shouted something unintelligible, and laughed. Annie gave a weak smile and waved back, shuddering as she imagined them toppling out of their windows.

'Italians are obviously mad as hatters,' was Ferguson's only comment.

In what appeared to be the old quarter the streets were full of workshops. They spilled out of the open buildings, many of them taking up half the pavement. Annie and Ferguson peeped inside some of them, and watched craftsmen making shoes and gloves and handbags. Some were bent over sewing machines, guiding colourful cloth with slender fingers. Annie thought how different it was from home, where all the women she knew did all their sewing by hand. Other men were moulding copper items or carving religious sculptures, and the chink of marble sounded like music to Annie's delighted ears. You could probably get anything you wanted in this busy street, she thought.

Annie took Ferguson's arm and they turned down another alleyway where the tenements were four and five storeys high, blocking out the sun. Small shop fronts were squashed together; some Annie could see were open at the back, leading to cramped living quarters. This was a much poorer street. Empty tins, meat bones, broken timber, newspapers, rags, even contents from chamber pots, were strewn all over. Stray cats and dogs zigzagged among the debris, sniffing for anything edible. To Annie's dismay, small barefoot children were playing among the rubbish, foraging for food.

'Mind!' Ferguson shouted, as he shoved her to one side. A cart brushed dangerously close, the owner brandishing a stick and shouting at the donkey whose ribs protruded through its mangy coat.

Annie shrank back against the crumbling wall.

'This place stinks.' Ferguson's tone was one of disgust. 'Rotting food and drains.'

Annie silently agreed. What she'd first thought were quaint narrow streets now felt as though they were closing in on her. Even the air was cloying.

'There's a big open square ahead,' Annie said. 'Let's walk all the way round, but we must remember we came out by the ice cream shop on the corner.'

'We'll treat ourselves on the way back,' Ferguson said, taking her arm.

They quickened their steps until they came to an elegant pink stuccoed building, the front lined with palm trees, its pedimented façade reminding Annie of Bonham Place. Instantly, she felt a pang of homesickness. Telling herself not to be so silly, she stopped to read the notice: MUSEO ARCHEOLOGICO NAZIONALE DI NAPOLI.

'It must be a museum,' she said. 'Let's have a look inside.'

'I'm not in the mood.'

'Well, I'm going in,' Annie said, surprising herself. 'You go on, and I'll meet you in an hour.'

'Where will you be?' Ferguson's tone was sulky.

Annie decided to ignore it. If he didn't want to come with her he wasn't going to stop her enjoying something she would never get another chance to see. 'I'll wait for you here, just inside the entrance.'

Inside, the eighteenth-century building appeared to Annie a cross between a cathedral and a fine country house. Even though she was used to the grand rooms at Bonham Place, it was a little daunting hearing the heels of her shoes echoing on the black and white marble floor, sharing the huge spaces with only a handful of visitors. But when she reached the art gallery she soon forgot any awkwardness. The soaring pilasters attracted her gaze upwards, where she strained her neck to admire the painted ceiling. It was a riot of pink cherubs, blue sky and silken white clouds, but too far away to be distinct. A real image of heaven, Annie thought, pleased with herself that in spite of Ferguson she'd made the decision to spend an hour here. She took her time as she stared at the paintings, wishing she knew more about the subjects.

In one of the rooms she was the only visitor. This was a tall, narrow room with a vaulted ceiling and an enormous arched window at one end. Slowly, she walked along the row of life-like busts and heads, perched on tall pedestals and columns, their blank unseeing eyes making her feel a little uncomfortable.

Some of them are quite cruel looking, Annie thought, as she left the Roman emperors and stepped over to a group of Greek gods and goddesses. Standing in front of a beautiful full- size female figure, she was thrilled to recognise her as one of the classical sculptures in the Great Hall at Bonham Place. Athena. It was like coming across an old friend. Annie knew from Sir Henry that Athena was no ordinary goddess. Once, when he'd found her deep in admiration in front of the cast at Bonham Place, he told her that Athena was the Greek goddess of war and love, and the protector of Athens. This particular image showed Athena wearing her helmet off her face, her shield in her left hand and her right hand raised high. It was a strong masculine stance, yet the drapery was very definitely feminine. She walked round the figure, her fingers briefly touching the smooth cold marble. Athena was carved in as great a detail at the back as it was the front, she noticed, as she marvelled at both the exquisite work of the sculptor and the woman herself. Yes, Athena was certainly a woman who knew her own mind, and would be a challenge for any man...or god. Her lips curved in a smile as she reluctantly moved to the next goddess.

Annie came to another gallery where a museum guide ex- plained in excellent English about Pompeii, a town near Naples, and what had happened to the residents when they were suffocated by ash from Vesuvius. Horrified at such a terrible event she hadn't known about when she'd stood on the deck of the *Orsova* to watch the volcano, her heart went out to the victims. She pressed her nose against the glass cabinets, determined to look closely at the artefacts and paintings they had left behind in their mad dash, absurdly wishing they could somehow know she was thinking of them.

She was sure Ferguson would have been interested in all that was on display. Why hadn't he wanted to come with her? She looked at her watch: ten past twelve. Five minutes to go. Sadly, there was no time to look at the mosaics. She began to make her way back to the entrance.

At twenty-five-past twelve Ferguson was still nowhere in sight. What should she do? She couldn't wander around Naples on her own, and even if she ventured outside she'd never find him. He *must* come along soon.

The guide called out something in Italian that she didn't understand, but the few remaining visitors wandered towards the entrance.

'We close for lunch,' the same guide appeared at her elbow.

Annie nodded and walked back the way she'd come. At the reception desk a family was choosing postcards.

'This is a good one of the harbour,' the gentleman said. 'We'll buy half a dozen.'

Maybe she could pretend she was with them. She slipped behind one of the postcard stands and after they'd made their purchase, followed them outside.

It felt as though Mrs Jenner had left her oven door open and ordered her to put her head inside. The sun burned the square with a full harsh light, stripping any colour, natural or man-made. How stark and baked everywhere looked. There wasn't a breath of air. It was unlike any weather she'd ever known; as though it were suffocating her. Yet everyone at home would be preparing for autumn and the long cold winter, and thinking how lucky Annie was. One of her shoes was pinching and she tried to stretch her swollen toes in the confined space as she turned this way and that, searching for her husband.

The family she'd followed walked briskly, as though they knew where they were going. The husband bent his head to say something to his wife and she looked up and nodded, giving him a loving smile. Annie couldn't help wishing Ferguson had stayed with her. They could have strolled round the square together like this family.

As if she'd read Annie's thoughts, the lady turned round and caught her eye.

'Didn't we see you in the museum, my dear?'

'Yes. I was waiting for my husband. He went to have a coffee. But he's late.'

'You shouldn't be walking alone,' the gentleman joined in, frowning and tipping his hat. 'Naples is a hotbed of crime. A woman on her own could get attacked.'

A shiver of apprehension ran down Annie's back.

'We were to meet at quarter past twelve but there's no sign of him.'

'Well, it's now...' the man looked at his watch, 'twenty to one. I hope nothing's happened.'

'I expect he's got talking to someone and forgotten the time,' Annie said, annoyed that she had to make an excuse for him. Ferguson had his watch and they'd agreed one hour. It really was too bad. She felt the full power of the sun scorching her face and instinctively pulled her hat lower down on her forehead.

'Why don't you join us,' the lady suggested. 'We're going to have a drink at one of the cafés on the square. We'll sit outside so you can see everyone who comes and goes.'

'It's very kind of you, but—'

'Not at all,' the man said. 'We'd better introduce ourselves. I'm Geoffrey Marshall and this is my wife, Doreen. Our twins, Bobby and Bertie.'

Gratefully, Annie walked in step with the Marshalls to the café in the far corner. Tired from her museum visit, her throat parched from the sun, even a glass of iced water would be welcome. Mr Marshall ordered a variety of cold drinks, and tea for his wife while she chatted to Annie. They were also on the *Orsova* but going to Sydney to see Mrs Marshall's sister.

'She emigrated three years ago and it's the first time I'll have seen her,' Mrs Marshall was saying as the waiter brought them their drinks.

'She must be looking forward to your visit,' Annie said. 'Is she married?'

She never heard the answer. As the waiter put a glass of something orange coloured in front of her she caught sight of a woman about to go into a small café opposite.

Adele.

'I'm so sorry,' Annie said breathlessly, jumping up. 'I've just seen a friend from the ship. She might have seen my husband. Please forgive me.' She reached for her purse. 'Can you tell me how much I owe? I'm afraid I only have English money.'

'You don't owe a penny,' Mr Marshall said, politely standing as she made to rush off. 'The boys will have your drink in no time.'

'If you're sure...' Annie said uncertainly. 'I feel so rude but—'

'You hurry after her, dear,' Mrs Marshall said. 'And do make yourselves known to us on the ship.'

'Thank you,' Annie said. But she knew she wouldn't. From their clothes and manners, Mr and Mrs Marshall's quarters were a long way from hers. Annie hurried across the square.

An old man was sitting outside the café where Adele had disappeared, and he garbled something to Annie which she couldn't understand. Feeling uncomfortable under his open stare she merely nodded and pushed open the door. It was as black as a cave and she blinked a few times, trying to adjust her vision.

'Adele! Are you in here?'

A woman rose from one of the tables.

'Annie! What—'

'Have you seen Ferguson?' Annie interrupted, too anxious to be polite.

'He had a beer earlier, then went looking for you. Why don't you join us? I'm sure he'll be back soon. Sit over there.' Adele pointed to a couple of chairs in a corner, close to her table, and threw Annie an intense look, then slid back into her own chair with her three companions. Black eyes switched from their cards as they turned to her. There was a pile of coins at each place setting. The biggest and untidiest pile was directly in front of Adele.

Annie sat in the gloom watching. So this was how it worked. She could see Adele was completely at ease, the way she called out the cards and pulled more coins towards her. The men gave a mirthless laugh and looked up as the door opened. A figure blundered in.

'I can't see her anywhere.' The man pulled a chair up at the table next to Adele, and even though it was dark, Annie saw the older woman glance at her and shake her head in warning.

Ignoring her, Annie rose to her feet and walked towards him.

'Are you looking for me?' she said, not able to keep the sarcasm from her voice.

Ferguson turned his head. 'Annie! Whatever are you doing here?'

'I could ask you the same question.'

12

Never, as long as she lived, would Annie forget that terrible Red Sea. Both male and female passengers, whatever class they were in, began to shed their jackets. One of the cooks told her it was the worst heat in thirty-seven years.

'We'll be serving ice cream for elevenses instead of beef tea,' he told Annie as he opened the heavy steel door for her that led to the sloping deck. 'That should cool you down. Not that you look in the least bit hot,' he added quickly, sending her an admiring glance while wiping the sweat from his balding head with his handkerchief.

Ice cream sounded wonderful, but after the long morning waiting for something refreshing, Annie found it was too hot to bother eating. Really, it was too hot to breathe. Her lungs felt they would burst. Perspiration soaked the back of her dress and under her armpits. Several passengers developed severe coughs, and children were forever crying with heat rash. Even with the division of classes, it seemed everyone was crowded in on each other, all twelve hundred of them if you counted the crew. One elderly lady had lain unconscious for hours until the doctor managed to bring her round. Annie wondered who and what would be the next emergency.

One evening, when she thought she would die of suffocation, the captain announced if anyone was feeling the heat too badly in third class they could sleep on deck. In the rush to find a space, Annie managed to find a corner by a coil of ropes. She was safe as long as she didn't sit up suddenly and hit her head on the roof of the iron steps above. But it was heaven compared with the stuffy cabin below, sharing with all those bodies.

The next morning, when she'd attempted to brush herself down, she couldn't help giving a wry smile at a notice pinned at eye level to one of the metal posts. LADY PASSENGERS SHOULD NOTE THAT IT IS NOT CONSIDERED CORRECT TO SIT OUT ON DECK IN THE DARK! Well, she didn't seem to have come to much harm.

She wondered how Ferguson was. He'd been subdued on the way back from Naples. She'd tried to question him as to why he was with Adele when he always ignored her on the ship or constantly warned Annie not to have anything to do with her. His explanation was that he'd been thirsty and gone into the nearest bar for a cold drink. Adele happened to be there. Annie was sure he wasn't telling the whole truth but she didn't feel the ship was the right place to have an argument. Maybe she was making too much of it, but for the moment she was annoyed with him, so it was just as well they were forced to live in separate quarters.

Until now she'd managed not to be sick, but as the days went by the weather conditions were worsening. One of the sailors said it was a monsoon as the ship tossed up and down and rolled from side to side like a toy boat in a child's bath. Annie crawled back to her bunk, her body trembling as she listened to the cries of women and children every time the lightning flashed and the thunder banged. How she wished she could comfort them, but she was too frightened to move.

She swallowed hard, then again, to keep the sourness in her throat from rising, but by now she knew she was going to be sick. She forced herself out of her bunk and stumbled along the passageways to the lavatories, her lips clamped together by sheer willpower. As she flung open the door the stench hit her. Women and girls were heaving over the line of washbasins, some of them with their dresses already soiled, their skins transparent. Groans and retching sounds spilled from the cubicles. Bile rose in Annie's throat. If only someone would come out so she could dash in. Now, she was oblivious to the ship's antics. All she could think of was to get her head over the pan. Please, God, let her get there in time.

At last a young woman appeared from one of the cubicles and Annie rushed in. Immediately, she brought up the contents of the previous night's sausages and bubble and squeak. She drew slowly up, feeling weak and a little ashamed. She took a piece of shiny toilet paper out of the packet to dab her chin, pulling a face at the foul taste in her mouth, desperate for a glass of water. If only Ferguson was with her. But no, on second thoughts she was glad he was at the other end of the ship, unaware of her plight. She couldn't bear him to see her in such a state.

The ship pitched again and a child screamed, 'I want me mam!'

Annie, holding the door open for the next woman who pushed past her with unseeing eyes, spotted the little girl trying to elbow an old lady aside. Frustrated that she'd lost her chance, the child promptly vomited all over the old lady's shoes.

'Now look what you've done, you naughty girl.'

'I couldn't help it,' the child whimpered, wiping her face with the sleeve of her dress.

Annie's heart contracted. She was only eight or nine, Annie guessed, and there was no sign of her mother. The little girl flew to another basin and retched over and over until Annie thought there could be nothing left inside. Where was her mother?

She had a vision of herself at the same age as the little girl when her own mother was ill. She must help the child find her mother. Annie looked around. More women had swarmed through the door, barely able to wait their turn, ignoring the others in their personal misery. Feeling a little better, Annie fought her way towards the child, who was still bent over the sink. She touched her on the back.

'I'm here, love. Don't be afraid.'

The little girl straightened with effort and looked round, the word 'Mam' dying on her lips as she saw it wasn't her mother. Her face was ashen, her eyes dull, her plaits hanging like two wet ropes. She mumbled something unintelligible, then gave a feeble cry and slowly crumpled to the floor.

Without stopping to think, Annie knelt down by her side and rapidly undid the top buttons of the little girl's dress. She rubbed the smooth young hand and leaned over her, praying the ship would stop rolling, even for a minute, so she could attend to the child without slipping and falling on top of her.

'Wake up…you're going to be all right. Please open your eyes. Please.'

The child's eyelids fluttered open in obedience. Her pale eyes were red-rimmed and glistening with tears. Annie gently pushed the strands of hair back from the little girl's forehead, then recoiled. Her forehead was covered in angry-looking blisters.

Dear God.

'I'm going to fetch some help.' Annie tried not to show her alarm as she let the little girl's fringe drop back. She put her arm behind the child's head to pull her up into a seating position. She leaned her against the wall. 'Where is your mother?'

The little girl shook her head and whispered, 'I don't know.'

'What's your name?'

'Rosie.'

By now, three or four women had formed a circle and were looking curiously down at the pair.

'What's your mother's name?' Annie's voice was gentle.

'Maureen.'

'Then I will try to find her. Stay here, Rosie, until I find your mother.' Annie's voice was decisive. 'Would you please keep an eye on her?' She appealed to a thin grey-haired woman. 'I promise I won't be long.'

'See you don't,' the woman replied. 'I've been sick meself and want me bed.'

'She's just a child.' Annie glared at the woman.

Annie instinctively lifted up her skirt as she staggered out of the lavatories and tottered along the corridor, conscious of odours of disinfectant and wax. She swallowed several times, letting her skirt free as she flattened her palms against the sides of the corridor to steady herself against the next wave. The only thing she must think about was finding the doctor. There was something about Rosie that frightened her.

She bumped straight into a man coming round the corner.

'Here, where do you think...?' his voice trailed off. 'Annie!'

'Ferguson! Oh, thank goodness.'

He put his hands out to steady her, and in her relief Annie forgot how cross she was with him.

'I came to look for you...see if you were all right,' he said.

'Oh, Ferguson.' Annie had to restrain herself from falling into his arms. 'I've been so lonely and sick...and afraid. I kept thinking the ship was going over and I'd never see you again.'

'Don't be such a goose. Of course you'll see me again. This ship's perfectly safe.'

'It hasn't *felt* safe to me these last hours,' Annie grimaced, 'though I feel better now.' She clutched the sleeve of his jacket. 'But there's a sick child in the ladies' lavatories.'

'Lots of passengers are sick with this storm,' Ferguson said, 'but thank goodness *I* don't feel anything.'

'It's not a case of seasickness. It's something more.' Annie looked round to see if anyone else was nearby. 'I think she might have smallpox,' she whispered.

'What makes you say that?' Ferguson gripped both her arms, his eyes intense.

'She's got a rash on her forehead and feels very hot.'

'Probably too much sun.'

'No,' Annie said firmly. 'It's not sun. I'm certain of it.'

'You didn't touch her?' His voice sharpened.

'Of course I did,' Annie snapped. 'I had to. It was only when I smoothed her hair back that I saw all the blisters. Gladys told me *she* had smallpox before she worked at Bonham Place and that's how hers started – on her forehead. It spread to the rest of her face in hours and two days later she said her whole body was covered.' Annie's voice rose. 'Ferguson, the child needs to see the doctor quickly.'

'Don't jump to conclusions,' he said. 'It could be measles. But I won't have you going near her anymore. I don't want you getting sick.'

'I've got to find the doctor. Unless *you* fetch him.'

'You poor girl.' Ferguson's grim expression changed to a smile. He put his arms around her but she shrugged him off. Why couldn't he understand the urgency? 'You've had a rough time, haven't you, dearest? You need to rest.'

'It doesn't matter about me. Ferguson, please—'

Ferguson dropped his arms. 'Oh, all right,' he said irritably. 'I'll go and look for the doctor. What's the child's name?'

'Rosie...that's all I know. Her mother is Maureen.'

Annie collapsed on to her bunk and lay flat on her back. She closed her eyes and took some deep breaths, trying not to fight the motion. Half awake, half drifting, an almighty crack suddenly echoed through the ship. She sat bolt upright, sure the ship was breaking up beneath her, her heartbeats ready to burst out of her chest. She felt rather than heard the presence of a figure in the cabin.

'Who's there?' she demanded.

'Are you all right, dear?'

Though Annie could only see the dim outline of someone in the darkness, she recognised Mrs Davey's voice.

'I think so.' She could barely summon the energy to speak.

'I'll get you some liver salts from the doctor,' Mrs Davey promised. 'I'll be back in two shakes of a duck's tail.'

'Thank you, Mrs Davey,' Annie whispered. She closed her eyes as she met the next roll head on.

Annie remained in her cabin until late morning of the following day, still too nauseous to eat anything. She slept fitfully but time moved to a crawl. She thought the night would never end. In her dreams she struggled to save Rosie from drowning. Dreams turned into a nightmare as she could never get near enough. Then just when she'd grabbed Rosie's hand, the child's fingers slipped from her own, and she could only watch in horror as the waves closed over the little girl's head, and she could still hear her crying for her mother. Annie awoke in a cold sweat. She lay still for a few minutes, thankful it was only a dream, wondering what time it was, and listening to the snores of her fellow passengers rumbling through the darkness.

She must have dropped off again for when she awoke something was different. She was alone in the cabin and the great ship was gently rocking her like a mother with her baby. She no longer felt bilious. Gingerly, she sat up, then moved to the edge of her bunk, her feet dangling over the side. Nothing happened. She came down the ladder, stood straight to test her balance, and blew her cheeks out slowly with relief. Her stomach gurgled and even the thought of the lumpy grey porridge did nothing to diminish the return of her appetite. Then she remembered Rosie.

What had happened to her? Was Rosie's mother sick in bed herself? Had Ferguson found the doctor? If so, had he diagnosed smallpox? Would it spread to the other passengers? Might little Rosie die? There were so many unanswered questions. She dressed quickly. She needed to find Ferguson.

Annie put her head in the dining room but there were only a few people finishing their breakfast. Just as she turned to leave, a male voice boomed over the megaphone.

'Your attention, please. This is your captain speaking. There is no need for alarm, but anyone who has been in contact with Rosie

Barber, a nine-year-old girl with long dark pigtails, please report to the hospital on the lowest deck immediately.'

As soon as the word 'hospital' was mentioned there was a buzz of voices.

'She must have something contagious,' one woman muttered, 'else why would they want to see everyone?'

'I'm going to catch it and die.' A girl sitting nearby, not quite grown-up, broke into sobs. 'I was close to Rosie yesterday.'

'Be quiet,' admonished the woman. 'You'll have the whole ship panicking. It's probably nothing.'

Annie fled from the dining room. There was no time to speak to Ferguson. She hurried down the stairs and joined a group of adults and a couple of children in a waiting room. She counted sixteen altogether, two of them crew members. A young nurse appeared and she ushered them into the doctor's surgery, one by one. Annie didn't have long to wait.

'Doctor Townsend will see you now,' the nurse informed her. She led Annie to an adjoining room where a dark-haired man in a crisp white coat sat behind his desk. At her approach he got up briefly, his height dwarfing the desk as he gave a half smile, then motioned her to be seated.

'At what point did you come into contact with the child, Mrs Bishop?'

'Yesterday afternoon.' Annie explained what had happened. His eyes never left her face as he listened, nodding when she told him how she'd noticed the rash on Rosie's forehead.

'I'm afraid your diagnosis is correct.' Doctor Townsend removed his glasses and set them down in front of him. 'She is highly contagious and has to be separated from everyone. Tell me...' he looked at her with intelligent eyes, 'have you been vaccinated against smallpox?'

'Yes,' Annie replied. 'When I was a child.' She wondered if his accent was Australian. He had a way of pronouncing his vowels, stretching them out, that was pleasant to listen to.

'Good.' Dr Townsend chewed his pencil thoughtfully, then raised his eyes to hers. She noticed they were grey, but not the steel grey of a November sky, more like the soft warm coat of a greyhound. She felt her cheeks warm as he continued eyeing her. 'Neither of the nurses has been vaccinated,' he added with an imperceptible nod, as though he had come to some conclusion.

'That's bad, isn't it?' she said, hoping he hadn't noticed her blush. 'They might easily catch it.'

'Exactly. I wonder, Mrs Bishop, if I could call upon you in this crisis.'

Annie felt her heart thump against her ribs as she heard herself answering: 'Yes, of course, doctor, if you think I can be of any use. What would you like me to do?'

24th September 1913, on board the *Orsova*

I feel quite upset today but all I can do is write it down in my precious journal.

It started when Ferguson and I were taking a walk round the deck this afternoon. I told him I was going to help the doctor with the smallpox patients. I thought he'd be pleased. Instead, he went pale, his eyes like blue marbles as he stared at me.

Why ever did you suggest such a thing?

I didn't, I told him. Dr Townsend asked if I would, and of course I said yes.

Yes, of course you would, he said, and there was a horrid edge to his tone. Then he looked at me as though seeing me for the first time. Do you realise what you're proposing, being among all those infected people, Annie?

Dr Townsend needs help desperately, I told him. His two nurses haven't been vaccinated, so they're not allowed to stay, but I have.

Well, I haven't been vaccinated. I've never had smallpox

112

so if I'm exposed to it through you—

Everyone who hasn't been vaccinated will be quarantined, I said. It would be nice if he'd asked about the patients. He didn't even ask how little Rosie was. I was worried to death about the child. I told him Dr Townsend had sent orders that no one would be allowed to disembark at any other ports until we reached Melbourne.

Being quarantined doesn't guarantee I won't catch it, he said, his face pink.

I told him Dr Townsend was doing everything to make sure it didn't spread.

I couldn't believe my husband was behaving so selfishly. It wasn't as though he hadn't been exposed to sickness in his own family. But then I suddenly realised. It was just because he had lost his brother and sister that he was trying to protect us both.

Let's not quarrel, dear, I begged, going up to him and kissing his cheek.

All right, he said, putting both his hands on the top of my arms and pressing them. A little warmth had crept back into his eyes. Just be very careful, was all he said.

He tried to make amends but I know he didn't really understand. Somehow that made me feel sad. I left him and went back to my cabin to collect my things. Dr Townsend said I would have to move into the nurses' room they used on night duty as I could be a carrier. Well, it won't upset me to leave that stuffy cabin. But how can I make Ferguson see it's something I simply must do?

13

Bonham

Ruby, September 1913

Three weeks have gone by. Annie and Fergus must be halfway to Australia. Why, oh why didn't Fergus pick me? It could have been me on the ship ready to start a new life. Maybe I would have to wait until I was sixteen but if I had Fergus I wouldn't mind. Can't he see how much better suited we are? He's always ready for a joke and I always laugh at them but Annie is very serious. Besides, I'm prettier. I haven't got that awful nose so I look better in hats.

Pa is getting more bad-tempered and everything I say is wrong. Ethel is the blue-eyed angel and I'm the wicked witch.

But I have some news. I haven't even told Pa yet. I have a job. I begged Pa to let me go to town on Monday and I went to the haberdasher's to get some ribbon for my hat. Mrs Dawson couldn't serve me for several minutes and I ended up helping a lady choose her buttons. Mrs Dawson let slip the assistant was ill and would not be able to work for a few weeks. I asked if I could take her place and she looked at me long and hard, then said I could. Pa will have a fit but he can't stop me. It's not as though it's going to be forever and it's only in the afternoons. Instead of going mad in the house all day I will have something to look forward to, meeting people and helping the ladies to choose pretty things to decorate their hats and dresses. Best of all I can start to save for my trip to Australia. If I don't take matters into my own hands I could wait forever for Annie and Fergus to send me the ticket money. And I'm not going to wait.

Pa made no attempt to stop me from taking up the position in Mrs Dawson's shop. He just grunted and said, 'So long as supper's on the table at six o'clock when I come through the door.'

I will have to prepare everything in the morning. Oh, how I hate cooking. At least Ethel will leave school next year. She's like Annie, loves cooking, so let her do it.

Mrs Dawson sacked me on my second day. I argued with a customer. She said the customer is always right, but it wasn't in the case of Mrs Gilly. Her voice penetrated every corner of the shop. She brought back a skein of wool which she insisted was flawed and demanded her money back. I refused because she had used up three-quarters, and had already wound the skein into a ball. So there couldn't have been much wrong with it and I told her so. She screamed out for Mrs Dawson, who was having a quiet cup of tea upstairs and was none too pleased when I called her down.

I tried to explain but before I got a word in Mrs Gilly told her a pack of lies, said that I had been rude, and reminded Mrs Dawson about the customer always being right. Mrs Dawson frowned at me and said she would see that I was punished. She gave Mrs Gilly her money back (I wouldn't have) and Mrs Gilly stormed out. By this time the other customers were really enjoying the scene. Mrs Dawson said in front of them, 'I'm afraid this isn't going to work, Ruby, so take your bag and leave without any more trouble.' I stood there furious, but there was nothing I could say which would persuade her to let me keep my job. The other three ladies in the shop could have told her the truth, but they kept their traps shut and nothing would prise them open. I tried to stick up for myself but Mrs Dawson went all stiff and said for me to go.

Now I have to tell Pa. He won't be pleased if he thinks I've forgotten my manners. He will probably believe Mrs Dawson and that bitch Mrs Gilly. So I'm doing the cooking and housework again. I feel like Cinderella, except there's no prince who will come to my rescue.

14

On board the Orsova

A week later the cramped ward in the bowels of the ship was full and all the passengers who had not been inoculated against the smallpox were strictly quarantined. It was frightening how many people Rosie had come into contact with, Annie thought, as she gave the patients their evening milk drink, but thankfully only eight were showing symptoms of smallpox. She was upset to see that one of the seriously ill patients was poor Mrs Davey, who lay very still and barely mumbled a word.

'How are you feeling, Mrs O'Neil?' Annie asked.

Mrs O'Neil was the thin grey-haired woman whom Annie had ordered to keep an eye on Rosie when she'd rushed out of the lavatories to find the doctor.

'Call me Minnie,' Mrs O'Neil whispered. 'Am I going to die?'

'Of course not, Mrs...Minnie,' Annie replied, crossing her fingers behind her back.

She didn't know much about smallpox, only that children and older people who contracted it were more likely to succumb. She eased a thermometer under Minnie's tongue for the second time since supper, thinking how different the woman was now she had gone down with the disease herself. Her temperature was high but not alarmingly so; she would probably survive. Annie pencilled the result on Mrs O'Neil's report card for Dr Townsend to assess when he made his rounds.

Her eyes roved around the crowded ward. Except for Minnie

and Rosie the other patients were asleep or reading. She glanced up at the clock. Not quite seven. Her stomach began making grumbling noises but she ignored it. One of the cooks' assistants would be bringing them something in half an hour or so. She tiptoed over to Rosie who lay on her back, her eyes enormous, looking up at the ceiling. The child's face was flushed and beaded with perspiration, and her small hands gripped the edge of the sheet.

'You haven't drunk your milk, Rosie,' she said softly, worried that the child wasn't interested in any food or drink.

Rosie looked at her with eyes too bright, and shook her head. 'My mouth is all sore inside.'

'I know, darling, but you must try a little so you get better.' Annie put her hand under Rosie's head. 'Here, let me help you sit up.' She gently propped the little girl into a sitting position and tucked another pillow behind her. 'Come on, love. It's still warm.'

'Don't want it.' Rosie turned her head away as Annie held the cup to her small mouth.

'Just a few sips. Come on, Rosie. Your mam will be awfully worried if I tell her you haven't eaten or drunk anything.'

'Why doesn't she come?' Rosie asked listlessly.

'She will do. When you're feeling better. You don't want her to catch it, do you?'

Rosie started to cry.

'Try and sleep now and when you wake up in the morning I'll give you a piece of bread with real butter and jam.'

Annie wrapped the sheet and a light blanket round the child, stifling a yawn.

'That's enough, Annie,' Dr Townsend said, looking over his shoulder as he soaped his hands in the corner washbasin. He'd stopped calling her Mrs Bishop after the first day, without even asking if she minded, and though she would never have admitted it to anyone, least of all Ferguson, she rather liked it. 'Go and get some rest.'

'Don't dismiss me before I have something to eat, else I won't have the energy to come back tomorrow,' Annie joked. That was the best part of the day, having supper with Dr Townsend, quietly chatting and keeping an ear out for the patients, feeling rewarded that they were working together to get everyone well.

Dr Townsend dropped the towel into the dirty washing basket, his smile fading as he looked at her. Annie met his steady gaze.

'You've been up far too many hours this week, though I don't know what I would have done without you.'

'I'm all right,' Annie protested, though her legs felt they would collapse at any minute. 'You must be tired as well.' She flushed at the idea of commenting on a doctor's well-being, but she'd noticed the circles under his eyes deepen each day.

'We could really do with another person to help.' Dr Townsend frowned. 'Can you think of anyone?'

'Not really,' Annie said, mentally going through all those women she knew by sight or were in her cabin. She didn't have much confidence in any of them. Some of them were too young, though she admitted she probably wasn't much older. She just felt so, being married. But what about Adele? She hadn't been confined to her cabin so she must have been inoculated. 'There may be someone,' Annie said. 'I'll ask her.'

Annie had her chance the following day when she went up on deck for a few minutes before breakfast. It was not yet half-past five but she craved fresh air before the day started. Sometimes she felt stifled in the ward, so far below the passenger decks. If only the patients could smell the sea air and feel the breeze on their skin, she was sure it would do them good. Her hands grasped the rail as she looked as far out as she could, dazed by the sight of the ship cutting through the water leaving a thick foamy trail. She drew in long, deep breaths. The sun was rising, forming dancing patterns of reds and oranges and pinks over the waves, and she watched, entranced, for several minutes. She was just about to drag herself away when she spotted Adele coming up the steps.

'Where've you been lately?' Adele chuckled as she joined her. 'Sneaking off to see your husband?'

Annie felt her face warm. 'No, nothing like that.' She put her hand impulsively over Adele's on the rail. 'Adele, may I ask you something?'

'What's on your mind?' Adele turned her head to look at Annie. 'You look serious.'

'I've been helping in the hospital and—'

'You mean you've had no training as a nurse and you're exposing yourself to a disease which can kill?' Adele took a step back, her green eyes glinting in disbelief. 'Are you mad?'

These exact words matched Ferguson's outburst. Somehow she had to convince her friend.

'I've been injected against it,' Annie said, 'so I'm happy to help. But we're desperately short as the two nurses haven't been vaccinated so they've been confined to their cabins.'

'You're not asking *me* to help, are you?' Adele's eyebrows shot up in horror. She looked so aghast Annie had to smile.

'Yes, I am.'

'No fear. Not for you. Not for anyone. There must be loads of women who would love to play Florence Nightingale, but that role is not for me.' Adele tucked a stray golden curl behind her ear.

'You don't have to wash them or anything. I do that,' Annie said, still hoping to persuade her friend. 'All you'd have to do is give them drinks and food and read to them, or just sit with them. There are only two women who need more attention – Mrs Davey, who was in my cabin, and Minnie O'Neil. But the one I'm really worried about is little Rosie. She's only nine. She needs someone to encourage her to eat something…to sit with her and talk to her. Her mother's in quarantine. I haven't got as much time as I'd like because of all the other patients.' She looked imploringly at Adele. 'You'd be just the person for the job. And we get better meals than the ones in the canteen,' Annie added with a sly grin. 'Dr Townsend said it's from first class.'

'Now you're talking.' Adele's face brightened. 'Well, so long as it's just for the child. And I don't have to see no blood. I can't stand blood. Or sick.'

'No, no, there's no blood,' Annie rushed in. 'And if anyone's sick I'm used to clearing it up. Oh, Adele, Dr Townsend will be so grateful.'

Grateful wasn't quite the right word. Dr Townsend looked astounded to see Adele waltz in the following morning, fully made up, and wearing an entirely unsuitable dress of light-coloured material with a deep-cut lacy collar.

'Are you sure she's the right person?' he asked Annie in an undertone when Adele had gone to fetch another jug of water.

'She'll be fine.' Annie's eyes were mischievous. 'As long as she doesn't see any blood. If it's all right with you, Dr Townsend, I've put her in charge of Rosie. I think the child will take to her and she might get her to eat something.'

'Well, I'll reserve judgement.' Dr Townsend sounded doubtful. 'Keep an eye on her, won't you? And for goodness' sake give her the largest apron you can find.'

Rosie was fascinated with Adele from the start. It was probably because Adele didn't treat her as a child, Annie thought. After two days of Adele's company Rosie was sitting up in bed and laughing at something Adele was saying. Already the little girl's colour looked almost normal and she'd eaten a boiled egg with bread and butter that morning. Adele had even shampooed her hair and instead of the tight dark plaits, Rosie's hair fell softly to her shoulders. Annie was amused to see that she had tucked one lock behind her ear the same way Adele sometimes did hers. Even Dr Townsend was surprised.

'Looks like it's your doing, Miss Frost,' he told her, smiling, when Adele was closing the book she'd been reading to Rosie. 'I can see she's definitely over the worst.'

Adele gave him a flirtatious smile in return. 'Nothing I did, I'm sure. It's because you're such a marvellous doctor.' She fluttered her lashes at him but he gave the two young women a quick nod and turned swiftly away. Annie couldn't help joining in with Adele's giggles.

'Honestly, Annie, he's too serious for words. Bit of a looker, though. If you'd told me how handsome he was, I wouldn't have hesitated.'

'Do you think he's…?' Annie caught herself and blushed to her roots.

'Oo-er. You look like you've got it bad.' Adele looked at her from under raised eyebrows.

'What are you talking about?' Annie demanded.

'You like him, Annie.'

'Of course I like him,' Annie retorted, furious with herself. 'We all do. He's a wonderful doctor. And married, Adele.'

Adele's face dropped with disappointment. 'Did he tell you then?'

'Not in so many words, but he's bound to be.'

'Not necessarily,' Adele said. 'But it's a shame for all of us if he is.' She sighed, rose to her feet and stretched her arms above her head, opening her mouth in a yawn. 'Oh, well. I s'pose we'd better get those bedpans. I'll give them out but you can collect them when they're full,' she added slyly.

The two of them busied themselves for the next hour but Annie couldn't push the thought out of her mind that she wished Adele hadn't noticed Dr Townsend in quite that way.

'Just because his wife's not with him doesn't mean to say he's fair game,' Annie couldn't help saying when Dr Townsend left the ward to catch a breath of air. Why did she have to defend Dr Townsend? He was perfectly capable of sticking up for himself.

Adele's smile was lazy and all-knowing. 'All men are fair game,' she said, using Annie's words as she bent to make an untidy hospital corner on the clean sheet of Mrs Davey's bed.

Annie tucked the sheet neatly in on her side. She looked up. After the tiniest hesitation she said, 'Not Ferguson.'

But she couldn't help remembering the girls on the dance floor at home. The way Ferguson smiled that crooked smile of his when one of the girls put a hand on his shoulder in the 'Ladies' Excuse Me' and she'd have to watch the pair of them whirl away. But he always came back to her, didn't he?

'Even Ferguson.'

'No,' Annie said, looking steadily at the other woman until Adele raised her eyes heavenwards. She changed the subject to something safer. 'I've made the tea so let's put our feet up for ten minutes.'

'Good idea.' Adele followed her to the small kitchen in silence and pulled out two stools. Annie poured the tea but just as she was handing Adele a cup, a sudden swell sent half of it down her apron. Adele chuckled, breaking the tension. 'You still haven't found your sea legs, have you?'

'Adele, I've been wanting to ask you something,' Annie blurted.

'Oh?' Adele's brows rose. 'Last time you said that, I ended up here.'

Annie smiled. 'I know. And look how well it's turned out.'

Her friend grinned. 'That's as maybe. Well, go on then. What is it this time?'

'It's just...well, you seemed to know Amber Bay when I mentioned it that first night we sailed.'

Adele's face paled under the powder and Annie half wished she hadn't broached the subject.

'Go on.' Adele's voice was quieter than usual.

'I just thought, because I'm going to work there, and Mrs Scott-Lawson sounded so nice in her letter, that if there's something

123

bad, I would rather know about it sooner than later.'

Adele put her cup down on the workbench and swung round.

'You're partly right, Annie. But I only know *of* Amber Bay. I've never been there, but I knew Mr Scott-Lawson...' Adele paused, 'rather too well.'

15

Alex

Alexander Townsend had almost welcomed the smallpox epidemic. Except for seasickness and heat rash among some of the passengers, the ship's hospital had been quiet. One of the first-class passengers had badly stubbed her foot on a jutting piece of equipment on deck, and there were a few cases of men being the worse for drink. That was about it. With little to do the two nurses had become bored and tended to gossip and he'd had to find them jobs to keep them occupied.

Improper as it would seem if he told anyone, he was glad he finally had a challenge. His goal was to get everyone in the ward back on their feet and completely well before they docked. That was until he realised the two nurses hadn't been vaccinated. How the company hadn't checked for something so basic before they'd engaged those women to come on this crossing, he couldn't imagine.

But if they had been vaccinated he would never have come into such close contact with Annie Bishop.

He cursed quietly, remembering she was newly married. He wondered if Ferguson would make her a good husband. To be fair, he'd only met Annie's husband briefly when he'd rushed up the other day and said there was a child on board who may have smallpox.

'As I haven't been vaccinated I'm going straight to my cabin,' Ferguson had said, turning to leave.

'Just a moment.' Alex put his hand on the other man's arm.

'What did you notice on the child that caused you to suspect it was smallpox?'

'I didn't see her. My wife did. You'd better speak to her.'

'And you are...?'

'Ferguson Bishop.'

He couldn't get away quickly enough, Alex had mused, as he'd watched the figure disappear.

Now, he glanced round the ward. Everyone was quiet. The clock showed nearly midnight. It might be a good opportunity to take ten minutes. He strode over to the hospital kitchen and while the kettle was boiling put two heaped teaspoons of tea in the pot. Barely letting it stand he poured it out but the tea tasted bitter and he added another teaspoon of sugar. As he gulped his tea, burning his lip in his hurry not to be too long, he thought about Annie and Ferguson Bishop.

He was the last person who should be wondering if Ferguson would make Annie a good husband. He'd been a poor specimen to *his* wife. He drained his cup and closed his eyes, remembering two years ago almost to the month how he'd told Gwen he'd be home in time for them to have their first anniversary dinner. A romantic evening, he'd promised her; something they rarely had. She'd said it was important not to be late. She had something to tell him. If he'd taken the time to really look at her instead of kissing her quickly and rushing out, he might have noticed her smile hadn't reached her eyes. He'd thought she was going to tell him she was having a baby. With a sick feeling he remembered how excited he'd been all day. But it wasn't that at all.

She'd been complaining of headaches. He squirmed in his chair when he saw in his mind's eye how he'd left her with two aspirins on several occasions. She'd obviously suspected it was something more serious and consulted another doctor, who had sent her to a neurologist. That evening, on their anniversary, she told him she had a brain tumour, and the neurologist had said that unfortunately there was nothing he could do.

Desperate, Alex had gone to see the neurologist on his own.

'Is the verdict definite?'

'Nothing is definite.' Dr Shaw had looked him in the eye. 'You should know that better than anyone. But we might have been able to operate if it had been spotted earlier.'

Sick to his stomach, he'd asked, 'How long has she got?'

'Six months...at most.'

His wife was twenty-four.

The headaches worsened. One day, a fortnight after he'd spoken to Dr Shaw, he'd rushed home early, panicking as she hadn't telephoned that lunchtime as she usually did. Jabbing his key in the lock, he swung the door open and shouted her name. The hall was empty. There'd been no answer, just an echo of his own voice. 'Gwen!' he'd called again, taking the stairs two at a time. Their bedroom door was closed. He turned the handle, a feeling of dread squeezing his heart.

She was lying on top of the bed, her eyes closed, her mouth half open. He rushed over and grabbed her wrist. Thank God, it was still warm. He felt for her pulse. Nothing. No flicker of eyelashes. He held his hand over her mouth, but there was no soft breath to warm it. She must have lain on the bed in the last few minutes, closed her eyes, and gone to sleep forever.

He collapsed on to his knees by the bed, grasping her hand.

'Oh, my darling Gwen, what have I done?' He spoke the words aloud, his voice thick with despair.

He glanced at the bedside table. Stretched his hand out to the packet of tablets.

It was empty.

He stayed kneeling by the bed and wept his heart out.

Hours later he found her letter propped on the mantelpiece, telling him how sorry she was; how she loved him; how she'd so badly wanted to have a family, but now her dreams were in ashes.

The headaches had got worse and her eyesight was permanently blurred. She couldn't stand it. He was not to blame himself for anything. He was a wonderful doctor and a wonderful husband. The kindest man she'd ever known. She only hoped he would find someone else to love one day.

But he'd never wanted anyone else.

Then he met Annie.

16

Adele took a deep breath. 'I never knew Mrs Scott-Lawson, but I met her husband four years ago.' Annie opened her mouth to say what an extraordinary coincidence it was, but Adele carried on before she could say a word. 'I was a barmaid in one of the hotels in Melbourne and he used to come in twice a week, regular as clockwork.'

Annie was listening intently, her eyes never wavering from her friend. Adele continued. 'He was quite a bit older than me. Nothing special to look at but always very well dressed and clean. I like that in a man. We used to have a bit of a laugh. He'd always buy me a drink. I'd tell him I weren't allowed to drink on duty and put all my tips in a jam jar. They soon mounted up, I'm proud to say.'

Annie threw her a warm smile.

'Any rate,' Adele went on, 'he began to get familiar after a few weeks. Nothing much at first. Just paying me compliments on my hair, or my blouse. I quite liked the attention and didn't think much of it. Then one day he asked if I had a boyfriend. I weren't thinking straight and told him no one special. He asked if he could see me after work. I said no, we wasn't allowed to keep company with the customers. He said no one need know. We could just have supper. So I thought, what's the harm in going for a bite to eat? They were mean with rations at the hotel. So after work that same night I got into his motor car and he took me to a swanky hotel a few miles out. He took me into one of the rooms and...well, you don't want

129

to know the sordid details.' Adele broke off, a sour look in her eyes.

'Oh, Adele. He didn't hurt you, did he?'

'Let's say he weren't the gentleman he made out to be. I said we couldn't see one another outside of work ever again, but he asked why not. It would be our little secret. And he'd see I wouldn't get into trouble.'

'He'd make sure you didn't get sacked?' Annie broke in.

'No, you silly girl.' Adele's lip curled. 'He meant he'd see I didn't get caught with a bun in the oven.'

Annie blushed to her roots. She remembered Gladys had used that same horrid expression about poor Mollie.

'What on earth did you say?' She looked at her friend, and added, 'You don't have to tell me if you don't want to.'

'No, I'll finish it.' Adele's eyes held a steely glint. 'He said – the bastard – if I would let him bed me on a regular basis he'd set me up in business in a year's time so's I'd be independent. I weren't falling for that old chestnut. Can you imagine? Twelve months down the line, me saying I'm ready to get started on a business and him denying everything and telling me he'd get me sacked if I reported him to his wife. Oh, no. So I said I wouldn't do it. And I wouldn't hurt his wife. She'd done nothing wrong. He was furious and left in a right temper. I had to get a taxicab I could ill afford back to my hotel. Next time he came in he begged and pleaded, but I wouldn't do it. So he reported me to my boss. Told him I was rude, and that it weren't the first time. You see, he spent a lot of money there – and brought his friends. Mr King, my boss, didn't want to lose him as a customer so he gave me the push right there and then. I had nowhere to go because I lived in one of the rooms. So I'd lost my job and my digs in the space of five minutes.'

Annie sat in shocked silence, her tea going cold.

'So what did you do then?'

'I packed my things, but the one thing I made sure I took with me was my tips from an old teapot. I'd made near on fifty pounds by then. It was enough to buy a return ticket in what used to be called steerage, look up the family and then come back. Actually, this is my second visit home in four years. And I'm still in one piece.' She gave a hollow laugh.

Annie was horrified. What sort of a household was she going into? Could anything like that happen to her? No, she was a married woman and not nearly so attractive as Adele, with her golden hair and full figure. But already she disliked Mr Scott-Lawson before she'd even met him. And how much should she tell Ferguson, who had set his heart on this family and the two positions that had been offered to them?

'I'm so sorry,' she said, taking Adele's hand. 'But I'm glad we're friends and you told me this.'

'Just keep your eyes open.' Adele squeezed Annie's hand, then picked up their cups and took them to the sink. 'That means on the ship as well. Some of the men, especially the sailors, might think you're fair game.' She looked round at Annie. 'They've been without a woman for a long time. If one of them ever makes a pass at you—'

'They wouldn't,' Annie protested. 'They know I'm married.' She waggled the fingers of her left hand.'

'Yes, men will see you're a married woman with your ring an' all, but it wouldn't stop anyone determined.' Adele's green eyes flashed. 'As I was saying, if anyone makes a pass at you, shove your knee up as hard as you can between his legs. That'll stop him in his tracks.'

Annie felt the blood rush to her cheeks. Adele seemed so sure that no man was to be trusted.

'Have you got that, Annie?'

'Er…yes, I think so.'

'Just one more thing. Please don't repeat any of this to Ferguson, will you? Men always think it's the woman's fault for leading them on. He'd have a go at me.' She laughed at Annie's bewildered expression. 'No, not in that way – but he'd say I was to blame.'

'I'm sure Ferguson wouldn't,' Annie began, but Adele held up her hand to stop her.

'As I said before, men are all the same. I don't trust any of 'em.'

Annie's head was near to bursting as she carried out her duties in the ward, trying to take in all that Adele had told her. She wondered if Mr Scott-Lawson's wife had had any inkling. Maybe she had and turned a blind eye. Suddenly, Annie wished she were back in England. Back to the safety of Bonham Place where she knew the family and there were no dark secrets – at least as far as she knew – except Old Jimmy, the elusive ghost. If she told Ferguson, would he still want to work at Amber Bay? Would he be worried Mr Scott-Lawson might make an approach to her?

She turned the questions over and over in her mind. She was certain Adele was wrong when she said all men were the same – Ferguson would never behave like that. But she couldn't betray Adele's confidence. For one thing, she'd promised Adele, and for another, she couldn't bear it if Ferguson was unsympathetic...which he was likely to be.

Nevertheless, she was grateful Adele had warned her about her future employer. Somehow it made her feel she had found a real friend.

'I'm afraid Mrs Davey passed away an hour ago,' Dr Townsend told Annie two days later when she'd come back on duty after taking a longer lunch break at his insistence, though she'd been reluctant to leave the sick woman.

'Oh, poor Mrs Davey,' Annie said, looking down at the still body with a sheet already pulled up over her head. 'She was in my cabin and so kind to me the first time I was seasick. And she was going to see her sister who was to have an operation. It's so sad.' She looked up and caught Dr Townsend watching her. Their gaze hung for a few seconds. A little embarrassed, Annie broke the silence. 'I wish I'd been with her when it happened.'

'I'd hoped we'd be able to pull everyone through,' Dr Townsend said ruefully, taking off his glasses and pushing his fingers through his dark hair. 'But she had it the worst.'

'What will happen to her?' Annie dreaded his answer.

'She'll be buried at sea. We're too far away to keep her until we disembark. But little Rosie is on the mend now.' He smiled down at her. 'She's so happy her mother is visiting regularly. She'll be able to return to her cabin in a few days, all being well.'

'It's wonderful,' Annie said. 'And a lot of it was Adele's doing.'

'Yes, it was. She turned out to be exactly the right nurse for Rosie.'

'I told you so,' Annie laughed.

'And,' Dr Townsend added, putting out a hand as though to touch hers, then pulling back, 'my instinct was right about you, too.'

Annie smiled at him. For some reason his words sent a soft warmth to her cheeks.

'We're getting close to land now,' Dr Townsend said one morning after he'd been up on deck for a few minutes. Annie was so exhausted she was sure she wouldn't be able to drag through another day, and the thought of arriving in her new homeland had lost some of its charm. She supposed it was all the struggle to get the patients well to be the reason. 'Go and get some fresh air and don't come back until after lunch.' He smiled as he looked down at her, his grey eyes bloodshot from so little sleep.

'No, honestly, I'm all right,' Annie protested. 'Unless, of course, you really don't need me.'

'It's not that...'

Something in his tone made her start. They were standing so close she could smell the salt water on him. She took in his strong features; the wide mouth that was usually serious because of the situation, but sometimes broke into a smile that lit up his face.

133

'A looker' was how Adele described him. Not disagreeing with her friend, Annie nevertheless felt a little odd inspecting him in such detail. Flushing slightly under his gaze, she answered, 'Well…if you're sure.'

'I am.' He took her arm and propelled her gently towards the door.

It was the first time he had touched her. She looked down at his hand, then at his face. There was a strange light in his eyes.

'Are you disembarking in Melbourne or going on to Sydney?' Annie blurted, more for something to say, though suddenly it seemed important to know.

'I'm getting off here,' he said. 'Everyone's well enough to leave the ship, thank goodness, and there'll be a relief doctor coming on board to Sydney.'

'I'm glad,' Annie said truthfully. 'You'll get a chance to rest.'

'Not for long.' Dr Townsend smiled at her. 'I like being busy.'

A shadow passed over his face, and Annie wished she could ask him what had happened to make him look so sad, and if there was anything she could do. Then she realised – he must miss his wife terribly. Yes, that would be it.

'Thank you, Annie,' he said. 'Thank you for everything.' He hesitated. 'I've never asked you where you'll be working.'

'We're going to—'

'This is your captain speaking,' a voice blared through the megaphone, making her jump. 'Would everyone please gather on the upper deck to hear an important announcement.'

'He'll be telling everyone when we'll dock,' Dr Townsend said. 'Go, Annie. They'll all be up on deck and your husband will be waiting for you.'

Not daring to give him another glance, her arm tingling, and confused as to why she was taking so much notice of a man who wasn't her husband, she fled from the room. Thoroughly irritated with herself she hurried along the corridor until, breathless, she reached the main deck. A crowd had already gathered, everyone talking and excitedly pointing out to sea. She followed their gaze and was surprised to see a thin misty line on the horizon.

'Land ahoy!' several men shouted, throwing their hats in the air.

Annie's heart beat fast. Australia. All the months of planning and now they were only days, maybe only hours, away. A lump came to her throat. Everyone around her seemed to have someone to laugh with and share the news, except her. Where was Ferguson? If he was here she couldn't see him.

She'd had no word from him, no message, all the time she'd been helping to nurse the sick passengers. Of course, he hadn't been allowed to leave his cabin, she reminded herself. But Dr Townsend had lifted the ban several days ago. He'd told her he'd heard Ferguson was terrified to catch anything and had decided to stay in his cabin until they docked. Dr Townsend had given her a searching look, and seemed about to add something, but instead had begun to lay out his surgical equipment for the day.

Annie remembered how happy she should have felt at the news of the ban, but all she could think of then was that the two nurses would come back for the last week of the voyage and she would no longer be working with Alex...no, Dr Townsend, she hastily corrected herself. But it hadn't happened. There'd been no mention of returning nurses, and Annie had remained until the end.

Now a small voice in her head insisted Ferguson had stayed away not because he was still terrified of catching smallpox, but because he was displeased with her – she'd gone against his wishes.

'Well, I'm delighted to give you the news you've all been waiting for,' came the clear tones of the captain as Annie scrambled up the iron steps. 'We dock in Melbourne at eight o'clock tomorrow morning. Those of you leaving the ship should disembark quickly at the announcement, following orders from the crew. Others who are going on to Sydney will have the chance to look around Melbourne.

More details will follow early tomorrow morning.'

A cheer rose up at the far end of the deck. Annie spotted Ferguson with some other lads who were waving their arms and laughing. She tried to catch his eye but he wasn't looking in her direction.

'One more thing,' the captain announced. 'We have pictures and photographs of the *Orsova* for sale in the second-class lounge on third deck.' There was a pause. 'Of course, anyone in any class may take this opportunity as a reminder of the voyage. You may purchase them from now until seven o'clock this evening.'

As Annie jostled her way through the crowd towards her husband he suddenly turned as though sensing her presence, and smiled. So Ferguson wasn't angry with her; it must have only been the memory of his little brother and sister that had scared him. She smiled back happily as she reached his side.

'Annie, I've missed you so.' He put his arm round her and kissed her cheek. 'I feel I've been buried alive these last weeks, but everything's going to be all right from now on.'

'I've missed you, too,' she said, but she knew in her heart she wasn't being completely honest. She'd had no time to miss him with looking after the patients. In fact, she'd been relieved he'd kept to his cabin. That way she could concentrate on the job without having to argue with him. But he hadn't asked how *she* was. Or if the patients had all recovered. She thought of Mrs Davey and brushed away a tear.

'What's the matter, Annie?' Ferguson squeezed her arm.

She looked at him, her eyes brimming. 'Nothing. I'm glad it's all over, that's all. The voyage and everything else.'

'Me too.' His lips briefly touched hers.

She waited for him to say something more. That he understood. She felt a prickle of anger, immediately followed by guilt as she remembered her wedding vow: to always obey her husband. She'd only been married a few weeks and already she'd ignored his

136

wishes. But he'd been unreasonable. She'd *had* to volunteer when there had been no one else to help poor Dr Townsend. He was such a wonderful doctor. She would miss their conversations, and the suppers they shared in quiet contentment after Adele had left and all the patients were sleeping. Feeling a little disloyal to Ferguson, she told herself that husbands couldn't possibly be right *all* the time.

'Annie, what would you say if we bought a picture of the ship?'

'I'd say we can't afford it.'

'We don't know how much they are. Let's go and have a look. Give us a chance to see what second class is like.' He took her arm. 'Come on. It will be a laugh.'

The second-class lounge was a different world away. Third class didn't have its own saloon and Annie could see Ferguson's eyes taking it all in. Soft rays of morning sunlight picked out the hundreds of images of the *Orsova* which were set out on long trestle tables. Some had thick black frames and were propped up, but most were weighted down at the corners to be shown flat or rolled, ready for the buyers to take them away. There were pencil drawings and watercolours and oils, as well as prints and photographs and postcards. Annie handed over twopence for two postcards – one to send to her father and sisters, and one for Mr and Mrs Bishop – but everything else looked too dear. She was surprised how many people were buying pictures and wished she had a little money herself to buy one. She moved slowly along the tables with Ferguson and the rest of the crowd, inspecting everything.

'This is nice, Annie.' Ferguson picked up a watercolour of the ship, then laid it quickly back in its spot when he saw the price.

'I love that one,' she said, pointing to a print of an oil painting about two feet wide. It was a framed one of their ship in calm waters.

'And here's the other to make a pair.' Ferguson picked up one exactly the same size but this time the *Orsova* was battling stormy seas. 'What do you think, Annie?'

'Beautiful.' She bent over the table to inspect the ship in calm seas more closely. 'But I'm sure they'll cost a fortune.' She turned round to Ferguson. 'See the colour. It looks as though they've been finished off by hand. We could get a small print of both of them for a lot cheaper.'

'How much are these?' Ferguson held up the picture to ask the man behind the table.

'Five pounds the pair. Without the frames. They're extra.'

'Ferguson, we don't—'

'I'll give you three pounds.'

'Sorry, mate, there's no discount. That's the price. Take it or leave it.' The man looked down his thin nose as though Ferguson was an unpleasant smell.

Ferguson's face turned red. 'We'll take them both,' he said, not bothering to curb his annoyance.

'Ferguson—' Annie began.

'Leave this to me,' he told her, and pulled out five one-pound notes. With a flourish he put them on the table, then looked directly at the man. 'Would you roll them?'

The man nodded. He scooped up one picture from each of two piles which he swiftly rolled and tied with string. Ferguson muttered his thanks.

'Well, you can't say I didn't try,' Ferguson turned to Annie, laughing, as they left.

She was surprised. He'd seemed so cross in the lounge. But the burning question was, how had he got that much money? He must have been saving hard since they'd got engaged, she decided. Yes, that was it.

She smiled at him. 'They're perfect, Ferguson. A perfect reminder of the voyage.'

PART III

The Discovery

17

Melbourne, Australia

October 1913

No one was there to meet them. Even if there had been, they would struggle to find them in this confusion. How frightening it would be to arrive on your own, Annie thought. She wondered how Adele was faring, but of course her new friend had been through this before. Annie glanced down at the two second-hand suitcases, a battered trunk, and two new leather travelling bags, clustered in a forlorn group around their feet.

She drew in a deep lungful of air. The quayside at Railway Pier, Port Melbourne had the same underlying oily smell as Tilbury, but everything else smelled different, as though it had all been washed with soap. She couldn't tell whether it was the ships in the port, or simply that the country itself smelled new. The very tarmac she was standing on, the workmen rushing around in their spotless overalls, the gleaming cranes, even the passengers from other ships looked as though they'd put on their Sunday best for the occasion. Everything was quite, quite different. Even the light appeared clearer than at home. Breeze, soft as a feather, stroked her face. Strange how mild it was. Norfolk, when she'd left, had been cold and dismal, bracing itself for the upcoming bone-chilling months. Then she remembered England's autumn was their spring. Ferguson had told her it was an upside-down country but she hadn't quite understood the significance at the time. She had a sudden urge to unbutton her coat, snatch off her hat and unpin her hair. But, of course, she didn't.

It was both fascinating and alarming to hear so many men shouting, the cranes banging overhead, the clanging of chains and several ships' horns warning of their approach. And somehow, above all the noise, she could hear the screech of unfamiliar birds. She caught sight of a flash of rainbow wings, its body a riot of purple, red and orange as it soared high above their heads.

'Oh, look, Ferguson, isn't it beautiful? Like a parrot.' She pointed the bird out but her husband was looking as bewildered as she felt. By the time he bothered to lift his eyes in the right direction it had vanished.

Annie stood mesmerised, trying to take it all in. Mothers were dragging their reluctant children, and fathers were struggling with trunks and boxes and suitcases. Dockers rushed from the boats to the wharf, their cargo precariously balanced on their backs, or pushed sack barrows, stacked high.

'What do you think we should do now, Ferguson?'

'We were told to go to the Customs House to register, but we need someone to help us with the trunk.' Ferguson glanced about him. 'I'll scout around while you stay with the luggage.'

'No, Ferguson, we must stay together.' Annie's voice was surprisingly firm. She had just spotted two lads who had been helping some other immigrants close by. Without thinking, she hurried over to them and moments later the lads had either end of the trunk, nodding for the newly-weds to follow.

'Don't ever do anything like that again, Annie.' Ferguson's face was red and there were droplets of sweat on his forehead. He picked up his own suitcase and bag, gesturing to Annie to take hers.

'What do you mean?' Annie struggled to keep up with him as he strode ahead, his shoulders square like a barrier between them. Why was he so cross? Was it because she'd taken the matter into her own hands? Since her mother died she was so used to looking after everyone it was second nature. She hurried on but after a few minutes her neck and shoulders ached from carrying her case, and the handle of her travelling bag started to burn her fingers. She threaded her way through the mass, desperate to keep Ferguson in sight. Suddenly, she could no longer see him. She stopped. Panic spread through her. She took a deep breath.

'Keep moving!' Someone from behind pushed into her, and she almost overbalanced. As she tried to steady herself the side of her case knocked the legs of a passing gentleman. The case burst open. Annie watched with dismay as a corset, a nightgown, a hairbrush and her precious journal scattered on the ground. The gentleman swung round.

'Here, let me, miss,' he said in an amused voice. A voice she recognised. He stooped to retrieve the nightgown Ethel had embroidered for her modest trousseau. It had somehow managed to wrap itself round one of her boots. He handed her the intimate garment, then lifted his hat a fraction. She looked up and met the warm grey eyes.

'Dr Townsend,' she said. She bent her head low, heat flooding her face, unable to speak as she knelt to stuff the nightgown back in the case. Why couldn't he have been a stranger? Then she reprimanded herself. She was being foolish. She'd never see him again, so what did it matter if he'd seen her corset and nightgown? Snapping the catches into position she reluctantly stood up to face him.

'I'm sorry, I wasn't looking where I was going. I've lost my husband.'

Dr Townsend gazed down at her and removed his hat. She noticed again how tall he was, the strong, slightly uneven features, the dark wavy hair. 'A looker,' she fancied she heard Adele's voice. Her blush deepened, though she refused to lower her gaze. After a long pause he said, 'Did you lose him on purpose?'

'No, of course not,' she said sharply. He raised a black eyebrow and suddenly she burst out laughing, and he joined in. This was another side to him that she hadn't seen on the ship. Somehow the shared laughter felt natural.

143

'Then we must find him,' he said, still chuckling.

While he checked the case was safely shut Annie looked around her. 'He's nowhere in sight,' she said. Nor were the two lads who had taken their trunk.

'At least I can take you to Customs House, which will be the direction your husband will be going.' He handed her the travelling bag and without waiting for her agreement took the case as though it weighed no more than a string shopping bag, miraculously making a path for her through the crowds. Her thoughts flew as she followed him. Ferguson would be furious when he saw she wasn't even capable of carrying her own suitcase.

Dr Townsend was head and shoulders above almost everyone else, making it easy to keep up with him. He didn't hurry her and several times looked round to make sure she was close behind.

'Oh, Dr Townsend, I see him,' she blurted before she'd taken in the scene. Ferguson was standing near a large brick building, but he was talking to someone. Adele.

'Lead the way then,' said Dr Townsend.

Annie hurried in front, thoroughly confused. Why was Ferguson talking to Adele? What on earth could he be saying? A couple stepped in front of her and the next time she looked up, Adele had vanished.

'Ferguson,' she called as she got nearer. 'I'm here.'

'Where've you been? I thought you were following me.' He seemed preoccupied until he noticed she was only carrying her bag. His forehead creased. 'Where's your case?'

'Right here.' Dr Townsend was beside them.

'Ferguson, you remember Dr Townsend from the ship. I bumped into him just now and my suitcase fell open, and then…' She couldn't continue with her husband's eyes switching from her to Dr Townsend and back again. Almost as though he were accusing her of something.

Then to Annie's embarrassment Dr Townsend said, 'The case is too heavy for her.' The meaning in his tone was unmistakable.

Ferguson flushed with annoyance. 'Thank you for being so considerate to my wife, Doctor. I'll take care of it now. We have two boys helping us.'

'You must be very proud of your wife,' Dr Townsend said, an almost imperceptible emphasis on the repeat of Ferguson's words, but Annie was aware of it.

'Of course I am. Why wouldn't I be?' Ferguson's tone was challenging.

'She wouldn't have told you herself, but I couldn't have managed without her on the ship. She's a born nurse.'

'Well, she's going to be cooking, not nursing,' Ferguson snapped.

'Ferguson, we should go,' Annie said, smarting to be spoken about as though she wasn't there and thoroughly irked by her husband's tone. But she couldn't help enjoying the little glow from Dr Townsend's compliment.

'Well, I hope you both find my country to your liking,' Dr Townsend said, and with a nod and a smile to Annie and the lift of a dark eyebrow, he touched his hat and walked away.

'So...your Dr Townsend is based in Melbourne,' Ferguson said, his eyes on the retreating figure.

'He's not *my* Dr Townsend,' Annie retorted.

'I don't like him.'

'You don't know him. You should have seen the way—'

'I thought he was quite rude, if you must know. He didn't even acknowledge me, except to say I'd failed as a husband for not carrying your case.'

'He didn't say anything of the kind,' Annie rounded on him. 'He's a wonderful doctor. Everyone got better from the smallpox.' She hesitated. 'Well, everyone except Mrs Davey.'

'Oh, he lost one of his patients, did he?' Ferguson sounded almost pleased.

'I won't hear a word against him.' Annie pressed down a spurt of anger. How dare Ferguson speak of Dr Townsend when he had

145

no idea how hard he'd worked for all the patients; how exhausted he'd been, with no let-up for almost a month.

With a final surreptitious glance she saw that Dr Townsend had been swallowed up by the crowd. She tried to imagine him going home to his family and only hoped his wife appreciated him. She supposed he had a wife. He'd never mentioned her, never spoken about his family, but then neither had she. Well, a nice man like him was bound to be married. And a father. She was just thinking what a lovely father he must be when she saw Ferguson's eyebrows draw together in irritation.

'Let's forget him,' he said, as he gestured towards an imposing building. 'This is Customs House.' He waved his arm, sounding excited, and Annie was relieved he seemed too caught up with the job ahead to give any more thought to her rescuer. He glanced at Annie, hesitated, then handed her his bag and picked up her suitcase. Once again, he marched off.

Annie stood in front of Customs House while everyone moved around her. She tilted back her head to take in the whole of the building. It seemed to stare down at her with its intimidating air of grandeur, summing her up, deciding whether or not she was welcome in Melbourne. A tremor of anxiety passed through her body and she told herself not to be so silly.

'Come *on*, Annie,' Ferguson shouted over his shoulder, 'we haven't got time to stand around. We've got to get registered.'

She couldn't help herself. The building looked as though it were alternatively sucking in and spewing out the mass of people, not just from their ship, but others that had docked around the same time. Annie shivered. You could easily get trampled upon with everyone shoving their way towards the half-dozen desks. She wished the registration was over and they could be in their own room at Amber Bay. Oh, how long was this all going to take? She scanned the crowd and saw Adele's hat bobbing on the far side.

'Adele!' she called, but her voice was lost in the confusion.

'Annie,' Ferguson turned angrily, 'for heaven's sake leave her alone.'

Annie's temper suddenly flared. 'I'm sorry, Ferguson, but she's a friend and I'm going to find out where she's going.' Before he could stop her she hastened through the mass after the disappearing figure.

'Adele!' she called again, not caring that people stared at her. This time the figure turned.

'Annie.' Adele's smile of surprise was genuine. She was clutching her carpet bag close to her side.

'Where are you staying?' Annie asked boldly. 'How will I see you?'

Adele smiled briefly. 'You won't.'

'I don't under—'

'That husband of yours has made it perfectly plain that I would be unsuitable company for his new little bride.' Strong words, but there was no malice in her tone.

'Oh, it's not true,' Annie said. Adele raised a pencilled eyebrow. 'And even if it was,' Annie rushed on, 'he's no right to tell me who can be my friend.'

'That's not how he'd see it,' Adele said, an unfathomable expression in her green eyes. 'It's being possessed I can't abide.' She tugged her hat down more firmly. 'You get married and you're not allowed to think for yourself. They do it for you.'

The crowd was now pushing from behind. Annie and Adele were trapped.

'You must join your husband,' Adele said, while at the same time tapping a man smartly on the arm who had pushed in front of her. 'Do you mind?' She looked over her shoulder at Annie, and said under her breath, 'I'm at the Hotel Esplanade, St Kilda.'

'I'll write to you,' Annie promised, but her words were muffled by the shrieks of the seagulls.

*

Amber Bay was everything Annie could possibly have dreamed of.

'It's not exactly imposing,' Ferguson muttered. His mood hadn't really improved since the episode at the quay, but Annie put it down to tiredness and squeezed his hand. She received a faint smile. It had taken over two hours to get registered at Customs House, and another hour in a hired horse and trap to reach Amber Bay. She felt drained, but it would be no use saying anything to Ferguson. He was doing the grumbling for both of them.

As the horse had patiently trotted along she'd tried to take in her surroundings. The sight of streets, wide and new and devoid of litter, and the reflections of the water in the bay that winked and sparkled at her, lifted her spirits. The driver had pointed out the tram stop – only a few minutes' walk, he'd said – before he turned his horse into a long winding lane bounded by tall elegant trees.

'What's the name of those trees?' she called to the driver, ignoring Ferguson's shake of the head.

'Gum trees,' he said without taking his eyes off the road. 'There's plenty of them in these parts.'

'They're so different from ours at home,' she turned to Ferguson, her eyes shining. 'Those silver barks and dark leaves. They look almost blue from here.'

As she spoke, a sudden rainbow of birds, bright red, blue and green, streaked overhead. Annie gave a small shriek of delight.

'Macaws,' the driver informed them. 'Do you get them in the Old Country?'

'No,' Ferguson answered in a brisk tone. Annie gave him a sideways glance. Where was his sense of adventure? Surely this was what they'd come all this way for. To see different things. But he didn't seem at all interested in his new surroundings. The voyage must have affected him more than her, she thought. Probably, the worry of catching smallpox. He'd soon feel better once he was settled.

Amber Bay was tucked away at the end, beyond a smattering of pretty Victorian houses, overlooking one of the inlets. The driver brought the trap to a stop and helped Annie alight, then he and Ferguson pulled the luggage down. In a trice the horse and trap vanished up the driveway.

Now, standing in the grounds of the house, her arm through Ferguson's, she felt prepared for whatever was in store.

Amber Bay had been built in the Greek classical style. Forming a magnificent entrance were four widely-spaced black marble columns which supported an ornate balcony above. Annie pictured herself walking up the few shallow steps, through the columns to the heavy cream-painted front door, but there her imagination stopped. She looked up at the row of tall windows on the upper floor. The ground floor windows were even taller, running from floor to ceiling in height. All of them had shutters, which lent the façade a sleepy air. Annie loved the house on sight.

'It's not what I expected.' Ferguson sounded disappointed, his eyes squinting in the bright sun.

'I think it's beautiful,' Annie said. 'It reminds me of Hatherleigh Hall, only smaller.' She turned to Ferguson, hoping he would be pleased with the comparison to his old place of work, but he only raised his eyes heavenwards.

'We better go round the back,' was all he said.

The tradesman's entrance was much plainer and overlooked the water. She could see several coloured boats bobbing up and down. Between the grounds and the bay wound a road almost free of traffic, and from where Annie stood, it looked too far away for anyone in the house to hear when a horse and cart or motor car came by. Soaring eucalyptus trees defined the boundaries, and sweeping lawns fell right to the edge of the road, keeping an open view to the bay itself.

Ferguson rang the bell. No answer. He pulled the cord again and this time they heard someone. The maroon-painted door opened to reveal a young girl in a dark dress with pristine white apron, not a wisp of hair peeping from under her neat white cap.

'Yes, please, sir?' she bobbed.

'Mr and Mrs Ferguson Bishop,' said Ferguson importantly, trying to look over the maid's shoulder into the shadowy hall.

'Oh. We weren't expecting you until tomorrow, sir.' Looking flustered she opened the door wider. 'But please come in.'

'I don't understand,' Ferguson said. 'We—'

'Who is it, Emma?' called a light female voice. The voice didn't wait for an answer and seconds later a slim young girl appeared.

'I'm Louise,' she said. 'Are you Annie and Ferguson Bishop? If so, you're a day early.'

The two stared at this apparition. Louise moved like a colt the way she tossed her head, causing her loose fair hair to swish around her slender neck. She laughed at their bewildered faces.

'You *are* Mr and Mrs Bishop?'

Annie recovered first. She nodded. 'There seems to be some misunderstanding, but we did say in our letter that we would be here this morning.'

Ferguson frowned as though to warn her *he* should be the one to speak. To explain.

'I'm sorry. Mother and Father expected you tomorrow. Oh dear. There was nobody to meet you at the harbour. You must be worn out.' She spoke in short, jerky sentences, but her friendly manner made Annie feel slightly less nervous. 'I'll tell cook to make some tea. Emma will show you your room. When you're ready, go to the kitchen. Through there,' she pointed to a white-painted closed door, 'down the steps, first on the right.' And with that she tossed her head again and was gone.

18

10th November 1913, at Amber Bay

This is the first time I've had a chance to write down my thoughts. We have been here for nearly a month and I'm settling in. It's odd how the weather is getting warmer as we approach what we think of as winter. I love being in the kitchen. Mrs Wilson doesn't have to cook for such a large family as Mrs Jenner and they don't entertain as much by the look of the calendar, so she has more time to go over the menus with me and likes to know what dishes we used to prepare at home. Unfortunately, Ferguson is not so happy. And I don't really know why.

For me, Amber Bay is everything I could wish for. We have a lovely large room on an upper floor which even F cannot fault. It has a view over farmland and is so much lighter than the room I shared with Gladys. I'm glad I didn't try to stop F from buying the two pictures of the *Orsova*. Ferguson has pinned them on either side of the fireplace. It makes the room oddly feel like home but they'll look even better when we can afford to get them framed.

I was dreading meeting Mr Scott-Lawson. He was away the first few days, which made it easier in one way so I could meet the rest of the family, but bad in another way because I kept worrying about it. Anyway, Mrs S-L was very nice. Louise is 15. She's cheerful and friendly. Her sister Daphne is 11 and mad on horses. We didn't see Russell because he's joined up. There's talk of war even here. I pray F doesn't have to go away and fight.

I finally met Mr Scott-Lawson. My heart was pumping nineteen to the dozen but he barely glanced at me and just said very politely he hoped I was settling in. I couldn't help thinking of Adele. Could she have been exaggerating? He's not a big man – shorter than Ferguson. Thinning brown hair and a moustache. The sort of man Mum used to call dapper.

She paused for a minute or two. How was Dad coping? she wondered. She glanced up at the clock in its mahogany case which she'd stood on the mantelpiece; a wedding present from her father and sisters. Ten minutes to four. Silly, she knew, but just to look at it and hear it ticking made them feel nearer to her. Closing the journal she lifted it to her nose, smelling the soft leather, her eyes stinging as she pictured her father's face when he'd given it to her. She closed her eyes, and her thoughts turned to Ferguson. He worried her. He wasn't the happy-go-lucky man she was used to. Maybe it was the strain of a new job and working for a new family, and once he'd properly settled in he would be back to his old self. But she couldn't help thinking about their recent quarrel.

It had happened the day before when they'd finished work and were settled in their room. Ferguson had never stopped grumbling. The house was not in the same league as Hatherleigh Hall – or even Bonham Place, he'd added slyly. No one of any importance came to dine, leaving generous tips like they did at Hatherleigh Hall. Mr Scott-Lawson had flown into a temper that morning because Ferguson couldn't produce his favourite cufflinks. The Scott-Lawsons weren't titled like Lord and Lady Hamilton at Hatherleigh Hall. They were too mean to have a full team of servants. He went on and on until Annie thought she would scream if he mentioned Hatherleigh Hall one more time. She reminded him that he often used to criticise the Hamiltons and the way the house was run. Now, according to him, they were perfect employers in the finest house in the country with the best-trained staff.

'We're so lucky,' she told him. 'Amber Bay is a beautiful house. You just haven't looked at it properly to appreciate it. We have a lovely room, we're warm and comfortable, the work isn't hard, the food is good. What more do you want?'

'I wanted to get away from being in service,' he'd said, his blue eyes flashing. 'I thought we were taking this job as a temporary measure. I always said that. I didn't know you were actually going to *enjoy* it.'

'You should be pleased I've settled,' Annie retorted.

His forehead creased in exasperation. 'I don't want to settle here.' He got to his feet, a sullen expression crossing his good-looking features. He marched over to the fireplace and seized the clock. Annie watched as he angrily wound it, then shoved it back on the mantelpiece, but remained with his back to her.

'What are you thinking about?'

He swung round. 'You know what I want. To work on a sheep farm.'

Not that again.

'I wouldn't want to see all that slaughtering.'

'Not meat,' Ferguson said impatiently. 'I've been reading about merino sheep. For their wool. It's the biggest thing here. They export it all over the world. Even England.' His face was alight with enthusiasm. 'We might even have to move to Sydney for me to get experience. Then eventually we could have a small farm of our own. I'd be my own boss.' His eyes met hers. 'I'm not giving up on it, Annie.'

Annie's heart plummeted. She'd hoped Ferguson had let go of such a notion. One of his many mad ideas. She hated the thought of being on a sheep farm. The isolation didn't appeal to her at all. On the road which led from Amber Bay there were buses and trams and carriages and ponies and traps. On a sheep farm with hundreds

153

of acres she'd be lucky to go to Melbourne once in a month – if they were still in Melbourne. Ferguson said they might have to move to Sydney but she would put her foot down about that. Common sense told her it was not the time to argue with her husband. They hadn't been at Amber Bay very long. He'd get used to it, she was sure, and stop dreaming of sheep farms.

Now, sitting in her room at the desk, writing her journal, another man's image invaded her head: Dr Alexander Townsend. Her cheeks flushed as she remembered their last meeting. Whatever must he have thought? She shook her head, wiped her pen, and scraped back her chair. There was no time to write more. She would begin a letter to her father and sisters that evening.

In the kitchen Mrs Wilson greeted Annie warmly.

'Come in, dear. Kettle's boiling. We'll have our tea and then we must put a move on. We've got some special guests tomorrow night, did I tell you?'

'No, you didn't, Mrs Wilson.' Annie thought how different she was to Mrs Jenner, who would be flapping like a hen, talking about the special guests for days before they arrived. 'Who's coming?'

'Mr and Mrs Richard Claymore and Mrs Claymore's brother, Rupert. Oh, and another gentleman – I forget his name – he's not been before.'

Annie's eyes sparkled as she skipped down the back stairs the following morning. The Claymores would be the first guests to stay overnight since her arrival and she wanted to impress Mrs Wilson with her cooking skills. Maybe she could suggest the fish dish. Being on the coast, the fish was excellent. Sea trout, if they had any in this region, would be wonderful simply baked with lemon and toasted almonds. Yes, she decided, we shall have watercress soup, the trout, followed by lamb as the main dish, then cheese and biscuits, and a chocolate soufflé. Annie stopped. Mrs Wilson might be offended. She'd have to be tactful.

To Annie's delight Mrs Wilson was only too happy to hear her suggestions. She smiled as she thought of Mrs Jenner. That particular cook would never have discussed menus with someone below her in status.

Ferguson wasn't impressed with the 'special guests'.

'When you think of all the distinguished people we used to have at Hatherleigh Hall...' he'd said under his breath after lunch, when Mrs Wilson had retired for a few hours. Irritation distorted his handsome features. 'I've never heard of these people.'

'That's because we're thousands of miles away from anyone we know,' Annie replied, a little tartly. 'I thought you'd show a bit more interest.'

'I would, if I had proper butler's duties. Can you believe Mr Scott-Lawson pours his own wine? *I* should be doing that. They've got no idea what an English butler is supposed to do.'

'It's different here,' Annie said. 'They're not so formal as the English.'

'You wouldn't be so keen if you were back to changing beds and lighting fires.'

Annie looked at Ferguson in surprise. 'We came to Australia to get away from those sorts of jobs, remember?' she challenged. 'That's what you told me when you were trying to persuade me to come here.' She noticed the corners of his mouth turn down. 'I thought you'd be pleased I was doing something more interesting.'

'I *am* pleased,' he said. 'But it's not what I expected.' He looked at her. 'Anyway, let's not quarrel. We're here now.' He gave a half smile but he didn't put his arms around her. A moment later he left the room. And for once, Annie didn't go after him.

'Can you make a start, Annie?' Mrs Wilson stood at the kitchen entrance, ready to go to the market. 'I want to be sure to get the trout – enough for eight – and we'll need more lemons. Can you think of anything else besides the watercress?'

'There's plenty of eggs for the soufflé, and we had the other vegetables delivered yesterday.'

'I'll be off then. I shan't be long. No more than an hour.'

'I'll get started,' Annie assured her.

But Mrs Wilson came back from the market with a grim face.

'He's let me down,' she said, taking off her jacket and dropping on to one of the kitchen chairs. 'There's no trout today. He palmed me off with salmon instead. I don't know what we'll do with it.' Mrs Wilson closed her eyes and gave a deep sigh.

Mrs Wilson didn't have Mrs Jenner's confidence at all, Annie thought.

'It will do very nicely,' Annie said truthfully. 'I saw a lovely recipe for salmon when we were looking through the menus…one with hollandaise sauce.'

'Can you make it?' Mrs Wilson looked hard at Annie.

'Yes, of course,' Annie said, crossing her fingers behind her back. 'You only have to follow the recipe.'

Annie realised it would be the first time she and Ferguson had worked together. In England she'd never heard of any female servant being allowed to help serve food in the dining room or hand round drinks and canapés at parties. It was always the job of the footmen and butler. But things were less regimented here and she was looking forward to taking part.

At two minutes to eight Ferguson and Ronnie, one of the house boys, appeared in the kitchen. Without speaking, Ferguson seized the tureen of soup and Ronnie followed him through to the dining room with a large basket of bread rolls.

Fifteen minutes later the two of them pushed through the scullery door, carrying the empty soup plates. 'Everything ready on the next course?' Ferguson asked Annie in an unusually curt manner.

Surprised at his tone, Annie nodded as her husband picked up the platter of salmon which she had skinned and cut into succulent portions. Ronnie carried a tureen of vegetables and Annie followed with the hollandaise sauce. As she entered the dining room and stepped over to the sideboard she caught a fragment of conversation Louise was having with one of the guests seated to her left.

'Yes, it's been in the family for simply ages. In the style of Louis XIV, which seems fitting, don't you think, being the male version of *my* name?' Louise giggled.

'You're both perfectly named,' the man said in an amused tone. 'It's certainly a magnificent piece. You're very privileged to live in such a beautiful house.'

Annie never heard Louise's reply. The sauce jug slipped off its saucer and fell with a muffled thud. Ferguson swung round, his shocked eyes meeting hers.

Daphne gave a loud, high-pitched giggle.

'Hush, Daphne,' Mrs Scott-Lawson told her daughter. 'It's bad manners to laugh or make a comment when someone's had an accident.'

Annie hadn't seen the guest when she'd walked in as he was half masked by the silver candelabrum centrepiece. It didn't matter – she knew his voice. With shaking hands and burning face, she bent to retrieve the jug, thanking her lucky stars it hadn't broken. But there'd be no sauce to go with the salmon now. It had taken a painstaking half hour for her to make it as the first time it had curdled. Now it dripped down the sideboard and on to the carpet. She would have to come back with a cloth. And the salmon would be nothing without the sauce. Oh, it was a disaster.

'Allow me.'

Dr Townsend was there beside her with a napkin soaked with water he must have got from the water jug. He began to wipe up the splashes.

'Please let me do that, sir,' she said to him under her breath. 'You're a guest.'

'Don't worry, Alex,' Mrs Scott-Lawson called. 'One of the maids will clean it up.'

'I think I've got most of it,' Dr Townsend answered his hostess, making a ball of the cloth and putting it neatly in one of the bowls on the sideboard. As Annie caught his eye he gave her a deliberate wink.

'It's not a disaster,' he said in an undertone, smiling at Annie. 'The smallpox on the *Orsova* was a disaster.'

He'd used the very same word she'd thought.

'Thank you, sir,' she said softly, sending him a fleeting smile. And he could take that which way he pleased, she thought, still mortified by the spill. She picked up the bowl and cloth Dr Townsend had used, and escaped to the kitchen where Mrs Wilson was preparing the cheese board.

'Oh, Mrs Wilson, I've had an accident upstairs.'

'I've had worse,' the cook said with a chuckle when Annie told her what happened. 'Once when I was serving I spilled gravy down one of the guests – right down the front of her frock. She did look a mess.' Mrs Wilson started to laugh again. 'She was furious. Said I should be sacked. But I wasn't. So don't you worry, my dear.'

'But what will Mrs Scott-Lawson say?' Annie persisted.

'She'll let it pass. She won't want to lose you for something that could happen to anyone.'

But Annie knew it was the unexpectedness of seeing Dr Townsend that had caused her to drop the jug.

'I've got to face going in the dining room again.'

'You don't have to. Ferguson and Ronnie can finish the evening. I'll make some parsley butter for the fish. It won't take more than a minute.'

'No, I'll take it in, Mrs Wilson. I have to show I'm not a coward.'

Everyone was talking and laughing when three minutes later Annie entered the dining room carrying Mrs Wilson's parsley butter. Ferguson shot her a questioning look but she pretended she hadn't noticed. She knew she'd have some explaining to do later in their room, but for now she must concentrate. Only once did she steal a glance at Dr Townsend. It was just natural curiosity, she told herself. His dark head was bent towards Louise, laughing at something she'd said, but as though he felt Annie's eyes on him he turned, the smile lingering on his lips. She caught her breath and busied herself rearranging the dishes on the sideboard that were already perfectly set out.

Ferguson was taking the rest of the salmon round the table to offer a second helping but everyone refused, except Dr Townsend. Annie watched Ferguson's bland expression as Dr Townsend steadied the plate, saying 'marvellous' as he helped himself to another generous portion.

'Careful, Alex, we want some left to make fishcakes for tomorrow's lunch,' Mrs Scott-Lawson trilled.

What a remark, Annie thought. Even though housemaids had not been allowed to serve in the dining room at Bonham Place, she knew the hosts would never have commented on what their guests were eating. Embarrassed on Dr Townsend's behalf she wondered how he would answer.

'Sorry, Stella, I'm only used to tinned and this is so delicious,' he chuckled, and his twinkling grey eyes met Annie's.

A tiny part of her was pleased he'd acknowledged her; had, in fact, tried to help her. She wouldn't let herself dwell on his smile, or his secret wink.

In bed that evening, after Ferguson had carried out his nightly ritual (as Annie described it to herself) and was recovering his breath, his eyes half closed in satisfaction, he suddenly said, 'So your Dr Townsend knows the Scott-Lawsons.'

'I wish you wouldn't keep calling him *my* doctor.'

'Did you know he knew them when you were working with him on the ship?'

'No,' Annie said truthfully, 'we never spoke of anything personal. All we cared about were the patients. We didn't have time for chit-chat.' Which wasn't quite true, of course, but she brushed the fib away.

'So it was the surprise of seeing him that made you drop the sauce jug.' Ferguson turned on to his side, thumped his pillow, and propped himself up on one elbow. He looked down at her, half amused, half suspicious.

Annie turned away to pick up the glass of water from the bedside table. 'Don't be ridiculous,' she said, her voice tense, keeping her back to him. 'It was strange, that's all, coming across him again. I haven't been sleeping too well, and I expect I was tired and not looking at what I was doing.'

'I wonder.' Ferguson yawned as he lay back down, moving away from her. 'Though I must admit, I'm worn out myself.'

At Hatherleigh Hall he would have worked twice as hard that evening than here at Amber Bay. After all, there were only four extra guests. She was about to remind him of this but Ferguson was already breathing rhythmically. Just as well – she was desperate for a good night's sleep. They'd be up again at quarter to six.

As she was busy in the kitchen, Annie didn't catch a glimpse of the house guests the following morning. Mrs Wilson had left a note saying that she'd be late and asked Annie to do breakfast. Soon, the satisfying smell of kippers and fried bacon permeated the kitchen. Only scraps from last night's salmon were left over, so Annie decided to stir them into the scrambled eggs, all the while picturing Dr Townsend telling his hostess he only ate tinned salmon at home. She couldn't help smiling to herself. Mrs Scott-Lawson hadn't had an answer to that.

Annie tipped a pan of sautéed potatoes into a heated serving dish and checked there was plenty of toast and coffee. Breakfast was the trickiest meal, Mrs Jenner always said. You had to make sure everything came out together, piping hot, and you needed to keep your wits about you. She tried hard to empty her mind of last night's dinner party, and the sauce jug, and Dr Townsend coming to her aid, but she was still smiling as Ronnie came in to take the dishes through.

Mrs Wilson's heavy lunch menu was one Mrs Jenner would have produced in winter. In this intense heat it would have been crisp salads and chilled soups, and Annie thought longingly of those summer lunches.

'When you have guests, doesn't Mrs Scott-Lawson discuss the menus with you?' Annie asked Mrs Wilson as they were peeling potatoes.

'No, she usually leaves it to me, unless it's someone *very* special.' She looked at Annie with affection. 'What about you, dear? Are you enjoying the cooking?'

'Yes, I am,' Annie responded with enthusiasm. 'It's more than just a job. I think food should be prepared with love.' She stopped. Had she been too outspoken? But Mrs Wilson beamed at her.

'Good girl. That's the idea. Well, enough of this. We must get on. They want lunch early as they're all going for a drive in Sir's new motor car.'

'How long have you been at Amber Bay?' Annie asked when they stopped five minutes for a glass of squash. Her heart beat fast as she waited for the answer. Did Mrs Wilson know about Adele?

'Coming up two years,' she said. 'It's the best position I've had.' She glanced at Annie. 'Though Mr Scott-Lawson has an eye for the ladies,' she added. 'Still, I'm safe enough.' The older woman laughed, and Annie lowered her eyes. 'Don't you worry, dear. His wife keeps a strict eye on him. She's had a bit of trouble with him in the past, so I heard, and he wouldn't get away with anything like it again.' She looked at Annie. 'Least said, soonest mended.'

So Adele hadn't exaggerated.

*

Two hours later, sitting down to their own lunch, Annie and Ferguson, with the rest of the house servants, were startled by the noise of the front door banging open. Loud voices from the hall penetrated below stairs. Everyone stopped eating, knives and forks in mid-air.

'What on earth—?' said Ferguson.

Annie jumped up but Mrs Wilson put a cautioning hand on her arm. 'Don't worry yourself, my dear. It'll be Mrs Claymore's brother, Rupert. He's a bit of a drinker. I expect he's fallen over. It wouldn't be the first time.'

'How awful,' Annie said. 'But don't you think we should see if we can do something to help?'

'Just make him a hot water bottle,' Mrs Wilson advised. 'He'll go to bed like a lamb. It happens practically every time.'

As Annie was putting the kettle on, Mrs Scott-Lawson appeared at the door, breathless and shaken.

'There's been an accident,' she said. 'Bring some ice.'

'What did I tell you?' Mrs Wilson said. She jumped up, extracted a bag from the ice-chest and made for the door.

Annie rushed after the cook, her shoes sliding on the polished floor. When she got to the hall she saw Mr Scott-Lawson, his back to her, hovering over someone. Poor Rupert, she thought. Her employer looked over his shoulder as the two women ran in.

'I tried to avoid a damned cat,' Mr Scott-Lawson said as Mrs Wilson handed him the ice. 'Clipped a tree.'

'Oh, sir, are you hurt?'

'Not a bit,' Mr Scott-Lawson said, 'but he is, poor devil.' He stepped back to reveal the figure. Annie gasped. It wasn't Rupert at all.

The man who was slumped in a chair with blood pouring from his head and down his face, where it dripped on to the black and white marble floor, was none other than Dr Alexander Townsend.

19

Dr Alexander Townsend was very demanding for a guest who had been forced to stay beyond his initial invitation, Annie decided with a wry smile as she carried his tray of mid-morning broth and a fresh water jug upstairs. Quite different from the kind, considerate and hard-working doctor she'd known in the ship's hospital. He'd obviously been in his professional stride then, working all hours to control what could have been a much more serious epidemic. Maybe this was his true personality. Or was he just impatient now he was on the other side of the desk, as it were?

Dr Brooke had arrived an hour after Dr Townsend had been helped in, and said it looked worse than it was – heads were notorious for bleeding from only a slight wound. In his opinion it didn't need stitching. He'd ordered Dr Townsend to rest for a couple of days, here at Amber Bay if possible, where he could be watched for any signs of delayed concussion.

'Good, it's you,' Alex said, his smile lighting up his face as Annie stepped in. 'Stella keeps on apologising every time she puts her head in the door.'

'Mrs Scott-Lawson is naturally concerned.' Annie set the tray on the bedside table.

'Oh, I know she is.' He hoisted himself up on the three plump pillows and took the tray Annie handed him. 'She also feels guilty. She thinks the accident was her fault.'

'What do you mean?' Annie wouldn't normally dream of

questioning a houseguest, but after all, Dr Townsend wasn't a stranger. She was relieved to see that he didn't appear to notice anything untoward.

'Stella saw the cat first and shouted a warning to Bertram. He swerved without knowing what he was supposed to avoid.' Alex stopped to taste the broth. He glanced up. 'Delicious. Did you make it?'

For some extraordinary reason Annie felt shy. 'Yes, sir.' It felt strange calling him 'sir' after she'd always called him 'doctor'. She'd even thought of him as Alex in her private moments. This relationship of houseguest and servant was very different and she didn't really like it. On the ship they'd worked together, but this new situation brought home to her the gaping difference between the classes. But the time they had spent on the ship was over. She must put it out of her mind.

As though he had read her thoughts, he smiled and said, 'Please don't call me "sir" when we're on our own. I'd much prefer you to call me Alex. Especially as we know one another.' He twinkled at her. 'Even worked together. I wonder what they'd say if they knew.'

'If you mean Mr and Mrs Scott-Lawson, then I'd be grateful if you wouldn't say anything,' Annie said. She looked at him steadily. The last thing she wanted was Mr Scott-Lawson mentioning to Ferguson what a coincidence that she'd helped Alex to nurse the patients on the ship. That would be sure to set him off again.

Alex raised an eyebrow.

'It's just that…I'd rather keep it between us.'

'It will be our secret, I promise. And,' his eyes danced, 'the other secret is when you lost Ferguson just after we docked.'

Annie's pulse raced as the scene at Melbourne docklands replayed. Dr Townsend bending down to retrieve her cherished nightgown. She'd prayed he wouldn't mention that encounter. She looked at the far wall, unable to answer him.

'We *are* friends, aren't we?' Alex spooned the last of the liquid from the bowl. He put it back on the tray, then looked up at Annie.

'It's different now...' she answered, bringing her gaze back to him, '...sir.' Alex's mouth twitched. 'Well, I must go.' She caught a whiff of tobacco from Alex's pajama top as she picked up his empty glass on the bedside table. She glared at him theatrically. 'Tell me the truth. Have you been smoking?'

He looked like a naughty schoolboy who'd just been caught stealing a child's pencil.

'How did you know?'

She went over to the window and fully opened it.

'It wasn't difficult.' She turned. 'Well, I'm pleased you're feeling better.'

'I loathe being in bed,' Alex said. 'And being a patient, but if it means I can see you sometimes, it's worth it.'

She wasn't close enough to read the expression in his eyes. Then he smiled again. It was a beautiful smile which softened the lines of his face, and made her feel he knew everything about her, faults and all; that she was accepted in spite of them.

Her blush deepened. He really shouldn't say such personal things but it wasn't her place to admonish him. Instead, she threw him a look of disapproval which made his smile even broader.

'I must go,' she said again, catching a glimpse of the bedside clock.

'Will you be back with lunch?'

'So you're expecting lunch, are you, sir?' Annie kept a straight face and for a moment Alex looked disconcerted. Serves him right for being presumptuous, she thought, holding back a smile.

Two days later Dr Alexander Townsend left Amber Bay without saying goodbye to Annie.

She doubted she would ever see him again. Somehow the thought depressed her.

165

20

April 1914

'You're putting on weight,' Ferguson remarked as he drew her to him one night when they had been at Amber Bay some months. 'You must be eating more since you've been working in the kitchen all day. Temptation with all that lovely food, I expect.' He chuckled.

Annie wasn't paying much attention. She was trying to muster the courage to tell him she didn't want to do it every night. Her breasts were sore with his nightly caresses and the act itself had begun to feel like an invasion of her body. It was strange. At first she had given herself to him with all her heart, but lately he didn't seem bothered whether she was happy or not. When she told him she loved him he would give her a squeeze in reply, but he rarely told her he loved her, too. She began to wonder whether she was there solely for his convenience.

She felt ashamed and remembered her mother's words. It was her duty, her mother had said, to give her husband pleasure. But wasn't *she* allowed to have pleasure too? Once, a few weeks ago, when he was inside her, a peculiar tingling started between her legs and travelled up through her belly in wave upon wave, gaining in intensity until her head felt it was spinning out of control; then there was an overwhelming sense of letting go, leaving her breathless, until she sobbed as though her heart would break. Ferguson had immediately been concerned, asking her what was wrong, holding her and stroking her head, but she hadn't been able to speak.

'I expect you're homesick,' he'd said, before he turned over and went to sleep.

As Annie approached the kitchen next morning she was overcome by nausea. She dashed to the lavatory and was violently sick. Beads of cold sweat stuck to her forehead, reminding her of the *Orsova* and how ill she'd felt in those storms. At least she was now on solid ground, she thought, rinsing out her mouth under the cold tap. Towelling her face she felt better, though still shaky when she made her way back to the kitchen.

Mrs Wilson, who was drinking her second cup of tea, glanced at her sharply. 'Are you ill, Annie?'

'I was, but I'm all right now, thank you, Mrs Wilson.' Annie poured herself a cup.

'What's the matter?'

'I must have eaten something.' Annie sat at the kitchen table opposite the cook, who surprised her by smiling and nodding as she looked her up and down, pausing for a second or two on Annie's waist.

'When was the last time you had a show?'

Annie was puzzled.

'Your monthly.'

Annie felt hot all over. 'I don't remember,' she said, truthfully. 'What's that got to do with anything?'

Mrs Wilson chuckled. 'You're going to have a baby, my dear – you see if I'm not right.'

After Mrs Wilson's proclamation, Annie had difficulty in keeping her mind on her job. She cooked the family breakfast and washed up on her own as Mrs Wilson had already left for the market. Unthinkingly, she placed the butter and remaining bacon on the dresser, and it was only as she was taking the dirty plates to

167

the dining room that she realised what she was doing. Muttering about being a perfect idiot she rinsed the last dishes, trying to recall the last time she'd bled. With all the excitement and worry of the new country, new job and new home, not to mention new husband, it had completely slipped her notice. And until Mrs Wilson had explained, she hadn't realised the significance. If it really *were* true, what would Ferguson's reaction be? A flicker of doubt crept over her. They'd always talked about having children in the future. But not yet. They hadn't been at Amber Bay long enough to become secure with Mr and Mrs Scott-Lawson. Her employers wouldn't want a baby in the house, crying and demanding attention. She and Ferguson might be turned out; sent home. A baby would change everyone's lives.

When Mrs Wilson returned, Annie tried to listen to her chatter, but all she could do was say 'yes' and 'no', and nod in what she hoped were the right places. If only she could just go up to her room to think.

'Annie, would you bring in some parsley and dill from the herb garden. Take your time. You probably need ten minutes' quiet.'

Annie could have hugged her. 'Thank you, Mrs Wilson. I won't be long.'

The morning air was already full of the promise of another hot day, as she picked her way through the kitchen garden and into the herb border at the bottom. The smell of fennel, reminding her of the aniseed balls she'd loved as a child, wafted upwards. Absentmindedly, she plucked a sprig of mint, holding it to her nose, breathing in its sharp peppermint aroma. Feeling a little light-headed she reached a small wooden bench and sat for a few minutes until her heart began to beat more steadily.

A baby. Someone of her own to love and cherish. Instinctively, she put her hand on her stomach, overcome by a feeling of exquisite tenderness. Not that she didn't love her husband, of course, but she admitted to herself that she didn't always feel entirely comfortable

168

with him. He seemed to get easily irritated, though she always tried to find excuses for him. He had all the responsibility of a job he'd had little training for, which must be worrying enough. So how would he cope with that and a baby? That is, if they were allowed to stay. She rubbed her hand along the arm of the bench, and picked at the peeling green paint. A splinter tore her finger and she watched the scarlet trickle. *Mrs Wilson might be wrong.* Oh, but how she wanted Mrs Wilson to be right. Well, there was no need to speak to Ferguson until she knew for sure. Only a doctor would be able to confirm one way or the other.

Mrs Wilson had suggested she write to the surgery for an appointment and for the reply to be sent care of Mrs Wilson herself. Two days later she handed Annie an envelope with a triumphant nod and a knowing smile. Annie turned her back and tore open the envelope. Dr Brooke was asking her to come in on Thursday, her day off. Usually she and Ferguson were given the same day, but this week they were told they would have consecutive days because of the amount of work that needed doing – more guests would be arriving at the weekend. Ferguson grumbled but Annie was relieved to be able to see the doctor without having to explain where she was going. By now, she was sure Mrs Wilson was right. She'd been sick almost every morning. Everything made her feel sick – fatty food, coffee, even certain colours like brown and fawn – but deep inside herself was a glow such as she'd never experienced. She was going to have a baby. She knew it.

If the Scott-Lawson's family doctor confirmed it was true she could share her precious news with Ferguson. She carefully counted out two pounds from her secret savings, hoping that would be enough, and quickly put the notes in her handbag, feeling guilty she was doing something Ferguson knew nothing about.

Mr Scott-Lawson was to drop Daphne off to school that morning and Annie boldly asked if she might have a lift into town.

'Doing some shopping?' her employer asked, looking at Annie appreciatively and giving her a wink.

The gesture immediately put her on her guard.

'Yes, I need a few items for Mrs Wilson,' she said, thinking she must ask Mrs Wilson if she needed anything.

'How will you get back?' he said, smiling as though he had the solution.

'I'll get the tram,' she said quickly.

Mr Scott-Lawson insisted Annie sit beside him in his yellow Delaunay-Belleville tourer, and ordered Daphne in the back. To Annie's deep embarrassment, he nodded and smiled as though he were royalty to the shoppers' incredulous stares. Annoyingly, he stopped opposite the surgery, patted her gloved hand, and sprang out to help her down. She bent to say goodbye to Daphne, then raised her eyes level with her employer's.

'Thank you very much, Mr Scott-Lawson. This is perfect.'

He wished her good day but she felt his eyes on her as she deliberately walked past the surgery. When he drove on she retraced her steps and approached the reception desk with a confidence she didn't feel.

'I have an appointment to see Dr Brooke.'

'Your name, please.' The receptionist barely looked up.

'Mrs Ferguson Bishop.' It still felt awkward saying it. Where had 'Annie' disappeared to?

'One moment, please.' The woman was brisk as she wrote down some details. She glanced up. 'Please go into the waiting room and wait to be called.' She gestured to a door with a half-glazed panel and resumed her writing.

Annie squeezed into a chair between an overweight woman and a child with a runny nose. One by one the patients were called in, some not reappearing for fifteen minutes or more. She began to feel queasy surrounded by so many people and their chatter, as though they were closing in on her. She shut her eyes.

'Mrs Ferguson Bishop,' called a nurse, breaking into the fog in Annie's head. Annie jumped to her feet and followed the nurse down a short hallway.

'Mrs Ferguson Bishop, Doctor,' the nurse said as she opened the third door.

'Please show her in,' came a familiar voice, and Dr Alexander Townsend rose from behind the desk.

Dear God, no. Where's Dr Brooke? Oh, what to do? She couldn't talk to him about her changing body. Bad enough with the nightdress episode. Now this. And how would he examine her anyway to tell if she was having a baby or not? She would probably have to take her clothes off. It didn't bear thinking about. If only—

'Dr Brooke is out on an emergency.' Alex Townsend interrupted her whirl of thoughts as he came towards her with that smile she knew so well. 'I'm his locum. He was the one who introduced me to the Scott-Lawsons.' His smile broadened. 'I must say, that was a surprise to see you there. A very nice surprise...particularly when you looked after me when I banged my head...' he gave her a mischievous glance, '...on purpose.'

'What?' Annie's mouth fell open.

'Just joking,' he grinned, putting his hand lightly on her arm. 'Come and sit down. Let me look at you.' He towered over her, making her feel even more at a disadvantage. 'You look a little pale. They're not working you too hard, are they?'

She heard his voice as though from a distance and there was a roaring in her ears. Her arms flailed. She was falling down a black hole. Then oblivion. The next thing she felt was a hand on the back of her neck, pushing her head down between the folds of her skirt towards her feet. The room swam and Annie desperately fought for control.

'It appears it's my turn to look after *you*.'

Annie heard a voice floating above her and felt an arm round her shoulders gently easing her upright.

'What...what happened?'

'Nothing. You fainted, that's all. Here...take a sip of water.' He held a cup to her lips. 'How are you feeling now?'

'I...I'm all right. Really I am.'

'Good. Take your time. Now tell me why you're here. Obviously not to pay me a social visit.'

Annie waited a few seconds until she could trust herself to speak.

'I had no idea you knew Mr and Mrs Scott-Lawson.' She hadn't meant to sound so ill-mannered and a little warmth crept into her cheeks.

'I had no idea you were working at Amber Bay.'

She stared up at him and met a smile in his eyes. The moment hung between them.

He cleared his throat. Annie dropped her eyes. It was no good. She grabbed hold of the arms of the chair to stand up.

'Annie, please.' Alex Townsend pressed his hand gently on her shoulder. She sank down again. 'It's best if you sit quietly for another minute or two. I don't want you getting dizzy again.'

'Really, I'm all right. But I have to go.'

'No. You came to see a doctor, so you must tell me what's the matter.'

'I...I'm unwell...in the morning and—'

'Are you sick in the morning?'

'Yes,' Annie whispered.

'And?'

'I think I'm having a baby.'

Dr Townsend nodded as though in agreement. 'Then let's examine you. Will you let me do that?'

Annie nodded, her face burning. It was too late for shyness now. She needed a doctor's opinion, and what was the difference if it was Dr Townsend or some stranger examining her? She took a deep breath.

'I'll need you to remove your skirt and petticoat, just leaving your undergarments,' he said, gesturing to the screen. 'Then you can slip this on.' He handed her a thin white gown. 'When you're ready, lie on the bed.'

She looked over at the narrow surgery bed that was pushed against the wall.

Biting her lip and clutching the gown to her as though she were already naked, she stepped behind the screen.

Dr Townsend was clinically professional. She lay nervously on the bed, pulling the sheet right up to her chin.

'When did you last menstruate?' he asked matter-of-factly.

She closed her eyes. It was bad enough when she had to tell Ferguson that she couldn't 'do it' because of her flow.

'It's all right, Annie. Take your time,' Alex said gently.

'It...it wasn't long after we arrived here,' she said finally, twisting her neck to the wall. 'I'm sorry, I can't remember exactly.' She paused, trying to work it out. 'The end of November I think.'

He put his hand on her abdomen and pressed lightly. The warmth of his hand spread into her body. She flushed even deeper.

'So we're now the 13th April. It seems to me you're about fifteen to sixteen weeks along. So we're probably looking at the end of August.' He looked down at her. 'Is this news going to present any difficulties?'

She was relieved Dr Townsend – she must stop thinking of him as Alex – was talking about practical matters.

'I don't know what Mr and Mrs Scott-Lawson will say. Maybe they'll sack us.'

'I don't think it will come to that.' Alex smiled reassuringly. 'They don't strike me as unreasonable.' His face became serious. 'What about your husband? Will he be pleased?'

'I...I don't know,' Annie answered truthfully. 'I hope he will, but he'll be worried about our jobs...as I am.'

'I think you should tell him sooner rather than later. Get him used to the idea.'

21

Alex

After Annie left the surgery, Alex Townsend sat at his desk, pondering the events of the last few weeks. He'd never thought he would set eyes on Annie again when the ship had docked. The trouble was, he'd begun to look forward to seeing her smiling face every time she entered the ward in the ship's hospital. He'd longed to really talk to her, to ask her about her family, what she enjoyed. Anything that interested her. But they'd both been swept up in trying to combat the smallpox epidemic. He'd admired the way she only had to be briefed once before she got on with the job. Somehow she knew how to bring comfort to the patients with her gentle words, encouraging them to take a little food and drink, changing the beds, and even assisting the cleaner when it got too much for one person. She'd been simply wonderful.

He'd never discovered the reason why she and her husband were making a new life in Australia. All he'd gathered was that they were newly married and had jobs to go to, but he didn't know where. It was only when she'd bumped into him at the docks and he'd helped her with her suitcase that her husband had told him in no uncertain terms that Annie was a cook. Else he wouldn't have even known that.

He hadn't cared for Ferguson's tone, and noticed Annie had been embarrassed at her husband's rudeness. He wondered why she'd married him. Was it to get away from her family? Or a job she didn't like? He shrugged, and took out the notes for the next patient. It was none of his business. Disappointing though it was, she was married and that was the end of it.

Until that evening in the dining room of the Scott-Lawsons. At first he'd honestly thought he was imagining things. Now, sitting at his desk in the surgery, he couldn't help smiling as he went back over the scene. Annie had dropped the jug, but not because she was clumsy. He of all people knew she wasn't that, after watching her with the patients on the ship. But she'd been caught unawares, just as he had. He was sure of it.

It was his good luck that Bertram had swerved the car and he'd knocked his head. Because being a patient at Amber Bay had given him enough hours to know that he was completely and utterly head-over-heels in love.

But he would never be able to tell her. She was not long married. And now she was going to have a baby.

He leant his elbows on the desk, dropped his head in his hands, and covered his eyes, his fingers meeting at the bridge of his nose. He gave a deep sigh.

God, this whole situation was depressing. Not that Annie would soon have a child, but because the child wasn't his. She seemed very unsure how her husband would take the news. How could she possibly love someone who was going to be the father of her child and be so worried what he would say? He and Gwen had planned to have children and that hope had been snatched away. Now, seeing Annie, the dearest woman he'd ever set eyes on since his beloved Gwen, and who was dreading telling her husband she was going to have a baby, was almost more than he could stand. He swore under his breath and tried once more to concentrate on the next patient's notes.

'Mr Blackwell to see you, Doctor,' the nurse announced, and he became the doctor once more.

*

Night after night Alex sat alone in his room, trying to read but not able to concentrate. This particular evening he took another gulp of whisky, wondering what on earth he could do. He'd had enough of sailing to and fro from Australia to England and back again.

At first it had helped after Gwen died, having a change of scenery, even if it was mostly sea. Now he felt numb. Memories of Gwen, both happy and sad, bubbled to the surface. He didn't want to volunteer as a ship's doctor any longer. But he equally couldn't run the risk of meeting Annie again. There was no future in it. Until the end of his contract he would have to continue his temporary position assisting Dr Brooke, which included looking after the Scott-Lawsons. Which would bring him nearer to Annie. His blood raced at the thought. But it was no good. He would have to say he was busy if Stella asked him to any more dinners.

In the meantime, he would put in for a transfer. Sydney might be the answer. That should certainly be far enough away.

22

Annie let another week slip by without saying anything to Ferguson. For one thing it never seemed to be the right time. Ferguson was either too busy or too tired. After his duty finished for the day he usually went up to their room and retreated behind the newspaper he brought back every evening when Mr Scott-Lawson had done with it. When she tried to speak to him he was often abrupt. But if she were honest she admitted that she was really worried. Then in the next breath she would tell herself not to be so silly. He was her husband. He might be shocked at first, but when it sank in he'd be just as happy as she was. Somehow they would manage and keep their jobs. Even Alex had been sure of that.

She wouldn't keep it from him any longer. Ferguson had to know. This morning she vowed that after the staff lunch had been cleared away and they were back in their room she would tell him. He'd be nice and relaxed with a full stomach.

'Ferguson?'

'What is it?' Ferguson's voice was muffled from behind the newspaper. Without waiting for her reply, he said, 'You know there's going to be a war, Annie. One involving a lot of countries on the Continent. Mark my words.'

He made out that he'd thought it up himself, but she knew it came from the pages he was reading. She'd got into the habit of skimming the newspaper herself before it went out to the rubbish, desperate to know what was happening at home. Her father had once remarked that newspapers always exaggerated and distorted the facts to make their papers sell, but at least she felt she was keeping up with the news.

Ferguson obviously didn't expect her to comment. He crackled the paper as he turned a page.

'Ferguson, would you please put that down a minute and listen to me?' Why was she so nervous? Did other wives feel the same when breaking such exciting news?

No answer. Ferguson was obviously completely absorbed.

'I'm going to have a baby.'

The newspaper went still. Ferguson's fingers were white as he gripped the paper. Slowly he put it down. At least now he was paying attention. Her husband sat there and stared at her, his mouth open, his eyes bulging. He didn't say a word. Finally, his eyes strayed to her belly.

'Are you sure?' His voice was a croak.

'Yes. I've been to the doctor.'

Please don't ask me which doctor.

'It's too soon for us to have a baby. You're too young.'

Annie gazed at him. He was in shock. She'd take it slowly.

'I'm not too young to be a wife,' she said, making her tone as reasonable as she could muster. 'And look at all the practice I've had with my sisters.'

'That was different. They weren't babies. Babies need attention night and day.'

As if she didn't know that.

'I can't pretend I'm happy,' he went on. 'We'll lose our jobs, for one thing – no question of it.'

This was worse than she'd imagined. She was prepared for him to be worried, but this cold manner of his completely took her by surprise. It was as though some stranger was taking her husband's place. She felt the tears prick the back of her eyes. She wouldn't cry. She wouldn't give him the satisfaction.

'Alex...I mean Dr Townsend—'

'Dr Townsend? Or *Alex*, as you call him. He pops up everywhere. What's *he* got to do with this?' Ferguson's face was contorted.

'He was standing in for Dr Brooke,' Annie said, furious with herself for letting his name slip out. 'Don't look like that, Ferguson. I didn't know he was in the same practice, let alone that he'd be on duty. He said it was due at the end of August, and that he was sure Mr and Mrs Scott-Lawson would make some arrangement so we could stay on.'

'I'm not having him tell me what to do.' Ferguson leapt up. 'I'll speak to him. After all, I *am* the father.'

'Ferguson, please don't. I'm asking you not to.'

'And why not?' Ferguson's eyes gleamed like marbles. 'You're acting as though he means more to you than your own husband.'

'That remark is completely out of place.' Annie's voice was hard. 'I'm not listening to any more of this nonsense.'

She left the room, giving the door a satisfactory slam.

She needed to be alone to think.

The evening air soothed her as she sat on the garden bench, the hard wood digging into her back, barely noticing that the hydrangea was in glorious purple bloom. Why had he changed? What had happened? She heard Mrs Jenner's warning in her ears as clearly as though she were sitting beside her. *You don't know them until you marry them.*

All Annie had wanted was to see her husband's face light up when she told him her news. For him to put his arms around her. Tell her that it wouldn't be easy but he'd be with her. That he loved her. That he was proud they were going to have a baby.

But instead he'd acted as though it were all her fault.

And why was there always trouble if she mentioned Dr Townsend? Or Adele, for that matter. The image of Adele floated before her. She couldn't help liking and admiring her friend, even

179

though she was so different from anyone she'd ever known. She took risks the way Annie would never have dared. Seeing off Mr Scott-Lawson that time (thank goodness she had never told Ferguson about that) and getting a job in a hotel. Adele was so brave. And she'd been marvellous with little Rosie on the ship. She'd helped out, which was more than you could say for Ferguson.

Yes, Ferguson had taken a dislike to both Alex and Adele. He'd made it quite clear that Annie was not to have anything to do with either of them. It was almost as though he were jealous.

'I'm sorry, Annie, really I am,' Ferguson whispered as Annie lay stiffly in bed with her back to him. 'I don't know what came over me. I seem to have such black moods lately, and this one is a real worry. But it's not your fault, dearest. Please turn round and let me make it up to you.' He kissed the back of her neck.

She tried not to shrink away. She knew what Ferguson meant. She closed her eyes, pretending to sleep. After a few long minutes, she heard him sigh, turn over, and begin to snore.

Mrs Scott-Lawson was sympathetic when Annie confessed about the baby.

'Oh, my dear,' she said. 'You mustn't overdo it. I know exactly what it's like.'

'I...we don't want to lose our jobs,' Annie faltered.

'Good gracious, child. No chance of that. Mrs Wilson said you were the best assistant she's ever had, and my husband is getting used to Bishop. He's doing a fine job.'

'Thank you, ma'am.'

'Now, run along. No more worrying. Things have a habit of sorting themselves out.'

If only it were that simple, Annie thought. She supposed it was easy for people with money. They only had to ring a bell and someone would appear and do everything for them. But she shouldn't have such uncharitable thoughts. Mrs Scott-Lawson had been wonderful and she was truly grateful, though she still had to convince Ferguson.

Ferguson seemed a little happier now he knew they would be keeping their jobs, but something else was bothering Annie. He no longer insisted on the nightly ritual. He told her he didn't want to hurt her, and once he even added 'or the baby'. She was relieved as it had begun to get awkward with her growing bump, but it was another change in her husband. Something she knew was important to him, and about the only time he seemed more his old self. The other change was that he'd taken up smoking, which she didn't think they could afford now they were going to have a baby, but it was no use saying anything. How she longed for a friend to tell her troubles to, but there was no one. Mrs Wilson was kind but she was old enough to be Annie's mother, and if Annie couldn't have her own mother she didn't want anyone else in her place.

Towards the end of June, just two months away from Alex's calculation of the birth, Annie sat down to write to Adele, feeling a twinge of guilt that she hadn't kept her promise and written sooner. It had been the best part of a year since they'd arrived in Melbourne and there had been no word. Adele might not even be at the...what hotel was it? She racked her brains. Oh, yes, the Hotel Esplanade. It sounded very grand. She wondered how far away it was. Adele had mentioned another name, maybe the road. She couldn't remember, but someone was sure to know the hotel.

The baby gave a sudden kick and instinctively Annie put her hand on her belly. Why waste time with letters. She would go and see Adele on her extra half-day off and make some excuse to Ferguson about going to the market. Frowning, she wondered if this was going to be a pattern in her marriage.

*

Two days later Annie was at the tram stop. To her relief the last weeks had been cooler. That morning she'd drawn back the curtains to a sky black as a widow's weeds. The rain had held off during her walk up the lane, but now she heard a faint rumbling and just as she glanced upwards the heavens opened.

'Drat,' she spoke aloud. She'd been so intent on leaving without being questioned by Ferguson or Mrs Wilson that she'd forgotten to take an umbrella. She turned up the collar of her rain cape but it gave little protection; her hat was soaked in seconds. As she was about to run for shelter a motor car drew up. The driver leaned across and spoke through the open side.

'Good morning, Annie. You look as if you're drowning. May I take you somewhere?'

It was Alexander Townsend. He was smiling and gesturing for her to get in. She hesitated, staring down at him, meeting those twinkling grey eyes. No. It wouldn't be right. She blushed and told herself she was being ridiculous. He'd obviously taken her hesitation for a yes, as he sprang out and opened the door for her. She felt, rather than saw, the couple at the tram stop eyeing her curiously. There was nothing to do but clamber in.

'What a pleasure to see you, Annie,' he said, briefly turning to smile at her. 'But you look as wet as an otter. How long have you been waiting?' His voice was light.

'Only a few minutes. It wasn't raining when I left the house.'

'Lucky for you I came along.' He looked round, released the brake and steered the motor into the traffic. 'Any longer and you could have caught cold. Where are we going?'

'Do you know the Hotel Esplanade?'

He smiled. 'Funny you should say that. That's exactly where I'm headed.' She started in surprise and he grinned. 'I'm teasing. But I know where it is. It's actually a little way from here – in St Kilda.' He gave her a quick glance. 'Why are you going there? Aren't you happy at Amber Bay?'

Annie shifted in her seat. Dr Townsend was a friend of the Scott-Lawsons. She needed to be cautious. The last thing she wanted was any gossip.

'I have a friend who works there,' Annie finally confessed. She didn't need to mention any names. 'I promised I would write to her and I never have. It's been almost a year since I've seen her.'

'Do you know if she'll definitely be there?' Alex Townsend cursed under his breath as a cyclist almost clipped him.

'No, but I thought I could leave a message if she wasn't.'

Alex nodded. 'We'll be there in about fifteen minutes. How long do you think you'll be? Half an hour?'

No, Annie decided. I am not going to be timed by someone. This is my free morning and I'm going to use it as I please. She was astonished at herself. Normally she would fall in with others' arrangements. She was putting her foot down. And she was enjoying it.

'I wouldn't want to keep you,' she said firmly. 'I'm really grateful for the lift, but I will be perfectly all right coming back on the tram. And I honestly don't know how long I'll be.'

'As you wish.'

She felt she'd offended him. They went the rest of the way in silence, until Alex turned the steering wheel to the left where the sparkling bay of St Kilda looped round in a huge semi-circle. Annie gasped at its beauty. Several boats were far out in the bay, with others bobbing at the edges. Seconds later Alex pulled up outside an imposing building. The façade reminded her of a postcard her friend Sarah had once sent of a row of white rendered hotels with columned entrances along Brighton seafront.

'Here you are,' Alex turned to her. 'Hotel Esplanade.'

'I'm really grateful for the lift,' she repeated, 'but please don't wait.'

Alex opened his mouth to say something but apparently changed his mind. He jumped out to open the door for her and grasped her arm, gently guiding her on to the pavement. He paused a moment, then got back into the driving seat, and she awkwardly climbed the steps, still feeling the pressure of his fingers, knowing he was watching her.

Adele was the first person she saw as she entered the reception hall, which was no smaller than the one at Amber Bay. Her friend was wearing the hotel uniform, a navy suit, brought to life by bright pink lipstick and dangling earrings which swung as Adele's golden head snapped round in recognition.

'My, my, if it isn't little Annie…only not so little now.' She stared straight at Annie's protruding stomach, and Annie felt her face go hot. Adele came out from behind the desk and took one of Annie's small rough hands in her own creamy-smooth one. 'I thought you'd forgotten me. Or that husband of yours had forbidden you to write.' Her eyes were questioning as she looked Annie up and down.

'Oh, nothing like that, Adele,' Annie said, trying to laugh off her friend's remark, only too well aware of how near the truth she was. 'And if he did, I would still have come.'

'Mmm. Quite an independent miss.' Adele's eyes gleamed. 'Well, as you can see, I'm working, but I might be able to have an hour. We've got some catching up to do. I'll get one of the other girls to cover for me.'

'Oh, please don't,' Annie protested. 'I half expected you'd either be working and wouldn't have time to see me, or even be out on a day off. I've got a note already written, in case. You mustn't get into trouble for me.'

'No one's going to tell me off, Annie,' Adele declared. 'You see, I own the hotel!'

23

Alex

Alex gazed after Annie for a minute or two until she had mounted the steps and disappeared through the heavy door of the portico. Reluctantly, he turned and pulled his car door open and sat in the driving seat, deep in thought.

He worried about her. It wasn't as though she couldn't take care of herself, but there was something in the set of her chin, the tightness of her lips, that had stopped any questions he'd badly wanted to ask. Questions like what happened when she told her husband about the baby? Did he react the way she'd thought? If so, is he getting used to the idea by now? But he'd asked none of these things and they'd journeyed almost in silence.

If only she had let him wait for her. He realised as soon as he'd said it that she wasn't pleased to be offered half an hour. Well, he would have waited longer. Could have done an errand or two – after all, this was his day off – and then returned for her. Maybe they could have gone for something to eat. Then he told himself not to be such a fool. Far too dangerous. Mostly for her, but if he valued his position with Dr Brooke, even though it was only temporary, he must stick to the rules.

What should he do now on his day off?

There were several options. He could take a boat trip on the river. But he didn't fancy it on his own. Besides, it was still drizzling. He could go to the library. He could go to one of the gentleman's clubs that welcomed doctors. But none of them appealed. He just wanted to be with Annie. To listen to her voice. To hear her opinion on things. How badly he wanted to cup her face in his hands. To look into those luminous eyes, navy-blue in certain lights. To watch that mouth curve in amusement. He remembered how she would sometimes laugh in the ship's hospital at something Adele had said. He'd wanted to join in, ask what the joke was, but he'd had to maintain his professionalism.

Oh, to pull the pins out of her hair and run his fingers through the tumbled waves. He imagined how long her hair was, visualising it falling to her waist. That once-slim waist, thickening now with her coming child. He gave a wry smile. She needed that baby more than anything in the world right now. Something of her own to cherish, as it didn't appear as though she had much cherishing from her husband. Alex only hoped he himself would be around when she most needed him.

Sitting here worrying wasn't going to do any good. With a deep sigh he got out and went round to the front to crank the motor.

24

Annie's jaw dropped in amazement. She'd never heard of a woman owning a hotel.

Adele laughed at her incredulous expression. 'Everyone looks like that when I tell them. 'Specially the men. They always ask how I got the money. Well, it's none of their bleedin' business.'

Flinching inwardly at the swear word, Annie knew she would never have been so impertinent as to ask such a question, and wondered if Adele had said this to warn her.

'I'm pleased for you, Adele,' she said. 'Really I am.' She decided to risk one question. 'Does it do well?'

'It gives me a decent living.' Adele tossed her golden curls. 'Annie, why don't you sit down over there in the booth,' she pointed to a dark corner where there was an oak table with a moquette corner seat, 'and I'll order some coffee for us. We can have a nice chat. Catch up on things.'

Annie would have rather sat near a window in the light, but she obediently crossed the reception area and sat at the table Adele had indicated. Her eyes flicked over the polished bar and dark-brown furniture, the brocade curtains and flowered carpet. Adele must have spent a lot of money to create such a comfortable atmosphere.

'May I get you something, miss?' a waiter enquired. Although he smiled politely, Annie didn't take to him. He was too short and too slight, with a narrow face, slicked-back brown hair and a knowing expression.

'No, nothing, thank you.' She looked up at him. 'I'm just waiting for Miss Frost.'

'You are acquainted with her?'

To Annie this was too personal a question. 'Yes,' she said, rather abruptly.

The waiter raised both eyebrows.

'It's all right, Heppel, I'm looking after the lady.' Adele stepped towards them carrying a tray of coffee. She set it down in front of Annie.

'Certainly, Miss Frost.' The waiter bowed to Annie and turned to another table.

'He's nosy, is that one,' Adele grimaced, looking after him. 'Now, Annie, I see you have some exciting news.' She looked down at Annie's extended belly.

'Oh, Adele, it's all happening at once. The baby's due in two months.'

'That's wonderful,' Adele said. 'I'm really happy for you.' She sounded wistful as she poured out two cups, and for the first time Annie wondered if she regretted not having children. She passed a cup to Annie. 'And how are they treating you at Amber Bay?' Adele scrutinised her.

'They seem kind,' Annie said. Should she mention Mr Scott-Lawson's wink and the smile which had made her feel wary? No, it would make her seem as though she was looking for trouble because of Adele's warnings. Surely he'd meant nothing by it. 'I suppose that sounds strange when you had such a bad time with Mr Scott-Lawson,' she said instead. 'I don't have anything to do with him, of course,' she added hastily, glancing at Adele to see how she was taking it. Adele merely looked skeptical. 'Ferguson and I only had one room, being a couple, but when I told Mrs Scott-Lawson I was having a baby she's let us have one of the gardeners' cottages. We've got two bedrooms. We've only just moved in but Ferguson's already painting one of them for the baby.'

Adele smiled as she took up her cup. 'So you're keeping your husband out of mischief.'

Mischief?

'Don't look so worried,' Adele patted Annie's arm. 'It's just a saying. But I'm surprised he's let you come and see me.'

'Ferguson doesn't know where I am,' Annie blurted. 'He's working. I've got a few hours off because I did lates four nights last week. They're always fair if that happens.'

Adele wrinkled her nose and Annie decided this time she wouldn't ignore it. Maybe it was the family who regularly complimented her on her cooking; maybe it was the growing child inside her; but she felt more confident these days. She could even stand up to Ferguson when she needed to, without going to pieces.

'Adele, you never finished telling me what happened to you after you lost your job at the bar. What did you do when you came back to Melbourne?'

'Well, I only had the clothes I stood up in. But I'd already got a waitress job here at the Esplanade before I went back to England to visit. Trouble was, it wasn't live-in. Luckily I'd got a friend who took me in. I told him I needed a bed for a few weeks till I could work out what to do. He's a bit of a gambler and took me horse racing. It was just a lark. I'd only ever played whist and gin rummy. I didn't have any money to speak of, just a bit by me under the mattress. So I decided to blow the lot. I couldn't be much worse off. But I got lucky and won a lot of money that first week. And more the second. Beginner's luck, my friend called it, until I won the third week in a row. I didn't push my luck any further though. Good job, because it wasn't long after that the owner of this hotel told me he intended to sell. I jumped at the chance and said I'd like to buy it. You should have seen his face!' Adele chuckled at the memory and gulped down her coffee. 'He said, "I suppose your money is as good as anyone's." I only had enough for a down payment but the bank did the rest. I'm paying them back every month. I'm independent.

No man telling me what to do. So the old bugger did me a favour.'

Annie struggled to take this all in. Adele was certainly a confident woman, but she enjoyed gambling, which Annie found disturbing. Yet she felt a fleeting stab of envy that Adele was in full control of her own life. What must it be like to make all the decisions; to tell others what to do; to run a business? How had Adele learned? Annie was lost in her thoughts when she felt the baby give a vigorous kick. Perhaps it was reminding her of its presence. Feeling ashamed, she put her hand on her swelling stomach and told herself how lucky she was. She had Ferguson and the baby, who would soon be born. It was all she'd ever dreamed of.

She wondered whether she could ask Adele about that time in Naples when Ferguson had gone to the same café as Adele, drinking beer with her. Had he been playing cards as well? But before Annie could open her mouth Adele abruptly changed the subject.

'Have you heard from your sisters?' Adele drained the last of her coffee.

'They take it in turns to write to me. Ruby wants to come here. Ethel's a real homebody. I suppose I fall somewhere between the two of them.' She smiled, almost to herself. 'Ruby made me promise to send for her once I got settled but it'll be ages before we can afford it. I shall try to find her a position near Amber Bay so I can keep an eye on her.' Annie leaned forward despite her bulk. 'The trouble is, Ruby hates domestic work and I'm not sure what else she could do, but once she makes up her mind about something, she'll do it. And she definitely wants to come to Australia.'

Annie caught the tram just outside the Hotel Esplanade, her mind going over everything Adele had told her. The tram stop was even called Hotel Esplanade, Annie noticed. Fancy having a friend who was a businesswoman and practically had her own tram stop.

'You be careful now,' Adele had cautioned as she'd warmly embraced her.

A faint tremor passed through Annie. She was sure Adele was referring to Mr Scott-Lawson, though she told herself she must stop reading things into nothing. Her employer wouldn't dare try anything under the same roof as his wife. She gazed out of the tram window hoping she wouldn't go past her stop. But she needn't have worried. Just when the area was beginning to look familiar, the driver slowed down and called out, 'Amber Bay.'

'Where've you been?' Ferguson demanded, catching hold of her arm as she was just about to slip into the kitchen. 'I've been looking for you.'

'I went out.' Annie was aware of her heart beating.

'Where?'

'Just in the town, having a look around.' She didn't want to lie but on the other hand she didn't want to go into Adele's story when they were on duty. One of the housemaids passed them, looking curious. 'I'll tell you later,' Annie muttered.

'You should be careful, what with carrying the baby and all.'

It was strange, Annie thought, that Ferguson echoed Adele's same words of warning.

'So where did you go?' Ferguson asked her again when they were back in their cottage before the evening shift.

'Actually, I went to see Adele.'

'Adele! I thought I told you to stay away from her.'

'I'm sorry, Ferguson, but I wanted to see her again. I like her.'

'She's nothing but a doxy.'

'That's a horrible word,' Annie snapped. 'Adele works hard and pays her bills.' She paused. Would Adele mind her telling Ferguson? She badly wanted to put her friend in a good light where Ferguson was concerned. She plunged in. 'Did you know she *owns* the Hotel Esplanade?'

'Yes, I did. She got it through gambling. A woman who

gambles, Annie.' Ferguson's voice was rough.

'Well, it must have been won legitimately. If she'd been a man you would admire him.' Annie felt anger flare up in her.

'I forbid you to have anything more to do with that woman. You're soon to be a mother, and I won't have my wife going off without my permission. Do you promise, Annie?' He looked at her. 'Annie?' he repeated, drawing out the two syllables.

She shook her head. 'I'm sorry, Ferguson,' she said firmly. 'I can't make that promise. It's unreasonable.'

Ferguson threw her a furious look and stormed out of the house. Annie dropped down in the cheap velvet armchair. She winced as she heard the front door slam. She put her hand on her stomach as though to comfort her unborn child, her eyes full of unshed tears.

25

28th July 1914

The thing we've all been dreading has happened. War was declared over Europe today.

Oh, I can't write any more. It's too awful.

30th July 1914

It seems the Austrian Archduke and his wife were shot dead in a street in Vienna by a Serbian student last month. I don't even know where Serbia is. The Archduke was the heir to the throne and this is what has set it all off. How can something like that, terrible though it is, have such a shocking effect on the rest of Europe? I'm trying to understand what's happening by grabbing the newspaper every time Ferguson puts it to one side. I hope it won't be long before I hear from my father and sisters but I fear it will be difficult for letters to get through. Ferguson says they will need the ships for the troops, not to act as post offices. Everyone's saying it will turn into a world war. Ferguson says Australia is sure to be dragged in.

Increasingly, Annie found it difficult to carry out her duties and another girl had been hired to help Mrs Wilson. Mrs Scott-Lawson had told Annie this was only a temporary arrangement until the baby was born, and then she could go back to work. Although it all sounded sensible enough, Annie was worried Mrs Scott-Lawson might take to the new girl and decide to keep her on. Even more worrying was who would look after the baby when she went back to work.

But right at this moment something else was preying on her mind. Ferguson had begun to go out two nights a week and whenever she confronted him he would answer,

'Isn't a man allowed a night out with his mates occasionally?'

Annie would bite her lip and try not to say anything, but one evening when he was even later than usual she lost her temper.

'Don't you care if I worry?' she demanded. 'You could have had an accident or been taken ill. How am I to know?'

Ferguson had the grace to look ashamed. 'Of course I care. But I'm only out with the lads. They're friends. Nothing for you to worry about.'

'Some friends,' she flared. 'And you've been drinking. I can smell it on your breath. You're spending money we can't afford. We're supposed to be saving.'

'Don't you tell me what to do with my money.' Ferguson's voice held a warning note. He slumped into the facing armchair. 'I'm earning the money for both of us now you're in the family way.' He made it sound like an accusation.

'No, you're not. I'm still working as much as I can.' Her whole body shook with indignation, and she put a hand on her belly to calm herself.

Ferguson was silent.

'I want to know where you're going when you leave here after work,' Annie persisted. 'Most people are getting ready for bed at that time.' Her palms felt clammy, dreading the answer if he told her and ready to be angry if he didn't.

'If you must know, I'm winning some money.'

'What do you mean, winning money?' It had crossed her mind more than once that he was seeing another woman. The ugly thought had reared up when she'd tentatively put her arms round him in bed on two or three occasions recently. He continued to make the excuse that it was too awkward for her and might damage the baby. All she'd wanted was for him to hug her and tell her he loved her, and that he was looking forward to seeing the baby. She'd brushed away the tears, feeling rejected. But gambling? Yes, she'd caught him playing cards in that bar in Naples but that had only been a game. This was serious. She studied Ferguson's face and knew he was telling the truth.

'Just placing a bet here and there.' Ferguson's tone had become like a defiant schoolboy's.

'But you're gambling with *our* money.'

'And I've made twelve pounds.' Ferguson could hardly keep the pride from his voice.

'But you could just as easily lose it,' Annie said, ignoring the voice in her head that whispered how useful the money would be when the baby came.

'I'm not that stupid,' he said. 'I'd stop if I started to lose.'

A sudden thought struck Annie as she heard Adele's words. *Beginner's luck, they said it was. But it was enough to put down a deposit on the hotel.* Was Adele mixed up in this then? Is that what they had been discussing on the quayside that day?

'Ferguson, has this got anything to do with Adele? You said she got the hotel through gambling.'

'What are you talking about? I barely know Adele.'

'Oh yes you do,' Annie said, trying hard not to sound triumphant. 'You were drinking with her at that café in Naples – and I expect you were playing cards then. That's why you didn't come back to the museum. *And* I saw you talking to her on the day we docked.'

'When you dropped your case for Dr Alexander Townsend to come running?'

'Please don't try to change the subject.' Annie's voice was quiet. 'As your wife, I'm entitled to know what you and Adele were talking about.'

'I wanted to know if she'd seen you,' he said. 'She hadn't, but she kept on yapping about a load of nonsense.'

Annie could not let the matter rest. The thought burned day and night in her head that Adele was behind all this. She'd have to confront her.

Every time she thought she might have a spare two hours, something happened that kept her at Amber Bay. A week had gone by before she had her opportunity. She was tired, her feet hurt, and the baby's weight was pressing down on her bladder, but she was determined. She knew the route now, and half an hour later the tram dropped her outside the hotel. With trepidation, Annie opened the door and trudged over to the reception desk. Adele was nowhere to be seen. She picked up the bell and jangled it. Finally, the same thin waiter appeared.

'I've come to see Miss Frost,' Annie told him.

'She's not in today.'

Annie swallowed her disappointment, yet there was something about the little man's expression she didn't quite believe. She was about to ask if he had any idea where Adele might be when a sudden cramp in her stomach forced her to stoop over.

'Anything wrong, miss?' He was looking at her curiously.

'No, nothing.' She drew herself up as the pain subsided. 'It's just a stitch.' She caught his eye. 'Do you know where she is? It's very important I speak to her.'

Without a word he turned and vanished through one of the rear doors. Ten minutes later Adele came in, looking as though she'd just woken up. Her hair was dull and dishevelled, and her lips weren't painted their usual defiant red. She smoothed her crumpled skirt as she went towards Annie, but her smile was genuine.

'Annie, what a pleasant surprise. You're lucky to catch me in. It's my day off.'

Now she was facing Adele, Annie felt tongue-tied, not knowing where to start. Seeing her look of discomfort, Adele said, 'Do you want to come up to my room? We can be private.'

'Yes, I'd like that,' Annie said, and followed her out of the same rear door the waiter had disappeared through, then along a passage, up a flight of stairs, and in the first door on the left marked PRIVATE.

Adele nodded for Annie to take the only chair.

'Now, what's this all about?' she asked, sitting on the bed. 'You look a fright, if I may say so. Even worse than me.' She laughed, then became serious. 'Something or someone's upset you.'

Annie didn't answer immediately. She had no idea how Adele would take it when she confronted her. To stall for time she looked around. Clothes were strewn over the bed, undergarments were spread on a clothes horse to dry, shoes were flung here and there, and the dressing table was a jumble of toiletries and cut-glass bottles. The room smelled stale with smoke.

'The cleaners will be in shortly,' Adele said, following Annie's gaze. 'It's difficult to keep order in such a cramped space. I need all the other rooms for guests. It's the only way to keep in profit.'

'Adele, I must ask you something,' Annie plunged in, hardly hearing her friend's words. 'Ferguson's been gambling.' She looked at Adele, who was watching her intently. 'He stays out late and comes in reeking of beer. He's even admitted it.' She was at the point of tears. 'Please, Adele, don't lead him astray. Please stop him from betting.'

Adele burst into laughter.

'Will you do that?' Annie pleaded.

'Annie,' Adele looked directly at her, 'I haven't been any influence on that precious husband of yours. Ferguson found out I'd had a lucky streak in my time and asked me to place some bets on the horses for him when we got to Melbourne, but I'd already met you and liked you. I told him it was a dangerous game.' Annie opened her mouth to speak but Adele raised her hand. 'No, let me finish. A dangerous game is what I said, with him being newly married and

197

all. The short answer is, I refused. I've seen better men than him lose everything through gambling: their house, their job, everything. When I got into it, I didn't have much to lose and everything to gain. I was lucky. But I quit while I was winning. Most people – most men – don't. I imagine your husband has got tied up with a bad lot. They'll be the ones leading him astray. Not me.'

Annie listened to Adele in shock but somehow she knew in her heart, by the open expression on her friend's face, that Adele was telling the truth. Before she could answer she convulsed with another griping pain.

'What's the matter, Annie? Are you having a contraction?'

'I-I don't know… I had a bad pain when I got here,' Annie stuttered, trying to catch her breath.

'Do you think you'd feel better if you stood up?'

Annie flung her arm across her belly as she bent forward.

'I c-can't. Another one—'

The next moment she felt warm liquid pour from her, soaking her skirt.

'Adele, what's happening?' Annie cried, grabbing the arm of the chair and struggling to her feet. Trembling, she turned round, and was horrified at the puddle she'd left. 'Dear God—'

Adele was at her side, steadying her.

'It's all right, Annie,' she said. 'Don't be scared. But we've got to get you to hospital straight away. Your waters have broken. The baby's started.'

Time passed in a blur of pain. Annie had a vague recollection of being bundled into an ambulance wagon, though she clearly heard Adele's voice reassuring her that everything would be all right. She was grateful for Adele's hand gripping hers but the pains racked her body. Was this normal? She crushed her friend's hand as the next spasm winded her.

'Don't try to speak, Annie. I'm here. You're going to be all right. You're going to have the best baby in the world and Ferguson will be so proud of you.'

Adele and the driver pulled her out of the wagon and half-dragged her up the hospital steps. Another wave of pain bent her double. She prayed for somewhere to curl up and die.

'Tell Ferguson. Tell him where I am, won't you?'

Annie's voice sounded thin and far away to her own ears as a nurse undressed her and roughly pulled a cotton nightdress over her head. Between Adele and the nurse they managed to get Annie up on the bed.

'Of course, Annie.' Adele bent over her and stroked Annie's cheek. 'Don't worry. I'll let him know. Everything will be taken care of.'

'The doctor will be along presently to examine you,' the nurse said in a curt tone.

Annie clamped her mouth shut to stop herself from screaming with the next pain, a pain which felt it would rip her apart.

'Something's happening,' she gasped.

'Nonsense.' The nurse's tone was as starched as her apron as she straightened the counterpane. 'You've got hours to go yet, so don't make a fuss. You'd think you were the first woman to have a baby.'

'How *dare* you speak to my friend in that manner!' Adele demanded. The nurse paled, but Adele carried on. 'Mrs Bishop never makes a fuss. You can see she's in pain.'

'I'll be all right.' Annie's face was drawn. 'But I can feel something...' and with a low animal groan she turned on her side and pulled her knees up in the direction of her chin.

'I'm going to fetch a doctor,' Adele said, and flew off. Minutes later she reappeared, wearing a triumphant expression. Half walking, half running behind her was Dr Alex Townsend.

'Look who I've brought to see you, Annie,' she said. 'It's Dr

Townsend who we helped on the ship. You're lucky it's his day at the hospital.' Adele turned to beam at the doctor but he was already bending over Annie's bed. Taking the nearest limp hand, he gently pushed away the tendrils of hair, dark with perspiration, which stuck to her pale forehead.

'Don't be frightened, Annie,' he said, bending his head close to hers. 'It's me, Alex.'

'I'm not frightened now you're here,' she whispered, but in the next breath she twisted her head from him and gave an agonising scream. The nurse frowned and opened her mouth, but Dr Townsend stopped her with the flat of his hand. He gestured to the nurse to draw the curtains, all the while talking to Annie in a low, soothing voice as he pulled the covers from the foot of the bed and raised Annie's nightdress, pulling her feet up into the waiting stirrups.

'Bear down hard,' Alex instructed, 'every time you get a contraction.'

How long would this go on? Minutes, hours? Time rolled by and she couldn't work out how long she'd been lying there. She was dimly aware of women's voices, and every so often, through her dazed mind, she heard Alex.

'Breathe slowly…in…out…in…out. Don't think of anything else. Just concentrate on your breathing.'

His words floated around her – along with the pain.

'You're doing wonderfully well,' Alex said, coming to sit on her bed. He picked up her hand and smiled. 'Only a little longer to go. I can just see the baby's head.' He pressed her hand briefly and went back to the foot of the bed as the next wave of agony took hold.

She called out, then lay back panting, her eyes closed, a peculiar notion invading her mind. Was she dreaming? Alex was the father. Alex with his lovely, warm grey eyes, his capable hands, his melodious voice. He didn't need to say anything. She felt his love as though he had actually spoken the words. She visualised his dark head as he bent over to see if the baby was coming. Heat flooded

200

up her neck to her face. Dear God, Alex must never know what she had been thinking. Nor must Ferguson.

She shivered at the thought.

'All right, Annie?' It was Adele, wiping her forehead with a cool flannel. 'I'm still here.'

Then another contraction blotted everything out.

'Push!' Alex shouted.

Instinctively, she pushed with every ounce of energy and felt her insides tear as Frances Elizabeth slipped into the world.

26

24th September 1914

Something awful has happened which I need to write down. Ferguson has been acting oddly again, just as he did when he first told me about Australia. I dreaded what he would spring on me. Then he told me. It was worse than I could have imagined. He's joined up. I had to sit down I was shaking so much. Ferguson leaving me and little Frankie. Married men with babies were the last to be called, I thought, and told him so.

He wouldn't answer.

You've volunteered, I said. You might as well be honest and tell me.

He said he had to do his duty by his country and just because we lived in Australia it didn't change anything. He said if he'd been single he'd have joined up the day war broke out.

You haven't discussed this with me at all, I said. How could you do this? I think he was surprised at how angry I was. When were you going to tell me? I demanded. And what about Frankie?

I'll be home before she even realises I've gone.

And have you told Mr Scott-Lawson?

He understands, Ferguson said, looking me in the eye and daring me to say more.

He seems to have all the answers, though I know he was nervous by the way he tapped his fingers on the little table. I've joined the AIF, he said.

So it was just like before, at Bonham Place, when he had worked it all out for both of us that we would go to Australia.

I asked him what the AIF was.

The Australian Imperial Force, he said impatiently. It's like the British Army – it started up right after war was declared.

I didn't want to hear any more. I got up from our kitchen table and he had the nerve to ask me where I was going.

I wanted to scream at him. But all I said was somewhere to think.

9th October 1914

I said goodbye to Ferguson this morning. He couldn't get out of the house quick enough. So here I am, alone with Frankie, and he's off to Victoria Barracks to have his medical and swear his allegiance.

He was lucky I didn't tip his cup of tea over him.

Then I felt terrible. At least he is doing something honourable. No one can call him a coward. But where does that leave me?

13th October 1914

I worried for nothing. Ferguson has been discharged on medical reasons. He has flat feet so they turned him away. He wouldn't be able to march. He has come home furious that he can't fight for king and country because of something which seems so trifling. I'm so relieved but when I told him so he became irritable. He says he's bored with his job and wants to look for something else. How can he be bored when he has little Frankie? He was pleased to see her but he doesn't have much to say to me. I suppose every marriage goes through difficult times but we are so lucky with what we have.

I wonder how long this war will last. They say it will likely be over by Christmas. I wonder.

New Year's Day 1915

There's no sign of the war coming to an end. In fact it's getting worse. The headlines are so depressing that often I can't bring myself to read on. But it feels disloyal not to know what our boys are going through. And of course Mr and Mrs S-L are constantly worried about Russell, who is serving somewhere in the Middle East.

Sometimes I don't understand this country at all. Women have had the vote here for years, yet they are not allowed to take over the men's jobs like I've read they do in England. I wonder what the Suffragettes would say about Australian women. Mrs S-L is going to start a regular group at Amber Bay. She said at least the Red Cross encourages women to knit for the boys and roll bandages. I asked her if I might join in and she said she would be pleased to have me.

4th May 1915

I'm not keeping this journal very regularly these days. The truth is, there's only gloomy news. But I meet the ladies on several afternoons a week. All you can hear is the click-clack of knitting needles. One lady can make a whole vest or a pair of socks in two days. No one else is that quick. At first I felt uncomfortable being among the ladies as the other maids are either too busy or too tired. But now I'm used to it and most of them seem to accept me. Sometimes I think they almost forget I'm a servant when they include me in their conversation. I wonder if the same thing happens at Bonham Place. Somehow I can't imagine it.

6th August 1915

Frankie's first birthday. Strange that in England she would be a summer baby, but here it's cold and windy. Melbourne's winter. It's still not as cold as Norfolk in the winter though. Mrs Wilson baked a sponge cake especially for her but she didn't like it. It's been hard looking after her and working at the same time. Mrs S-L said so long as she's in her cot I could bring her into the kitchen. That worked when she was little but now she's in Daphne's old playpen. I told Mrs Wilson yesterday I was worried what would happen when she was walking but she said we'd manage somehow. There is sure to be a girl in the village who would be pleased to have a job at Amber Bay, she said. Everyone adores Frankie. She's such a happy and contented child. Sometimes I feel I'm pouring all my love into her.

30th November 1915

Christmas is just around the corner and the weather is becoming very warm, but things are getting even worse in Europe. Ferguson is still upset that he can't fight. Most of the young men we see nowadays have some horrible injury or limb missing. You would think he'd be relieved to be in one piece. Yesterday he said a couple crossed the street in front of him in an exaggerated manner and he heard them say 'coward'. People can't see anything wrong with him, that's the trouble. I do feel sorry for him when that happens.

2nd January 1916

Another New Year. More fighting. More soldiers dying. It's so senseless. Poor Mr and Mrs S-L. They must be going mad with worry.

27

June 1916

'Russell's been injured!'

Mr Scott-Lawson never appeared at the kitchen door and it took Annie several seconds to digest what he'd said. She sprang to her feet. 'How serious is it, sir?'

'We don't know.'

The last time the family had had a letter from Russell he was still in the Middle East, and they presumed it was Egypt. Ferguson told Annie he'd heard Mr Scott-Lawson explain to his wife only the other day at breakfast that their son was fighting to protect British interests in the Middle East and the Suez Canal. Mrs Scott-Lawson had snapped, 'Who cares about the Middle East and the Suez Canal? How does that have anything to do with us in Melbourne? And our only son?' She had flown out of the room crying.

Mrs Wilson collapsed on to one of the kitchen chairs, her hand to her mouth in dismay.

'Did they tell you where he is, sir?' Annie asked.

'The King George Hospital…in London.' Mr Scott-Lawson's voice was steady but his skin looked grey. Drops of perspiration glistened on his forehead and he took out a handkerchief to wipe them away.

'Poor Master Russell. And poor Mrs Scott-Lawson.' Annie felt sympathetic tears gather.

'Yes. It's not easy for his mother with him so far away.' Mr

206

Scott-Lawson gave Annie a long, hard look. 'When there's more news I'll let you know.' He turned to Mrs Wilson. 'Mrs Scott-Lawson won't be having any lunch today.' He nodded and left the kitchen, quietly closing the door behind him.

For some reason Annie felt uneasy. She told herself not to be so stupid. It was a shock to hear about Master Russell, and the quicker she got on with her job the better it would be for everyone concerned. She took up the spoon and broke up the skin which had already formed on the chicken soup she'd made that morning. As she stirred it her thoughts flew to her father and sisters. If anything happened to one of them it would take six weeks for her to reach them.

Annie's face drained as a boy wearing a peaked cap held out a yellow envelope.

'Morning, miss,' he said, touching his cap. 'Telegram,' he added importantly.

Hands shaking, she took it. She looked at the name on the envelope but the letters swam. Fear caught in her throat.

'Are you all right, miss?' The boy stroked his jaw, faintly shadowed with new bristles, as he watched her.

She couldn't trust herself to speak.

'Can you be sure to give it to Mr and Mrs Scott-Lawson?' the boy prompted.

She nodded dumbly.

'That's all right then,' he said. 'Oh, nearly forgot. You have to sign for it.' He reached in his bag and pulled out a book, then handed her a pencil. She scribbled her name and he shoved it back in his bag, then grabbed his bicycle from the wall and swung his leg over the bar. 'I hope it's not bad news,' he said as he pedalled off, his front wheel wobbling along the kitchen garden pathway.

Annie stared after him, then turned towards the back door. Absentmindedly, she picked up a small brown paper bag which had blown on to the path and threw it in the rubbish bin.

The telegram burned in her hand.

I'll give it to Mr Scott-Lawson, not his wife, she decided. If she hurried round to the front she'd just catch him before he left for work.

'Annie,' Mr Scott-Lawson appeared in the hall at the same moment, and took his hat from the hallstand, 'who was it at the door?'

'It was…it's a…a telegram for you, sir.'

'Here, girl. Let me have it, for God's sake.' He stretched out his hand.

Annie bobbed her head and handed it to him. She watched as her employer ripped it open, his eyes flying over the words. She knew she should have left him in private but the horror of what he might be reading rooted her to the spot.

A minute passed. He put his hand to his forehead, shielding his eyes. Finally, he looked at her, his eyes devoid of expression.

'Russell's dead.' His mouth twisted as he crunched the telegram in his hand. Abruptly, he turned and ran up the stairs.

It didn't seem possible that one piece of paper had the power to alter everything in this family, Annie thought, trembling from head to foot as she made her way back to the kitchen. As she opened the kitchen door she heard Mrs Scott-Lawson's blood-curdling howl.

The whole atmosphere of the house changed. It had always been a lovely light house, with the sun flooding through the windows and bouncing off the wooden floors in the hall and morning room, and Mr Scott-Lawson's study. Annie had always thought of Amber Bay as a happy house. Hearing Louise and Daphne laughing; Mrs Wilson chattering away, and cooing over Frankie; Mr & Mrs Scott-Lawson reading and writing in the library, or listening to music on the gramophone in the evenings – it all made for a contented household. Now, Mrs Scott-Lawson barely spoke to anyone, apart from the housekeeper, declaring that the house was in mourning and would remain so for six months. The maids had been ordered not to touch Russell's room.

'I hope she's not going to let the place go to rack and ruin,' Ferguson said one afternoon when they were taking Frankie for a walk in the grounds at the rear of Amber Bay.

'I'm sure she won't,' Annie said. 'Anymore than Mr Scott-Lawson would. She's in shock, that's all.' She tightened her grip on the pushchair as they picked their way through the light woodland, the sun flickering through the leaves like millions of candles. To lose a child. It must be the saddest thing that could ever happen to a parent. They must be sick with grief. She would do everything in her power to ease things for her employers.

Poor Russell. She'd never met him but she felt as though she knew him as part of the family. She'd often lingered by one of the photographs on the grand piano in the music room, showing a handsome young man in uniform. His broad smile and the mischievous light in his eyes were in complete contrast to the formality of his uniform. Annie would smile back at him. And now he was no more. Gone. All his future dreams, his career, in ashes. She gave a deep sigh. How much longer would this senseless war go on? She didn't dare think of Alex, who had been serving as an army doctor for the last year. Snippets of conversation between the Scott-Lawsons told her he was still alive, but that could change at any dreadful moment.

Dear God, keep him safe. Oh, please keep him safe.

The days of mourning slipped into weeks. Mrs Scott-Lawson looked as though she were in a dream, her eyes clouded with shock and disbelief. Annie's heart went out to the older woman but she knew it wasn't her place to talk about it. She had said how very sorry she was the day after the telegram, but even to her own ears it seemed sadly inadequate.

'Thank you, Annie, you're most kind,' Mrs Scott-Lawson had said, and passed by, barely pausing, her eyes red and swollen.

Annie and Mrs Wilson spent more time than usual cooking and presenting the dishes, trying to tempt Mrs Scott-Lawson's appetite. But every day her plate came back almost untouched, and soon her expensive and fashionable clothes began to sag on her bony frame.

'It's not our place to worry,' Ferguson said, when Annie voiced her anxiety that evening when they had tucked Frankie in for the night.

'I don't agree,' Annie said. 'If she's not careful she'll end up in hospital.'

'Well, it's for her husband to look after her,' Ferguson said, taking up his newspaper. 'There's no point in talking about it anymore.'

Mr Scott-Lawson had never missed a day of work in Melbourne since his son's death, but Annie noticed how pale and pinched his face looked, even two months later when she helped him on with his coat. He barely acknowledged the daily gesture as he picked up his hat and umbrella, which was quite unlike him, Annie thought, knowing his impeccable manners.

This particular morning as she handed him his hat he looked directly in her eyes.

'Annie?' he said, as though it were a question.

'Yes, sir?'

'Thank you for all you're doing. For my wife, especially. I do appreciate it. She's been very hard hit.'

'I know, sir. I'm happy to help in any way I can. So please don't worry.'

'I know I don't have to so long as you're here to take care of her.' He gave a half smile.

'Thank you, sir.'

'I was wondering...' He looked at her again with his heavy-lidded eyes.

'Yes, sir?'

'No, nothing. It's nothing.'

He turned abruptly but Annie watched his retreating back, trying to ignore a ripple of apprehension.

'I'm going into town this morning,' Mrs Scott-Lawson announced one morning at breakfast, as Annie was clearing the dishes from the dining room table.

'Do you good, dear,' her husband said, folding his paper. 'What do you have in mind?'

'I'm going to meet Marjory. She thinks I've got to get out, so I'm taking her advice.'

'Excellent.' He got up from the table and kissed his wife's cheek. 'Give her my regards. Tell her to come over for dinner one night. We haven't seen her since the—'

'Since the funeral,' Mrs Scott-Lawson finished in a flat tone. 'I know. I'll tell her.'

The house was quiet when they'd left. Mrs Wilson had gone to the market. It was Mrs Johns' and Lily's day off and Emma had been called on an emergency at home with a sick parent. Ferguson had taken Louise and Daphne to school in the pony and trap. He said he wanted to call in at the general store on the way home for some boot polish so not to expect him right away.

It feels peculiar being in the house completely on my own, Annie thought, as she washed up the breakfast dishes and wiped down the draining boards and the big pine table. It was the first time it had ever happened. She'd always been used to working with several other servants bustling about. Three of the gardeners at Amber Bay had joined the army, but when she glanced out of the kitchen window she saw Ronnie hobnobbing with Mr Clarke in the distance. Mr Clarke was too old to be called and Ronnie had asthma. She wondered how many staff were left at Bonham Place, and how they were coping. She'd written to Gladys twice but had

had no reply. Well, they were worlds apart now, in every sense. She shouldn't be surprised.

If it wasn't for the fact that there was a war on, this would have been rather nice. She could even pretend she was the mistress for an hour or two. Annie smiled at thinking such nonsense. Better get the bedrooms dusted and the beds made first. That would bring her down to earth. Still, there were only the two bedrooms which needed doing, so it wouldn't take long. They could easily be fitted in with cooking a light lunch today.

She climbed the staircase with its mahogany steps and wrought ironwork, stopping every so often to run her fingers lightly along the smooth surface of the banister, which Lily had polished early that morning before she'd taken off for the day. The staircase seemed to float through the air in a swan's neck curve, without any visual support. It was hard to believe it had been made by man and not the gods. Annie smiled at the thought.

The Australian spring didn't seem so far away when she craned her neck to look up at the domed ceiling which rose high over the landing. Sunlight poured through the glazing, instantly lifting her spirits. Surely the war couldn't go on much longer. Annie began to hum a tune from *Samson and Delilah,* happy that the mood of the house had brightened just the tiniest bit, from the moment Mrs Scott-Lawson announced she was going into Melbourne. Maybe this would be the start of the lady's recovery – to be with her friend and out among people again.

Annie was totally immersed in her thoughts when she heard the front door open.

Mrs Wilson must have forgotten her purse.

'Mrs Wilson,' she called, 'I'm upstairs making the beds.'

There was no answer. Maybe Mrs Wilson hadn't heard. Then she gave a start – it couldn't be Mrs Wilson. Or Ferguson. They would never come in through the front door. Annie listened, her chest suddenly tight. Heavy footsteps were coming up the stairs.

Heart beating fast, she grabbed the poker in the fireplace and stood behind the open bedroom door, barely breathing.

Someone came in. She could smell tobacco. Hear a man's harsh breath. Dear God, who was it? She couldn't stand here forever. Pulling in her stomach, her mouth hard, she slid from behind the door, holding the poker high.

'Annie!'

'Oh, Mr Scott-Lawson!' Annie's face flooded with embarrassment as she lowered the poker. 'I thought it was a burglar.'

He laughed. 'I'm sorry I frightened you. Here,' he gestured to the poker, 'let me take that. It could be dangerous. You looked as though you were ready to use it.'

'I was,' Annie retorted, then realised what she'd said. 'I'm sorry, sir, I didn't mean it like that. I meant I was pleased it was you.'

'Are you, Annie?' Mr Scott-Lawson came closer; so close she could smell his musky cologne. 'Are you *really* pleased it was me?'

'Yes...well...of course I'm glad it was you and not a burglar,' she repeated, feeling uneasy.

Mr Scott-Lawson smiled. 'I'm glad I'm not a burglar, too,' he said, as he went over to the bedroom door and softly shut it.

From what seemed a long way off she heard a click. What on earth—? She stood frozen with fear and disbelief, but before she could cry out he had closed the space between them. He caught her by the shoulders and bent his head, his mouth already moist.

Appalled, she drew her head back to avoid his heavy lips.

'Please don't, sir.' Annie tried to push him away but he was like a block of granite.

'Annie, my dear, you can't imagine what hell I've gone through lately.' His voice was thick and his grip on her shoulders tightened.

'I know,' Annie whispered. 'Poor Master Russell. I feel so sorry for you and your wife, but—'

'We're all alone,' he said, his eyes burning into hers. 'All I'm asking is a little comfort. You mustn't worry. I'll be very careful.'

'Mr Scott-Lawson, I'm a married woman.' She twisted her body out of his grasp and made for the door. She had her fingers on the knob, frantically turning it one way then the other, but it refused to open. Her head felt it was filled with cement and her heartbeat pounded in her ears as she desperately rattled the door.

Dear God, he's locked it.

He was behind her in an instant, dragging her away.

'Stop!' Annie shouted, pounding his arms, but he threw her on the bed in a heap. She cried out and tried to pull herself up, but he was too quick. Forcing her down he pinned himself on top of her. 'Please don't,' she gasped. 'Ferguson will be back any minute.'

'Annie, oh, little Annie,' he moaned, clumsily removing the pins holding her cap on, and burying his face in her hair. 'I've wanted you ever since I first set eyes on you.'

'You can't—' She couldn't finish. The very breath was being squeezed from her lungs.

'I can't what, Annie?' He pushed her skirts up above her knees and with a swift movement covered her mouth with his hand. She tried to bite the flesh but he pressed even harder. His other hand grasped the inside of her thigh until his fingers found her private place. 'Annie,' he moaned as he took his hand from her mouth and smothered her lips with his own. His breath tasted of stale tobacco and kippers, and Annie thought she would be sick. Suddenly, Adele's words rang through her as though her friend was shouting them in her ear.

Half sobbing with effort, and fighting the nausea, she wrenched her leg free from his weight. She brought her knee up as hard as she could between his legs. Cursing, he loosened his grip, grunting in pain. She dragged herself from under him and clutching the eiderdown, fell with it to the floor. She stood up and brushed down her skirt, all the while keeping her eyes on his face, letting him see she wasn't going to be intimidated. He sat on the edge of the bed, still groaning, his face red, his thick grey hair gone haywire. She knew she must look every bit as bad.

'Mr Scott-Lawson. I hope you will forget this. As I intend to.' The words came in spurts as she tried to catch her breath.

'You...little...fool,' he said, his eyes now blazing. 'You realise I can have you sacked.'

It wasn't a question.

'For what?' Annie tried to ignore her shaking, though now it was more from anger than fright. 'I've done nothing wrong.'

'No?' His eyes narrowed as he looked up at her. 'Maybe not you, but Bishop has.'

Annie's eyes flew wide. 'What has my husband done?'

What was he talking about? Ferguson hadn't mentioned any trouble. As far as she knew, Mr Scott-Lawson was more than satisfied with him.

Her employer hesitated, his Adam's apple jerking in his throat. She held her breath, waiting. He tried to straighten up before he spoke but she could tell it must have been too painful as he slumped forward again, holding himself. 'He's stolen money from my wallet.'

'I don't believe it,' Annie said, shaking her head. Ferguson was not a thief. But Mr Scott-Lawson's next words were little stabs.

'I'm afraid it's true. I caught the rascal red-handed. He begged me not to punish him so I relented. He's a good valet – excellent, in fact. Just weak-willed. All he needed to do was ask me for a loan. I might have given it. Instead, he decided to help himself.'

Annie didn't know what to say. If she said she knew Ferguson would never steal any money, she might as well tell Mr Scott-Lawson that he was a liar.

'I shall speak to him,' was as neutral as she was able to manage. She dreaded asking the next question. All she wanted to do was get away from this horrible man, but she had to know. 'How much money was it?'

'A ten-pound note.' He patted his jacket pocket. 'I'd slipped it in here. Bishop must have seized the opportunity when I changed for the evening.'

'I shall speak to Ferguson. Ask him—'

'There's no need to say anything. I told him it wouldn't go any further.' Mr Scott-Lawson threw Annie a sly glance. For a moment she forgot his shocking behaviour, and his accusation. It struck her how beaten he looked, and once again she felt sorry for him. He'd lost his son. No one deserved that. Then his next words wiped away her sympathy. 'But if it happens again you'll both be packed and on the ship back to England before you can say "Jack Robinson".' He reached for his shoes. 'Now, get to work before I change my mind.'

28

The more Annie repeated Mr Scott-Lawson's words in her mind about Ferguson stealing ten pounds, the more she was convinced her employer was deliberately lying. But why would he? Was it to frighten her so she didn't tell Ferguson that Mr Scott-Lawson had nearly…? She couldn't bring herself to say the word, even in her head. She burned at the memory. What would have happened if she hadn't managed to free herself? The man must be demented with grief to have suddenly acted like that, though it still didn't excuse him. But he hadn't been demented with grief when he'd suggested the same to Adele. What was his excuse then?

Her heart beat hard when she thought of Ferguson. He would be furious if she told him what had happened, and if he confronted Mr Scott-Lawson they'd be thrown out immediately. No, she couldn't say anything. She'd have to push it to the back of her mind; pretend it hadn't happened. But it had, and she knew she would never feel the same about Amber Bay again. She hated Mr Scott-Lawson for that.

But Ferguson stealing. No, never.

'You're late tonight,' Ferguson called from their little sitting room when Annie came into the cottage a few days later, soaked through from a sudden heavy downpour.

'Mrs Wilson wasn't feeling well so I told her I'd finish clearing up.' Annie took off her rain cape and hung it on the kitchen hook before joining him in the sitting room.

'Come over here.' He stubbed out his cigarette and smiling, stretched out both arms without getting up from the chair.

Annie hesitated. This was more like the old Ferguson, but she wasn't used to it. She went over to him, wondering what he wanted.

'Where's Frankie?' she asked as he pulled her down on his lap. She felt like an awkward bundle and badly wanted to get up but didn't want to hurt his feelings, especially as he seemed in such a good mood.

'Upstairs asleep.'

'Did she have her bath?'

'Yes.'

'Did you feed her?'

''*Course* I fed her.' A note of irritation crept into his voice. 'I'm not completely daft.'

'I didn't say you were.' She felt her throat fill with hot tears and buried her head in his shoulder. 'Don't let's argue, Ferguson. I can't bear it now after—'

'After what?' Ferguson turned her face towards him so sharply she felt her neck click. 'After what, Annie?'

'N-nothing. I told you, I'm just tired. I'll be all right tomorrow.'

'Something's upset you and I want to know what. You've been quiet for days. Please, Annie, tell me. Has someone been unkind to you? Your eyes look red, as though you've been crying.'

Annie gave a start of surprise. He never seemed to notice anything about her nowadays.

'I'm just tired, that's all.' At least that was partly the truth.

He examined her closely, as if she were a piece of silver he was contemplating on the best way to clean.

'I don't believe you. You're trembling.'

'I told you, it's nothing.' She felt her face go pink. 'You know I get a bit homesick sometimes.'

'We'll get Ruby out here soon as we can,' Ferguson said,

kissing her cheek. 'You'll feel much better then.'

'I didn't think it would be such a long time before I saw anyone from home,' Annie said, thankful to change the subject.

'I know.' Ferguson shifted a little. 'Well, if you're sure you're all right.' He gently pushed her off his lap. 'Sorry, Annie, leg's gone to sleep.' He got up and followed her to the kitchen. 'Is there any of that soup left?'

Annie lay in bed gazing at the ceiling that slanted just above her head. Ferguson was still downstairs reading the paper. What should she do? Should she tell him? If only he didn't always flare up when she tried to discuss something with him that he didn't want to hear.

But as a married woman, shouldn't she tell her husband what had happened? From now on she would be on the alert, but, thank the Lord, Mr Scott-Lawson had made no further gesture or sign when she'd helped him on with his coat the last few days. She'd dreaded having to come that close to him, but he'd just nodded and left without a word.

Then there was the matter of the ten pounds. Ferguson would lose his temper if she told him what Mr Scott-Lawson had said. But it wasn't right she should keep such accusations to herself. Ferguson must be allowed the chance of defending himself. Even a criminal would be allowed that much. She felt her face redden at such a word. Ferguson, a criminal? Was she losing her senses? Was she beginning to wonder if what Mr Scott-Lawson had told her was true? She shook herself. No. Whatever troubles she and Ferguson had, he wasn't a thief. She pressed her lips together. Maybe it was better to say nothing.

She heard Ferguson's tread up the stairs. Closing her eyes she began to breathe rhythmically, feigning sleep.

Annie turned the problem over and over on how to clear up the matter of the ten pounds. It was there when she was stirring the cake mixture, or dressing the joint for lunch, or helping Lily do the washing up. Had Ferguson really taken any money? If he had, it was stealing. And if so, it was only by the good grace of Mr Scott-Lawson that they hadn't been sacked on the spot. *Good grace.* Her stomach tightened. She was sure Mr Scott-Lawson was using it as a form of blackmail so he could take advantage of her. But if she told anyone, who would believe her? That Mr Scott-Lawson had attempted something so preposterous with the assistant cook!

After agonising for another week she decided to go and see Adele. Adele would know what to do.

'Well, I thought you'd forgotten your old friend.' Adele smiled as she saw Annie enter the hotel foyer. She was wearing a new uniform in bottle green with a white collar and cuffs. It suited her. 'Let's have a look at you then. My, you're looking more grown-up every time you visit.'

'Older, you mean.' Annie smiled ruefully. 'And that's because I'm usually in a state when I see you. And today's not much different. I badly need your advice.'

'Sounds mysterious,' Adele said. 'I'd better order some tea.' She snapped her fingers and one of the waitresses came over. 'A tray of tea, Lucy, and some of those almond biscuits.'

'Yes, ma'am.' The waitress scuttled off.

'So what's the matter?' Adele settled into an easy chair beside Annie, in the usual dark corner. Today, Annie was glad. It was the most private table in the room.

'It's about Ferguson,' Annie started, hating herself for discussing her husband with the very person he detested.

'Isn't it always?' Adele laughed.

'It's serious, Adele,' Annie said. She took a deep breath. 'I might as well come out with it. Mr Scott-Lawson told me Ferguson stole ten pounds from him.'

220

'Really?' Adele's eyes widened in surprise. 'I can think of several things that husband of yours is capable of, but I doubt stealing's one of them.'

'Do you really mean it?'

''Course I do. You know me. I wouldn't say it if I didn't mean it.' Adele looked at her sharply. 'Why would Scott-Lawson tell *you*? I should've thought he'd sack Ferguson on the spot if it were true.'

'If it *is* true – which I don't honestly believe it is – maybe he would have sacked us if it hadn't been for—' She hesitated, twisting her wedding ring, smarting from the image of Mr Scott-Lawson's face above hers. The humiliation that he'd put her under.

'For what? Come on, Annie, tell me.' Adele put her hand on Annie's arm and pressed it.

'Mr Scott-Lawson…he…he…tried…'

'I see. He tried his tricks on you, didn't he?'

Annie nodded dumbly.

'The bastard.'

For once Annie didn't flinch.

'What did he do to you?' Adele demanded.

'I was alone in the house,' Annie gulped. Adele nodded for her to go on. 'Probably no more than twenty minutes. Mrs Wilson had just popped out. He came back. I was making their beds…it was Lily's day off and Emma had an urgent call from her family. He… he…' Annie swallowed hard. 'He threw me on the bed and put his hand up my skirt. He had his whole weight on top of me. It was awful. I couldn't breathe, but then I remembered what you'd said. I pushed my knee up into…into his…'

Adele threw back her head and chortled. 'Right in the balls!' She looked at Annie, her green eyes gleaming with admiration. 'Well done. I never really thought you had it in you.'

'Oh, Adele, he said if I tell anyone he'll pack us straight off to England. I shouldn't be telling you this but I've been so miserable. Ferguson keeps asking me what's the matter.' She looked up at her friend, tears running down her cheeks, then turned her head away as Lucy came into view and set the tray down on the coffee table. The girl disappeared.

'Let me pour you some tea and you'll feel better. Just take your time.'

'I haven't got long.' Annie used her finger to wipe her eyes, then took the cup gratefully and sipped a few mouthfuls. 'I'm on duty this evening. But I've got to get to the bottom of it…somehow. I must know the truth.'

'Then ask him how much there is saved up for Ruby's fare.'

'That wouldn't work. I'm the one who looks after the money now since Ferguson gambled that time. I know to the penny how much we've got.'

'Well, check it again. If there's more than you think, you'll have to talk to him.'

'No, he'd never add to the savings,' Annie said quietly,. 'He'd know I'd be suspicious, and he wouldn't risk our jobs just to get Ruby here. Mr Scott-Lawson must have accused him and Ferguson thought I'd never find out.'

'Except you don't believe he took any money.'

'No, of course I don't.'

But a horrid little voice deep down whispered that Ferguson had changed in so many ways that he might have done.

Ferguson caught her as soon as Annie arrived back at Amber Bay and walked into the kitchen. She was relieved to see that Mrs Wilson had gone to her room and they were on their own.

'Where've you been?' he asked.

'I'm tired of you always wanting to know where I am every minute,' Annie said, the words popping out of her mouth before she could stop them. 'I don't ask *you* where you go.'

'That's different. You're a married woman.'

'And you're a married man. And a father. You should be at

222

home with your wife and daughter in the evenings when you've finished work.'

Ferguson's jaw dropped open. 'I'm not sure I heard right,' he said finally, and slammed the door as he strode out of Mrs Wilson's kitchen.

Annie cradled her head in her hands. Marriage was not turning out to be all she had thought. She had too many secrets from her husband, and it seemed he had secrets from her. Wasn't love supposed to surpass everything? Didn't it make difficult things easier to talk about when you knew the other person loved you above everyone else? That they would understand and love you even more for confiding in them? Comfort you when you needed comforting, and rejoice with you when you were happy?

She sighed as she raised her head. There was work to do, and if she didn't get on with it there'd be even more trouble.

10th August 1916

I decided not to say anything to Ferguson about the £10. If he's innocent he might confront Mr Scott-Lawson, and then we would lose our jobs. And with a two-year old it wouldn't be easy finding another position. Also, Mr S-L would assume I'd told F about the other thing. And if F took the money I have to respect Mr S-L for saying he would forget about it if I didn't mention what he did.

I'm going to try to put it out of my mind and carry on as usual.

Christmas 1916

Another Christmas and still no sign of any let-up in the war. Frankie enjoyed the day. When the S-Ls were out visiting after church I took her into the hall to see the Christmas tree. Ferguson played games with her and generally looked after her while I was busy with Mrs Wilson. Thank heavens she's such an easy child.

20th January 1917

Unless something really important happens I have decided not to write in the journal until the war ends. I don't want to use up the precious pages for minor domestics.

11th November 1918

At 11 o'clock this morning the war was declared to be over. Oh, thank God. It's been four long, terrible years. I dread to think how my family managed with such food shortages. I do miss them so. The S-Ls made us all sit with them at lunch. Ferguson was excited to dine with the gentry, and Mrs Johns looked as though it was her rightful position, but I could see Mrs Wilson and the maids looked uncomfortable – as I felt. Mr S-L opened a large bottle of champagne. He passed us all a glass.

Let's toast the end of the war, he said. We raised our glasses. To absent friends, he said. Then he looked at his wife. Especially to our son, Russell. He downed a full glass of champagne. Mrs Scott-Lawson took a sip, then burst into tears and fled from the room. There's no peace for her.

2nd July 1919

Ruby is coming in October. I'm so happy.

29

October 1919

'It's almost exactly six years ago since *we* arrived,' Annie reminded her husband, as she waited anxiously by his side at Railway Pier, Frankie's hand held firmly in her own. A warm spring breeze fluttered over her as she watched the ship slide into port. From where they stood they were close enough to read its name: the *Themistocles*. She closed her eyes to shut out the noise, wondering how to pronounce it. For a few moments she conjured up her own voyage on the *Orsova*, remembering the storms and the dreadful seasickness. And, of course, the outbreak of smallpox. Poor Mrs Davey. She never did see her sister. Annie shuddered.

What a lot has happened since we came, she thought. She and Ferguson had their darling Frankie; she loved cooking with Mrs Wilson and was fond of Mrs Scott-Lawson, though she remained wary of that lady's husband; and a war lasting four years, with Russell Scott-Lawson one of the many hundreds of thousands who had given their lives. And what had it all been for?

Where did Ferguson belong on the list? He seemed to have finally settled into his position as Mr Scott-Lawson's valet, but she had no idea if he was happy. It had been his dream to come to Australia, yet he didn't seem to have adapted as well as she had. Once he'd turned on her and said, 'My dream was to have our own sheep farm. And you refused to even consider it. As far as I'm concerned we're still in service, which was *not* my dream.'

A stab of guilt sliced through her. Sometimes she had a struggle not to resent how disappointing her marriage was. She'd thought by now she and Ferguson would have grown companionable together, become closer, but it hadn't happened. It was almost as though Ferguson was leading a separate life. Certainly, she knew none of his friends. Were most marriages like hers after the initial happiness? Any intimacy was over with as quickly as possible these days and she felt more and more isolated.

But everything would change now Ruby was coming. Annie wanted to call out to anyone within reach that she would soon see her sister, and impulsively gave Ferguson's arm a little squeeze of excitement. He looked at her and gave his boyish, crooked smile. For a few seconds the years seemed to dissolve, and to her surprise she felt her heart turn over, just as it used to.

'You'll feel differently about things when you have Ruby close by,' he said unexpectedly, as though he'd read her thoughts. 'I know it hasn't always been easy for you.'

She was taken aback. This was the first glimmer of understanding he'd shown her in years. She hadn't been able to give him the attention he demanded when Frankie was born, and it got worse instead of easier as Frankie got older. The little girl was into everything, rather than lying contentedly in her basket as she'd done when she was a baby. Luckily, Frankie had started to entertain herself for hours at a time with her books and a doll Louise had given her. And now she was attending school it had taken away the worry of Annie and Ferguson having to check her all the time to make sure she was safe.

Annie's eyes still on the *Themistocles*, desperate to be the first to spot her sister, she admitted that Australia was a marvellous country. Amber Bay was home now. Any bouts of homesickness were mostly for her family, and that was soon to change. Her heart beat faster knowing Ruby would appear at any minute.

And thank God Alex was safe. Goose pimples ran across her

226

shoulders although the sun was warm this morning. She gave an involuntary intake of breath. He'd only been to Amber Bay once since he'd been home from the war. That was a year ago.

She'd heard the bell clang at the front door early one evening and had gone to answer it.

'Hello, Annie.'

She'd had to hold on to the edge of the door.

'Al...Dr Townsend.' She couldn't get further than his name. She just stood there looking at him. He took off his hat to reveal the dark wavy hair. There was a hint of silver which she'd never seen before. He looked older but his familiar grey eyes sparkled.

'You're thinner,' she said, and could have bitten her tongue out for making such a personal comment.

'I'm not surprised with what we were given. But I'm glad to see *you* looking so well, Annie.' He gave her his slow, beautiful smile which lit up the new contours of his face, and there was not a hint of reproach.

She suddenly felt ashamed. The family and servants at Amber Bay certainly hadn't gone without, but poor Alex, and all the other young men like him, had existed in shocking conditions. In muddy trenches being shot at, wet and cold, sick and wounded. She knew this by the relentless daily accounts in the newspapers and couldn't begin to imagine their fear.

'We've been so lucky in this country,' she managed, still gripping the edge of the door. 'I only wish I could have done something.'

'You were,' Alex said. 'You were looking after the family.' He smiled. 'Aren't you going to ask me in?'

She moved back and he was there, right next to her, towering over her. The warmth of him. His fresh, clean doctor smell. She turned away, and with a shaking hand closed the door behind him.

'How's Frankie?' he asked, as she helped him off with his coat and hat.

'Getting to be a big girl now.'

Her voice didn't sound like her own. She had to stop herself from wrapping her arms around him with sheer relief; from telling him how often she'd thought of him, how thankful she was he'd come through the war unhurt. As though he was aware of her tumult, he turned to face her.

'Annie, my dear,' he said softly, 'I hoped so much I'd see you. Is everything well with you?'

'We're all well, thank you, Doctor,' she answered, trying to keep her voice steady. He raised an eyebrow at her deliberate misunderstanding. 'Except poor Russell.' Annie's eyes glistened.

'Yes, of course. Poor chap. I've come to offer my condolences to them. There can't be anything more terrible than losing a child.'

The Scott-Lawsons had invited Alex to supper but Annie didn't see him any more that evening. It was Mrs Wilson who'd told her at breakfast the next day that Dr Townsend had put in a transfer to a new hospital in Sydney. That's why he hadn't visited for so long. She wished he had had the chance to tell her himself, rather than it coming from Mrs Wilson.

Now, standing at the quayside to meet Ruby, his face sprang into her mind as clearly as on that last evening. She pushed the image away. What Alex was doing and where he was going was none of her business. But his image lingered.

With effort she dragged her mind back to her sister.

Waiting for Ruby seemed interminable. She watched half a dozen fishermen lowering their great circular nets into the water from the pier. They were crumbling some sort of food above the openings of the nets to attract the fish, and a few minutes later one of the men raised his net of thrashing silver pilchards to the broad grins of the others.

'Poor fishes,' Frankie said, looking worried. 'They're s'posed to be swimming in the water.'

Annie smiled down at her daughter. She was a serious little girl with her gold-tipped lashes and hair the colour of ripened corn.

'Let's go and find Daddy,' she said, hoping to distract the child.

Ferguson had wandered over to a group of men who were shouting to one another as they stacked the cargo they'd unloaded from the latest goods train, ready to be reloaded on to the various ships. Even from this distance she could smell the sweet, earthy perfume of lanolin emanating from the bales of wool.

'That's the smell you'd get all the time on a sheep farm,' Ferguson said as he came hurrying towards them. 'Isn't it marvellous?'

When was he going to forget that nonsense?

'I want to see the sheep,' Frankie said, running to her father. He picked her up, laughing.

'We will, one day. But first, we've got to meet your Aunt Ruby.'

Excited though Annie was about seeing her sister, she couldn't help feeling apprehensive as to what Ruby would make of Australia. Ruby hadn't come for just a holiday – she'd found her a position at one of the neighbouring houses. Annie didn't know much about the owners, Mr and Mrs Barton, only that they lived more modestly than the Scott-Lawsons, and wanted a girl who could turn her hand to anything. She hadn't dared tell Ruby any details, knowing how much her sister hated the idea of going into service, in case she turned it down. No, the position wouldn't suit Ruby at all, but at least she'd be near, and something better was bound to turn up sooner or later.

'When will we see Aunt Ruby?' Frankie tugged on her father's hand.

'Won't be long now.' Ferguson craned his neck towards the ship. 'They're starting to come down the gangway.'

'There she is!' Annie waved frantically to her sister, who was one of the first passengers to appear. You couldn't miss her, Annie thought, with her copper-red hair pulled back off her face; even from a distance she realised her sister had grown into a vivacious young woman. Her head was topped by a navy-blue hat, a shade deeper than her travelling outfit which showed off her waist to perfection.

It couldn't have been easy for Ruby with me gone and the new responsibility of Dad and Ethel, Annie was thinking, as her sister rushed towards her.

'Annie! I told you I would come, and here I am. Though it took long enough, didn't it?' She kissed and hugged her sister, then turned to Ferguson. 'Oh, thank you, dear brother-in-law!' Ruby laughed as Ferguson planted a kiss on her cheek and picked up her suitcase.

Ruby's eyes were darting around at everything, a wide smile on her face. Annie looked on amused, remembering how she herself had felt when she'd first stepped on to Australian soil. That newness. She hoped Ruby would notice it in the same way. After a few moments Ruby's eyes rested on Annie.

'Was it a pleasant voyage?' Annie asked.

'Long and tiresome,' Ruby replied. 'Six weeks with nothing to do except play childish games and talk to other passengers – when they weren't being sick, that is. Luckily, I wasn't.' She laughed and tossed her head.

Annie felt a twinge of envy at her sister's strong constitution. The memory of how ill she'd felt in stormy waters was still powerful.

'Say hello to your Aunt Ruby.' Annie gently pushed her daughter forward.

'So this is Frankie,' Ruby said, bending slightly. 'You *are* a big girl.'

'I can read now. I'm the bestest in my class.'

'That's very good.' Ruby straightened up, her eyes skyward. 'I believe I've brought the sun with me.' She looked around her, eyes sparkling as she spread out her arms in an excited, childish gesture. 'Oh, Annie, I'm so happy. I can't believe I'm really here.' She snatched off her hat and her hair fell to her shoulders like a shower of bright copper coins.

That was exactly what she'd wanted to do, Annie remembered, when she'd first arrived. She'd curbed herself, thinking Ferguson wouldn't like it. Curiously, she turned to see her husband laughing

230

at Ruby's exuberance. So he wouldn't have minded at all, she thought, smiling. It was nice to hear him laugh. She hadn't heard it for a long time.

'How's Ethel and Dad?' Annie asked Ruby as they followed Ferguson to Customs House to get her registered.

'Pa is Pa – he doesn't change except to get older. He misses you. He doesn't say as much to me or Ethel, but I catch him staring at your wedding photograph sometimes when he thinks no one's looking. He compares my cooking with yours. I know I'm not as good as you, but Ethel loves being the little cook. Just as well as I've been working for Mrs Johnson. You remember her?' Ruby put her hat back on and stuck a pin through it.

Annie nodded. May Johnson was a widow who'd opened a hat shop. The local gossips loved discussing how she'd got the money to do it. Her hats were provocative and eye-catching – not at all the kind of hats Annie would have chosen.

'This one came from May's.' Ruby gave a twirl.

'It's made for you,' Annie said, truthfully. 'The colour exactly matches your eyes. You look adorable. A lovely young woman. I can't believe it.'

Ruby flashed her small white teeth. 'I'm twenty-one. Got the key of the door and Pa couldn't do anything about it,' she chuckled.

Annie's heart ached for her father – to have two daughters so far away, knowing he would probably never see them again, must be so difficult. But Ruby didn't appear at all perturbed.

Customs House was nearly as crowded as before, but Ferguson managed to find them some seats. It looked like another long wait.

'I want to sit next to Aunt Ruby,' Frankie piped.

'No, Frankie,' Ruby said firmly. 'I need to talk to your mother. Go and sit with Daddy and be a good girl.'

Frankie screwed up her face but before the tears came Ferguson had gathered her on to his lap, whispering to her and making her giggle.

Ruby didn't mean to upset the child, Annie told herself. There was simply too much for her sister to take in all at one time. Everything was bound to fall into place, particularly when Ruby was settled with her new employers. And she would come to love her niece, Annie was sure. But deep down she knew that Ethel would have loved Frankie immediately.

'Have you met them?' Ruby asked Annie that first evening in the cottage, stretching her legs out in an unladylike fashion as she sat watching Annie darn a hole in one of Ferguson's socks. 'The Bartons, I mean.'

'Not yet,' Annie admitted. 'Mrs Barton invited me to see your room but I was shown it by one of the maids. It's a large attic room and—'

'*Attic* room?'

'It's bigger than most English attic rooms,' Annie tried to assure her. 'Don't judge it before you see it.'

'I hate it already.' Ruby's voice was petulant. 'I certainly didn't expect to be shoved into an attic.'

'Really, Ruby, wait until you see it.'

'Well, if I don't like it, I'll leave. I'll stay with you in the cottage. Frankie can have a mattress in your room, and I'll arrange with one of the maids to have a bed put in the nursery.'

Ferguson sat reading the newspaper but Annie was quite certain he was listening to every word. She was right. He suddenly put his paper down and looked at both of them.

'I'm sure if Ruby is unhappy with the arrangements we can help in some way.' He went back to his paper but not before he returned Ruby's smile of gratitude.

That's not what I want. Annie tried to push such an uncharitable thought away. She enjoyed having her own home and although she loved her sister, she hadn't dreamed Ruby might want to live with them. She suppressed her annoyance that Ruby hadn't had the good

232

manners to wait to be invited to stay, and felt unreasonably cross that Ferguson had taken Ruby's side.

'Let's wait until you meet Mr and Mrs Barton,' was all Annie said.

Ruby was like a wind blowing through the cottage. Sometimes it was a brisk and stimulating breeze, and sometimes it caught you off guard and was disturbing. It was only when Ruby left the cottage that the wind rushed along with her, leaving Annie to calm the turmoil her younger sister had left behind. But she was glad Ruby had been given her chance. After all, hadn't she herself made a new life? Now one of her dearest dreams had come true – her sister was here.

As predicted, Ruby instantly disliked her new lodgings. She wasn't pleased with the new job either.

'I'm worn out,' she complained, flopping into one of the two easy chairs in the cottage which happened to be Ferguson's. 'I'd never have agreed to come if I'd known. I'm housemaid, kitchen maid and any other maid. If they didn't have a scullery maid I'd be doing that job too.' Ruby almost spat the words.

This was worse than Annie had feared.

'I thought I was going to be a lady's maid, but Mrs Barton isn't nearly grand enough. I should have known when she didn't have a title. I hate it. Oh, Annie, how could you possibly have thought this would suit me?' She turned a fierce blue gaze on her older sister. 'Ma would never have let me come to this.'

At the mention of their mother, Annie flinched. Ruby was right. She should never have dragged her sister over here into such a menial position when Ruby was so pretty, so talented, so capable of doing something better. It was only that she had longed to have someone from her own family close by. She'd been selfish, not waiting for the right position for Ruby. But Ruby had been determined to come at the first opportunity.

'And the Bartons are not nearly as generous as the Scott-Lawsons are with you,' Ruby complained. 'Even the food's not the same. Well, it is for *them*, but we get very plain meals, I can tell you. When I worked in the hat shop for May Johnson, she used to send out for our lunch every day. And on Saturdays we had a glass of ale.'

Annie said nothing. If it was only one glass of ale a week, she supposed it couldn't do much harm. Nevertheless, she was glad she could keep a watchful eye on her sister.

'I *hate* my room in the attic. It's large enough but it's not even mine. Didn't Mrs Barton tell you?' Ruby glared at her sister. 'I have to share it with Clara, the fourteen-year-old *scullery* maid.'

She made it sound as though poor Clara didn't deserve to share a room with such a grand lady as herself, Annie thought, steeling herself for what was coming.

'So can I stay here, Annie?' Ruby pleaded, her dark-blue eyes luminous with tears. 'I promise you won't even notice me. I can take Frankie for walks while I'm looking for another position.'

Annie hesitated. It would be a wonderful way for Ruby to get to know her niece. Perhaps it would work out. Ruby just needed careful handling, that's all. 'I'll talk to Ferguson,' she promised.

To her surprise Ferguson put his foot down. 'We're all right as we are,' he said. 'It's only a small cottage and we've got Frankie to think of. She needs her own room. If we put her in our room she'll get used to it and we'll never get any peace. Tell your sister she'll have to stay where she is.'

'That wasn't what you said the other evening.'

'I didn't promise anything.'

Annie looked at him in astonishment. She was about to argue when he added, 'I've thought about it and we don't have the room.'

*

But Ferguson hadn't reckoned on Ruby's powers of persuasion, Annie grimaced, when Ruby came over a week later on her next day off.

'Have you had a busy day, Fergus?' Ruby asked. 'Here. Sit down. Let me put your slippers on.'

Annie put down the wool stocking she'd been darning on the small table beside her chair and watched, fascinated, as her sister took hold of his boot and untied the laces. Ruby fitted his slippers as carefully as the prince did to his Cinderella, then looked up at him coyly. Annie noticed Ferguson's Adam's apple jump and his body tense. He was obviously ready for an argument. She hid a smile. Ruby could get round anyone. Her sister's copper curls, loosely pinned off her face, shimmered in the gaslight.

'Would you like a beer?' Ruby asked, looking straight into his eyes.

'I know exactly what you're doing, young woman.' Ferguson laughed, sounding a little nervous.

Annie glanced across at her husband in surprise. Why should he be nervous with Ruby? She shrugged and took up the stocking again.

'Well, what do you want?' Ferguson said, and now his voice was impatient.

'I can't stand it at the Bartons. I hate my job. I hate my room. I hate the Bartons. I hate *everything*.' She sat on the floor by his feet. 'I don't know why I came to Australia. It's not how I imagined it would be at all.' She covered her face with her hands and burst into tears.

'Ruby, stop behaving like a spoilt child.' Annie's voice was unusually firm. 'You haven't even given it a chance.'

'I don't have to give it a chance. I hate it!'

'There, now, don't cry.' Ferguson produced a clean white handkerchief that Annie had ironed that morning. 'I'm sure we can find you another job. Just stay where you are for the moment.'

'No, I won't.' Ruby stood up and stamped her foot. 'You got

me here under false pretences. I've given in my notice today and I'm not going back tomorrow except to collect my things.'

True to her word, Ruby took Frankie out for a walk every afternoon, but every morning she disappeared for hours, merely saying she was looking for another job if Annie questioned her. Worrying over Ruby was taking away the excitement Annie had felt when her sister first arrived.

'I'm beginning to think it was a mistake to send for Ruby,' Ferguson said one night as he lay with his arm loosely around her.

'What do you mean?' she asked, her eyes closed, dreading what he had to say.

'She's too high-spirited. Uncontrollable.'

'You make her sound like an untamed horse.'

'That's probably a good description,' Ferguson said. 'I think we should send her home. She's never going to settle here.' He paused. 'Come on, Annie, you know I'm right.'

'That's not a very nice thing to say.' Annie opened her eyes, feeling a prickle of guilt that the same thought had once or twice crossed her own mind.

'If you was honest, you'd agree with me.'

She couldn't bring herself to say the words. It would be too disloyal. But she wished her sister wouldn't take everything for granted, thinking she could do exactly as she wished. Mrs Scott-Lawson had already remarked that she couldn't be expected to provide Ruby with her food.

'I should have tried harder to find something more suitable. I'd forgotten what an independent girl she is.'

'She's not a girl any longer, Annie,' Ferguson said, and it sounded to her ears almost a warning.

'She is to me.' Annie turned over with her back towards him. 'She's my little sister, and I love having her here. She can stay as long as she wants.'

She closed her eyes again, wondering what had made her side with Ruby when she privately agreed with Ferguson that it wasn't working. Even though she was tired out, sleep evaded her.

A month after Ruby had moved in with Annie and Ferguson she made an announcement.

'I've got myself a job,' she said. 'It's live-in so you won't have to put up with me any longer.'

'Where is it?' Annie asked, secretly relieved, then immediately worried that her sister had taken things into her own hands without mentioning anything to her.

'In a hotel.'

'Cleaning a hotel is hard work,' Ferguson said, frowning.

'Oh, I shan't be cleaning,' Ruby said, smiling at him. 'I've had enough of that, thank you very much. I'm going to learn how to run the bar.'

'Oh, Ruby, don't you think—' Annie began.

'I don't approve of it,' Ferguson interrupted, glancing at Annie. '*We* don't approve.'

'Approve or not, that's what I'm going to do.'

'How did you hear about the job?' Annie asked.

'It was advertised in the post office. I've met the owner, Adele. Apparently you know her. She sent her best wishes to you.'

Annie tried to hide her dismay. Adele was her friend but she certainly didn't want her sister to be working where there was alcohol, though if she warned her about it, Ruby would be even more stubborn. Also, there was that waiter with the funny name. Heppel. He gave her the creeps. No, the Hotel Esplanade was definitely not the place for Ruby.

Before she could protest, Ferguson spoke up again.

'As your brother-in-law, responsible for your welfare, I forbid you to go and work for that woman.'

'What's wrong with her?' Ruby's voice was raised.

237

'I don't need to go into details. Just take my word for it.'

'I'm sorry, Fergus, but you're my brother-in-law, not my keeper. You may be able to control Annie, but I'll run my own life. I start on Monday.'

Annie looked at Ferguson for support to forbid her sister from taking the job, but Ferguson was gazing at Ruby, his face flushed red.

30

Ruby

It was all I could do not to fling myself into his arms and tell him, that day when I docked. I was surprised Annie didn't notice anything queer. All she was interested in was Frankie. I tried to be loyal to my sister, I really did. But I want Fergus more than anything else in the world. And it's only a matter of time before he'll realise he feels the same.

He smiled down at me that day I arrived and kissed my cheek, and the clean, manly smell of him, after being cramped with sweaty, unwashed people on the ship, made my blood sing. But I didn't want a kiss on the cheek. I wanted a proper kiss. Like the one Benjy gave me when he came to the hat shop to fix the plumbing. He grabbed me, forced open my mouth with his thick lips and stuck his tongue in. It felt like a snake darting all around my mouth. It was horrible and I pushed him away. But if Fergus did that to me, I'd die of happiness.

Fergus behaves like an affectionate brother-in-law. He gives me a peck on the cheek when he says goodnight, he cleans my best pair of shoes before I go out, and seems concerned that I hate my new position. But when Annie's safe at work I get him on my own – pretend I want his opinion on things.

'I don't know why you're asking me,' he said once, laughing. 'You never take my advice.'

'You never tell me what I want to hear,' I said.

239

He gave me a strange look, searching my face. After a few seconds he blinked as though to remind himself who I was. Then he turned and left the room.

Now he makes sure he's never alone with me. If he only knew how it makes me more determined. But whatever I do he laughs it off. It's gone on for a month now, and I can't bear being in the same house as him, let alone the same room. It's like a knife in my heart when I see him with Annie. It wouldn't take much for me to spill out my secret longing. I have to get away. But when I told everyone I was going to the Hotel Esplanade to work for Adele, Fergus tried to stop me. And his face went all red. Is that a sign? Does he want me as much as I want him?

I'd been working at the Hotel Esplanade a couple of months when I decided I had to do something; make some excuse to Adele that Annie needed me for a few days. I told Adele Frankie was ill and Annie had asked me if I would look after her so she could still go to work as they were short. I *had* to make Fergus fall in love with me and I couldn't leave it to chance.

I packed my case with care, folded my best Sunday dress, and laid it on the top.

I couldn't believe my luck when I saw Fergus was there to greet me at the cottage.

'Annie's working,' he said, as he lightly embraced me. I trembled at his touch as his fingers seemed to linger on my waist. Had he noticed? 'She's made up your bed in Frankie's room,' he added, watching me.

I swallowed hard. He'd said the word 'bed' and almost smiled.

'Is Frankie back at school?' I asked him.

'Not yet. Louise has taken her for a walk. Frankie loves her.'

His tone becomes gentle when he speaks of his daughter.

'We're all alone, then,' I said.

Fergus locked his eyes to mine, and I saw passion spring. 'Is this what you want, Ruby? Is this what you've come for?'

He caught me to him, his hands raking through my hair, and kissed me properly for the first time. A shot of exquisite joy flared inside me and I pressed myself into him, my lips feeling soft and full under his. I put my tongue into his mouth, heard him gasp and pull away. For a moment I thought I'd ruined everything, until I saw the gleam in his eye.

'Wild Ruby,' he laughed. 'Where did you learn to do that?'

'Nowhere,' I lied. I wasn't going to tell him about Benjy. 'I just wondered what it would feel like.'

'It feels like this,' he said.

'I wanted you the minute I set eyes on you at the docks,' he confessed, as we lay squashed together on the narrow bed. 'But I didn't want to hurt Annie. And it's too dangerous. We can't do this again.' He threw back the sheet. 'Annie could come in at any time.'

He leapt up and finished dressing.

I turned my head to the wall, furious. I was aching and exhausted. All I wanted to do was rest in his arms and sleep. And dream of my first lovemaking with my one and only love. And he'd gone and spoilt it, good and proper.

'Come on, Ruby, get up.'

I sat up then, not caring that my breasts were fully on show, and stared at him.

'Just go,' I said.

If he thought he could get rid of me that easily, he was wrong.

I went to the cottage as often as I dared, and as often as I could get away from the hotel. Adele always wants to know where I'm going but it's none of her business. Nothing matters except Fergus. Every time I see him he says we shouldn't, but I always get round him. I've begged him to leave Annie but he's made every excuse.

'You don't really love me,' I told him. 'You're just saying the

241

words to keep me happy. Well, I'm *not* happy. I shall tell Annie. I can't understand why she's never suspected anything was going on.'

'She trusts me,' Fergus said. 'And she's busy with Frankie, and work at the house.' A warning look darkened his eyes. 'Don't threaten me, Ruby. Keep Annie out of this.'

'She has to know sometime.'

'I can't make promises I can't keep. I have a child, remember.'

'How can I forget?'

He turned away from me to leave the cottage, but I stopped him.

He faced me. 'What now?' I could tell he was angry.

'Do you still love me?' I unbuttoned my blouse, and reached my hand inside to pull out a breast. I licked my middle finger, then teased the nipple erect, my eyes never leaving his face.

With an animal groan he bounded over, pinned my arms to my sides, and buried his face in my hair. I only just made out the words.

'You know I do.'

Weeks later, when Adele gave me two days off, I went to Amber Bay. I timed it when I knew Annie would be safely at work and Fergus would be having a quick smoke outside the cottage before he served lunch.

'Oh, hello, Ruby,' he said, looking annoyed. I guessed it was because I'd caught him smoking.

'Don't worry, I shan't say a word to Annie,' I said, putting a hand on his arm.

'She doesn't like me to smoke. Says it's bad for Frankie. She's probably right...she usually is.' He gave a nervous laugh.

'Fergus, I have something to tell you. I don't know what you'll say but—'

'I need to talk to you, too,' he interrupted me, his tone hardening. 'We've got to stop this. I mean it. Annie suspects something. And it isn't right. We both know it isn't right.'

I was taken completely by surprise. Fergus was going to toss me aside like some old rag. We'll see about that, I thought. I smiled at him.

'I'm afraid it's too late for that, Fergus, dear. We're going to have a baby.'

He looked thunderstruck. Then went white.

'You...no, it isn't true...y-you can't be,' he stammered. He looked at me with glazed eyes, then pulled on his cigarette and pounded it on the cottage wall until it was pulp.

'I'm afraid it is,' I said firmly, not taking a blind bit of notice of his temper. 'And I want to know what you're going to do about it.' I waited for his answer, scarcely breathing.

All I know is that I love him. Nothing and no one is going to stand in my way. It's a pity he's married to Annie, but when I tell her the truth, she'll never forgive him. Then Fergus will come to me for comfort. I'll have a beautiful baby boy and Fergus will never want to leave me and—

'I'm not going to do anything,' Fergus interrupted my thoughts. I watched him as though through a fog. He wouldn't look me in the eye. But he seemed to have recovered his wits and his voice was quiet as he carried on. 'There's nothing I can do. Annie's my wife.' He paused a few seconds, then blurted, 'Besides, she's going to have another baby.'

I stood very still. I could hear my insides churning with fury. Then I screamed at him. '*Annie's* going to have a baby? You got us both up the spout at the same time? You said you loved me! And all the time...when were you going to tell me, Fergus *dear*?'

I was gratified to see his handsome features flush. 'Annie wanted to tell you herself.'

I thought my head would burst. How *dare* Fergus make a fool of me!

'Well, she can tell me...and then I'll tell her *my* news.'

For a split second I realised my sister would be destroyed when

I told her the truth. But just as quickly I dismissed it.

'Ruby, please don't. I'm sorry for the trouble I've caused you. It's all my fault. You're so beautiful, I couldn't help myself. I just don't want to hurt Annie. She hasn't done anything unkind – ever – to either of us.'

'Shame you didn't think of that before you carried on with me.'

'It takes two.' Fergus's voice suddenly turned to ice.

'What do you mean by that?'

'The way you led me on. You're a tease, Ruby, and I'm a normal man.'

My laugh was hollow. 'You were ready to be led.'

'Well, I can't alter what's happened. But my place is with Annie.'

So he wasn't going to stand by me.

'Ruby, don't you see?' Fergus changed his tune and was pleading with me. 'Annie's your sister. We can't hurt her. You must never tell her I'm the father. And anyway,' his blue eyes held mine, 'how do I know I am?'

'You think I'm lying?' I went up close and before he realised what I was about to do, I smacked his face hard. 'How dare you! Of course you're the father. I've never been with no other man. There weren't any left. Don't you remember there was a war on for four years?' I didn't bother to hide my sarcasm. '*You* might not have noticed, but *we* did at home. All the men with an ounce of energy enlisted. And either didn't come back or they were good for nothing when they did.' I glared at him. He remained silent, just looking at me. I had to goad him into saying something. 'What do you take me for?'

'I just wanted to be sure, that's all.' He tried to light another cigarette but his hand shook so badly he flung it in the bushes. Serves him right.

'I'm telling you for the last time.' I went up to him and put my head on his chest. 'Put your arms round me. Look at me. Tell me that you don't love me.'

I raised my face to his and smiled my slow, seductive smile, knowing he wouldn't be able to resist me, but he flung me away, his breath jagged.

'Stop it, Ruby. Annie or anyone could come along at any moment. Can't you understand? I've made up my mind. I'd made it up before you told me about the baby. I must have been mad. It's Annie I love. You'll find someone else of your own one day and—'

'Who's going to want me with a bastard?' I shouted, pleased to see him flinch at the word. 'And what am I supposed to do for money? I won't be able to carry on working. No, Fergus, I won't do it. I won't keep quiet. Either you tell Annie or I will.'

'I forbid you to,' Fergus warned, 'and that's the end of it.'

That's where he was wrong. It wasn't the end of it. And the sooner Annie knows, the better. She'd be bound to give him up and Fergus will realise it's me he loves. Then I'll have him for my own, forever.

31

Amber Bay

5th May 1920

I posted a letter to Dad and Ethel today telling them my wonderful news. And that I was certain this time I would have a boy and we would call him Harry. How I miss Dad and Ethel. How I long for them to meet Frankie, and see the new baby. Will I ever see them again? Of course I will. I mustn't keep thinking like this. It's bad for the baby.

20th May 1920

I told Ruby she was putting on weight. She broke down in tears. I'm having a baby, she said. I was shocked as I didn't know she was even courting. I asked her who the father was and she looked at me with tear-stained eyes and said one word. Fergus.

Dear God, I can't write any more.

23rd May 1920

Ruby's baby is due in November, the same month as my own. I was so thrilled when I first knew I was going to have another baby, but Ferguson—

Annie brushed the tears angrily away as she heavily underlined her husband's name.

—is the father of both our babies. I don't know what to do. He refuses to talk about it except to say it isn't true, and that he is astonished I believe my sister. I hardly see him anymore. He says he has some new friends. I can't bear to look at Ruby. My own sister. I feel betrayed by them both. How can I ever forgive them? All I want to do is go home.

Annie dipped her pen back into the bottle of ink and tried to write more but she was drained from crying. She placed her pen in its holder and paced up and down by the window trying to think. What should she do? Leave her husband? Where would she go? She wouldn't get another job now she was expecting a baby. Even Mrs Scott-Lawson was not so amiable about this second one, reminding her that she still had a job of work to do. Ruby had proudly announced she would carry on as usual, right up until the birth of her own child, and that Adele would stand by her. Adele who was supposed to be *her* friend, Annie thought, with unaccustomed bitterness.

Annie reread her last few words. *All I want to do is go home.* But that would be running away. And she couldn't bear the look of pity on her father's face. Then there was Ethel. How could she tell Ethel such sordid details about her own sister. Annie shook her head in despair.

She had to talk to someone. Adele. Yes, she would go to the Hotel Esplanade. It was Ruby's day off and she always went out. Maybe Adele could help her work out what to do.

Dizzy and ill with worry, she dragged up the front steps of Adele's hotel, feeling as though she were walking through mud. Adele was talking to a gentleman but as soon as she saw Annie and took one look at her face, she made her excuses and left him.

'Come up to my room.'

Adele sat her down in the one chair and poured her a glass of something Annie didn't recognise.

'Don't say a word till you've drunk this,' she ordered.

Annie looked at the glass. 'What is it?'

'Just drink it,' Adele commanded.

Annie took a sip, then coughed as the liquid ran like fire down her throat to her stomach.

'And another.'

'No. I—'

'It will do you good,' Adele said, leaning over and taking the glass. She put it to Annie's lips. Annie took another mouthful and coughed again.

Adele perched on the side of her bed. 'Tell me.'

'Did Ruby tell you I'm having another baby?' Adele nodded. 'And...Ruby...I don't know how—' To Annie's shame the tears streamed down her face and for some minutes she couldn't speak. She felt Adele's arm slip round her shoulder and wept anew at the small kind act. 'Has Ruby told you who the father of her baby is?' Annie finally gulped.

'She didn't have to. I guessed.'

'You knew...before me?'

'I think Ruby needed someone to talk to.'

'*Ruby* needed—' Annie began, sobbing afresh.

'Don't let it make you bitter,' Adele said, offering Annie a handkerchief. 'Or cause a rift between you. These things happen. A pretty girl, a weak man, and before you know it—'

'But my *sister* with my own husband.' Annie's voice choked with tears of rage.

'Do you think you're the first wife it's happened to?' Adele raised an eyebrow. Annie stared at her, horrified. 'Because I can assure you, you're not. Come on, Annie, you look as pale as a workhouse girl. I don't suppose you're eating properly. You're too thin, and that's not good with you expecting.'

'I do try,' Annie said, fighting for control. 'The trouble is, I'm sick all the time. I was only sick a few times with Frankie.'

Adele grimaced. 'How *is* Frankie? You haven't brought her to see me lately.'

'She's changed. I think she senses things aren't right between her father and me and she's vying for his attention. In a way I'm relieved.'

'What about Ethel? Have you told her?'

'No.' Annie felt her voice wobble. 'She knows I'm having another baby but I couldn't bring myself to write and tell her the whole truth. Oh, Adele.' She shuddered.

Adele wrapped her arms around her. 'How do you feel towards your husband now, Annie?' she asked softly.

'Nothing. I feel nothing.'

19th November 1920

Everything has gone so very wrong. My head will burst if I don't write this down. I sometimes think I'm going mad.

I was sick for much longer with this baby and suffered badly from headaches. Ferguson tried hard to be patient. I know he hoped the new baby would bring us closer. I was sure it would be a boy this time. I went back to the same hospital, longing for it to be over, longing to see my new baby – the only good to come of this whole rotten mess.

The hospital smelled of disinfectant and blood and turned my stomach. The doctor was much older than Alex, with a stern face, but the nurse I had this time was very kind. I was in labour for sixteen hours. When I thought I couldn't stand it a moment longer the doctor used some sort of instrument. It was as though a red-hot poker had stabbed me. I heard screaming. Was it me, or one of the other mothers? I bit down on something that tasted like rubber, and clung on to the nurse's hand. I felt the sweat run into my eyes. It would all be worth it, I kept telling myself, as the doctor clamped a gauze pad over my mouth and nose.

The next thing I knew Ferguson was sitting by the bed,

holding my hand. His eyes were bloodshot.

How long have I been asleep? I asked him.

About four hours. His voice was unusually gentle.

Have you seen the baby? Is it a boy? What you wanted—

Yes, Annie, a beautiful baby boy.

A son. We'll call him Harry. I couldn't help smiling. I looked at Ferguson. Maybe we could repair some of the hurt. I could tell he had something important to say to me but he seemed to be having difficulty getting the words out. He squeezed my hand so tight my wedding ring cut into my finger.

Annie, the baby—

Where is he, Ferguson? I haven't seen him yet. Is he asleep?

Ferguson's usual ruddy complexion had turned pale.

Ferguson?

Annie, dearest, you have to be very brave—

A coldness crept through every part of my body until I was numb. I turned my head to see him properly. His Adam's apple was jumping up and down, and I watched it, hypnotised.

The baby was stillborn, Ferguson said.

Then he squeezed my hand again, even more tightly, but this time I didn't notice any pain.

There must be a mistake, I said. They were talking about the wrong baby. My baby was just asleep.

Ferguson looked like death.

No, no, oh please, God, no. I began to shake. My head started to swim and bile came up in my throat.

You mustn't upset yourself, Annie. There was nothing anyone could do.

I wanted to scream. To hit out at him. My beautiful baby.

Alex – if he'd been here he would have saved my baby. Where was he when I needed him?

I must have said those words aloud because Ferguson frowned, though all he said was that I must get some rest and he would be in to see me again tomorrow. Then he kissed me on the forehead and left me.

Left me with my demons. The hospital. My baby. Ruby. Ferguson. Even Alex.

Adele had sent word to Annie that Ruby would give birth at the hotel and that she would personally see that Ruby had the best care. She said she realised Annie was too unwell to see her sister at the moment, but she would be welcome whenever she felt fit enough. And of course she would send a telegram to let Annie know the minute there was any news.

Annie's mouth hardened as she skimmed the note. She had been ordered by Dr Brooke to stay in bed for at least a fortnight, even if it meant missing the baby's funeral. But it wasn't any baby, she'd wanted to scream to the doctor. It was her darling Harry. She'd only been allowed a brief look at him before they'd taken him away. A little mite, his eyes closed so she hadn't even seen their colour.

And sooner or later she would have to face seeing Ruby's baby, knowing Ferguson was the father. Tell Ruby how sweet her baby was without being swamped by her own pain at losing little Harry. No, it would be more than she could bear.

It was enough to worry about Frankie, though Ferguson had quickly got into a routine of feeding and bathing his daughter every evening before going on duty. Mrs Wilson came over to the cottage every day with Annie's lunch and would stay awhile to make sure she ate it. Although Annie tried to please her, attempting to swallow almost made her choke.

'Come on, Annie, please drink this soup. It's got all lovely vegetables and herbs in it. The best thing to have if you want to get strong.'

Annie half-heartedly put the spoon in the bowl and sipped a few mouthfuls but it tasted like ditchwater. She knew it was delicious because Mrs Wilson was known for her soups, but everything tasted sour or bitter on her tongue. She picked at the slice of unbuttered bread, hoping it might quell the nausea that threatened her whenever she even looked at any food.

'I'm worried about you,' Mrs Wilson said, as Annie put her spoon down. 'You've become so thin. You must get strong for Frankie's sake. It's so sad about the baby but you'll have another one in time.'

'Never!' Annie spat the word. 'I don't want him near me again.'

Mrs Wilson drew back in surprise. 'But you said he's been good helping you since all this happened.'

'What could he do? He couldn't just abandon me. Well, yes, he could. He's done it before. He only thinks of himself. His own pleasure. His adventures. It's all Ferguson, Ferguson. He's never grown up. Well, I hope he's satisfied he's destroyed my feelings.' She heard the words tumbling out as though they poured from someone else's lips. It couldn't be her speaking. She sounded like some fishwife. She turned her head on the pillow towards the wall, not wanting to see the horrified expression on Mrs Wilson's face.

'All men are children,' Mrs Wilson soothed as she tucked another pillow behind Annie's head. 'You'll feel better in a few weeks' time. Don't worry about anything. I must go now, dear, as I have some shopping to do. Will you be all right?'

'Yes, of course. You go.' Annie, ashamed of her outburst, pushed her hair back from her forehead, feeling it lank and sweaty. Goodness knows what she looked like. 'I don't know what I would have done without you, Mrs Wilson.' She gave the cook a rueful smile. 'I seem to be saying that often these days, don't I?'

'Don't you worry about a thing.' Mrs Wilson picked up the tray. 'It's getting you well that I'm interested in.'

Annie lay back on the pillows and closed her eyes in misery. It had been the longest week she could remember. Every minute had dragged. All she had to look forward to were her visitors, but everyone seemed to be acting differently around her. Ferguson only briefly looked in, and seemed either nervous, as though he couldn't wait to get away, or preoccupied. Frankie whispered when she talked to her mother, as though she was worried she would disturb or upset her. Annie missed her daughter's laughter. Even Mrs Wilson was disappointed in her. But Mrs Wilson didn't have children, so how could she possibly understand the pain of losing one?

Annie thought of Mrs Scott-Lawson. The poor lady had also suffered the tragedy of losing her son. Rich or poor – there was little difference in the end. But she didn't want to end up like Mrs Scott-Lawson, a woman who had let herself sink; who barely took any interest in Louise and Daphne, her two lovely daughters. She mustn't let that happen to her darling Frankie.

Annie lay there a few minutes longer and made her decision. She wasn't going to wait out the fortnight. Harry's service was tomorrow. She must be there for him. She threw back the covers and sat up. Then she swung her legs over the edge of the bed and set her feet on the floor. She pulled herself up by holding on to the sturdy bedside table, but she hadn't bargained on her legs misbehaving. They felt as wobbly as Mrs Wilson's blancmange and she almost fell over.

Gritting her teeth, she managed to stumble to the marble-topped washstand where Mrs Wilson had thoughtfully filled up the jug with water. Slowly, she washed herself and got dressed.

'It's nice to see you up,' Ferguson said when he came in after finishing for the day. Annie was sitting downstairs in the front room. 'You're looking better.' He knelt by her chair and put his arm around her shoulder and kissed her cheek.

'I can't stay in bed,' Annie told him. 'Everyone's working except me. It doesn't feel right. And I want to be there for our son tomorrow.'

In case you've forgotten already, with the excitement of yours and Ruby's baby due any minute, she was tempted to say. But she managed to bite back the words. What was the point of being bitter? Nothing would bring back little Harry. The muscles in her husband's face tightened as though he'd read her thoughts. He smoothed his hair from his brow and she tried to dredge up some sympathy for him. He'd lost his son, too.

'We have to put everything behind us,' he said awkwardly, as he straightened up. He threw her a sidelong glance as he took off his jacket. 'Start again. Do you think we can do that, Annie? It's what I want. I hope you do too.'

She couldn't answer.

25th November 1920

F and I and dear Mrs Wilson went to Harry's service. That's what I'm calling it in future. I can't bear the other word. Feel too numb to write more.

The following day a telegram arrived.

RUBY'S BABY BOY SAFELY DELIVERED. COME WHEN YOU CAN. ADELE.

Annie slipped the telegram back in its envelope. So it's a boy, she thought. He's alive. As my baby should have been. Not being buried in the cold earth, all alone, without knowing his mother. Never knowing how she loved him. Her eyes filled as the image played in her mind, over and over. How long would it be before Harry didn't come to haunt her? She hadn't told anyone her nightmares. They wouldn't understand. Except one person, perhaps. But she wouldn't whisper his name, even to herself.

Letter dated 30th November 1920

Dearest Annie,

I want you to know that I am being looked after well by Adele and a nurse comes in every day. The baby cries a lot. Sometimes he screams and it's difficult for me to get any rest. The nurse says it's because I'm not making enough milk.

I'm longing to see you. Please come when you feel strong enough. I've never really said how sorry I am that you lost your baby but it's now brought home to me how hard it must have been for you. I think you will like the baby, especially if he's not crying when you see him.

   Please forgive me and come.

   Your loving sister, Ruby

One sentence jumped off the page as Annie read her sister's short letter. *The nurse says it's because I'm not making enough milk.*

Her own breasts were full to overflowing and woefully sore. The nurse had shown her how to extract the milk with the help of a breast pump, but it was a painful process, and the very reason why she was doing it caused her to break down and weep every time. She should be suckling her baby, the way she had with Frankie.

It was time to go and visit her sister.

3rd December 1920

I've been to see Ruby. She was already up and dressed even though the doctor said she should be resting.

I was afraid you wouldn't come, she said.

I didn't tell her how much I'd been dreading it. But she knew.

She wants to go back to work as quickly as she can. Adele said she must wait a few weeks at least, but she is determined. I must say she looks very well.

She asked me if I would nurse the baby. She handed him to me (she hasn't given him a name yet) and I slipped the buttons off my blouse and rested his head at my breast. Oh, the sheer joy of feeling him there. He began to suckle immediately, as though he didn't know the difference between his mother and his aunt. It was the most natural thing in the world for both of us.

Afterwards, when I put him over my shoulder and made him burp, Ruby asked me if it would be possible for me to look after him for a few weeks until she could see to him herself. You have plenty of milk so he'd be far better off in your care anyway, she said.

It was so unexpected. I never dreamed she'd let me take the baby away.

I said I still needed my job at Amber Bay, but she said no one would expect me to go back for a few weeks, and the Scott-Lawsons had expected another baby within the household anyway. In the meantime she'd be really grateful if I could just help out. I said I would have to discuss it with Ferguson.

'Ruby has asked if I'll look after the baby for a few weeks so she can get properly back on her feet,' Annie told Ferguson that night in bed.

'She can't be serious.' Ferguson had been lying on his back, telling her about the special guests. Now, he rolled over to face her. 'And what do you mean, "get back on her feet"? She can't go back to work yet.'

'She wants to as soon as she can,' Annie said, trying to still her heart that raced every time she thought of Ruby as a mother…and Ferguson's mistress. 'She's as strong as an ox. But the worst thing is, she's not producing enough milk so she gave him to me and he took it like a lamb.'

'So you'll be saddled with the baby and *you* won't be able to go to work for a few weeks. No, Ruby's responsible and she'll have to look after it.'

'It's not an "it", it's a "he",' Annie corrected. 'And I would have been "saddled", as you call it, anyway if my baby had lived.' Her voice wobbled as she spoke the words, but now she'd started she couldn't stop. 'And after all, this one's *your* son too. I would have thought you'd be pleased to have the opportunity of seeing him.'

'You only have Ruby's word for that,' Ferguson snapped. 'I don't want you to take in the baby because I don't want anything to interfere with our jobs.'

Annie lay quietly. There was no point in arguing. She'd made her decision.

32

January 1921

Ferguson was more observant than Annie had given him credit for.

'I know you're punishing me, Annie,' he told her one night in bed when he began to stroke her arm. She felt her body stiffen and pull back. 'No, don't try to deny it – it's as plain as that nose on your face.'

He was obviously in one of his moods.

'I've got something important to tell you.' He sat up. 'Are you listening, Annie?'

'Yes.'

'We never get a chance to talk, what with me working, and you looking after Frankie…and Ruby's baby.'

Annie blinked back the tears. If only Ferguson would admit that he was the father, maybe she could start to forgive.

'I'm afraid it's serious.'

Annie jerked her head towards him. 'What is?'

'We don't have any savings. And now there's no more opportunity without the two wages.'

'Please don't joke, Ferguson,' she said, turning over with her back to him. 'I'm not in the mood. I'm tired.'

'It's not a joke. We've run out of money.'

Annie tensed. She turned round again and stared up at Ferguson. Even at this angle she could see a little pulse beating fast in Ferguson's neck. His face was hard and tense.

257

'Run out of money? Of course we haven't. We've got nearly sixty pounds saved up.'

'We haven't.' Ferguson's voice was low. 'It's all gone.'

'Gone? Where has it gone?' But sick with dismay, she knew.

'Annie, don't—'

'You lost it gambling.' Spittle flew from her mouth.

'If only you weren't so tired all the time, I wouldn't have gone around with the boys.'

'That's nonsense and you know it,' Annie flashed back.

'I know what you're thinking.' He looked hard at her. 'I'm not blaming you…just trying to explain. And a married man does have rights, after all.'

He tried to kiss her but she pulled away, twisting her head from the smell of beer.

'I'm exhausted, Ferguson.' Her voice was cold, angry. 'How could you think I want you to—' She couldn't bring herself to say the word 'love'. It was all she could do to stop herself from telling him she never wanted to be intimate with him as long as she lived. 'You've blown all our precious savings while I'm trying to keep my job and look after you and Frankie and the baby, and clean the house.'

'Leaving precious little time for me.' Ferguson's voice rose as he flung back the bedclothes. He pushed her over to one side, away from him, then pulled her buttocks tight against his stomach.

She tried to loosen from his grip but his hands were firm on her waist, pulling her closer.

'Ferguson…I don't want to.'

But he was panting hard. Had he heard her? She clenched her teeth to stop herself from crying out as her body went rigid under his grip. 'Ferguson…please, no!' she called out, but he was already pushing himself into the passage which was still raw from her ordeal. After a few fierce thrusts it was over. She could only thank God he'd been quick. Her eyes stung but she was determined not to let him see her cry. A terrible silence fell between them.

'I'm sorry, Annie, but I'm still your husband.'

'Just leave me alone.' Annie's voice trembled. She shifted her nightdress that had rucked under her hips from Ferguson's frenzy and drew the blanket up under her chin. She was shocked that he could do such a thing to her. The pain between her legs had become a dull throb and she felt the beginnings of a bilious headache. Were all husbands like Ferguson? Doing whatever they pleased whether their wives wanted it or not? She watched him as he left the room, his head bowed, quietly shutting the door behind him, and vowed she would never allow it to happen again.

'I won't forgive you for that,' Annie hissed when Ferguson slipped back into the bed an hour later.

'It wasn't how I wanted it, Annie. But you never show me any affection nowadays.'

'Can't you understand why?' She kept her voice deliberately quiet.

'I'm sorry, Annie,' Ferguson said, his voice thick, his eyes on the ceiling rather than her. 'Really sorry. For everything. Even though I know you don't believe me. I don't want us to go on like this. You've had a rough time. It's not how I thought it would be. We used to be happy. But I still love you.'

She moved her head slowly from side to side on the pillow. Love.

'You do believe me, don't you?'

'I don't know what to believe anymore,' Annie said, her eyes blurred with tears. 'But there's one question I want to ask. Do the Scott-Lawsons know you've been gambling?' Her breath seemed to leave her as she waited.

'Yes.' Ferguson's voice was so low she could hardly hear him. 'They've given us four weeks' notice.'

'*Four weeks?*' Annie shot up in bed. She looked down at Ferguson in disbelief. 'To pack everything and look for another post? When were you going to tell me we'd been sacked?' She didn't wait for him to answer. She wanted to shake him until his teeth rattled. Steeling herself to keep calm, she said in a quieter tone, 'Where are we going to find something?'

'We won't find anything here. We've got to go back to England because Mr Scott-Lawson said he wouldn't give us a reference.'

'No, he wouldn't,' Annie said bitterly.

'What do you mean?'

'I just wish we'd never heard of the Scott-Lawsons.' Annie hugged her knees, desperate to rid herself of the memory of Mr Scott-Lawson's body weighing down on hers, the reek of his breath, that wild light in his eyes... A cold tremor swept through her.

'What makes you say that?'

'He tried something once with me, that's all.'

'*All?*' Now Ferguson sat up, his eyes ablaze as he stared at her. 'I'll kill him. What did he do? Tell me, Annie.'

'It's a long time ago, and nothing happened.'

'Something must have else you wouldn't have said it. Tell me,' he repeated.

'No,' Annie said. 'It happened after Russell died. He wasn't thinking straight. But he'd be the last person to give us a reference. We'll find something here without any help from him. Frankie's settled in school. She won't want to leave her friends.' She was grasping at any possibility to stay in Melbourne.

'We've got no choice. The government have deported us.'

Annie grabbed his arm. 'What are you talking about?'

'Gambling debts,' he muttered.

She bit her lip, shocked to the core. After a minute's silence she said, 'And where are you suggesting we live when we go back to England?'

'With your dad and Ethel, I suppose,' he said meekly. 'Just for a few weeks anyway...till we sort ourselves out. Actually,' Ferguson threw her a darkly suspicious look, 'I thought you might be pleased to be going home. You always used to be on about how homesick you were.'

But home's here now, she wanted to scream. Desperately trying to still the thumping of her heart, she said, 'Why did you leave it this late to tell me?'

There was no answer. Annie waited a full two minutes, feeling waves of anger sweep over her body. Her scalp burned. Her nerve endings felt as though they had been set on fire. Her muscles were as hard as rolling pins. That he should use her the way he did, purely for his own satisfaction; that he would not admit to being the baby's father; that he and Ruby had betrayed her trust; that he had gambled their savings away; that they were forced to leave Australia under a cloud – it was more than she could bear. But she had to bear it. She had the children.

'Did you ever steal any money from Mr Scott-Lawson?' It was out before she could stop herself.

'Annie, do you know what you're saying? What you're accusing me of?' He shifted his pillow behind his back and looked at her with bloodshot eyes.

'He said he'd caught you red-handed,' Annie said miserably.

'When did he tell you this? Why didn't you come to me?' Ferguson's voice rose in anger. He stared at her. 'Was that when he tried to do something to you? The bastard.'

'It doesn't matter when he told me,' Annie said, her stomach tightening.

'Was he talking about a ten-pound note?'

'Yes.' The image of Mr Scott-Lawson and what he had tried to do to her before he'd told her about the missing money swam in front of her eyes again. She began to shake.

'He gave me his trousers to clean,' Ferguson explained in a resigned voice. 'I went through the pockets to make sure he hadn't left anything in them, and found the note. I put it in my pocket meaning to hand it to him when I next saw him, but he stopped me on the stairs before I had a chance. He said he hoped I hadn't tried to steal it but I soon put him straight.' He looked at her. 'You do believe me, don't you?'

Annie nodded. Yet one of them was lying. She distinctly remembered Mr Scott-Lawson patting his jacket pocket, saying the ten-pound note had been in there. Ferguson's version was that the note had been in his employer's trouser pocket. But what did it matter now? They were being sent back to England in disgrace.

'So we have to book a ticket for the next ship going to England,' Ferguson said, running his hand through his hair.

'And how do we pay for our fares?' she asked him.

He just shook his head.

Dear God, how much more? But there was something else she desperately needed to know. She could hear the uneven rhythm of her heart thudding in her ears.

Open your mouth, Annie, and say it now.

'What about the baby?' She almost choked on the words. 'What's going to happen to Ruby's baby?'

'Ruby will come back with us,' Ferguson said firmly, as though he'd thought it all through, 'and learn to bring up her own child. I told you not to take him in. Ruby's a spoilt child. She'll have no idea how to look after him because you've done it all up to now.'

Annie felt if someone breathed on her she would blow away. Looking after Ruby's baby was all that was keeping her sane. He was a fractious little boy and rarely gave her a moment's peace but she didn't care. She was grateful for his demands. It kept her busy and blocked out some of the hurt. And when she put him to her breast it eased some of the pain. She could play her game of make-believe...that the baby was her own Harry. Ruby didn't want him. She hadn't even given him a name yet.

'She won't want to leave Australia,' Annie said. 'She likes her job. And being with Adele. I know her.'

'If it wasn't for you she wouldn't be able to keep her job.'

His voice dripped with contempt and she looked at him sharply. Had he ever been in love with Ruby? If he had, it didn't sound as though he had much time for her now. In fact, for someone who had so badly wanted to begin a new life in a foreign country, he didn't sound particularly upset at the idea of going home. She tried to picture what it would be like to be back in England. If she were honest, she didn't want to return. She'd grown to love Australia, its land, its people. And if she left she'd never see a certain face again.

'I'm not going!' Ruby shouted, as the three of them sat round the kitchen table in the tiny cottage.

Ferguson threw her a furious look. 'Of course you are. We're all going.'

'Not me. I like it here.' Ruby twisted a stray bronze curl round her finger. 'Adele wants me back at the hotel. As head receptionist. Going up in the world, I am.'

'We're all going back together,' Ferguson snapped.

'Why should I? I'm not the one who's lost all the money. Why should I have a miserable life because of your—'

'Ruby, stop—' Annie shook her head to warn her sister.

'Enough!' Ferguson roared, banging his fist on the table. 'I won't have it. *I* make the decisions here.'

'Maybe for Annie,' Ruby fumed. 'But not for me. I make my own. And the baby's. And by the way,' she stood up, eyes fastened on Ferguson, 'the baby's name is Harry. I feel I owe that at least to my sister.' She glared at him and charged out of the door.

By the time Annie caught up with her, Ruby was halfway down the vegetable garden, sobbing.

'Ruby…Ruby, wait. Sit down a moment. We must talk.' Annie got hold of her arm and pulled her on to a bench.

'There's nothing to talk about.' Ruby brushed away the tears with the back of her hand, but they continued to fall.

'Yes, there is. If you stay here, how are you going to work and look after a baby?'

A dart of anxiety flitted across Ruby's face. 'Are you really going, Annie?'

'We have to. I don't want to go any more than you do.' She pressed her sister's hand, thinking how young Ruby still was, even if she *was* twenty-two. *She's starting to realise she'll be here alone without any family.* 'Ruby,' Annie said gently, 'you haven't answered me.'

Ruby burst into fresh tears. 'I don't know,' she cried. 'I can't look after him. I don't know how. He'll have to go to foster parents.'

'You can't do that.' Annie tried to keep the panic from her voice. 'I'll look after Harry while you find a new job when we get back to England. Somewhere near me.' She held her breath. If she could just keep Harry a little longer, look after him, watch him grow, she might one day find some peace.

'All right.' Ruby's shoulders slumped with relief. Her eyes met Annie's. 'He'll be better off with you.'

Annie released her breath in a long sigh. 'So you'll come back with us,' she persisted. It was essential that Ruby understood the plan.

Ruby nodded.

The two sisters sat for a minute without speaking. Then Ruby looked at Annie, her eyes shiny as ink.

'Annie,' she said, a tremor in her voice, 'I don't have a husband and I need to earn my keep. You lost your baby. Will you look after Harry? Keep him and bring him up as your own son? Then you won't need to tell anyone I'm his mother. He'll grow up thinking you're his mother and I promise I'll never tell him different.'

Annie thought her heart would burst. She was just about to answer – say there was nothing she would like better – when she thought of Frankie. And *her* little Harry. He never got a chance at life. If someone said she would have to give up Frankie to be brought

264

up by someone else, she would tear their eyes out. She would scrub floors for her daughter forever, if need be. If she kept Harry, Ruby might never forgive her. She'd say it was all arranged in the heat of the moment. That Annie had persuaded her.

She took a deep breath.

'Ruby, you'd regret it one day. And blame me.'

'I don't know how to be a mother.' Ruby's face was running with tears. 'And I don't *want* to be a mother. I only want to know he's safe. Please, Annie.' She raised her eyes imploringly. 'I'm sure you'll soon love him.'

'Oh, Ruby, I love him already as though he were my own.' She tilted her sister's face and looked deep in her eyes, still worried that Ruby might not understand the sacrifice she was making. 'You need time to think. Why don't we talk about it when we get back to England and you're more settled?'

'I've already thought. Ever since Fergus—' Ruby's face flushed, but she went on, 'ever since he said he was going to stay with you. I can't look after a baby and earn my living all on my own. I mean it, Annie. I've made my decision and I won't change my mind.'

'If you're sure that's what you really want.'

'I'm sure.'

Annie held out both arms and her sister fell into them.

33

February 1921, letter dated 18th November 1920

My dear Annie and Ruby,

*I hope you are both keeping well. I'm afraid I have some
very sad news. Our dear Dad died yesterday. The doctor said
he had a heart attack. I was there when it happened. It was so
awful. The funeral is this Sunday. I wish you were both here
with me. By the time you get this letter it will all be over.*

I can't write anymore.

Your loving sister, Ethel

Annie wordlessly handed the letter to Ruby whose eyes darted
over the short note.

'Maybe it's for the best. He's never been the same since Ma
died,' Ruby said, putting the letter on the chiffonier, and speaking
in a matter-of-fact tone. But when Annie looked at her sister, she
noticed her lovely eyes glistened with tears.

'I'm glad we're all going home.' Annie's throat felt it would
choke her. 'We can give some comfort to poor Ethel.' She rushed
out of the room and flung herself on the bed she shared with her
husband. Her dearest father. And she hadn't been with him. Never
even knew the exact time he'd died. Been oblivious. She lay on her
side, her knees drawn up into a ball of misery. But no tears fell.
She had fallen into a troubled sleep by the time Ferguson came to
find her.

'If you don't let me stay, you can't have Harry!'

It was early morning, the day after Ethel's letter. Annie had her back to Ruby and was stirring the porridge, which had just begun to thicken, trying to shut out the memory of her father keeling over. Imagining Ethel's fright and despair, discovering it was too late. Now, Ruby was making her own announcement. Was there no end? Annie swung round, the wooden spoon still in her hand, splattering porridge on the wall behind the stove.

'But, Ruby, we agreed—'

'Well, I've changed my mind. If you force me to go back to England, I'll keep Harry. If you let me stay, you can have him – just as we agreed,' she mimicked her sister's words. There was no trace of the tears or pleading of yesterday. Ruby stood there, tall and still, her copper hair falling loosely to her shoulders, and her chin set in that determined fashion Annie recognised.

'You don't have any family here, darling,' Annie said, trying to sound calm, but fear gripping her stomach. 'You'll be miserable. At least when I came here I had Ferguson—' Annie broke off, suddenly aware of what she was saying as she saw Ruby's frown.

'There's nothing for me in King's Lynn,' Ruby said, a fierce expression settling on her pretty features as she sat down. 'I like it here. But if Fergus insists,' her voice quavered, 'I'll look after Harry myself. Mind you, I'll have to leave him with somebody while I go to work.' She threw Annie a challenging glance.

Annie's eyes brimmed. She couldn't let little Harry go to some stranger; it wouldn't be right. Somehow she had to keep him within his own family. Couldn't Ruby see that? But if she said her sister could stay in Melbourne, Ferguson would be furious. Dear God, what should she do?

'Annie?'

It felt to Annie as though the kitchen itself was holding its breath. A minute passed. Annie was conscious that in the next few moments she would be making a decision that would have repercussions on all their lives. But what choice did she have? The kitchen clock ticked by another thirty seconds. She took a deep breath. 'If you promise you'll stay with Adele,' Annie conceded, 'and if the time comes that you change jobs, you'll always keep in touch with her. And that you'll write to Ethel and me regularly. You must always let us know how and where you are.'

'I promise.'

'And promise that you'll never breathe a word to Ethel unless you talk to me first.'

'I won't tell her.'

'And Harry...you'll be his loving aunt. The same as with Frankie.'

'Yes, Annie, I promise.' Ruby's gaze didn't flinch. 'I just want to ask you one thing.' Annie braced herself, wondering what was coming next. Then she heard her sister's clear voice. 'Will you one day tell Harry the truth?'

Annie felt a shiver of apprehension. What if someone found out she wasn't the legal mother? Could they put her in prison? Ruby's eyes never left her face, waiting for her reply. It was as though she knew exactly what Annie was thinking. They must both keep strong. They were doing this for Harry. To give him the best possible life. But a little voice whispered that if she were honest, Harry was the baby she'd lost...her son who had come back to life...who would be the child to restore her.

'One day, darling, I'll tell him the truth,' Annie repeated softly, taking her sister's hand. 'When the time is right.'

Ruby caught her small front teeth on her bottom lip. Then she pressed Annie's hand in return, and nodded.

At the end of the following week, Annie hurried back to the cottage and retrieved a letter from under the newspaper lining of one of the drawers in the chiffonier.

Letter dated 24th January 1921

My dear Annie,

I have only just heard the news that you are returning to England. Bertram S-L told me. It was quite a shock. Are you sure you are doing the right thing? It's a big decision. I know your family are all back in England, except Ruby, of course, but you have a new life here and things might not be exactly as you imagine them there. Please think about it again. I know I'm being perfectly selfish, but oh, Annie, I'm going to miss you so terribly.

With much affection,

Alex Townsend

She'd only had the chance to look at the postmark before Ferguson had come to find her. She looked at the envelope again. Sydney. Now, she read and reread every word, pausing at each sentence, her heart racing. Eventually, she folded the letter back into its creases and carefully tucked it into its hiding place. This small secret isn't harmful, she told herself. It's just a friendship. But if it was so harmless why couldn't she tell Ferguson?

5th February 1921

This is the last time I intend to write in my journal. When I look back to the voyage over here and my feeble entries I wonder why I am taking the trouble. It served me well when I was going through that time but now it's of little use. And now dear father is no longer alive I don't have the heart anymore for this journal he gave me.

Annie sank down at the table, cradling her head in her arms. The tears streamed down her cheeks until she thought there could be no more left. She wept for her father, for Ethel, for her stillborn baby, even for Ruby and Ferguson. They surely wouldn't have meant it to happen. Her outburst woke Harry and he began to howl. Angry with herself she swept the tears away with the heels of her hands and rushed over to the cot.

'Shhh, shhh,' she murmured as she picked him up. 'Mummy's here.' For a few moments she forgot Harry was not the baby she'd carried inside her. She cradled him in her arms and rocked him as she walked up and down the room, singing a lullaby to him, but it wasn't enough. His face grew bright red as he began to bellow. Holding him tightly to her, she sat down and struggled to put him to her breast but he pushed it away with his little hand, jerking his head from side to side. His screams pierced her ears and shot through her head. Something was wrong.

She heard footsteps on the gravelled path.

'Oh, you're here, Annie,' Ferguson said, not bothering to wipe his boots. 'I heard Harry crying and I was just checking on him.'

'He won't stop crying,' she said, about to hand him over to see if Ferguson could calm him. 'He's not well.' Then she froze. Ferguson was peering down at the journal she'd left open on the table.

'What's all this?' he said, picking it up. 'I didn't know you were keeping a diary. You never told me.'

'You never asked,' Annie returned boldly, trying to ignore the thumping in her head as she held out her free hand. 'It's not a diary, it's just a journal. The one Dad gave me. Just to record things. Please give it to me, Ferguson. It's private.'

'There's nothing private between husband and wife,' Ferguson snapped, his face reddening as he flipped over the pages. 'This makes interesting reading. I see my name's down here.'

'Along with lots of others,' Annie said, watching helplessly as Ferguson read through one entry, then another. All of a sudden he grabbed several pages, ripped them out, grabbed some more and tore them all to shreds. He tossed the book back on the table.

'What a loyal little wife you are!' he shouted. 'How dare you write about me!'

Harry's wail reached an impossible pitch.

'What on earth's the matter with him?' Ferguson made an impatient sound and stormed towards the door. As he opened it Susan stumbled in. Annie watched with a kind of detachment as the girl glanced at her, then at Ferguson.

'I only left him for ten minutes,' she said, her face pink.

'It's all right, Susan,' Ferguson told her. 'As you can see, we're both here.'

Susan narrowed her eyes, looking from one to the other as if trying to weigh up the situation.

In that split second Annie knew without a doubt that her husband and the girl who was supposed to be looking after Harry were lovers.

Annie didn't say anything to Ferguson about her suspicions. It was odd – she didn't feel any more hurt. She'd been betrayed by her husband and sister and nothing else seemed to matter – only the children. Harry must get better. Now he was sleeping peacefully, but several times in the night she stumbled out of bed to check him, praying he would still be breathing in the morning.

'Sleep, little one,' she whispered to him in the dark, determined that if he hadn't improved by morning she would take him to Dr Brooke.

Morning came and Harry began bellowing again. Even Ferguson looked concerned.

Annie, worn out with so little sleep, picked Harry up and rocked him in her arms. 'I'm taking him to the doctor. Now. You'll have to let Mrs Wilson know.'

'Do you want me to take him?'

Annie looked at her husband with surprise. His tone was kinder than usual. But she had to do this herself; had to know exactly what the matter was, and what she had to do to get him well.

271

'No,' she said. 'Thank you for offering, but it's easier for me to go.'

'If you're sure,' he said. 'Try not to worry. He's different from Frankie. Boys are always more trouble. He'll be all right.'

Annie's eyes flew wide when she saw it was Alex on duty.

'I thought you'd transferred to Sydney,' she blurted, her heart making peculiar leaps as she put Harry over her shoulder and rubbed his back. He had stopped screaming in the waiting room and was whimpering with exhaustion.

'It didn't work out so Dr Brooke asked me back.' He looked closely at her. 'I'd heard there was an addition to the family,' he smiled, 'but tell me, who's the patient?'

She noticed his eyes had lost their usual twinkle.

'It's Harry,' Annie said. 'I'm worried sick. He's been unusually quiet through the night, though yesterday he cried for hours. And he wouldn't have his feed this morning, which is not like him at all.' She handed him the baby.

Alex gently placed him on a thick towel on top of the same bed from which he'd once examined Annie. Silently, he ran his hands over the little body. Then he put the stethoscope on Harry's chest. Annie tried to read his expression, but it told her nothing. He turned the baby on his stomach and eased a thermometer up his bottom, left it for a minute or two, extracted it, carefully wiped it and read the result.

'Exactly as I thought. Normal.' He looked at her and smiled. 'Don't upset yourself, Annie. It's nothing to worry about. Just a touch of colic. He's quiet now because he's worn himself out, but I'm afraid persistent crying is one of the symptoms.' He placed Harry back in her arms.

'Why has he got it? Frankie didn't.'

'Sometimes babies get it when they have a traumatic start in life,' Alex said, looking at her intently. 'They become sensitive. He might have it now and again, but they grow out of it. You have to be patient. In the meantime you can get him some gripe water from the chemist. That should help.'

He went over to the sink and she watched him clean the thermometer, then wash and dry his hands. The relief made her light-headed and she clung on to Harry, who started to grizzle.

'Annie?' Alex strode over, his voice full of concern. 'Here, give him back to me and come and sit down. Something else is wrong, I can tell. Is it to do with Harry?'

She nodded. It seemed wrong to burden him with her troubles but he was a friend. The sickening thought stole over her that she would never see him again.

He sat on one of the visitors' chairs, rocking Harry gently in his arms, and she took the chair next to him.

'Harry,' she began, as he turned to her, 'isn't…isn't mine. He's Ruby's.' She swallowed hard. 'She had a baby the same time as me. I'm looking after him for the time being.'

'Go on,' Alex said, his eyes never leaving her face.

'Ferguson—' She felt the familiar stinging at the back of her eyes.

'I think I see,' Alex said quietly. 'He's the father of your sister's child, isn't he?'

Annie could only nod and stare at the floor.

'But what happened to your baby? Dr Brooke mentioned when he last wrote that you were having another.'

'He…he was stillborn,' Annie gulped.

'Oh, Annie, I'm so sorry.' Alex tightened his grip on Harry and released one of his hands to briefly close over her own.

'Is your husband aware that you know about him and Ruby?'

Annie nodded again.

'What's he done about it?'

Her head whipped up. 'Nothing!' She almost shouted the word, hardly aware of the surprise on Alex's face at her outburst.

273

Harry let out a cry of alarm. 'It's all right, Harry,' she said, reaching over to stroke the baby's head. She looked into Alex's eyes, full of sympathy. 'I thought I'd got over it by now. But Ferguson keeps saying it's not true...that Ruby's lying to make things difficult between us. He won't face up to it.'

'Is there anything I can do to help?'

'No.' Annie held his gaze. 'You've been wonderful. The most important thing is that Harry's not got anything serious. I don't know how to thank you.'

'There's nothing to thank me for. I'm just doing my job.'

'I don't know what I would have done without you,' she tried again, as she rose to go.

'Don't go for a minute.' He put out a restraining hand. 'It's me who doesn't know what I'm going to do without *you*.' He paused. 'Did you get my letter?'

She nodded.

'Annie?'

'We sail in two days' time,' she said in a low voice.

'So this is to be our last meeting?'

Annie bit her lip. 'Yes.' There was nothing else to say.

'What about Ruby?'

'She refuses to come with us. She's made up her mind to stay at her job with Adele. And she's put Harry into my care, to bring him up as my own, though we're not telling anyone.'

'It's probably for the best,' Alex said with feeling. 'I'll miss you terribly but your father and sister will be glad to see you.'

Annie stared at him, her face crumpling as she burst into tears.

'Oh, Annie, please don't cry. Things will turn out well for you – I know they will.'

She opened her handbag and thrust a single sheet of paper into his free hand. He read it, his face grim. Harry had quietened and stared up at Alex with unfocused eyes, his face blotched. Alex handed back the letter, his fingers briefly touching hers.

'Oh, Annie, I'm so sorry. So very sorry. I don't know what to say.'

'I got it from Ethel last week,' Annie sobbed. 'It isn't right. Why did he have to die before he saw his grandchildren?'

'I'll get you some water. Stay where you are.' He set the baby back on Annie's lap.

She looked down at Harry, thankful he'd stopped crying. She smiled through her tears and kissed the top of his head. Gratefully, she accepted the glass of water Alex held out for her.

After a minute or so, she said, 'I must go. I've taken up far too much of your time. You have other patients to see.'

'I don't like to let you go in such a state.'

'I'll be all right.'

'Annie—'

'Don't say anything.' Annie rose unsteadily to her feet with the weight of the baby and stepped towards the door.

Alex leapt forward, and as he brushed past her to open the door she was once again aware of the nearness of him, his crisp white coat, the warmth of his breath as he stood in front of the door. She only had to put Harry down on the bed and she could melt into the safety of his arms.

'Annie,' he said again. 'I can't let you go before I tell you—' He looked down at her with such intensity, and this time his eyes shone with love. 'You must know by now how much I care.'

Annie's chest twisted in pain. Words she had longed to hear. But too late. Too late for everything.

'Alex, you mustn't say—'

'No, I must,' he interrupted. 'I know I can't say more. I wish I could. You're married and it wouldn't be fair to you. But if you *ever* need me, send word. You can always get me through the surgery. If I'm not here, Dr Brooke will send any message on.' He gripped her arm. 'Promise me you'll do that?'

Annie nodded. 'I promise.' She looked at him, not wanting

to tear her eyes away from his face...ever. The dark hair which he habitually brushed away from his forehead; his warm grey eyes which twinkled when he was teasing her; the nose, not quite straight. His lips. Oh, just one kiss. Only one. To last her a lifetime. Her throat filled with tears. 'I so wish things could be different.' She choked on the words.

'So do I, my love.'

He'd called her his love. She wanted to sing with joy. Hear him tell her over and over... He was so close. How easy it would be to reach out. Fold herself in his arms. She made a tiny movement towards him – then stopped. He was right. She was a married woman with two children. She had no business to feel anything for him except as a friend. She tightened her hold of the baby.

But I love you. Oh, Alex, how I love you.

Clutching the baby to her chest she stumbled through the door. Harry began to sob.

In the final rush of packing and saying her goodbyes, Annie couldn't find her journal. She made a last frantic search, but it had disappeared. Maybe it was just as well.

34

Alex

He'd wanted to kiss her. Oh, how he'd wanted to kiss her. But it was impossible. She'd had Harry in her arms, for one thing. For another, she trusted him as a friend and he could never do anything to betray that trust. But he knew now Annie felt something more than friendship for him. He'd felt the spark of attraction leap between them so many times – so strongly she *must* have felt it too. Sometimes he thought he'd seen a question in those dark-blue eyes of hers. Then they would cloud over and the moment would pass. But only minutes ago he could have sworn she was about to tell him she loved him.

God, he was a fool. He should have chanced it. Told her he loved her, so she would know without any doubt. Now he'd lost her.

Annie, don't leave me, Alex groaned to himself as he drove back to his lodgings. Why hadn't he told her he loved her? The question tumbled over and over until he thought he would go crazy. Why hadn't he told her life wasn't worth living without her? That he could look after her so much better than that wastrel of a husband. Then he imagined the contempt in her eyes. She'd tell him he'd got it all wrong. That he was imagining things. That she respected him as a doctor and even a friend, but she loved her husband and there could never be anything between them. And he couldn't stand that – not having any more hope. Yet the way she had just looked at him, her eyes filled with tears, he was certain she loved him in return, even if she hadn't admitted it to herself.

His comfortable rooms looked dreary in the fading light. Normally the plain colours were balm to his nerves after a long, tiring day, but tonight the whole atmosphere seemed joyless.

Scrambled eggs on toast would have to do this evening. He couldn't raise the energy to cook a proper meal. Or even to think straight. Annie was leaving in two days for England. Two days, and his life wouldn't be worth living. He had what? Thirty, forty, maybe more years left, all of them to be faced without Annie.

He ate his eggs without tasting them, and poured himself a large whisky. Then he let the pan and plate soak in the sink, and sat by the small coal fire. He opened his book but the words appeared as a jumbled blur and he closed it and put his head in his hands. He must have sat there for several minutes. When he felt the tears streaming down his face he realised he was crying for the first time since Gwen's funeral.

PART IV

The Return

35

Tilbury, England

March 1921

Surely Ethel will be here to meet us.

Annie leaned over the deck, her hand firmly clamped on her hat which threatened to join the freewheeling seagulls. Twisting her neck this way and that she tried to spot her sister, reminding herself that Ethel would now be twenty-one. A young woman. It was impossible to imagine.

She couldn't see anyone who could be her. Annie tried to dislodge the lump in her throat. It had only been the thought of seeing Ethel which had stopped her from howling like a wounded animal at being forced to leave Australia and return to England.

He called me his love.

Sick at heart she pushed a strand of hair from her eyes and saw a young couple waving madly from the quay. Something about the way the laughing young woman had both arms in the air reminded Annie of Ethel when she was really excited, and Annie couldn't help a half smile. Some passenger was going to have a wonderful welcome.

Ferguson stood mutely at her side, holding Harry. He'd spoken very little on the long voyage but to his credit he'd been good with the children. Frankie hung on to her father's other hand, chattering, and Ferguson looked down at his daughter and smiled indulgently. When Annie caught Ferguson in these small acts of kindness and love she could almost fool herself into thinking that she did indeed have a normal happy marriage.

We're going to Australia to better ourselves. Annie clearly remembered Ferguson's words that day in the servants' hall at Bonham Place. Ironically, they were in a worse financial situation than before. Thank goodness she'd taken the advice from her mother: 'Always try to put a little money to one side and don't tell your husband. You may need it in an emergency.' If she hadn't done so they wouldn't have had the money for the fare home. That would have been even more shameful.

She cupped her hand over her left eye to comfort herself against the pain that was threatening to become another of her bilious headaches. However bad it got she wasn't going to let anything spoil seeing her beloved sister. If she was here, that is. Annie took her hand away and looked around. The same young woman was practically leaping in the air and waving like a mad traffic policeman. Annie narrowed her eyes. As the ship drew closer her heart leapt. Impossible to believe. She could clearly see now that it was her dearest Ethel, all grown-up, and in spite of the headache she jumped up and down and waved back.

She glanced across at Harry. He'd worn himself out with crying and had fallen asleep, his head in the crook of his father's shoulder. Like an angel, Annie thought, grimacing at the memory of his last outburst. Not a bit like Frankie; this one had bellowed from the start. On the journey it felt as though he was protesting instinctively at being rejected by his natural mother and forced to travel halfway across the world to a foreign country. But Ruby hadn't really rejected her baby, Annie thought. She'd just known he'd be better off with his aunt, who could give him more love and attention than she was able to. And she mustn't judge Ruby for that. Besides, Annie loved Harry. Loved him wholeheartedly, just the way she loved Frankie. Maybe it was easier, she reasoned, that Harry's real mother was her own flesh and blood.

For the hundredth time, Annie wondered how her sister could

give up her own baby. Ruby was simply too immature to be a mother, but what if the day came when she asked for him back? She brushed the thought away. It was too dreadful to think about.

Ferguson shifted the baby to his other arm. Maybe one day they could settle into some kind of companionship. But loving Ferguson – trusting him, relying on him, knowing he would always love her – that had vanished.

'Come and hold my hand, Frankie,' Annie called to her daughter. 'Look, there's your Aunt Ethel.'

'Where?' The little girl jumped up and down trying to look for someone she'd never seen in her young life.

'Over there.' Annie pointed. 'We just have to get off the ship and then we'll all go home together.'

Home. The word tasted bitter.

As soon as they disembarked Ethel came rushing through the crowd towards them, smiling and holding out her arms.

'Oh, Ethel, it's so wonderful to see you!' Annie hugged her sister. 'I didn't recognise you at first. Look at you! All grown-up.'

'And with a husband,' Ethel laughed. She turned to a tall, lanky man standing a little to one side. 'Johnnie, this is my sister, Annie.'

'As if I hadn't guessed,' Johnnie beamed.

'Ethel's husband?' Annie said, bemused. She looked from one to the other. 'When did all this happen?' She glanced at Ethel, who was smiling broadly. 'You didn't tell me!'

'Yes, I did,' Ethel answered. 'I think three or four of my letters must have gone astray over the years as I didn't always get answers to my questions. I wondered why you hadn't mentioned it. Almost as though you disapproved,' she laughed.

'I never would,' Annie said. 'But the last letter I got from you was just before we sailed, and you told me about Dad.' Her eyes brimmed. 'It must have been so difficult for you.'

'It certainly hasn't been the same with you on the other side of the world.'

'Well, I'm here now,' Annie said, trying to keep up her smile.

Ferguson cleared his throat loudly and the two sisters turned in unison.

'This is Annie's husband, Ferguson,' Ethel turned to Johnnie.

The two men shook hands.

'And who is this darling girl with hair like Goldilocks?' Ethel bent down to Frankie, who was half hidden behind her father.

'Frankie, say hello to your aunt. Don't be a silly girl.' Ferguson's tone was impatient.

'She's tired,' Ethel said. 'Leave her be. We'll get to know each other very soon, won't we, Frankie?' she said to the little girl, who nodded. Ethel turned to Ferguson, who was still holding the baby. 'And this little chap must be Harry. Or that's what you said you'd call him if you had a boy.' Ethel smiled at her sister.

Annie nodded, trying to swallow the lump in her throat.

'He's beautiful.' Ethel dropped a kiss on top of the baby's head and glanced up at her brother-in-law. 'He looks more like you, Ferguson, and he's got your eyes, but his hair – why, it's the exact colour of his Aunt Ruby's!' she laughed as she chucked Harry under his chin.

It was as though her sister had turned a knife in Annie's heart. How long would it be before Ethel would guess? To hide her dismay, Annie bent her head low as she pretended to help Frankie with her shoelace. She wondered what Ferguson was thinking.

'Ferguson,' Ethel's voice was serious, 'thank you, thank you for bringing my dear Annie home.' She swung round to her sister. 'Oh, Annie, how I've missed you. And Dad. He missed you dreadfully. If only he could have seen these two little ones.' Her eyes filled with tears. 'But where's Ruby?' She gazed this way and that, as though her sister might materialise at any moment.

'Ruby has decided to stay in Australia,' Annie said, her calm voice not ringing true even to herself. 'She loves it out there and it suits her. I didn't want to leave her but maybe she's made the right decision.'

'Oh, but—'

'We'll talk about it later, dearest,' Annie said firmly. 'Come on!' She grabbed Frankie's hand and linked her other arm through her sister's. 'I'd forgotten how cold it would be in England. Let's go home.'

Ethel wanted to hear everything in detail about Ruby's decision to remain in Melbourne, but Annie had already decided not to tell her that Ruby was Harry's real mother. As far as Ethel need know, Harry was Frankie's little brother. She'd never written to Ethel about Ruby having a baby at the same time. That would have been too upsetting. Thank goodness Ruby was no letter writer. It was more than likely that she too, had never mentioned to Ethel that she was expecting a baby. Annie only hoped Ruby would keep her promise. In a peculiar way she still felt some kind of loyalty towards her wayward sister.

She reminded Ferguson when they had a minute on their own not to divulge the baby's birth.

'I've told you over and over, I don't know who the father is,' Ferguson began, but Annie cut him short. She stared at him and he turned his face away.

'Please, Ferguson, stop pretending. I deserve better than that. Let's keep to our agreement. No one is ever to know any different that Frankie and Harry are brother and sister and we are their parents.'

Now she had to face her youngest sister. Ethel was a serious girl but rarely taken in by anyone, let alone Ruby.

'How long is she going to stay in Australia?' Ethel's expression was puzzled as she poured them tea in the front room of their old home. She suddenly brightened. 'Do you think she's courting and that's why she didn't want to leave?'

'Not as far as we know,' Annie replied truthfully. 'Sometimes you have to let Ruby be. She thinks Australia has the opportunities she's been looking for, though I wouldn't be surprised if she gets homesick after a few months with no family there, and comes back to us.'

Harry began to whimper. Annie picked him up, putting him over her shoulder and patting his back, but he turned an angry red, screwed his eyes and yelled.

'Let me have him, Annie.' Ethel held out her arms to him from her chair. She rocked him back and forth, singing softly and stroking his head until he began to droop against her chest and finally fall asleep.

'That's a miracle, Ethel,' Annie said, feeling a twinge of envy that her sister had such a knack. 'He usually takes ages to calm down with me. The trouble is, he gets colic. Alex…' her face went bright pink, and she hurriedly corrected herself as Ethel gave her a curious glance, '…that is, Dr Townsend, said he'll soon grow out of it. It's hard sometimes when I'm tired. Frankie was a happy child from the moment she was born.'

'They're both adorable.' Ethel gently laid the little boy in the cot she'd borrowed and tucked him in. She put a few more pieces of coal on the fire. 'He'll soon settle down. It's a shock for all of you to be home, I expect.'

Annie had spoken too soon about Frankie being such a happy child. They'd only been back a few weeks when a change came over her daughter. She took a long time to settle down at night, and when she did she wet the bed and blamed it on her 'friend'. She picked at her food and she wouldn't let her father out of her sight. At first Ferguson was amused with his daughter's attentions. He regularly listened to her read from her storybook and most evenings read her a bedtime story. But it wasn't long before the novelty wore off and he began to make excuses as to why he didn't have the time. Frankie would end up in tears. This evening had been the worst.

'I'm not reading to you anymore,' Ferguson told the child. 'You're old enough to read your books yourself.'

Frankie jumped down from her chair, her face screwed up with fury, and flung the book on the floor.

'Pick it up at once, Frankie.' Ferguson's voice was stern.

'I shan't. I hate you and I hate Mummy. I want to go back to 'Stralia.' She ran out of the room sobbing, and a minute later Annie heard Ethel talking to Frankie in gentle tones.

Head thumping, Annie sat on the bed in her mother and father's room and wept. She cried, knowing she must finally accept she would never see her father again; she cried over Ferguson, who was friendly and polite but showed no real interest in her; she cried for little Frankie, who hated her new school where the other children taunted her for speaking funny; she cried for Harry, who would never know his real mother; she cried for her own lost Harry; she cried over the kindness of Ethel and Johnnie, giving up their room for her and Ferguson and the children. And finally, she cried for someone on the other side of the world. Someone who she knew loved her with a steady heart, even if he hadn't uttered the words. Someone she'd lost forever.

Her tears spent, she got up and went to the chest of drawers to find a handkerchief. As she unfolded the small soft triangle of cotton, she noticed the faded initials, E J R. Eleanor Jane Ring. Her mother. More tears streamed down her face as she tenderly laid her mother's handkerchief back in the drawer and searched for a plain one, but even after she'd blown her nose loudly and washed her face she didn't feel any better. Her eyes were an ugly red and Ethel would notice. She'd have to tell her she thought she might be coming down with a cold. Reluctantly, she went downstairs to help Ethel with supper. She had to keep going – if only for the children's sake.

'I still can't understand why Ruby wanted to stay out there without any family,' Ethel persisted a few days later as they washed up the breakfast dishes. 'Are you sure she hasn't met someone? She's always been rather secretive and maybe hasn't told you.'

'The hotel where she works isn't that far from where we were at Amber Bay,' Annie said, keeping her voice level, 'and we used to see her often. She never mentioned anyone special.'

Except Ferguson.

She swallowed the bitter thoughts. It did no good going over and over all that had happened, though she longed to unburden herself. But it wouldn't be fair. Ethel would hate Ferguson and might even end up hating Ruby.

'Let's hope she'll meet a nice young man who she can settle down with and have a family,' Ethel said, her blue eyes bright with enthusiasm. 'Though of course,' her face suddenly drooped, 'Australia's too far away for us to all go over for the wedding.'

'I'm sure she'll meet the right man one day.' How long could she keep up the pretence?

Ethel put the last of the plates in the rack. 'What about you, Annie?'

'Me? I'm already married.' She laughed, pretending to misunderstand her sister. 'One husband's more than enough.' But the flippancy was gone as soon as it started.

Ethel opened her mouth to say something, then closed it. Finally, she asked, 'Is it so awful being back in England? I know you feel the cold, but that shouldn't make you cry. And you've been crying a lot. I wish you'd tell me what's troubling you.'

'It's just that when I left, Dad was here.' At least it was partly true. 'Now he's gone. And I wasn't here when he died, so I keep expecting him to come in any minute and ask where his dinner is. You haven't told me exactly what happened.' She watched as Ethel folded the damp tea towel and hung it on the oven door. 'Come and sit down and tell me about it.'

'Well, he went to the print shop as usual that morning,' Ethel began, as she joined her at the table, 'and came back at lunchtime not feeling very well. He wouldn't eat anything. Just said he'd be going back to work by and by. After half an hour he got up. He didn't make it any further than the front door.' Her sister shuddered at the memory. 'One moment he was walking, the next he'd fallen in a heap.'

'Whatever did you do?'

'I kept slapping his face, begging him to say something. Then I held a mirror up to his face and it stayed clear. I knew then. Poor Dad. He was heartbroken after Mum died. It couldn't have been easy bringing up three daughters. Then you left...'

'Oh, Ethel, I'm sorry.'

'No, it was right you followed your husband. But Dad missed you so much. He loved your letters. So did I.' Ethel gave Annie a smile. 'I thanked God I had Johnnie. I don't know what I would have done without him. He was wonderful helping with the funeral and everything.'

'I'm glad you've got him,' Annie said slowly. 'He's a good man. Perfect for you. How did you meet him?'

'Dad brought him home one evening. He asked me if I could stretch the supper. He'd only just started at the printing works and I think Dad felt sorry for him, being in digs and all. We liked one another straight away.' Ethel smiled at the memory and Annie fought a twinge of envy at how happy her sister seemed. 'I wonder what Ruby will say. Probably that he's dull, I shouldn't wonder.'

'I'm sure she wouldn't say anything of the kind,' Annie said, but it was the sort of comment Ruby would make about a quiet man who took his job and his wedding vows seriously. She felt the familiar empty feeling in her stomach.

'She was always worried sick that I would meet someone before her, even though I was the youngest. I told her she wouldn't be on her own for long – not with her looks.'

Annie gulped. To busy herself she went over to the sink to fill the kettle. Almost without thinking, she turned round. 'I told her the same but I didn't think she'd—' She caught her lower lip between her teeth.

'Didn't think she'd what?' Ethel prompted.

'Nothing. It's nothing, really.' Dear God, she mustn't say anything now. Not at this late stage. Not when she and Ruby had made the decision to keep it a secret from everyone. Ethel was looking at her curiously, waiting for an explanation. 'I wish she was happy, like you,' Annie finished lamely.

'And what about *you*, Annie?' Her sister's clear gaze, so like their mother's, met her own. 'Don't take offence, dear, but you and Ferguson don't seem to see eye to eye very much these days. That is, when he's here, which isn't often.'

Annie felt a warmth spread over her face.

'We're an old married couple now,' she said, trying to laugh it off. 'You can't keep up the honeymoon forever.'

'Johnnie and I will,' Ethel said, without a touch of fanfaronade.

36

Bonham

13th May 1921

I've decided to keep a diary again, even if it's only in this exercise book. I wonder where I put the lovely leather one Dad gave me just before I boarded the *Orsova*. Someone is sure to find it one day. I only hope it doesn't fall into the wrong hands.

I'll always hate Friday 13th from now on. I didn't used to be superstitious but Ferguson's latest bombshell is that he wants to go to America. He was serious. Is he mad? He's working at a hotel in Norwich so I only see him one day a week. Nothing's ever resolved. He hates his job and wants to go to America as soon as he can. He says he'll find work easily in New York because Americans don't usually have butlers and it will be a novelty for a wealthy family to have an English butler. I don't know where he's found out all this information. I told him I'm not moving anywhere else. This time I will not be going with him. I mean it.

I still can't believe he's even thinking about such a thing after all we've been through. He said he will go on his own if I don't go with him. I don't know whether it is just a threat, or whether he really intends to go. Why can't he see what he's doing to the children? Harry's still a baby but Frankie knows there's something in the air and she's started to misbehave again. I told him if he went, not to come back. I meant it at the time but I don't know how I would feel if he really goes.

8th August 1921

> Ferguson is leaving at the beginning of next month! I'm determined not to try to stop him. I've learned from the past that it's no good. And I refuse to use the children to make him change his mind. He must have arranged this as soon as we got back to England and never told me about it. I think he knew I wouldn't go with him. Maybe he's relieved. I can't think clearly anymore.

30th August 1921

> Ferguson obviously cannot wait. He goes in three days.

'Can we go to the park today?' Frankie rushed in, her pale gold pigtails flying.

'Not today, Frankie.' Annie bent down to give her a hug. 'You know Daddy's leaving this morning. We won't see him for a while, so we have to be here to say goodbye.' Annie gulped on the last word. It still didn't make sense that her husband should be leaving them all.

'I don't want Daddy to go.' Frankie began to cry.

'What's this all about?' Ferguson appeared at the doorway. He swept the little girl up in his arms. 'Daddy won't be long before he sends for you. I just have to find a job and somewhere to live first.'

'I don't want to come without Mummy and Harry.'

'No, of course not. I meant all of you.' As Ferguson spoke the words he caught Annie's eye.

'Breakfast is ready,' was all she said.

Frankie broke into fresh tears.

'Frankie, do you understand what I'm saying?'

Frankie shook her head vehemently and nuzzled her face into the arc of her father's neck and shoulder. Annie watched her daughter, her heart breaking to listen to the child's sobs.

'Come on, that's enough.' Ferguson pushed her gently away and lifted her down to the floor. 'You're a big girl now. You've got to be brave and help Mummy. Can you do that for me?'

'No!' Frankie shouted, and tore out of the kitchen.

'She'll get used to it,' Ferguson said, refusing to meet Annie's eyes. She noticed his voice wobble. So he *did* feel something for his family – but obviously not enough. It was as though a curtain had slipped between them and at that moment Annie vowed to herself that she, with the help of Ethel and Johnnie, would see that the children didn't suffer. They would all somehow get through the next months without Ferguson. She left the kitchen without a word and went to wake Harry.

Johnnie had already left for work. It was an awkward little group that sat round the breakfast table. Frankie refused to eat more than a bite or two of her boiled egg. She sat staring at the opposite wall, her face set in a determined fashion, like a person way beyond her seven years. Then all of a sudden she rushed from the table, sobbing. Even Harry was quieter than usual.

Ferguson wiped his mouth on his napkin and stood up. Ethel disappeared into the kitchen and soon a louder clattering than usual emanated from the sink.

'We'd better get started,' Ferguson said, giving Annie an apologetic smile. 'I'll just go and fetch my case.'

She ignored the smile; hardened her heart. 'Goodbye, then.' She looked directly at him.

'Aren't you going to see me off?'

'No.' Annie drew her lips firmly together.

'That's a fine thing. What will it look like if you don't come?'

'No worse than it looks that you're leaving me and the children,' Annie flashed.

Ferguson's face reddened. 'I told you I'll send for you when I get settled. It's not forever, but the way you're talking—'

'To me it *is* forever.'

The last thing she remembered about him was the trail of spicy cologne.

For the next few weeks Annie felt like a widow – numb, disbelieving, and lonely. What she hated most was her embarrassment when she tried to explain to well-meaning neighbours that her husband was going to try his luck in America and would send for her when he was settled. When they voiced their surprise that he was prepared to go away again so soon, and without his family, she heard herself making excuses, until finally she got tired of trying.

In the end, Annie said as little as possible. If people wanted to gossip, then so they must – she wouldn't worry about it. There were too many immediate problems which required her attention, especially the urgent one of finding a job, and quickly. But where, when she had two children to look after?

'...so I'll look after the little ones.' Ethel broke into her thoughts a week later as they were cleaning the downstairs rooms.

'Oh, Ethel...no...'

'Yes,' Ethel said firmly. 'I've already decided. I don't have anything much to do except look after Johnnie.'

'You're a dear, but Harry's such a handful.'

'He'll be all right. They both will. And anyway, Frankie's in school.' Ethel smiled as she dusted the only photograph they had of their father and mother together on their wedding day and set it back on the chiffonier. 'Don't you trust me?'

'You know I do but...' Annie trailed off.

'Then the matter is closed,' Ethel said. 'We hope to have our own one day, but until then, we'd love to have them. Johnnie is in complete agreement. Says it will be good practice for me—' she broke off, chuckling. 'Even when I have a baby, I can still look after them.'

'Of course I'll pay you as soon as I find a job,' Annie said, her heart leaping with gratitude.

'We'll see about that when the time comes,' Ethel said firmly.

'Johnnie was promoted last month so he'll earn a bit extra from now on. You don't have to worry about anything.'

'I'd rather you than anyone look after them,' Annie said, thinking how different her two sisters were. 'You're so good with little Harry.'

'I love him like my own,' Ethel said. 'But I hope I'll be able to have a baby one day.' She looked at Annie and gave an embarrassed laugh, but Annie thought she saw a tear glisten in her sister's eye.

'Of course you will, dear. It'll happen when you least expect it.

'What about Bonham Place?' Ethel said, after Annie came home from the village late one afternoon, exhausted from another fruitless search.

'I've already inquired there even though I don't really want to go back. That part of my life is over.' Her eyes pricked at the thought of those years, learning to cook under Mrs Jenner's stern eye. 'Gladys says there's a new cook. Mrs Jenner retired but she comes in on the new cook's day off, so I wouldn't be needed. Anyway, I've changed too much to fit in. They're used to me being a maid, not a cook.'

Ethel nodded as she cut two slices of fruit cake.

'I've talked to Mr Lincoln at the post office. He doesn't know of any job going but he said he'd let me know if he hears of anything. Then there's the children to think of,' Annie continued, 'though Ferguson has been good and sends money for them regularly.'

'Don't make me cross,' Ethel said, her jaw tightening. 'He had no business going in the first place, leaving his family, and the few dollars he sends every month barely covers their food.'

Annie bit her lip. Her sister rarely made such a strong judgement, but it was true. And Frankie would soon need new shoes and a coat for the coming winter. Harry was bursting out of his clothes. She couldn't impose upon her sister and Johnnie much longer.

*

Going to the park was the one outing in which Frankie showed any kind of pleasure since her father had left, and Annie made sure she took the children as often as she could. Once or twice she even went on her own to give herself some time to think in the fresh air, but no matter how she tried to understand her husband's motivation, wondering what he was planning, or what she was going to do with her own life, she couldn't come up with any answers.

One particular afternoon she was glad of Ethel's company as she watched Frankie laughing with some other children as they spun round on the small roundabout. The mother of the other children gave it another push whenever it began to slow down. Harry was unusually quiet in his pushchair, focusing on the three children, his coppery head turning this way and that as he followed the movement.

'Annie,' Ethel interrupted her thoughts, 'do you realise we haven't heard from Ruby, not even once since you came home?'

'I know,' Annie said quietly. 'She's not the best letter writer.'

'Was there anything troubling her? You know, before you came back?' Ethel went on.

Annie got up to fetch the teddy bear Harry had thrown out of his perambulator, thankful that he'd diverted her sister. 'If you throw it away, Harry, you might not get it back the next time.'

As though she'd shouted at him, he immediately opened his mouth wide and bellowed.

'Harry, stop that.' She sent him a warning look.

He screamed even louder. His hair clung to his head in damp curls, his face almost purple as he held his breath for what seemed like a minute after each howl before he let rip again.

Ethel reached into the perambulator and picked him up.

'There, there,' she soothed, rubbing his back and turning her ear as far away from his mouth as possible. 'Let's take him on the roundabout, Annie. He just wants to join in with the other children.'

'He's too young,' Annie protested, but Ethel was already marching over to the roundabout.

'Oh, if you're going to stay with the children I'll go and see to baby,' said the woman who had been pushing the children. She looked harassed and relieved at the same time as she raced off without waiting for any reply, her long skirt flapping in the breeze.

To the amusement of the three other children and Frankie's outright embarrassment, Annie and Ethel sat on the roundabout, both holding the wriggling, screaming Harry. But as soon as Ethel pushed with her foot to make it turn, Harry's mouth stopped open in mid bellow.

'You rather take after your Aunt Ruby,' Ethel laughed. 'And it's not just your hair. She used to have quite a temper.' She turned to Annie. 'Does she still?'

'Not really. Well, sometimes, when she's...she's...' Annie stuttered, her chest tight all of a sudden. She clutched the metal rail with one hand, the other trying to still Harry, and averted her face.

'Annie, what's the matter? Every time I mention Ruby you either change the subject or don't give me a proper answer. I *know* something happened in Australia. Please tell me. She is *my* sister too.'

'There's nothing to tell.'

'You've never lied to me before, Annie. Please don't do it now. It's something to do with Harry, isn't it? And I think I've guessed what it is.'

Annie froze.

'Look at me,' Ethel persisted. Annie turned, and Ethel looked directly at her. 'Ruby's his mother, isn't she?'

Annie's head whirled, exaggerating the motion of the roundabout. She couldn't catch her breath. Swallowing hard, she shot her foot out to stop the machine. Her shoe dragged along the ground for a few seconds, raising a swirl of dust, before the roundabout came to a halt.

'Mummy, what are you doing?' Frankie shouted from the other side of the roundabout.

'I-I'm just going to sit down for a while with Aunt Ethel.' Annie got up, her legs shaky, testing the ground beneath her. 'You can keep it going.'

Ethel held her arm as they made their way back to the bench. Annie wondered if her sister could feel her trembling. On the adjacent bench the harassed mother was absorbed in rocking her baby in the perambulator, and Annie felt her sister's fingers clutch a little more firmly.

'I'm right about Ruby, aren't I?' Ethel said as soon as they'd sat down. 'She's his mother.'

'Yes,' Annie whispered.

'Why isn't Harry with Ruby and his father?'

'I let Ruby live with us,' Annie swallowed. Ethel was silent, waiting for her to explain. She didn't want to tell Ethel the truth. But if she didn't tell her she'd be treating Ethel like a child.

'I thought she had a position near your people.'

Annie drew in a deep breath. 'Ruby hated her lodgings at the house where she worked. In fact, she hated everything about her employment. She got a job with Adele – I told you about her – and so I couldn't keep an eye on her. She's a little wild, you know. I think they began to see one another—' The tears started to roll down Annie's cheeks.

'Oh, Annie.' Ethel put her arm around her older sister's shoulders. 'This is so hard for you, but I think you'll feel better for telling me.'

'Maybe.' Annie pulled a handkerchief out of her bag and blew her nose. 'Anyway, Ruby began to put on weight. And she seemed terribly upset about something. But I didn't guess she was going to have a baby until she confessed. I was shocked, I can tell you. But these things happen and I was prepared to accept the father. See them get married.'

'He's obviously Australian. That must be why she wanted to stay out there. But I still don't understand. Didn't she want to get married?'

Annie shook her head.

'Oh, I see.' Ethel made a tutting noise and nodded her head. 'He's already got a wife. That's why he can't marry Ruby. That's it, isn't it? Oh, poor, poor Ruby.'

'You're right,' Annie said flatly. 'He's married.'

'So who *is* the father?' Ethel asked. 'Did you ever meet him?'

Annie's tear-soaked eyes never left her sister's face. 'Can't you guess?' she said in such a low voice Ethel strained towards her to hear the words.

The two women sat looking at one another without speaking. Then Ethel's eyes widened in horror as the truth dawned.

'Oh, dear Lord. Oh, Annie. Not Ferguson. Don't let it be Ferguson.' Her face paled in shock.

As though a storm had broken out deep inside Annie, she threw herself into her sister's arms and cried and cried until her stomach ached and there were no more tears left.

'Come on, dearest. We should go home,' Ethel said after a few minutes, still stroking Annie's hair. 'The children need their tea.'

Frankie had climbed down from the roundabout and was staring at her mother.

'Why is Mummy crying?'

'She's just a bit upset, that's all,' Ethel said, patting her hand and smiling at the child. 'Grown-ups cry sometimes, too, you know.'

Frankie looked unconvinced. She turned to her mother. 'Mummy?'

'Don't worry, darling. I'm all right now.' Drained of all emotion, Annie stood up and kissed her daughter.

'We'll soon be home and then I'll put the kettle on,' Ethel said, smoothing down her skirt. 'We'll have a nice cup of tea.'

'The cure for all ills.' Annie gave her sister a watery smile.

'Something's worrying me, Annie. Have you and Ferguson adopted Harry officially?' Ethel asked over tea.

'No. I wanted to but Ruby said there was no need. And Ferguson wouldn't admit that he was the father anyway.'

'*What?*'

'He always denies it.' Annie took a gulp of her tea. She pulled a face and added another spoonful of sugar. 'If he'd said he was sorry, I might have been able to forgive him.'

'I'd like to give that husband of yours a good slap,' Ethel said, her face unusually grim. 'What about Harry's birth certificate?'

'I've got that. But nothing to say I'm his guardian. Ruby simply asked if I would take him as my own. We didn't sign anything because it was to be kept secret. Just between sisters – and Ferguson, of course.' Annie set down her cup, her eyes brimming.

'Annie,' Ethel covered Annie's hand with hers, 'once it dawned on me Harry was Ruby's baby, not yours, I realised something awful must have happened. Oh, Annie, what happened to *your* baby?'

'I had a baby boy as well…but they only let me see him for a few moments. They wouldn't let me hold him. You see, he was… he was…' Annie convulsed into sobs.

Ethel rushed round the table and put her arms around Annie. 'He didn't live, did he?' she whispered.

Annie shook her head. The lump in her throat was hard as stone.

'Did you name your baby?'

'Yes,' Annie swallowed hard. 'I called him Harry, as I'd intended.'

'Is that why Ruby named *her* baby Harry?' Ethel asked, her own eyes filling with tears.

'At first she didn't call him anything,' Annie said dully. 'Then when I looked after him while she went back to work, she said she was going to call him Harry. She said it was the least she could do.'

Ethel shook her head in disbelief. 'Did that upset you? That she chose the same name?'

'No. I was so thankful I still had a baby to care for and love while Ruby worked, it didn't matter what she named him. Somehow calling him Harry sounded right. I only dreaded the time when she could look after him herself.'

'She never planned to,' Ethel said, her voice unusually hard. 'So then she asked if you would take him back to England?'

'Yes. I told her to think about it. That it was a serious decision she might one day regret. But she kept repeating he would be better off with me. I thought at least Harry would have his own father. I took Harry to bring up as my own child because Ruby begged me to. It was selfish, but I knew it would help to heal the pain of losing *my* little Harry. After a few weeks of caring for him I sometimes forgot he wasn't mine. I still do. Is that wicked?'

'Of course not, dearest. But one day he's going to find out you're not his mother. Does it say on the certificate that Ferguson is his father?'

'No. It just says "father unknown".'

37

'I wish I knew what to do.' Annie looked round the familiar little dining room as they were eating their porridge. It reminded her of her first breakfast on the *Orsova* and she told Ethel what had happened to the porridge bowls when there'd been a storm at sea.

'I don't think one of us got our own bowl back,' Annie said, smiling as Ethel chuckled. 'But seriously, I must get a job.'

'Will you try to find a cooking situation?' Ethel asked.

'It's the only thing I can do.'

'Why don't you write to Lady Hamilton?'

'Oh, I couldn't. What would Fer—?' She stopped herself. What did it matter what Ferguson said or thought? She must get out of that habit.

'At least you know what they're like,' Ethel continued. 'They were kind employers and paid well, and you never know.'

Annie's mind whirled. Ferguson always said the kitchen staff at Hatherleigh Hall were nosy and liked nothing better than to gossip. 'How could I explain my husband has left me and the children to go to America?'

'Tell the truth,' Ethel answered simply. 'And then say how you are looking forward to an early reply.'

Annie was silent. Was it possible that she could work at the same place where Ferguson had worked all those years ago? She looked at Ethel who smiled gently at her. Ethel was right.

She might be the youngest but she was the wisest.

To Annie's astonishment she received a reply two days later.

Dear Mrs Bishop,

My husband and I were delighted to hear from you. It seems you might be the answer to our prayers. We have had two cooks since Mrs Gold retired and both are no longer in our employ. Would you come to see us? The sooner the better. Unless I hear otherwise I will send Sidney with the motor car this Friday at 10am.

Yours most sincerely,

Jean Hamilton

Lady Hamilton offered Annie the position on the spot, despite not being provided with any references from the Scott-Lawsons. She said it was enough that Annie had worked for her great friend, Lady Bonham. Annie was to start on the Monday. She didn't know whether to laugh or cry when Sidney brought her home and she spilled the news to her sister. Ethel was thrilled, which made Annie feel she had made the right decision. Later, when the children were tucked up and Annie lay on the bed in what used to be the box room, she counted her blessings.

The children were well. Frankie had begun to settle and had even called Johnnie 'Daddy' that morning, although she'd instantly realised what she'd done and rushed out of the room. Time would heal Frankie, Ethel assured her. Annie wondered if it would have the same effect on herself. But at least she had a job with good employers. She was well. Her sister was to look after Frankie and Harry. But there were some terrible gaps. In spite of everything she missed Ferguson and Ruby. She missed Adele's friendship. But most of all, she finally admitted to herself in the tiny windowless room, she missed Alexander Townsend.

*

'We've had a letter from Ruby at last,' Ethel declared, holding out a long white envelope. 'I haven't opened it yet as I wanted to wait until you came home.'

Annie glanced at the return address. Ruby was still in Melbourne. She also saw that the name on the envelope was Ethel's. Fighting a tiny thread of jealousy that her own name didn't appear, she said to her sister in a calm voice, 'You open it, dear. It *is* addressed to you.'

Ethel frowned as she slit it open with their father's letter-opener, then broke into a relieved smile. 'It's for both of us,' she said. 'Shall I read it out?'

'Yes, do.'

Letter dated 10th November 1921

Dear Ethel and Annie,

I hope this finds you both well. I am keeping well this end. We are very busy at the hotel but I enjoy all the company and Adele is a good friend. She keeps an eye on me like an older sister. She asked me to say hello to you, Annie.

I don't go out much as the bar is full every evening.

How are Frankie and Harry? Please send me a photograph of them when you can. And remind me of Frankie's birthday. Harry is probably walking and talking by now. Sometimes I wish I wasn't so far away, but I am very happy here.

I ran into Dr Townsend the other day when Adele sent me to the chemist. He said to give you his kind regards next time I write. So I am.

Your loving sister, Ruby

Annie momentarily squeezed her eyes shut at the mention of Alex. She felt a heat rise from her chest all the way to the top of her head. She put her hand to her cheek and found her face was burning. He'd sent his 'kind regards'. Well, what else did she expect?

Ethel looked at her curiously. 'Dr Townsend. Isn't he the doctor you helped on the ship?'

'Yes.' Annie's mouth tightened. She didn't want to discuss Alex with anyone, even Ethel.

'You said how hard he'd worked in the hospital. Always putting the patients' needs first.'

She'd told Ethel about the smallpox outbreak, and though she'd only referred to him as Dr Townsend, it had been a strange relief just to say his surname aloud. Now she wished she'd never mentioned him.

'That's what doctors are supposed to do,' Annie managed.

'But you made Dr Townsend sound special.' Ethel looked closely at Annie.

'He's a very good doctor. And a very nice man,' Annie finished lamely.

Ethel smiled. 'Is he married?'

'I've no idea,' Annie returned, her cheeks flaming. 'But what difference does it make if he is or he isn't?'

'I don't know,' Ethel said seriously. 'I just like the sound of him, for some reason.'

Later, much later, in her tiny bedroom, Annie admitted to herself that it would make all the difference in the world if she knew for certain whether Alex Townsend was married or not.

38

Melbourne

Alex, November 1921

Lost in thought, Alex Townsend didn't notice anything particular about the young woman in the queue in front of him in the chemist's. If only Annie hadn't been forced to return to England. He knew she had begun to think of Australia as home. What a shock it must have been to have to pack up and leave with so little notice. To change countries again when he was sure she had finally settled in Melbourne. What a disgrace that husband of hers had brought upon her and the children. She'd had no choice. Ferguson had gone through all their savings and they'd had nowhere to go. She'd had to face so much, yet she'd taken little Harry as her sister had begged her, and promised to bring him up as her own son.

How he wished it were in his power to help. To stand by her whatever happened. He shrugged. Annie was her husband's responsibility, not his. Then Annie's lovely face misted in front of him. Her beautiful eyes, so sad at each new hurt. He longed to be the one to bring back the sparkle. It was no use. His heart felt as though it were losing its power to beat as he told himself he would never see her again. Nearly a year had passed and he had to face the fact that Annie would never return to Melbourne. She was too loyal to leave her husband. And ask him for a divorce? No, Annie would say it was out of the question. Her place was with her husband. Not that they'd actually discussed it, but he knew it to be so. He sighed. The worst thing of all was that he would never get the chance to tell her he loved her. And that he thought about her and missed her every single day.

He bent his head in despair.

It was only when the young woman spoke that Alex was jolted back to the present. 'I've come to collect Miss Frost's prescription.'

Her voice. Impossible. He was hallucinating. Annie was on the other side of the world. He was more tired than he realised and he'd been thinking about her, that was all. But this young woman just mentioned a Miss Frost. Could she be talking of Adele? He wanted her to turn round so he could see her face but she stood with her back to him. Thick, wavy strands of copper hair fell from under a small hat perched on top of her head. He couldn't tap her on the shoulder, or start a conversation. He could only watch as the pharmacist looked along his shelves and pulled out a small brown paper bag.

'I'll need you to sign for it,' he told her.

The young woman scribbled something, put the packet into her bag and turned. Her eyes fixed on his with a gleam of appreciation.

'Good morning, sir.' She stopped in her tracks. 'My goodness. Are you all right? You look as though you've seen a ghost,' she laughed.

'I'm so sorry—' he began, heart racing. This young woman's hair was lighter, yet her eyes were exactly the same shape, the same deep blue as Annie's. She must be, had to be, Annie's sister, Ruby. The young woman waited, one dark eyebrow raised.

'I didn't mean to stare. I mean…are you…? I feel I've met you,' he stuttered.

'Well, I'm sure I'd remember a handsome man like you if we had.' She sounded amused.

Alex felt his face warm. Annie would never have made such a remark. And yet she reminded him so… He had to ask.

'You're Annie Bishop's sister, aren't you?'

The young woman stepped back, her eyes widening with surprise.

'Yes, but how on earth did you know?' She cocked her head to one side, her jaunty little hat looking as though it might fall off, as she scrutinised him.

Their voices would have been identical if this young woman's had been softer, Alex thought, a little unkindly.

'When you spoke. Your accent. You sound so alike, and there aren't too many English women in Melbourne.'

'That's right. I'm Ruby.' She fluttered her lashes and smiled her bold lipstick smile. 'And who, if I might ask, are you?'

She was openly flirting with him. So different from Annie, he almost laughed.

'Alexander Townsend,' he admitted.

She looked at him intently. 'Ah, *Doctor* Alexander Townsend. Annie's mentioned you.'

His heart turned over. 'Has she?'

'Several times. You delivered her baby, if I'm not mistaken. Frances Elizabeth.'

'Little Frankie. Yes. Have you heard how your sister is, now she's back in England?' He couldn't bring himself to say 'home'.

'She writes often. I'm not that much of a letter writer, I'm afraid.' Ruby giggled. 'But last time I heard, they were well. The children are growing.'

He felt he detected a slight catch in her voice. Of course. She must feel sad at times without her family. And, of course, baby Harry. There was an awkward silence. He wanted to get away. It was too painful talking to Annie's sister.

'Are you still working for Miss Frost?' he asked, forcing himself to be polite, though in truth he wasn't the slightest bit interested.

'Adele? Oh, yes,' Ruby was enthusiastic. 'I'm learning a lot about the hotel trade. You should come in and have a drink one day, Doctor. Just the ticket after a hard day's work delivering babies and things.'

308

'I don't get much time off,' he said, thankful he had such a perfect excuse. And if he did, he certainly wouldn't want to spend it with Annie's sister. If he couldn't have the real thing, no substitute would do.

'Don't say you haven't been asked,' Ruby said, tossing her head in a provocative manner. 'Well, you know where I am in case you change your mind.'

'I do, indeed. Remember me to Miss Frost. She was a good friend to your sister. And please give An...I mean, your sister,' he hastily corrected himself as Ruby lifted an eyebrow, 'my kind regards when you write to her next. And now I must be on my way to visit one of my patients. It was nice to meet you, Miss—?'

'Oh, call me Ruby. Everyone does.'

It was eerie how alike their eyes were. Both so dark, they were almost navy. But where Annie's were soft and warm with gentle humour, Ruby's were stained glass.

'I'll remember that, Miss Ruby,' Alex said, tipping his hat.

He could feel Ruby's eyes boring into his back as he hurried away, the ache in his heart worse than ever. It was only when he was back at the surgery that he realised he hadn't brought back the new dressings Dr Brooke had asked him to collect.

39

Bonham

8th January 1922

It was a quiet Christmas. Just Ethel and Johnnie, me and the children. But we made the most of being together and Frankie was happy with the stocking Father Christmas had left her. Harry was curious as to what was going on and cried when he became overtired but Ethel was marvellous with him. He calms right down when she cuddles him. Maybe he senses I'm anxious half the time.

23rd February 1922

Lady Hamilton seems to be satisfied with the dishes I cook for them. And who would have guessed who the first footman is? Only Eric, the new boy at Bonham Place, who passed me the note from Ferguson all those years ago! The note which changed both our lives. He is a nice enough man and very proud of the way he has bettered himself. I think he has taken a shine to me, but I'm not interested.

I continue to hear from Ferguson, but every time a letter is delivered with American stamps it's a shock. He is so far away. Several months have gone by since the children last saw their father. They won't recognise him when they do. Whenever I open a letter of his, I wonder if this could be the one telling me he's made a mistake and is coming home.

He's working in some boatyard – it seems as though it's

more difficult than he thought to find a family who wants an English butler. But there's no hint he's unhappy, except he says he misses us all and is looking for lodgings big enough to take us. At the moment he says he's in one room. Why can't he accept that I won't be joining him?

19th April 1922

I haven't heard from Ferguson for two months. I've written every fortnight and usually hear back once a month. Is he ill? I don't know anyone who could get in touch with him and can only pray he's safe and well. Frankie constantly used to ask when Daddy was coming home. Now she's stopped asking.

20th June 1922

Still no word from Ferguson. I'm really worried. Also, we need the little money he sends for the children to help with their food and clothes.

21st June 1922

There is one piece of exciting news which was a perfect birthday present. Ethel is going to have a baby. She and Johnnie are so thrilled. I am too. She will make a wonderful mother.

24th June 1922

I have had a letter from Alex.

40

Letter dated 2nd April 1922

My dear Annie,

I hope this letter reaches you. I have sent it to your sister's address as I presume you are staying there. If not, maybe Ethel will have forwarded it to you.

Ruby came to see me yesterday. She still works at the Esplanade and she's walking out with someone. She told me the worrying news that your husband went to America last year but you and the children haven't joined him.

I plan to come to England for a long-needed holiday. Annie, may I come and see you? Please say yes, for the sake of our old friendship. I will arrive Tuesday, 8th July so I hope you get this letter in time. I'm sorry not to be able to give you more notice but will risk it and come to see you anyway.

Affectionately yours,

Alex Townsend

Annie bit her lip as she read the letter, forcing herself to concentrate on Alex's news of Ruby. Ruby had met someone. Thank goodness. She hoped it was someone her sister could be really happy with. She reread the letter, trying to imprint the words in her brain before she reluctantly folded it and laid it carefully in her father's chiffonier. Her blood raced. Alex was coming to England. He wanted to see her. How did she feel about it? Her heart beating wildly, she conjured up the image of his dear face. She could almost see his tall form in her parents' house, his head brushing the ceiling. How she wished he could have met them both. She drew in a deep breath. Did that mean she was going to allow him to come and see her?

Leaning back in her father's chair, she imagined the familiar whiff of tobacco from his rolled-up cigarettes in her nostrils. It made her throat ache just to think about it. But although she had still never forgiven herself for not being there when her father had had his heart attack, she knew she was lucky in many ways – even without Ferguson. Harry seemed to have settled. He was becoming a chatterbox, even though he was not yet two, but was perfectly quiet when someone told him a story. Although he would never have an even temperament, he could turn on the charm when it suited him. And Frankie was fitting in better at school now she'd managed to lose her accent.

When she looked at Ethel and Johnnie so happy together waiting for their first child she was glad for them, but then she would rush back to her stuffy little room and put her head in her hands. In these weaker moments she admitted to herself she was lonely. But now Alex was coming to see her, and she wasn't going to let him see a tired, tear-stained woman. Before he arrived she would catch the train to King's Lynn. She'd buy a new dress and go to the hairdresser's.

The day before Alex Townsend was due to arrive in England she heard from Ferguson. Some American dollars fluttered to the floor as she pulled out the single sheet. The letter was undated.

Dear Annie,

I am not sure how to tell you, but I have met a very nice woman called Margaret—

Annie stopped reading and sat down heavily. She read the same few words over and over. Then her eyes moved on.

—who I know you would like if you met her. Things are going well and I have decided to stay. I thought long and hard about the children and they are best left where they are in England, with you. I am working in a very nice restaurant which is part of the hotel. In fact, that is where I met Margaret. I am sending some money for you and the children.

I hope you are keeping well. I would like news of Frankie and Harry and a photograph if possible. You can reach me at the above address.

Try not to think too badly of me. We were happy once.

Yours,

Ferguson Percy Bishop

Annie's eyes skimmed to the top of the page but the Sandown Park Hotel meant nothing to her.

Ever since she'd received the letter from Alex telling her he was coming to England, Annie had felt guilty. In her heart she knew he didn't mean it to be merely a social call, but she wouldn't allow herself to think any further. If she wrote to say Alex couldn't come, he'd never get the letter in time. At least, that's what she'd told herself. And anyway, she was still married. She still wore her husband's ring. And what about Alex? Did he have a wife?

Ferguson's letter felt smooth and cold to her fingers as she held it with both hands, but she read it through again, just to make certain she understood the message. Then she slowly put the sheet of paper back in the envelope. She needn't have felt guilty. All the while Ferguson had been with someone else. No wonder she hadn't heard from him for so long. She picked up the dollar notes and counted them. Fifty dollars. It didn't seem much for a marriage.

*

Alex had written again to say he would take a cab to her sister's house. He'd been recommended a small guesthouse which he hoped was not too far away, and as soon as he'd met the landlady and had been shown his room, he would come straight over. Ethel had tactfully taken the children to the park though Annie had begged her to stay.

'I'll meet him soon enough, dearest,' Ethel told her. 'You must see him first on your own.'

Annie didn't know whether to feel relief or fear. Fear that when Alex saw her again he would wonder why he had troubled himself to seek out a servant. Yet when she was with him she wasn't aware of any class difference. Maybe it was because when they'd first met on the *Orsova* and he'd asked for her help, they'd worked as a team.

There was a knock at the door. Her heart pounding out of all control she opened it.

He stood there smiling at her.

'Hello, Annie.'

All the weeks and months dissolved and it was as though they'd seen each other only yesterday. She found herself staring at him, her heart full. She couldn't speak. Self-consciously, she offered him her hand. He caught it and pulled her to him, hugging her before she could protest. Before she could stop herself she was hugging him back. A little breathless, she drew away from him.

'Do you think we'd better go in,' Alex said, his grey eyes sparkling with mischief. 'We don't want the neighbours talking.'

Smiling happily, and flushing a little, she stood aside. He filled the narrow hallway.

'It's wonderful to see you again, Annie.' Alex looked down at her and the warmth was unmistakable. 'I've missed you. And it's wonderful to be in England again.'

'I'm glad to see you too,' Annie said, loving the familiar clean smell of him. 'You came at exactly the right time – just when I was beginning to get homesick for Melbourne.' She smiled up at him. This lovely, lovely man who had encouraged her, helped

315

her, comforted her…and delivered darling Frankie. 'Let me get you a cup of tea. Or do you require something stronger…' she paused, keeping her face straight, 'sir?'

Alex laughed. 'You can stop that nonsense right away. You might have called me "sir" at the Scott-Lawsons but you didn't really mean it. I think that's why I like you.' He paused as he scrutinised her. 'I'm not sure about the new hairstyle.' His grey eyes glinted as he touched the edge, letting his finger brush her cheek. 'Though maybe I could get used to it.' He looked down at her again. 'You know, it *does* suit you.'

'Do you think so – really?' She knew she was behaving like a young girl as her hand automatically went to feel the back of her shingle. 'I'm not sure whether I should have done it.'

She could still feel the sensation of his touch.

'I never saw your hair loose,' Alex said, 'except when you were having Frankie,' he chuckled.

At one time Annie would have blushed at such talk, but now she couldn't help laughing. 'What a long time ago it seems,' she said.

'Well, you certainly don't look the shy girl I first knew. The one who let the contents of her suitcase spill out on Melbourne docklands, just to get my attention.' He darted her an affectionate smile as she opened her mouth to protest. 'You look more confident, but if anything, even younger with your new short hair.'

She turned her head from side to side like a mannequin.

'Yes, I approve,' he laughed, and the surge of joy made her tremble.

Any embarrassment she thought she would feel disappeared. He sat in her father's chair as they drank tea and talked, and it seemed so right to see him there. She listened to his voice, enjoying the sound of his familiar accent, as he gave her all the news of the family at Amber Bay.

'Have you seen Ruby again?' There was only a faint edge to Annie's question.

'Not since that last time. She seemed happy enough with her life, though it's hard to believe she's your sister, she's so different.'

She noticed his eyes darken with concern. 'I'm all right about her now,' she said in a low voice. 'Do you think she's serious about the man she's walking out with?'

'I don't think you could ever be sure with Ruby but I wished her the very best.' He leaned forward, a hand on each knee. 'Tell me about the children.'

'Frankie loves her new school. She doesn't mention her father anymore. She's quieter. I'd like to see her laugh the way she used to. But she's a good girl and adores Harry.'

'And how is Harry the Handful?'

Annie laughed. 'He always wants his own way. I have to be firm with him as he does have temper tantrums. But he's a bright child. He likes repeating long words even though he has no idea of their meaning.'

Alex smiled and she drank in every detail as though for the first time. His thick, dark, wavy hair, the contours of his dear face, the way he really looked at her whenever she spoke, the way he listened so intently to what she had to say.

'It must have been hard for you,' he said, when she told him about Ferguson's sudden decision to go to America. How he'd promised to send for them, though she admitted she wouldn't have gone anyway.

She got up and showed him Ferguson's letter.

He quickly read it, then leaned back in her father's chair. 'What are you going to do now?' he said. 'Spend the next twenty years hoping he'll leave her and come back to you?'

'No, I won't do that,' Annie said firmly. 'I've waited for him too long already. I gave up a year ago when his letters almost stopped. I knew something had happened. He'd either had an accident or was ill...or he'd met someone. I'm glad it's nothing bad. He's still the children's father.'

'Hmm.' Alex sounded unconvinced. 'Give it a year or so and he'll realise what a fool he's been to lose you, and he'll want to come back. Then what will you do? Take him back, I suppose.' He seemed resigned to have answered his own question.

'I don't want to talk about it,' Annie said. Instinct made her add, 'I don't want anything to spoil your visit.'

The weather for once was glorious. They took the children on picnics, to the zoo, and to the playground. This particular afternoon they decided to listen to a band playing music in the park. It was a mix of English folk songs and popular tunes but only fifteen minutes after the musicians had started to play, Harry began to grizzle. Alex looked enquiringly at Annie and she nodded. He picked Harry up and they shuffled from their seats to a few frowns and the clicking of tongues. When the little boy was strapped into his pushchair, Alex guided it with one hand, and tucked Annie's arm through his as Frankie ran ahead.

Was this the time to ask him? She glanced up and he turned and smiled at her.

'You look as though you have something on your mind.'

'Well,' she hesitated. 'It's never been my place to ask—' She felt nervous but decided she had to know before it was too late, although she wasn't sure what it might be too late for. 'I just wondered if—' A flush crept over her cheeks.

'I *was* married,' Alex said.

'How did you know that was what I wanted to ask you?'

'It's natural you'd want to know.' He pressed her hand.

'You said "*was* married".' Annie steeled herself for his reply.

'She died.' His tone was matter-of-fact.

'Oh, Alex, I'm so sorry.' Annie stopped, and anxiously searched his face.

'It was ten years ago.' He smiled as he looked down at her. 'Too long ago to be sad.'

'It doesn't matter how long, it's still sad.' After hesitating, not knowing how she wanted him to answer, Annie asked, 'Have you any children?'

'No. We both wanted them but she had a brain tumour, so by then it was too late.' A shadow passed over his face. 'She was only twenty-four when she died.'

'She was so young,' Annie said, her eyes liquid.

'Yes,' Alex agreed. 'She was a dear girl. You'd have liked her. I'll tell you more about her one day, I promise.' After a few minutes chatting about Melbourne, he smiled at her.

'Shall we go home?' he said.

She nodded, feeling somehow even closer to him.

After only a few days Frankie asked, 'Is Uncle Alex going to stay with us forever?'

'No, darling, he has to go back to Australia, where he lives. But not yet,' she added quickly, seeing Frankie's face drop. 'He's still got lots of time with us.'

'Can we go back to 'Stralia with Uncle Alex?'

'No, darling. You've started your new school. What would your new friends say?'

'I don't care – I hate them. I want to live in 'Stralia again.' She dashed off to find her Uncle Alex.

Annie dreaded to think how Frankie would be when Alex went back, to the point where he became impatient with her for constantly reminding him they didn't have many days left.

'Don't worry about the future,' he said. 'Just enjoy the moment.'

Annie had already resumed her work at Hatherleigh Hall. She'd asked Lady Hamilton if she could go home every evening after supper for the last week, feeling guilty that her employer had immediately agreed. What would Lady Hamilton say if she found out it wasn't Annie's husband who had returned, but some unknown Australian doctor? Where had Annie, the obedient little maid, gone? It was so absurd Annie couldn't help smiling.

Alex had slipped into the habit of collecting her from Hatherleigh Hall in a car he'd hired from the local garage. Normally Ethel and Johnnie would already have eaten, but this last evening they all ate supper together. Eventually, Ethel and Annie cleared the table while the men sat back contentedly in the front room, smoking their pipes, and finishing the rest of the wine Alex had brought.

'He really likes you, Annie,' Ethel had said more than once. And this evening in the kitchen she whispered, 'Can't you see he's in love with you?'

'Nonsense,' Annie said, her heart somersaulting. Although he seemed happy in her company, he'd never mentioned love. It was as though they'd never had those last moments in the surgery just before she'd left Melbourne, when she'd taken Harry to be examined. 'I'm just one of the servants he accidentally got to know a little better, that's all.' She didn't sound very convincing, even to herself. 'And then of course he was very kind when I was expecting Frankie.'

'You weren't in service when you first met him,' Ethel said triumphantly. 'You were a substitute nurse on the ship.'

'Well, I suppose he thinks of me as a friend.' Annie smiled at her sister's expression.

'If that's all you are, then explain why he's come halfway round the world to see you.'

'He doesn't have any family in England, so perhaps he just wanted to see someone he knew. He loves England,' she finished lamely.

Ethel didn't look convinced. 'Are his family all in Australia?'

'Yes, but his mother is Italian. They went out to Australia when Alex was only twelve or so.'

'That explains the black wavy hair,' Ethel laughed. Then she looked serious. 'And you said his wife died?'

'Yes,' Annie said. 'Two years before I met him on the ship. She had a brain tumour and died a few months later. There was nothing anyone could do. I know Alex was devastated.'

'Poor Alex. But it hasn't changed my mind about his feelings for you. You see if I'm not right.' Ethel wiped her hands on the kitchen roller. 'What would you do if he asked you to marry him?'

'Don't be ridiculous, Ethel.' Annie's voice was unusually sharp. 'I'm still married.' She saw the hurt look on her sister's face. 'I'm sorry.' She put her arms round Ethel. 'You've been so good taking care of the children and me, and I'm being horrid to you.'

'You're upset because he goes back tomorrow.'

Lady Hamilton had allowed Annie to have the day off on Alex's last morning provided she worked on her next day off. The children had said their goodbyes. Alex's train was due to leave that afternoon.

He was unusually quiet as they lingered over lunch.

'I don't want to go, Annie,' he said abruptly. His next words came in a rush. 'You know, I've often thought of working in England. What would you think if I did?'

She couldn't speak. The idea was too overwhelming.

'I'm sure I'd find a vacancy in a doctors' practice,' Alex went on. 'My qualifications would transfer.' He got up and walked over to the fireplace. Leaning on the mantelpiece he said, 'You haven't answered my question.'

'I thought you loved Australia,' was all she could manage.

'I do – or rather, *did*. Now I'm not so sure. If you're not there—' He held out his hand to her. 'Annie, come here.'

Slowly, she crossed over to him. He took both her hands in his and raised each one to his lips.

'We didn't really finish our last conversation in Melbourne, did we?'

She trembled, waiting.

'I haven't said anything until now because I didn't want to rush you. I wanted you to be sure. But I want to be with you every moment. You must know that. I want to help you to bring up Frankie

321

and Harry. I want to be a husband to you.' Annie's eyes flew wide. 'Oh, yes, I know you're married,' he went on hurriedly before she could protest, 'but Ferguson isn't even in the same country and he's unlikely to come back. I knew you were special the first time I set eyes on you on the ship. You didn't even hesitate when I asked if you'd be prepared to help me with the smallpox outbreak. But when you bumped into me on purpose at the docks,' he chuckled, 'that's when I fell helplessly in love.'

'I did not bump—'

But Annie didn't get any further. Alex was kissing her softly, drawing both her hands behind his back, and holding her as though he would never let her go. Her mouth tingled the moment she felt his lips touch hers; her head swam and she was floating. Then she gave herself up to him, pressing her lips firmly on his, fiercely kissing him back, holding on to him as though she would sink to her knees if his arms no longer supported her. 'Annie,' he murmured, and kissed her again. This time his kiss became deeper and more stirring, until finally, breathless, she eased away, not taking her eyes off him.

'Oh, Annie, you don't know how many times I've wanted to do that.' His voice was thick. 'And I don't care who knows it and I don't care whether you're married or not, though I would love it if you were married to me. I love you so much.' He kissed her again, and it seemed as though he were reaching to the very core of her.

In a daze she stroked his face, over his cheekbones and along his jawline, marvelling that she was finally allowed to touch him in such a way. Tenderly, she stroked his eyelids and smoothed his eyebrows, then ran her fingertips across his mouth, giving little intakes of breath at how soft it was to her touch...oh, the scent of him...the nearness...it was making her dizzy with longing.

'So what do you think, my darling?' He clasped her hands again in his.

Annie looked down at their hands, her thoughts flying. Was he asking her to live in sin? Would Ferguson give her a divorce?

If so, she would be the talk of the village. No one she knew in the neighbourhood was divorced. And moving in with a man who was not her husband... What Alex was asking was something so shocking, so against all her beliefs...such madness...and yet so wonderful.

She looked into his eyes, full of love, and knew in an instant that she never wanted to let him go. If she did it would tear her heart out.

'Alex...dearest,' she faltered, 'you know what you're asking of me?'

'Yes, I do.'

'And you're willing to risk your reputation...as a doctor?'

'If *you* are. As a married woman it will be worse for you. But by taking the risk we'll be together. We'll be so happy, my darling.'

41

Christmas Day 1922

The candles on the Christmas tree threw their soft light on to the features of the family grouped around her. Annie's glance fell on her sister. What a dear girl she was. At that moment Ethel's attention was riveted to the Moses basket by her side even though the baby was sound asleep. She smiled. Ethel had christened the baby Eleanor, after their mother.

'Can I open another present?' Frankie was hopping up and down on her spindly legs.

'Yes, if you're a good girl and wait your turn.' Annie sent her daughter a loving smile. 'Ethel, for you.' Annie handed her sister a parcel. 'And Johnnie.' She gave him a small packet.

'Here, this one's for you, Frankie, from Uncle Johnnie.'

The child carefully unwrapped the coloured paper and shouted out, 'A paintbox! Oh, thank you, Uncle Johnnie.' She flung her arms round him and kissed him. 'Has Harry got a present?'

'He's a bit too young to open it,' Annie explained.

'I can open it for him. Where is it?' She turned to her small brother, who started to cry.

'He doesn't understand Christmas yet,' Ethel said, picking him up and making soothing noises. 'In fact, I think he'd be far better to have a little nap. Wouldn't you, my love?'

'I'll take him upstairs,' Annie said, but Harry screamed as Ethel handed him over.

'He's tired,' Ethel said tactfully.

Annie threw her a grateful smile.

The child was heavy in her arms as she carried him upstairs. Although he'd been walking for some time he often cried to be carried. The little boy needed a father. Annie tried to picture her husband but the image was foggy. How easily he had substituted one family for another. I won't be bitter, she thought, as she laid Harry in his cot, but she felt the tears gather. Angrily, she brushed them away.

'I want story,' Harry shouted in between the sobs, pushing her away with his little fists.

'Please, Harry,' Annie said, leaning over the cot, desperate to quieten him. 'Mummy will read you a story if you stop crying.'

'Can I help?'

She grabbed the rail of the cot. Held her breath. Slowly straightened up. If she looked round, she might find it was only her imagination running wild.

'Annie?'

A glow spread through her entire body.

Strong, warm arms caught her own and turned her round, pulling her firmly to his chest where she could feel his heart beat loud and fast.

'Alex! You weren't supposed to be here until next—'

He stopped her with his kiss.

'I wanted it to be a surprise,' he laughed. 'Are you pleased?'

'It's the best Christmas present I ever had.' Her eyes flashed with delight as she laughed too.

'Mum-mee,' Harry shouted from his cot. 'Sto-ree.'

With Alex by her side holding one of her hands, Annie sat and read Harry a story about a little boy who was crying because he'd lost his way home. He met a dragon who made his tail into a flaming torch and guided the little boy back to his house where his mummy and daddy were waiting for him with a piece of chocolate cake. But all the while she read to Harry she was conscious of Alex, their shoulders touching, and the warmth of his hand. She knew he was watching her, impatient for her to finish the story, yet dear enough to understand she needed to give Harry her attention for as long as he needed.

'He's fast asleep,' she finally whispered, still not quite believing Alex was really here.

'Good,' he said, but before he took her hand to lead her from the room he bent over the cot and gently kissed Harry on his forehead.

Annie thought she would explode with happiness.

Frankie was overjoyed to see her Uncle Alex again, and even Harry responded, offering him wide grins and begging for stories. Not for the first time did Annie think what a wonderful father Alex would have made. She even told him so one evening.

'*Would* have made?' Alex repeated, sounding a little hurt. 'Oh, Annie, darling, this is not the way I planned, but I intend to be the best substitute father to those children I can possibly be. And one day we might—'

Annie knew he didn't dare finish the sentence.

It only took a few weeks before Frankie began calling Alex 'Daddy', and Harry quickly followed suit. Annie knew Alex was secretly delighted.

The only worry was finding somewhere to live. Even though Ethel had told them to take their time, it was becoming impossible in her parents' old house now Ethel and Johnnie had their baby.

'As soon as I get settled we'll have our own place.' Alex kissed the top of Annie's head. 'We could rent something cheap in the meantime, but I don't think it would be good for the children to have the upheaval of moving twice. So long as Ethel doesn't mind.'

It was taking longer than he'd hoped for Alex to find work, and somehow Annie kept the fear to herself that he'd made a terrible mistake coming to England. Was he having such difficulty because he was Australian? She couldn't bring herself to ask him. He'd managed to fill a locum's vacancy in King's Lynn when that unfortunate doctor had been killed at a railway crossing, but the position was only a temporary arrangement.

Several weeks passed before Alex's luck turned. A doctors' practice in King's Lynn was ready to dissolve because one of the partners was suddenly forced to retire from ill health. The workload was crippling for the remaining doctor, who was frantic to find the right person, and it had only taken an hour's interview and Alex's Australian references to be read before Dr Stanley Linton gave Alex the good news.

Maybe things would now start falling into place, Annie thought, as she put Harry in his pushchair ready for the daily walk to collect Frankie. The sky was gloomy. Probably more rain to come but at least the air was warm. So far they hadn't had much of a spring and it was now early May. She steered the pushchair around an extra large puddle and past the last row of cottages before the road leading to the school, when she stopped so abruptly that Harry pitched forward, his reins tightening.

There in front of her was a 'To Let' sign with an arrow pointing to a red-brick house, set back from the road in its own garden. She could only glimpse its outline as a couple of tall trees masked part of the property, but she habitually glanced up the drive on her way to Frankie's school, wondering who lived there. The same thought always crossed her mind: what a lucky family they must be to own such a house. And now it was to be let. She was sure the sign hadn't been there yesterday. She'd have noticed it.

Heart thumping with excitement, she put the brake on the pushchair, whereupon Harry immediately began to grizzle. Ignoring him for once, she squinted her eyes, trying to gauge the size of the gardens, and making a quick decision, turned the pushchair towards the house. If it was going to be let, surely it wouldn't be unusual for someone to venture up the drive.

Even to her inexperienced eye she could tell the gardens had once been properly planned, though now they were sad and neglected, which probably meant the house was too. But this was the house she'd always dreamed of. It was built like a child's drawing, with a pair of windows top and bottom on each side of a central door.

Flower borders, so full of weeds it was difficult to spot any actual flowers or shrubs, lined the sides of a path which led to the front door. There was no sign of anyone at home, and she was mindful not only of the time, but that she was trespassing. She gazed up. Ivy had been left to creep wherever it wanted and was already as far as one of the upstairs windows. The windows themselves were streaked with dirt.

She looked around her, daydreaming. Her own garden. This one would need a lot of attention and they might have to hire a gardener. That is, if they could afford one.

She mustn't get too excited. But if Alex loved the house too, maybe they could have a dog. She knew he loved animals but they'd never talked about owning a dog. There was still so much to learn about one another. She smiled to herself. They had a lifetime ahead of them.

'Do you like it, Harry?' she said, bending down to the little boy. 'There's a big garden for you to play in.'

'Want to play,' Harry said, his face brightening.

'Well, be a good boy and you shall,' she told him, searching for a piece of paper in her bag to write down the address on the sign.

Whatever would Alex say when she told him? Oh, he must see it before someone else fell in love with it. Smiling with sheer joy at the thought of Alex and the house she was somehow sure would be theirs, barely able to contain herself, she almost ran with the pushchair to the school gates, Harry gurgling with laughter at the new game. Frankie was already waiting for her at the gate, an anxious look on her face.

'I thought you weren't coming, Mummy.'

'I'm only a few minutes late.' Annie bent and kissed her daughter. 'I think I might have found us a new home.'

Frankie hopped up and down. 'A new home, a new home,' she sang. 'We've got a new home.' She looked up at her mother. 'When will we move in?'

'It's not ours yet, darling,' Annie laughed.

But it would be, she was absolutely certain of it.

'I've found a house for us,' she told Alex the minute he walked through the door.

'That's marvellous!' He laughed at her enthusiasm, sweeping her into his arms as he always did when he came in. 'Where is it? What's it like inside? How many bedrooms?'

'So many questions!' She kissed him. 'I've not been inside. Why don't we have a look now, while Ethel's cooking supper? It's only ten minutes away.'

Hand in hand they walked along the lane and down the road, past the row of cottages.

'It's up there,' Annie said excitedly, pointing triumphantly up the short drive. 'You can just see it through the trees.'

'I already like it,' Alex said, eyes gleaming as the house came in view.

'You're not just saying it?'

'You know me better than that. Let's see if there's anyone at home.'

But no one came to the door, no matter how hard they knocked.

'It feels abandoned,' Annie said, frowning. 'I don't know who we can ask to let us in.'

'No one at this time of the evening. We'll have to find out who owns it.'

They walked back down the path and turned right towards the row of cottages.

'Look, there's someone in their garden.' Annie pulled her hand away. 'Excuse me,' she called. The woman was putting her rubbish in the bin and looked round in surprise. 'Do you know if anyone lives at the house for rent?'

The woman shook her head. 'It i'n't been lived in for years.'

'But the notice has only just gone up.'

'That sign's been up and down like a yo-yo. Hooligans from the village keep taking it down and dumping it in the woods. Then the rental people put it back.'

'Who used to live there?' Alex asked.

'A family. One kid. The husband's been gone a couple a year or more,' the woman said, her head bobbing with tightly coiled pipe cleaners. 'He were an alcoholic. So then the wife went to live with her mother, taking the kid with her. But you can speak to the old codger who's got a key. He lives just up the road. The one with the picket fence next to the pub,' she pointed.

'We haven't got time now,' Annie said reluctantly. 'But we'll come back tomorrow.'

'Suit yourself.' The woman nodded to them in a not unfriendly fashion and disappeared indoors.

'Shall I go and ask the man with the key to show me round on my own tomorrow?' Annie took Alex's arm as they walked back to Ethel's house. 'Then at least I'll know if it's right for us.'

'I'd love to come with you,' Alex said, 'but I've got a full day. You go and have a look. But don't be too disappointed if it's in a bad state.'

Annie could hardly sleep that night, with the dream of moving into their house. She mustn't keep thinking of it as 'theirs', she told herself. They didn't know who owned it and anyway, the owner might take a dislike to them. Or her worst fear – he might not agree to a couple renting his house who couldn't produce a marriage certificate. She deliberately put Alex's warning out of her head that it might not be in a fit state.

By ten o'clock the next morning, Annie was outside the house the neighbour had pointed out. The sun shone thinly on the peeling red door of the cottage. She tightened her wool scarf and looked for a bell. There didn't appear to be one. This house, too, seemed deserted. Where was everyone? She used the knocker but no one came. Deliberately lifting the handle of the knocker high so it would make as much noise as possible, she let it slam down again. Then waited for a minute before she did it for the third time. At that, a thick voice, followed by a cough, came from the other side of the door.

'All right, all right, I'm coming.'

The door opened a few inches and an old man put his head round.

'Clear off. I don't want to buy noth—'

'I'm not selling anything,' Annie interrupted. 'I've come to look at the house in Brown Lane. The one at the end with a "To Let" sign. May I see inside?'

'How many are you?' the old boy wheezed, wiping his nose on his sleeve.

'Just my...the two of us, and our two children.'

'Where are they all, then?' He opened the door a little wider and looked beyond her with rheumy eyes. Annie took a step back from the fishy smell of sweat and stale cigarette smoke which enveloped him.

'He's working. He's a doctor. Our daughter's at school, and my sister looks after our son.'

'Hmm.'

'Are you the caretaker?' Annie asked, curious, suddenly wondering if she'd got the right place.

'The caretaker?' He looked astonished. 'Is that what they told thee?'

'Well, one of the neighbours said you had a key and—'

The old man threw back his head and let out a chesty roar. 'The caretaker? Oh, that's ripe, that is.'

Annie was becoming impatient. Either he had the key or he hadn't.

'I was told to come and see you and you'd let me look around.'

'Tha' can go without me.' He shuffled backwards from the door. 'I'll see if I can find the key.'

Annie felt a bit uneasy. Who was this old man? She was just about to give up when she heard the shuffling feet again and he reappeared.

'Here it is.' He handed her a large key, dangling on a piece of grimy string. 'I wish you luck.' He cleared his throat.

'You haven't asked my name,' Annie said, taking the key and stepping back quickly to avoid the stale smell. 'It's Mrs...Townsend.'

'Well, you look honest enough, Mrs Town...whatever it is—' The old man broke off to cough. Annie surreptitiously turned her face away, wishing he had used a handkerchief. 'Just see tha's back here in twenty minutes. Don't be later, mind.'

The key triumphantly in her hand, Annie half ran back along the road, her heart leaping as the house came in sight. As she hastened up the path she noticed a small apple orchard beyond the sprawling overgrown lawn at the side. It looked as though it belonged to the house, and she imagined herself making jam and chutney, and Alex's favourite: apple pie. Her lips curved into a smile at the thought.

She put the key in the lock, breaking several cobwebs as she did so and disturbing two spiders. Although it was a little stiff at first, she felt it turn. She pushed the door but it didn't move. Checking she had definitely unlocked the door she tried again. There was a tiny movement. With her right shoulder hard against the door and her left hand flat on it, she gave it a hefty shove. It opened and she nearly fell inside.

The hall was wide and empty. To the left, at the back, a sturdy staircase wound its way to the upper floor. Conscious of how little time she'd been given she half ran to open the nearest door. She stood there, her eyes widening in disbelief. Someone must have emptied their rubbish bin over the floor. There was no other explanation. Her nose wrinkling at the overriding musty stink of damp mixed with stale tobacco smoke, rotting vegetables, and an unidentified sourness, she warily stepped forward.

Fearing that she might tread on a dead mouse among the debris of papers, cigarette ends, and empty milk bottles, she slowly picked her way through the mess, old newspapers crackling under her shoes. The wall by the window looked the worst. It seemed to be where the damp was coming from. She slid her finger behind the broken seam of a stained piece of striped wallpaper and it began to roll off under her hand; the old paste, long dried, was spotted with mould. The window frames themselves were black with fungus, the sills rotten and the glass filthy, as though there were a heavy fog outside.

She'd seen enough. It wasn't worth looking any further, she thought, sick with disappointment. But just as she was leaving she decided she'd have a peep at the rest of the house. On the other side of the stairs she opened a panelled door to what she presumed would be the dining room. It was not in quite such a state as the front room, and had a pretty Victorian fireplace with a large floor-to-ceiling window to the rear garden, exposing another area of lawn. She pictured the children playing in the fresh air, where she could see them. This room didn't smell of damp but was deathly cold. She shivered and pulled the door behind her.

The house was bigger inside than it appeared. She found a long narrow room, one wall completely glazed, with a door to what was once the kitchen garden. Vases of flowers, their stems in putrid slimy water, were lined up along a wooden bench. She pulled a bunch halfway out of one of the vases and reeled with the stench that erupted.

The kitchen was as large as the front room at home. Annie

looked at the old-fashioned range flanked by various cupboards and shelves. In a flash she could visualise herself cooking meals for her family, the range warming the room; and copper pots, the kind Mrs Jenner used, adorning the shelves; Harry in his high chair, rattling his spoon impatiently on his little table. What must the kitchen have been like when it was new? When there was a family eating and talking and laughing.

Annie peeped into a doorway at the far end of the kitchen. The scullery. The old boiler was still in place and a Belfast sink with wooden drainer stood on the opposite wall underneath a filthy window. Below the sink there were dozens and dozens of empty bottles. She picked one up and wrinkled her nose at the pungent smell of stale beer. She looked down at the linoleum, so encrusted with dirt and stains she couldn't really tell if it was supposed to be brown, or even if there was a pattern underneath.

She knew it was getting late. There'd be no time to look upstairs at the bedrooms. She must have been gone at least twenty minutes and it would take her another five to get back to the old man's house. Just one more door on the ground floor. She peered in.

And reeled back in horror.

Two black eyes gleamed at her.

42

'Tha's been gone more 'an half an hour,' the old man grumbled when a white-faced Annie handed him the key. 'Well?'

'I-I don't think it will suit,' Annie's voice trembled.

'What's wrong with it?' His eyes pierced through her, and when she failed to answer he said, 'All right, I admit it needs a bit of tidying up.'

Annie looked at him, incredulous, not knowing whether to laugh or cry. Did the old man really think it only wanted a tidy up? She thought of her own home which was neat as a pin. Always smelling fresh. But it wasn't her home any longer: it was Ethel's. The house she'd just looked at would have been perfect, even with the work which was needed, except for— Annie shuddered.

'Lost your tongue, has thee?' The old man backed into his hall. He paused and looked her up and down. Seeming satisfied, he said, 'Tha's better come in.'

Annie hesitated. The fetid air which drifted around the old man made her stomach churn but it would seem rude not to take up the invitation. Reluctantly, she followed him inside where he waved her into a small, cramped living room. She looked around in amazement at the hundreds of picture frames and photographs and prints which were leaning against every possible table, chair, cupboard, fireplace and wall.

'Little hobby of mine,' he said, his eyes following hers as though seeing the disorder for the first time. 'Sit ye down,' he told her. 'I shan't bite.'

Flushing, Annie sat on the edge of the nearest armchair, having first to persuade a large ginger cat to make room.

'Would thee care for a cup of tea?' he asked, after he'd already sat down and put his feet up on a footstool. Then he rubbed his feet together, reminding Annie of a fly.

'Oh, no thank you,' she said, not trusting the condition of his kitchen, or his hands. 'I need to do some errands.' She hesitated. 'You said you weren't the caretaker, Mr—'

'So who am I?' he finished. 'I'm the owner, that's what.' He clutched the arms of the chair and leant forward. 'So the house i'n't suitable for your wants?'

He was close enough for her to notice some stiff grey hairs sprouting from his nostrils.

'Not really. It…well…' she trailed off. There was a long silence. The old man waited for her to continue. She gathered her courage, hoping he wouldn't take offence. 'Have you been down there lately, Mr, er, Mr—?'

'Jackson's the name.'

'Mr Jackson.'

'Not for a few months. Haven't got the heart. Is it bad?'

The full horror of what she had seen in the study danced in front of her. The stench was as though someone had tipped raw sewage on the floor. Books which looked as though they had been snatched off the shelves in anger were flung everywhere. Shards of glass from smashed lamps littered the desk or had dropped on the carpet like hailstones. A shattered bottle of what was once whisky was strewn over the hearth. But it was the rats. There were dead rats everywhere. There must have been a dozen or more, some of them the size of small cats. One had had its head bitten off. By another rat? Annie shivered in disgust.

'Rats,' Annie whispered. 'All over the study floor. And I saw a live one. It looked at me as though *I* was the intruder.'

The old man's eyes became misty. 'I couldn't go back in there after they took him away.' He pulled himself up and ambled over to the window. 'I should've got the place cleaned up. I hoped someone would take it on so I wouldn't have to see it again. But no one has shown the slightest interest.' He turned to her. 'I suppose that i'n't surprising if it's as bad as tha' says.'

Who was he talking about? Who had been taken away?

Mr Jackson looked so forlorn Annie wished she was brave enough to say she would take it. Then she thought of the rats and the filth and the general state of the house. No, she couldn't. Alex would think she'd lost her mind.

'The booze got him in the end, see.' Mr Jackson broke through her thoughts.

'I don't understand.'

'Of course tha' don't,' Mr Jackson's voice quavered. 'I'm ashamed to say he was my son.' He put his head in his hands and his shoulders shook, but no sound emanated from him.

'I'm really sorry,' Annie said, feeling sympathetic, but longing to escape into the fresh air.

Mr Jackson pulled his hands away from his face and looked at her, his eyes moist.

'Nothing tha' can do. I'm skint, that's all. Always lending him money. Never getting a penny back. But when it's your own flesh and blood...' He took out a grey, paint-stained piece of material and blew his nose. 'And look at the good it did me. His wife don't want to know, and I never see my granddaughter. But I tell thee something,' a spark of hope leapt into his eyes, 'tha' can have it for five pound a month.' He threw her a sly glance. 'And the first six months at half price. That'd help do it up a bit. Now I can't say fairer than that.'

Five pounds. It sounded a fortune. And it would take goodness knows how much money to make it properly habitable. Besides the state of the study, there was the damp, among other things. Mr

Jackson should be responsible for that but he might not have the money to do it. The house needed decorating from top to bottom. Maybe she could bargain with him. She remembered that day on the *Orsova*. She'd been so upset with Ferguson, and then Adele, when they'd bargained with the stallholders. It hadn't seemed right. But with two children, and Alex only recently finding permanent work… She took a deep breath.

'I don't know,' she said, quite truthfully. 'Five pounds is a lot of money considering the condition it's in.' She was curious to see what his reaction would be.

He shook his head. 'I could do four pounds ten,' he said. 'A bargain, if ever I saw one.'

'My husband would have to see it,' she said, the word 'husband' falling naturally from her lips for the first time.

'Did you see the house, darling?' Alex said, as soon as he had kissed her that evening.

'It wouldn't be right for us,' she said, dishing out the potatoes. They were on their own as Ethel and Johnnie had gone to visit Johnnie's mother who was in hospital.

'I thought we both agreed it would be perfect.'

Annie proceeded to tell Alex about the state of the interior, her face screwing up with the memory when she described the study. To her amazement, Alex threw back his head and roared with laughter.

'Annie, what did you expect? The house hasn't been lived in for years. All nature has probably passed through it at one time or another. We just need the rat catcher. I can assure you after he's been through the house you wouldn't see another one. And to make certain, we'll get a nice hungry cat.'

'It needs a lot of money for the repairs,' Annie said, seriously.

'Did you ask him what the rent is?'

'Five pounds a month. At least that's what he said at first. Then

338

he reduced it to four pounds ten. Not much of a reduction. Oh, and the first six months at half price to help do it up a bit, he said.'

Alex's head shot up. 'We'd never get anything that big that cheap around here. Tell him we'll take it.'

'But you haven't even seen it,' Annie protested.

'I don't need to. I've seen the outside. I've seen the gardens too – a bit overgrown but we can sort that out. We can have a music room and listen to my gramophone records. You'll love them. We might even get a piano. You've often told me about your mother and how well she played, and how much you enjoyed it. Maybe you should learn too.' He ignored her protesting hand waving in front of her face. 'Or one of the children. And there must be at least four bedrooms. Maybe even five. Gives us an excuse to fill them with babies.' His eyes shone. 'Honestly, Annie, it's perfect. We'll make it a wonderful home for us and the children.'

Annie was surprised at the speed Alex organized the repairs of Camellia House. It wasn't the real name, but a beautiful camellia grew near the front door, so that was what Ethel started calling it and the name stuck. Annie advertised for a couple of girls in the village willing to get rid of the mess, assuring them the rat catcher would do his job first. The girls tackled the worst of the cleaning, and Annie and Ethel did the final clean after the decorators had finished.

'So now you have a beautiful home,' Ethel said without a trace of envy as she looked round, admiring their handiwork.

'I couldn't have done it without you,' Annie said, standing the broom in one of the tall cupboards. 'It's been such fun working together. Oh, Ethel, I'm so excited! I'll soon be in my own home. You will come and see me, won't you? Bring Eleanor and when she's old enough she can play in the garden with Frankie and Harry.'

'Of course I'll come, dearest. Just you try and stop me.'

*

339

'Am I causing you any embarrassment, Ethel,' Annie asked her sister as they were taking the children for a walk the day before the move, 'with Alex and me not being married?'

'It's none of anyone's business,' Ethel said quickly.

'I overheard somebody in the greengrocer's talking about a couple who lived in sin.' Annie felt her cheeks grow hot. 'It's such a horrid expression. I suppose that's how they'll talk about *us*.' She hesitated. 'Maybe that's who they *were* talking about.'

'Don't take any notice.' Ethel stopped pushing and scrutinised Annie. 'Does it worry *you*?'

'A little, if I'm honest, but not enough to let him go. Alex would like us to be married but I said I couldn't love him more just because we had a marriage certificate. You *do* like him, don't you, Ethel?'

'I adore him,' Ethel said, laughing. 'After Johnnie, of course. Seriously, why don't you ask Ferguson for a divorce?'

'I have,' Annie said. 'Twice.'

'And?'

'I never get a reply.'

How wonderful to be in their own home, Annie thought, sad though it had been to leave Ethel. Still, her sister wasn't far away. She hung the two pictures of the *Orsova* in the sitting room over her parents' chiffonier, the treasured piece of furniture that Ethel had insisted she take with her to Camellia House. Mr Jackson had done a first-class job of framing the pictures. He'd used gesso and painted the frames a shiny black, just like the ones on board the ship. She smiled. It had been Alex's idea to give him the business.

'You said how short he was of money, Annie. So why don't you let him frame the *Orsova* paintings?'

'You haven't seen his house, or his workroom,' Annie said.

'Let's ask him anyway,' Alex said.

Now she stood quietly for a few moments gazing at them. She did this often, never tiring of looking at the proud passenger steamship riding the stormy seas, or the second picture where the *Orsova* was gliding along in the calm. Somehow it represented all she'd felt ever since that first day when she'd left everything she knew and sailed away to an unknown destination.

Ferguson had wanted to take them with him to America, but in the end he'd decided to travel with only one bag. How very glad she was that he'd left them behind.

Their voyage to Australia. Ferguson had been so enthusiastic at the thought of a new life. Tears pricked her eyes. No, she mustn't dwell on sad memories, Annie told herself. After all, it was on the *Orsova* that she'd met Dr Alexander Townsend. Alex, who loved her and the children. She only hoped Ferguson had found the same happiness.

She smiled. She, too, was sailing in calmer seas now.

43

21st June 1923

Annie opened her eyes barely wide enough to notice the bright light that peeped through the spaces along the top of the flowered curtains in their bedroom, slanting narrow rays of sunshine across the wooden floor. Still sleepy, she turned over in the bed to give Alex a morning kiss, but his side, though still warm, was empty. She ran her hand over the space he had left, imagining she could feel the imprint of him under her fingers.

Flinging back the covers, she pulled on her dressing gown, and put her head round the door of Harry's room. She smiled as she watched his little chest move rhythmically up and down while he slept. It was the only time he was ever quiet. She took the stairs two at a time, and the smell of burning hit her as her foot came off the last tread. She rushed into the kitchen.

'Happy Birthday, Mummy!' Frankie hopped up and down with excitement. 'Daddy's making you a special breakfast, and I'm helping. But he burned the toast.'

'Never mind, darling. We can have bread and butter instead.'

Alex, whistling a tune, turned from the stove and smiled at her over Frankie's fair head.

'Happy Birthday, darling.' He kissed her. 'Go and sit down. It's your turn to be waited on. We'll be there in a moment. Harry's probably still asleep.'

'He was when I looked in just now.' Annie smiled up at

342

him. 'But I'll go and get him.'

It wasn't a whole family without Harry at the table, even though he usually grizzled, wanting all the attention. She lifted him out of his cot, which was getting too small for him, and set his sturdy little body on the linoleum, managing to give him a hug before he thrust her away.

'It's time for breakfast, Harry. Everyone's downstairs waiting for you.'

He wobbled after her to the top of the staircase, turned himself round and crawled backwards down each step, as she anxiously watched him, her heart contracting with love. From nowhere, Ruby's image danced in front of her. Would she be interested? Would she wish she'd kept him? Annie shook herself. Today was her birthday. She mustn't allow any such thoughts.

By the time she'd settled Harry in his special chair, Frankie and Alex between them had set a boiled egg at everyone's place and a plate of bread and butter. Alex appeared carrying a pot of tea and the milk jug, with Frankie in tow holding a bowl of sugar. There were some envelopes with her name on by her placemat.

'Open my card first, Mummy,' Frankie demanded. 'I made it.'

The scene which Frankie had painted showed a family standing outside the front door of their house. The father was tall and dark, the mother was slim, also with dark hair, and a golden-haired girl was holding the hand of a small boy with flaming red hair. Annie stared at it for several moments, tears pricking the back of her eyes.

'It's us, Mummy. Our family.'

'It's beautiful, darling. Absolutely beautiful. I'll always keep it.' She swallowed, and carefully set the card on the mantelpiece, then came back and kissed her daughter. Frankie beamed.

There was a card from Ethel of two horses with their riders trotting down a country lane.

'And you've got one from Melbourne,' Alex said, pointing to

an envelope with an Australian stamp. 'It went to Ethel's.'

'It'll be from Ruby,' Annie said, carefully slitting open the envelope.

But it was from Adele. She hoped Annie would have a wonderful birthday and said that Ruby was well and engaged to a nice man, though quite a few years older. Maybe he'd keep her in line, Adele had ended with an exclamation mark.

Nothing from Ruby. Annie bit her lip. She was grateful that Adele had assured her she was well, but it would have been nice to have heard that from Ruby herself, especially now she was to be married.

She came to the last envelope, fatter than the others, and took out the card showing a picture of a young woman sitting in a deckchair by the sea, reading a book. Two stiff pieces of card fell on to the table. She picked one up. It was a ticket for a Strauss concert to be held at the Royal Albert Hall in London in two weeks' time.

'Oh, Alex, how wonderful, but—'

'No buts,' Alex said firmly. 'Ethel is going to have the children, and I've booked a hotel near the concert hall for a couple of nights. It'll be like a honeymoon. The one we didn't have.' He smiled at her expression and began to sing a snatch from *Die Fledermaus*.

Music was something they both shared. Alex had a fine baritone voice and she loved hearing him sing around the house. If she recognised the song she'd join in. If she didn't, he'd teach her.

'You should have been a professional singer,' she said now, only half teasing.

'You think being a doctor's wife is difficult – try being a singer's.' His lips brushed hers, warm and full of promise, as he rose to his feet, ready to leave for work. 'You'd never see me from one month to the next.'

Alex had begun to call her his wife the day they'd moved into their home. The first time he'd said it she'd given a little start, but now she was used to it. One day, maybe, they really could get married. But she couldn't possibly be any happier than today, her birthday. Whatever the future held, Alex would be by her side.

She and Alex spent two glorious days in London, discovering St Paul's (Annie felt dizzy looking up at the inside of the dome), the National Gallery, where they admired paintings they'd only seen pictures of, and the National Portrait Gallery next door. They marvelled at the exhibits in the British Museum, and lingered at the window displays of several department stores. Annie was amazed at all the stores and their windows, but Selfridges had by far the most astonishing display. A fake pyramid formed the backdrop of a facsimile of Tutankhamen's burial chamber, which had only recently been opened in the Valley of the Kings near Luxor. The boy king of Egypt's funerary mask took centre stage, and golden statues of gods and goddesses, weapons, clothing and boxes of jewels he would need on his journey into the afterlife surrounded him. Garlands of flowers decorated a replica of the chariot he'd died in when he was only nineteen.

It was enough to entice them to step inside. Immediately, they could hear an excited buzz from a dense gathering of men and women, and there, to the left, was a whole section of exotic items, all from Egypt. It was like stepping into Aladdin's cave, Annie thought, as she gazed in awe at the display.

'I'll take you to Cairo one day,' Alex promised, when they'd bought a pair of Egyptian cotton sheets and pillowcases for Ethel and Johnnie as well as themselves. He steered her back through the crowd. 'But in the meantime,' he laughed, 'you'll have to make do with "pretend".'

On their second day Alex took her to a smart little restaurant for lunch. He ordered a bottle of champagne, but as they waited for their food to arrive Annie worried about the expense.

'We can afford it,' he reassured her, 'now I've been made a full partner.' He clinked his glass with hers. 'It's a double celebration.'

'Oh, Alex, that's wonderful news! When did you find out?'

'The day before we came away, but I didn't want it to over-shadow your birthday treat.' Alex took her hand and kissed it. 'So I waited until we came away.'

The concert in the Royal Albert Hall was heaven. Letting the notes wash over her, foot tapping gently, her mind flew back to the evening at Bonham Place, so long ago she felt as though she was a different person then. She remembered how she'd hunched up in the dark passage and strained to hear these same waltzes. Now, here she was, listening to a full orchestra, with Alex's hand warmly holding hers. She glanced at him, smiling at his rapt expression. How lucky she was to have his love. As though she'd spoken the words aloud, and still concentrating on the stage, he squeezed her hand.

'I wouldn't have missed our trip to London and all the things we did for anything in the world,' she told him that night as she snuggled against him in the hotel bed.

'There'll be plenty more,' he said, kissing her. 'I love you so much.'

'I love you too.'

'We must buy a better mattress,' Alex said when they were back in their own bed, facing one another, laughing and talking.

'We've been spoilt,' Annie chuckled, 'staying in such a grand place.'

'I want to spoil you,' Alex said seriously. 'I love giving you presents. You always look so surprised and pleased.'

'I am,' Annie said. 'And you've given me the best present I could ever wish for. One you don't even know about…' She kissed his mouth. 'Darling, we're going to have a baby.'

'Oh, Annie.' His voice was husky as he pulled her into the warmth and security of his arms. Then he held her away to look at her. 'Are you sure?'

'Quite sure.'

As long as she lived, she would never forget the pride and love in Alex's eyes as he began to gently caress her.

Alex worked long hours as a junior partner but he often found time to take the family on days out during the summer, exploring the Norfolk coast. Most Saturdays he took Frankie and Harry to the library where they were allowed to choose their own books, and it was he who taught the children a love of reading. In the winter, on a Sunday, Annie would wrap the children up and Alex would drive them into King's Lynn where they would go to church. Annie told herself they went to King's Lynn because it gave them all an outing as a family, but in her heart she knew it wasn't the real reason. She couldn't bear the looks of disapproval on some of the women's faces in the village church. The way they turned to talk to someone else rather than speak to her, a married woman living in sin.

'I want this baby at home,' Annie said one Sunday morning when they were walking down the road to where Alex had parked. Frankie was skipping ahead and Harry was asleep in his pushchair. 'And I want *you* to deliver it.' Her dark eyes were mischievous as she looked up at him. 'Do you think you can?'

'I'd be honoured, madam,' Alex teased her back. 'But I'd better do some revision. It's been at least a couple of days since I delivered a baby.'

A fortnight later, at five o'clock on 23rd December, Katherine Alexandra Townsend spent her first evening at Camellia House.

Frankie adored Kitty from the moment she was born. The child insisted upon helping her mother with everything to do with her brand-new sister, even changing nappies. It made Annie smile to see Frankie wrinkling her nose as her small hands carefully gathered the edges of the soiled cloth together and dumped it in the waiting bucket.

Harry was deeply skeptical of the new baby. He ignored her for the first few weeks, but eventually he, too, was captivated when Kitty fixed her large eyes on him and smiled at him for the first time.

44

September 1924

Much later, when Annie thought about it, she might have known her peace and contentment couldn't last. She'd been so busy that year with the children, especially with Kitty, who was more than a match for Harry, the way she craved attention the whole time, captivating all who came within her range. Annie smiled to herself. Kitty was a charmer and such a joyful baby, and Alex was besotted with her.

The house was taking shape and most of the rooms were decorated. In between times she and Alex spent hours wandering round junk shops and antique shops, often putting a deposit down on a table or a set of chairs or a rug. Alex's trunks which they thought had been lost forever had finally arrived from Melbourne, and excitedly they unpacked his books, a few watercolours, and his precious gramophone and collection of records.

She regularly visited Ferguson's mother and father. The first time she had only taken Frankie and Harry to see them. It had brought a lump to her throat, seeing the frail couple sitting in the front room of their little cottage, the same room where her and Ferguson's wedding lunch had been held. They didn't deserve the anguish Ferguson had caused them. He only wrote to them occasionally, they told her, and she could tell they were heartbroken that their son was so far away and had left his family behind, then met another woman.

On the second visit she decided to pluck up the courage to tell them about Alex. Yes, they'd heard plenty of village gossip, but she needed to tell them herself. It wasn't as painful as she'd feared, and they begged her to bring Kitty to see them, which she did on the following visit.

Her family was all she had ever dreamed of, and Alex was the husband she realised she'd never really found in Ferguson. In the early days when Ferguson had left for America, she'd often wondered if it was possible to truly know anyone, even if that person happened to be your husband. Sometimes she'd even felt guilty she'd been so emphatic in telling him she would not be following him to America. It was only when Alex found her that she'd understood for the first time how important it was to be true to herself. To stop making excuses. To follow her heart.

The longer she lived with Alex the more beloved he became, and if she thought of Ferguson – usually only when Frankie or Harry did or said something which reminded her of him – it was always with sadness that he had so lightly given up his family. What a naïve young woman she'd been, putting aside her own life while she devoted herself to the whims and wishes of her husband.

Alex never put her in such a position. Instead, he encouraged her ideas for the garden and was proud of her new sewing skills. He helped whenever he could with the older children so Annie could conserve her energy for Kitty who woke her every night, demanding to be fed. If only she and Alex could marry, but Ferguson had refused to divorce her, and she hadn't heard from him in over a year. Maybe one day Margaret would persuade him to get a divorce. Annie hung on to that hope.

That afternoon, when she'd finished earlier at Hatherleigh Hall, she dropped Kitty off at Ethel's so she could go to a sewing class in one of the women's houses in the village. Such heaven to spend two hours talking to mothers about their little ones, and cutting out material for a new coat for Harry.

On the way home she'd called in to the grocer's and the chemist, leaving herself plenty of time to do some ironing before Frankie came home from school. Planning what she was going to cook for supper, she hadn't taken any notice of the heavy-set man with the brim of his hat pulled firmly over his face, standing idly by the last gate of the terrace. As she put her key in the door, a voice from behind made her start.

'Hello, Annie.'

Her hand froze on the key.

Annie whirled round and gasped. She hardly recognised him, and not just because he was wearing glasses. He wore a smart light suit of which his flesh seemed to occupy every inch. The jacket buttons puckered over his chest and stomach. He made a move towards her and she saw the beginnings of a jowl.

'Aren't you going to invite me in, then?'

'Ferguson! You gave me a fright. What on earth are you doing here?' Her heart pounded as she looked at him, trying to think what this meant. What she should do. What she should say.

'I've come to see you, of course.' His tone was gentle, reasonable.

'I haven't heard from you all year.' She glared at him. 'You never replied to the last letter I sent. And now you suddenly appear.'

'Give me a chance, Annie.' Ferguson held up his hand in defence. 'Once I decided to come back I thought I'd be here before you got any letter from me. So here I am. Aren't you pleased to see me?'

Thank goodness Alex wouldn't be home for an hour or more, and that Harry and Kitty were with Ethel. But Frankie would soon be home from school. She pictured her daughter telling her about her lessons. It would be a terrible shock for her to suddenly come face to face with her father, whom she hadn't set eyes on for three years. As for Harry, he'd only been a baby when Ferguson had taken himself off to America.

'How did you find my address?' she demanded.

'I went to your mum and dad's old house to find Ethel. But she wouldn't tell me anything.'

Dear Ethel.

'I told her I'd come to see my children, but she pretended she knew nothing. Wouldn't even let me in.'

So he hasn't seen Kitty.

'One of your old neighbours spilled the beans,' Ferguson went on. 'She knew where you'd gone.'

He made it sound as though she had committed a crime. And if they stayed on the doorstep any longer there'd be more gossip. Reluctantly, she turned the key fully, opened the door and stepped inside. She turned her head round.

'You'd better come in,' she said, and closed the door behind him. She led him into the front room.

'This is nice, Annie.' Ferguson sat himself in the chair she thought of as Alex's and looked around. 'Very nice indeed. Looks like you've come up in the world.'

She was thankful the one framed photograph she had of Alex was safely in their bedroom on the mantelpiece. Still, it wouldn't take much for him to see that there was a man around. She noticed Alex had left his slippers under the very chair Ferguson sat in now. Well, it was too late. She had no chance to think up any kind of excuse. And besides, it wasn't in her nature. She must tell him the truth and take the consequences.

'It must be quite a penny to rent,' Ferguson went on. 'How do you manage it?'

Not with any help from you, she wanted to say, but she merely said, 'I work.'

'Why don't you sit down?' Ferguson said, smiling at her.

'I've got some ironing to do.' She didn't move.

'You can surely put it off.'

'I can't. That's how I've planned my afternoon.'

'I don't know. Ironing.' Ferguson gave a snort of laughter.

'You'd think there were more important things to do besides ironing. After all, it isn't every day your husband comes home from America.'

'And it isn't every day your husband leaves you and his children to *go* to America,' she retorted.

'I always meant for you and the children to follow.'

It was pointless to argue.

'So you're working.' He looked up at her. 'Where did you find employment?'

'Hatherleigh Hall.' Her eyes gleamed in defiance.

'Hatherleigh Hall?' he spluttered, half rising from the chair. 'How *could* you, Annie? You, of all people, be so disloyal.'

'Disloyal to whom, Ferguson?' Annie's voice was dangerously quiet.

'Why, me, of course.'

'That's a little ripe, coming from you.'

He had the grace to lower his gaze. 'What I meant was—'

'It was quite easy when it came to whether the children got fed or not,' Annie interrupted testily. 'You'd stopped my allowance for the children by then. Food doesn't appear out of thin air, you know.'

'But of all places,' – Ferguson wasn't going to let it drop – 'you didn't need to go there. Whatever did Lord and Lady Hamilton say? What did you tell them about me?'

'I told Lady Hamilton you'd gone to America. Nothing more. She needed a cook. That was all she was interested in.'

'I'll never be able to hold my head up in the village,' Ferguson said with feeling.

'Why would you want to? Your home is in America now... with Margaret. Or I presume it's still Margaret.' Annie watched Ferguson as he shifted in Alex's chair. She noticed a faint sheen of perspiration on his forehead.

'Where's Frankie?' he asked, deftly changing the subject.

'She'll be home from school soon.'

I'm not ready for this.

'I expect she'll be surprised to see me.' Ferguson gave a nervous laugh as he began to tap his fingers on the arm of the chair. She noticed how the material of his trousers stretched tightly over his heavy thighs. 'But she'll like the presents I've got for her.' He nodded to the large brown paper bag by his side. 'And two for Harry.' He hesitated, not quite looking Annie in the eye. 'He must be four by now, is he?'

'Nearly,' Annie said woodenly.

Is that what he thought? That he could buy back their love with presents? All he'd ever managed to do was send them a birthday card with the same message: he hoped they were well and that Frankie was being a good girl and looking after her mother. Sometimes he hadn't even managed that.

She heard the click of the front door.

'That will be Frankie now,' she said, a sick feeling starting in the pit of her stomach.

But she was wrong.

'Darling,' Alex called, as she heard the front door close behind him. 'I've got some—' he stopped dead at the doorway. 'Oh, I see you have a visitor.' His animated expression fell away. He caught Annie's eye and raised an eyebrow.

She gave a faint shake of her head, her heart beating heavily, her nerves twitching. She noticed Ferguson's knuckles tighten on the arms of Alex's chair.

'Do you remember Ferguson, Alex?' Annie desperately tried to make her voice sound natural. 'You met him once on the *Orsova*.'

'Of course. The only passenger who never came up for air, even when the smallpox quarantine was over.' Alex's tone was deliberately mild as he strode into the room. He looked down at Ferguson, frowning, then turned to Annie. 'What's going on?'

'I'm not sure.' She looked at him, her eyes silently begging him

353

not to start a quarrel with Ferguson. 'I was as surprised as you to see him.'

Alex swung round to face Ferguson. 'So what the hell are you doing here?'

Ferguson flushed with annoyance. 'Well, well, well. If it isn't Dr Townsend. Friend of the Scott-Lawsons, too, if I'm not mistaken. What a surprise. And what a cosy little hideaway for *my wife.*'

It was Annie's turn to flush. This was a nightmare. Maybe if she said her nine times table she would wake up and laugh at such a ludicrous situation. But it was real. And she didn't feel like laughing.

'Get the hell out,' Alex said, towering over the chair, his arm half raised over Ferguson.

'Please, Alex—' Annie watched with dread as the two men's faces contorted in anger. She'd seen Ferguson lose his temper plenty of times, but had never seen Alex so furious.

'No need to threaten me,' Ferguson said, his head back, his light-blue eyes fixed on Alex with a steely glint. '*I'm* not the one at fault here. I just want to speak to Annie on my own. I haven't come to cause her any trouble.'

'You're not bloody going to,' Alex said, dropping his arm. He shifted one of the wooden chairs into Ferguson's line of vision, and sat on it. 'So say what you've come to say and then leave.'

'Annie, I want to talk to you alone,' Ferguson repeated. He began to tap on the sides of the armchair. She knew the sign: he might be nervous but he was determined to have his own way.

'There's nothing to discuss that can't be said in front of Alex,' she said firmly.

'What I was going to say to you is none of Townsend's business.' Ferguson looked at her intently. 'I presume you're living in sin with him, Annie?'

Alex shot out of his chair and took a step forward, but Annie held out her arm.

'I wouldn't be "living in sin" as you call it if you'd agreed to a divorce,' she said. 'Alex and I would be married by now.'

Ferguson opened his mouth to speak but Annie stopped him with the flat of her hand.

'No, Ferguson. Listen to me. You've been gone for three years now, and I haven't heard from you for over a year. You wrote and told me you'd met another woman – Margaret – and that you thought it best I remain here with the children. And since that last fifty dollars, I've had nothing from you to support them. Yet you won't agree to a divorce.'

'I don't want a divorce.'

'I would have thought Margaret would want to be made an honest woman of,' Annie said tartly.

'Well, it's a bit more complicated than that,' Ferguson frowned, 'but I don't want to talk about Margaret. I want to talk about *you*, Annie. So would you mind leaving us on our own, Dr Townsend?'

'You can't come here and order Alex around—' Annie broke off, losing patience. 'You didn't want me and you don't want me to have anyone else. Even though you've got Margaret. You're like a dog in the manger.'

'My relationship with Margaret isn't serious,' Ferguson said. 'I don't love her the way I do you. And you're still my wife. I didn't have to marry you, you know, to go to Australia. But I did. To prove how much I loved you.'

'What are you talking about?' Annie flashed. 'We had to get married to get the permit.'

'No. It's what I told you and your dad. He'd never have let you come with me if you weren't my wife.'

Annie looked hard at him and he dropped his eyes away.

'You lied to me,' she said. 'That was the first lie. And it wasn't the last, was it?'

Ferguson's face flushed crimson. 'I love you. That's why I did it. So you'd be safe with me.'

The trouble was, Annie thought, Ferguson really believed what he was saying.

'You've always had a fine way of showing it.' Alex's mouth hardened. 'Right from the moment you left Annie to struggle with a heavy suitcase when you first arrived in Melbourne. Not exactly the thoughtful, loving husband.'

'And you're so considerate, are you?' Ferguson half rose, the blood rushing to his cheeks. 'You don't mind everyone yacking about Annie because she's living in sin? Everyone in the village knows I'm her husband. Most of them came to the wedding. Even if you don't worry about *your* reputation as a doctor, you should think about *hers*.'

'You've said enough.' Alex was out of his chair and had grabbed Ferguson's arms. 'Get out! We don't want to set eyes on you again. Which should be easy – your home is in America.'

'Take your hands off me.' Ferguson glowered, beads of sweat gathering above his top lip like a watery moustache. 'I can get up without any help from you.'

Alex let him go and Ferguson hauled himself out of the chair. 'Annie, we *must* talk.'

'I really don't have anything to say to you,' she said, not wishing to be unkind, but losing patience. 'I'm happy now and I hope you will be, too, someday.'

'Annie, please—'

'Come on, Bishop,' Alex said, pushing Ferguson towards the door. 'I've had enough of listening to this drivel.'

'You can't stop me seeing my children!' Ferguson shouted, twisting his neck round to Annie.

'Since when have you claimed Harry as your child?' she heard Alex demand as he opened the front door.

Annie closed her eyes, willing her heart to stop pounding. The front door slammed shut. She heard Alex go into the kitchen and fill the kettle. She wanted to follow him but it was as though she was rooted in her chair. Closing her eyes and leaning back she took some deep breaths. She listened to the normal sounds of cups and saucers being rinsed but things were no longer normal. She sat numbly, waiting for Alex to come back into the room.

He soon appeared, carrying a tea tray, his expression weary.

'Oh, Alex.' Annie jumped up and threw her arms round him. 'I couldn't believe it when I saw him. I'd just come back from the shop and there he was.'

'Don't worry, darling.' He put his hand on her back, holding her close and stroking her hair. 'He can't do anything to harm us. He's all talk and no action.'

'But what he said...about your reputation. That was horrible.'

'He's no threat. Believe me, doctors aren't always whiter than white. We're human. I'm not worried at all. And I don't want you to be.' He tilted her chin. 'Promise me.'

'I promise. But—'

'No buts. He'll soon realise he's on a lost cause and go back to New York.'

'I don't think he'll give up that easily,' Annie said, sitting down and gulping her tea. 'He's come to see the children, and he won't rest until he does. And I don't see how I can stop him. He's their father, after all, however much he's always denied being Harry's.'

'Well, the one child he's *not* going to see is Kitty,' Alex said firmly.

45

Every time Annie walked out with Kitty in Harry's old perambulator she was worried fate would make sure she bumped into Ferguson. She got into the habit of glancing up and down the road whenever she left Camellia House, and nervously looked in every shop window before she went in.

She had no idea how long he was staying, or if he was even planning to go back to New York at all. Surely he was. After all, he'd made a life there. Couldn't he see that she'd also chosen a new life? She bit her lip in annoyance. Ferguson was used to getting his own way and she felt on edge, expecting the unexpected at any moment.

Ferguson wrote to her every day from his parent's cottage, begging to see the children, and later threatening he would go to the school and meet Frankie. The very thing she'd dreaded.

She grappled with her guilt and anger, but in the end he wore her down. She wrote and told him he could meet them in the park on Wednesday afternoon at four o'clock.

'We're going to see your father this afternoon,' Annie said, as she was about to leave Frankie at the school gate that morning.

'My father? What, from New York? I don't want to see him.' She looked at her mother with anxious eyes; the same blue as her grandmother's, Annie thought. 'We're happy as we are, aren't we, Mummy?'

'Of course we are, darling, but your father would like to see you and Harry. He's only here for a short time. Will you do that for me?'

Frankie fiddled with the straps of her school bag, then dropped it on the ground. Annie knew her daughter was turning this unwelcome announcement over and over in her mind, this way and that, stalling for time, averting her eyes.

'But I love Alex.' Frankie finally looked up. 'I always think of him as my real dad.'

'Of course you do, and he loves you, but your father loves you as well. It's just that some people can't always show it.'

'Well, you see him if you want,' Frankie said, a determined look to her chin, 'but count me out. I'll go straight to Aunt Ethel's and wait for you there.'

'That's not what I expect from you, Frankie,' Annie said. 'Your father wants to see you before he goes back to America. It might be a long time before you see him again. Maybe years. And he'd be very upset if you didn't go.'

'Why? He never writes to us. Why does he want to see us now?'

'Because he asked me. And because I promised I'd bring you and Harry to say hello to him in the park. I can't break my word. We'll only be half an hour. Please, Frankie—'

'No.' Frankie raised her voice as she snatched up her school bag. 'And I'm surprised you thought it was a good idea.'

Really, Frankie was becoming impossible. Annie sighed. Maybe Frankie was right. Maybe it would have been best not to let Ferguson see the children. It was only going to upset everyone. But it was too late. She'd already agreed.

Without kissing her goodbye, Frankie sped off towards the school entrance.

'Frankie's become so difficult, Ethel. She refuses to see Ferguson.'

'I can't say I blame her,' Ethel said, settling Eleanor on her special blanket with her teddy bear. 'Ferguson's got a nerve. Trouble is, when all's said and done, he *is* their father.' She thought for a minute, then said, 'What about if I meet Frankie this afternoon and tell her we'll have a walk in the park, and if when we get there she feels unhappy in any way, I'll bring her back to mine?'

'I think that's a good idea,' Annie said gratefully. 'She always takes more notice of you.'

'What about Kitty?' Ethel asked.

'Alex hasn't got to work until this evening's surgery so he'll look after her.'

Annie dreaded another meeting with Ferguson, but at least in an hour's time it would be over.

'Come on, Harry, eat up your bread and butter.'

'Don't want to.'

His sudden sneeze made her jump.

'Oh, Harry, you're getting a cold,' she said, dabbing his dribbling nose and wiping his eyes with her handkerchief. 'Poor little chap. No wonder you're so miserable. Maybe I should keep you in the warm today.'

'No!' Harry bellowed. 'I want to go to the park.'

He began to cry. Annie felt helpless. He really ought to stay home and yet she'd promised Ferguson. Maybe the fresh air would do him good.

'All right,' she said. 'But we're not going until you've finished your tea.'

Ridiculously, she'd wanted the children to be on their best behaviour for their father, but what with Frankie's outburst this morning and Harry starting a cold which was making him fractious, Ferguson might pretend he hadn't seen them and slink away. Even though her stomach was churning with anxiety and frustration, she couldn't help feeling sad.

When she and Harry arrived at the park it was a few minutes to four. The day had been pleasantly warm and sunny but now the

360

clouds were beginning to form and it had gone dull. Annie glanced around her but there was no sign of Ferguson. Somehow she'd thought he'd be here early. There was only a handful of children and their mothers but in another quarter of an hour the place would be teeming. She spotted Ethel and Frankie in the distance; her daughter was pushing Eleanor in her pushchair, and they were both squealing with laughter.

Annie waved to her sister and settled herself on a bench. Harry immediately snatched his hand away and ran over to the swings.

'Auntie Ethel, will you push me on the swing?'

Ethel smiled at the child and lifted him on to the wooden seat, giving him a strong push.

'Harder!' Harry shouted. 'Push me harder!'

Annie kept her eye on the park entrance, expecting to see Ferguson appear at any moment. It was quarter past four. At first she didn't take much notice; he was often late. But as the minutes crept by she began to wonder if he was coming. Yet he'd insisted on this meeting so it was strange he wasn't here for something he'd said was so important.

'I think you should take Harry home,' Ethel said, when she brought him back a few minutes later. Frankie was keeping well back, restraining Eleanor, who was trying to climb out of her pushchair. 'He's been sneezing and you don't want him getting worse.'

'I know,' Annie said worriedly, looking up at the sky. 'I'll give him another ten minutes, just in case something's happened. Then we'll go.'

After a few more minutes Annie jumped up from the bench. 'I can't keep Harry out here any longer,' she told her sister. 'He's obviously not coming so we'll go home.'

'I told you he didn't bother about us,' Frankie said.

The postman delivered a letter postmarked New York exactly two months later.

My dear Annie,

In the end I decided not to come, though I wanted to see Frankie and Harry very much. I thought about everything for a long time. You are with someone else now and if he makes you more happy than I did, I decided it would be wrong to upset things when I know you have not had it easy these last years.

Tell Frankie and Harry I do love them and miss them and hope that one day, when they're older and more understanding, I will be able to visit them. Maybe they will also come and see me wherever I am. I hope so.

At least I saw Ma and Pa, so it wasn't a completely wasted journey.

Please forgive me, Annie, and I hope you will always be happy. You deserve it.

Yours,

Ferguson Percy Bishop

Annie let out a long breath of relief as she reread the letter. She put it back into the envelope and tucked it in one of the drawers of her chiffonier. No matter what had happened in the past, he wasn't really a bad man.

46

Christmas Eve 1926

Living with Alex seemed the most natural thing in the world to Annie as she laid a special supper table for their 'fourth anniversary', just one day after Kitty's third birthday, and the day before Ethel and Johnnie and Eleanor would walk over for Christmas lunch.

It would have been easier if they had moved to another village or town to escape wagging tongues, Annie thought, as she set out the knives and forks, and two wine glasses. They'd seriously considered moving to King's Lynn to be closer to Alex's surgery, but somehow living in a town didn't have the appeal of Annie's village. Also, Ethel lived nearby and was there to look after Kitty and meet Harry from school when Annie was working at Hatherleigh Hall. But the main reason for not moving was that she and Alex both loved Camellia House.

'Happy Anniversary, my dearest.' Alex kissed her and slipped off his coat. He sank into his armchair with a sigh.

She thought how worn he looked; his irregular features were more stark, and his grey eyes had lost some of their sparkle.

'You're working too hard,' she said.

'That's the penalty for being a doctor,' Alex smiled. 'Though I must say, I do feel tired this evening.'

'You haven't had any time off for over a year,' Annie reminded him. 'Can you ask for a few days?'

'Not at the moment. We're seeing more and more patients every day.' He turned his head and coughed.

'That sounds nasty,' Annie said, anxiety creeping into her voice. 'Do you think you ought to see a doctor?'

Alex laughed. 'Already lost your faith in *me* as a doctor, have you? Don't worry – it's only a bit of a cold.'

After supper, when Harry and Kitty were in bed and Frankie was in her room doing her homework, the two of them sat opposite each other in their armchairs, perfectly content. Annie studied him. There was something on his mind, she was sure of it, the way he kept patting his pocket and smiling. She was just about to say something when he reached in his pocket and pulled out an official brown envelope.

'I've got something for you to read.'

She looked curiously at the address. Although it was marked 'Private' it had been sent to Alex's surgery. She pulled out the folded sheets of paper from the already slit edge of the envelope, and smoothed them fully out on her lap. She picked up the first page, her eyes scanning the typed paragraphs. The words 'Camellia House' leapt out at her but she couldn't take in what it was about. Surely the rent wasn't going to increase. She picked up the second page, then looked up, her eyes shining.

'Alex, is this what I think it is?'

'Well, I've bought the house if that's what you mean,' he said.

'Are you sure we can afford it?'

'Perfectly sure,' he grinned. 'Are you pleased?'

'*Pleased?*' She jumped up, the papers still in her hand, and flew to him. He laughed and sat her on his knee. 'I can't believe it. I must be the happiest woman in the world.'

'I thought that was because you live with me,' his grey eyes gleamed, 'not because you're now a woman of property.'

'What do you mean?'

'Read the name at the end of the last page,' Alex chuckled.

'Annie Elizabeth Bishop.' She looked at him, puzzled. 'Where's your name?'

'It's not on there. I've put it in your name only.'

'I don't understand.'

'Because we're not officially married, my darling.' He stroked her hair. 'I wanted you to feel secure. You're my family, and this will be the children's inheritance.'

She grasped him round his neck and kissed his cheek. 'You're my chosen husband in every way. The best thing that ever happened to me. I love you. And I'm not just saying it because you've given me the house,' she added mischievously.

He laughed and turned her face to his with the tip of his finger. 'You'd better prove that to me,' he said. Before she could answer he bent his head. His kiss was deep and warm with love.

47

Alex, April 1927

He knew it was wrong not to tell her; not to share his anger, his fear, his sense of letting her down completely. But where would he start? Every time he looked at her and saw the love glowing in those dark eyes, her lips curving into a smile the moment he appeared, the warmth of her snuggled up against him in their bed, the sweet damp smell of her after they had loved one another – how could he pick the right time? No, he would wait a little longer. Let her think all was well for as long as he could. Until he could no longer hide it from her.

Yesterday's conversation with his partner had been grim.

'I'm sorry, old boy, but the results are in, and I'm afraid it's bad news.'

Alex tried to brace himself, knowing what was coming, but dreading it being confirmed.

Stanley held up the X-ray photograph against the light and Alex narrowed his eyes. There was an undeniable shadow on one of his lungs. So his guess had been right. At the moment it didn't look much bigger than a halfpenny, but he knew from experience that it wouldn't go away, that it would grow bigger. How rapidly, it would be difficult to judge. Still, he had to ask the question.

'Is there any new treatment I haven't heard about?'

'Only the gold treatment. And it's so toxic I'd be loath to recommend it. I think it does more harm than good.' He looked intently at Alex. 'No, your best bet is to take the air. Switzerland – if you can afford it. That might give you a bit longer.'

'How long do you think I've got?' Alex tried to keep his tone nonchalant but inside his heart was beating wildly.

'As you well know, we can never be sure.' Stanley hesitated. Alex nodded for him to continue. 'A year. Maybe two.'

Alex briefly squeezed his eyes shut. It didn't seem fair. He and Annie had only had four years together. She was his love, his life.

It was as though he'd been punched in the gut to have it confirmed by another doctor. He remembered the last time, not so long ago, he himself had diagnosed tuberculosis in a woman. He could see her now, her face red and distorted with coughing, tears streaming down. But she was old – well into her seventies. He should have had another thirty years, for God's sake. He opened his eyes and looked at Stanley's worried face. He mustn't break down. And the quicker he came to terms with it, the better prepared he'd be to help Annie. His eyes moistened and he blinked back the tears. Thank God she would never be without a roof over her head. No one could take away her home. That, at least, was some comfort.

With a racing pulse, he visualised her on her own again, but this time with the responsibility of three children. Dearest Frankie, impossible Harry, and his own darling Kitty. He would never see her grow up, get married, and have her own family. He tried to shake himself out of the maudlin thought. This was not the way to plan his remaining precious time. He needed to concentrate on how best he could make their paths as smooth as possible.

'It's particularly bad luck at only forty-two,' Stanley said. 'You should be in your prime.' He glanced at Alex. 'But you need to plan.' He walked over to the window and stared out, his back to Alex. 'Dammit! We've got the best practice in town.' He swung round. 'You're a damn good doctor, you know. I'm going to miss you. Don't know how I'll replace you,' he added gruffly.

'Someone will come along,' Alex said, the words almost sticking in his throat. He didn't want to think of someone else doing the job he loved and having a joke with Stanley. But his working days were numbered. No one would want to be looked after by a doctor with tuberculosis. Suddenly attacked with a coughing spasm, he felt for his handkerchief, covering his mouth with the piece of cloth until it subsided. Thank God there was no blood – yet. He folded it up and put it back in his pocket. If only he felt as calm inside as he was forcing himself to appear.

Pulling himself back into the moment Alex made a decision. He'd take Annie away, and the sooner the better. If they could just have one last holiday together. Maybe stay at a bed and breakfast by the sea for a few days. He'd ask Stanley if he could be spared. He'd also have a word with Ethel. He might even tell Ethel the truth, so she would understand he wasn't taking advantage of her kindness in always offering to look after the children.

He'd explain to Annie why he hadn't said anything before, and most importantly, it would give them a chance to live that week for each other, before they faced their short future together.

'Of course, old boy,' Stanley said immediately. 'Shame it's not summer. Warm weather is what you need. Take a fortnight.'

'No, a week's enough, thanks,' Alex said, sinking into the armchair. 'I've got my patients. I don't know what the standard practice is but I want to tell them…before it gets any worse.'

'How's Annie taken it?'

'I haven't told her yet.' Alex rubbed his eyes. 'I will do…when we're away.'

He told her on their last day by the sea. She wanted to go to Hunstanton, where her father used to take her and her sisters after their mother died. She told him how the rhythm of the waves always had a calming effect on her.

'Until we had a full-blown storm on the *Orsova*,' she said, pulling a face. 'Right before you begged me to help you with the smallpox outbreak. I might have known you had an ulterior motive.'

Her eyes danced with mischief and he couldn't help smiling though his heart felt as though a rubber band was binding it tight.

'You fell for it though, didn't you?' he managed.

She laughed. 'I know you need a holiday, Alex, but why not wait until June or July when the weather's better?'

'No, I don't want to wait. We need some time on our own.'

She looked at him with a hint of suspicion in her dark eyes, but didn't say anything.

This week had been an exception. Much warmer than usual for May, the sea flowed and ebbed with its soft furls of sea-horses. He'd booked them into a bed and breakfast, paying extra for the sea view, and they had spent an idyllic week together. Until this morning. The moment he was dreading.

'Annie—'

'I haven't eaten such a big breakfast in a long time,' she said with a satisfied sigh, neatly putting her knife and fork together, and leaning back in her chair. The landlady had brought them kippers followed by soft-boiled eggs and bread and butter, and a large pot of tea, but Alex had only managed to swallow a few mouthfuls. He glanced around the dining room and thanked God they were alone. It was late and everyone had already eaten and left. He'd delayed coming down to breakfast this morning so he could spend the very last hour of their holiday with his arms wrapped around her in bed as she slept. She'd laughingly berated him for letting her sleep so late, and he'd been pathetically grateful she hadn't heard his early-morning coughing fit.

Now, as they sat on hard upright chairs in Mrs Martin's cosy little dining room, she was smiling. He thought he had never seen her look so beautiful.

'What shall we do today, darling?' she said, then caught sight of his plate. She frowned. 'Are you all right? You've hardly touched anything.'

'It's nothing.'

'That cough seems to be hanging about.' She stared at him, her eyes suddenly wide and luminous. 'Alex, what's the matter?'

'If you've finished, let's go upstairs to our room.'

Without another word, Annie gathered her cardigan and bag and Alex followed her up the narrow staircase.

'Please tell me what's going on,' Annie said, as he locked the door. 'Tell me, no matter how horrible. I want to know.'

'Come and sit on the bed.' Alex patted the bedspread. Slowly, Annie moved across the room and sat down next to him. He took both her hands in his and kissed the palms.

'Annie, you've got to be brave,' he said. 'I've been talking to Stanley.'

'Stanley? What about? Are you ill? Is it your cough?'

'Yes, it's the cough,' he said, holding her hands tight. 'It's not going to go away.'

'Maybe it's bronchitis. A bad chest infection.' She caught her bottom lip with her teeth. He could see she was grasping for anything but the truth she knew he was about to spring on her.

'I wish that's all it was, my darling. But it's tuberculosis.'

'Oh, dear God, Alex, no!' Annie cried out. He saw the fear in her eyes as his words took hold. 'We'll take you to a sanatorium. Get you better,' she added quickly, taking one of her hands away and stroking the side of his face.

'No, it's too late to make any difference.' Alex took her in his arms. 'Stanley says I've probably only got a year.'

Annie pulled back to look at him, a flash of anger in her eyes. 'How can he be so sure?'

'He's as certain as one can be. That's why I wanted us to come away. Be on our own. And I've loved every moment this week, even though I've missed the children.' He tried to laugh but had to turn his head away to cough.

'We must be able to do something.' Annie clutched his arm.

'You're a doctor. You must know what to do. There must be some treatment that would work.' The words came tumbling out. 'Please don't die, Alex. I can't bear it. I need you. The children need you.' Tears poured down her cheeks and angrily she brushed them away.

Alex caught her hands again. 'You have to be strong, darling. We both have to, for the children's sake. I want us to enjoy every day we have left. As though we're normal. And we must both pretend I'm not ill. Not dwell on what's going to happen. Will you promise me that?'

He felt her hands go limp under his, and he squeezed them gently. 'Promise?'

She looked up at him, her eyes inky blue in the morning light. She nodded. There weren't any words.

'And Mother,' Alex said softly. 'When it happens, can you let her know? I've got her address in the chiffonier. She moved back to Italy after Dad died.' He hesitated, wondering how she would take his next comment. 'I do wish you could've both met, darling. Try to forgive her. She just couldn't get over the shock that I fell in love with a married woman. Her upbringing was so strict – Roman Catholic, of course. If she'd just met you once I know she would have loved you.'

'She might not.' Annie gave him a weak smile. 'I took her only son away.'

Alex had thought so often how religion had caused his mother to lose all the pleasure of seeing him regularly, and, of course, she had missed knowing Kitty, her only grandchild. He'd written to tell her about Kitty as soon as she was born, but he'd only had a brief message in return, saying that his mother was pleased for him and hoped he was still happy.

'I'll write to your mother,' Annie told him, 'but not for a long time yet.'

'It might not be that long,' Alex said. He saw her draw in her stomach and take a deep breath as though she was making a decision.

'I shall hand in my notice when we get home,' she said firmly. 'I'm going to nurse you back to health.'

'Darling, that's a wonderful thought and I'll always be grateful, but I still want you to promise me that we'll live every moment together...until the end. I love you so much. I always will. Do you promise?' He gave her a shaky smile.

She smiled back through her tears.

'I promise,' she whispered.

He drew her towards him. She was so close her breath was like a caress to his skin. He felt her arms wrap around his neck. He pulled her closer still. His dearest Annie. She would help him get through whatever was in store for him. Then as though she'd touched a hot iron she recoiled.

'What's the matter, darling?'

But he knew.

Annie's face was scarlet. 'I'm sorry, Alex. It's just that I'm frightened...' He saw her gulp as she gathered courage. 'It's not just me, but the children,' she added weakly.

'It's not contagious through kissing, thank goodness,' Alex said, stroking her face. 'Or touching. It's carried by air. So you don't have to worry. I would never let you or the children come to any harm.'

With not a second's hesitation Annie leaned into him and took his face in her hands. She looked deep into his eyes and he imagined he saw himself reflected in them. His fear and worry seemed all at once to dissolve in her love for him. And when she kissed him full on the lips, it was the sweetest kiss he had ever known.

48

February 1928

Every day that passed towards the time his colleague, Stanley, had predicted would be left to her beloved Alex, Annie prayed to God he'd go on living a few more months. But even though she never gave up hope, she couldn't deny he was getting weaker. He'd lost more than three stones in weight ('I was too fat anyway,' he told her, with the shadow of his old smile), and his dear irregular features were prominent in a face now skin and bone.

But somehow they were still happy, Annie thought humbly; they had become even closer, even though he'd insisted upon moving into the spare bedroom so he didn't disturb her. Stanley had encouraged Alex to conclude his work at the surgery within the month so he could have as much time as possible with his family while he felt in reasonable health. She'd kept her promise and treasured every moment spent with him, finding something wonderful in every day they shared. It might be Kitty's laughter, and the way the little girl would throw herself into Alex's arms, shouting, 'Daddy, can we sing a song?' and Annie would close her eyes and smile at the sweet sound of their voices blending. Or it might be a beautiful sunrise they'd watch together, or a visit from Ethel bringing one of her special ginger cakes, still warm from the oven. So many little things, but they meant the world.

But underneath these precious moments his sickness tore apart her dreams of all she wanted for her family. Stanley had been marvellous. He continued to pay half Alex's salary. 'For however long,' he'd said, clearing his throat noisily. Living simply they could manage, even without her earnings. But she knew Alex was desperately worried as to how they would all cope when he was no longer there. And that time was closer, she had to concede, now Alex rarely came downstairs.

'At least you've got the house,' he said, coughing now almost every time he spoke. 'Don't ever let anyone take it away from you and the children.'

'No one's going to take it away from me.'

'It may be all paid for, but you never know. If there's another war. If Germany—'

'You're talking nonsense,' Annie interrupted. 'Why would Germany start something again after the last disaster?'

'They've never recovered from losing,' Alex said, choking as he tried to form the words. 'That dreadful Nazi party. The Germans with any sense think they're a joke, but I distrust them. That fellow Hitler's hell-bent on power, if you ask me.' He tried to sit up in his agitation, but fell back against the pillows, coughing. 'It's you and the children I worry about,' he said, when he'd recovered.

'You mustn't worry,' Annie said. She wiped the sweat from his forehead, wondering if his temperature was making him talk jibberish. 'They always say it was the war to end all wars. So there won't be another one. Anyway, you mustn't fret about me. It's you we have to concentrate on. Getting you better.'

'Annie, we know I'm not going to get better,' Alex said, so softly Annie had to strain to hear the words. 'But we'll enjoy every moment God gives us. Just like we promised one another. You mustn't be sad, darling. I love you so much.'

'And I love *you*, dearest,' she said, kissing his lips, grown thin with the illness. She turned away to hide her tears. 'I'll get you some tea.'

She left the door open behind her so she could hear him call out if he needed anything.

'Is that for Daddy?' Frankie asked, coming into the kitchen as she was pouring out a cup. Annie nodded. 'Can I take it up to him? I want to tell him about coming top in arithmetic and geography.'

'Oh, well done, darling.' Annie smiled at her daughter, handing her the cup and saucer with two biscuits.

Annie sat at the table drinking her tea without tasting it. She ran a hand tiredly through her hair, then glanced at the clock. It was five. She knew she should start supper, but her legs felt as though they were rooted; that if she tried to get up from the table they wouldn't even support her.

She wondered what she could give Alex. Lately, he'd eaten less and less; just picked at his food. She made him soup every day and he always told her it was delicious, but he never managed more than three or four spoonfuls.

Her eyes brimmed with unshed tears. It wasn't that she minded nursing him. On the contrary, she loved doing things for him to make him comfortable. But instead of him getting better she had to admit that he was deteriorating. For the first time since he'd told her about his illness she glimpsed the future. A long, dark path where she was alone.

Stop it, she told herself furiously, pulling herself to her feet. You're not helping anyone. Just get on with making supper.

'Mum! Mum, come quick!' Frankie was shouting from the top of the stairs.

What did the child want now? Annie thought as she trudged out of the kitchen.

'It's Daddy,' Frankie sobbed. 'He won't answer me. I told him about the arithmetic test and he—'

'Hush, darling,' Annie said, her stomach making sickening leaps. 'He's just fallen asleep, I expect. You know how tired he is these days.'

Frankie held back as her mother pushed wide the bedroom door. Alex was lying on his back with his eyes closed, exactly as she'd left him. She stroked his hair away from his forehead.

'Darling, Frankie's come to see you,' she said, taking his skeletal hand in her own.

His hand was warm. The cup of tea was untouched.

'Alex, darling. Wake up. Frankie's got some exciting news.' She looked intently at him. 'Alex?' There was no steady rise and fall of his chest. No flicker of his eyes.

'Alex!' she called again, frantic now as she bent over him. *Please God—*

'Mummy!'

Dimly she heard her daughter from some place far away.

'Frankie, ring for Dr Stanley,' Annie said, without turning round. 'Tell him to come at once.'

She heard the sound of scuffling shoes as Frankie fled down the stairs.

Annie gazed down at her dearest love, gently squeezing his hand. He looked more peaceful than she'd seen him in a long time. In that moment she knew it was too late. He would never answer her. He had left her forever.

I can't live without you. She didn't know if she'd screamed the words aloud or if they were screaming inside her head. All she knew was that she hadn't said goodbye. Hadn't been there when he needed her. When he'd drawn his last breath. He'd been on his own. She'd only left him for five minutes to make him a cup of tea. She'd had no idea how close to death he'd been. Dear God, it wasn't possible that he could have died in such a short space of time. She'd never see him again. Never see him smile. Feel his arms wrapped around her. Hear him say he loved her. She couldn't bear it.

She gripped on to his hand and wept.

*

'Annie…Annie, dearest.' Dimly she heard her sister's voice, and gentle hands were prising her fingers, one by one, from Alex.

'No, no…don't…leave me alone.'

'He's at peace now, dearest,' Ethel said. 'Come downstairs. I've made some tea.'

'I don't want tea,' Annie sobbed. 'I want Alex. Oh, Ethel, I want my Alex. I don't know what to do. What shall I do?'

'There's nothing to do except carry on.' Ethel stroked her sister's face. 'It's what Alex would have wanted. Come on, dearest. You must be strong for the children.'

'I'm not strong anymore. Oh, Ethel, whatever shall I do without him?'

'You'll carry on. You have to. If you go to pieces then so will the children. But you know me and Johnnie will do everything we can to help. You're not alone, Annie. We love you. And don't forget, we loved him, too.'

Annie suddenly felt ashamed. She wasn't the only one who would mourn Alex. Frankie and Harry both loved him. But Kitty was so young to lose her father; she would forget him. Annie took the handkerchief Ethel handed her, wiped the tears and blew her nose, vowing never to let that happen. She would find something to tell Kitty every day about her father.

She thought she would have broken down completely without dear, calm Ethel and her Johnnie. Johnnie had seen to it all before, when their father had died. Now, he quietly made the arrangements for the funeral while she concentrated on looking after Frankie and Harry and Kitty, numb with misery, barely knowing what she was doing. Dreading the day of the funeral. Longing for it to be over.

Annie's fingers were sweating as she got dressed on the morning of Alex's funeral. She opened the curtains to see the sun for the first time in a week. She supposed it was preferable to all the rain they'd had lately, though that would have better suited her mood.

She tucked a blouse into her black pleated skirt, catching a glimpse of her pale face above the white frilled collar. Maybe she should have started making a black dress when Alex had first told her there was no hope. But she'd never stopped hoping.

'Where's my hat?' she heard Frankie shout. 'Have you taken it, Harry? If you have, I'll box your ears.'

She heard Harry shout something rude back to his sister. Why did they have to quarrel today of all days? Hoping to stop it developing any further, Annie grabbed a box from her wardrobe and rushed down the stairs.

'I know Harry's taken my hat,' Frankie said furiously. 'I can't find it anywhere. He thinks it's funny.'

'I've got a special hat for you,' Annie said. 'Let me put it on.' She arranged the hat over her daughter's thick fair hair. 'There. Go and have a look in my mirror. You look lovely.'

Frankie disappeared.

'I didn't take her stupid hat,' Harry fumed as he came into the front room. 'Why can't I go to the church? I don't want to go to school. Frankie's going. It's not fair.'

Even at this last minute Annie wondered if she had done the right thing to send Harry to school as usual, and Kitty to one of the neighbours. Perhaps all the children should have been allowed to say goodbye to Alex. She hesitated, biting her lip. But it was too late now.

'Frankie's older. You mustn't miss school, Harry,' she said, helping him on with his boots. He wore what she privately called his 'Ruby expression' when he was cross. His lower lip drooped and his face looked as though it might crumple at any moment. 'It's reading and writing this morning. You know it's your favourite.'

'It isn't. I hate it.'

Annie's mouth tightened. It was going to be a dreadful day for everyone and she mustn't make it worse. She was relieved when the doorbell rang and there was Ethel, ready to drop Kitty off.

'Kitty, Aunt Ethel's here,' Annie called up the stairs. 'Don't forget your book and puzzle.'

Her daughter came scampering down, her dark curls still in a tangle. She was humming a tune to herself and Annie couldn't help smiling, she so reminded her of Alex. Then her heart plummeted. Today she would be saying goodbye to her one true love. But Kitty? How could a four-year-old possibly understand she would never see her beloved daddy again?

'Go and get your comb, darling,' Annie said, drawing the child to her and giving her a kiss.

She ran off and was back in seconds. 'I've made a little song for Daddy.'

Annie's heart squeezed so hard she thought she would never be able to take another breath.

'Have you, darling?' she managed, as she combed her daughter's mop.

'Shall I sing it now?' Kitty pulled out of her mother's arms and opened her mouth.

'Not now, darling,' Annie choked. 'Mummy has to go to the church to say goodbye to Daddy. Save it for when I come home.'

'When will Daddy come home?' Kitty said, her face suddenly solemn.

'I'll tell him you love him and said goodbye,' Annie said, feeling sick. She turned away before Kitty could see her tears.

'I'll see you at the church,' Ethel said, looking at her sister with anxious eyes. 'Will you be all right, dearest?'

Annie nodded. She stood at the front door and watched them leave. Ethel was firmly holding Kitty's hand, but the little girl was abnormally slow. She kept glancing back and waving, getting out of rhythm with Ethel's firm tread. Harry had already shot out of the door and was running ahead of them.

Annie closed the door quietly and went upstairs to do her hair. She'd let it grow long after the bob she'd had when Alex first came

379

to England. It was easier to twist into a coil at the back of her neck than keep those short locks groomed. Besides, she adored feeling Alex's fingers through the long silky strands on their loving nights. And how, before he had become really ill, he sometimes brushed her hair before they went to bed, parting it at the back of her neck to kiss the smooth skin. What was the point of being fashionable? Alex was the only one she'd wanted to look nice for. And now he was gone, taking all the laughter and fun away with him.

As soon as Annie saw the bearers bring the coffin into the church she thought she would faint. The men lowered it gently and bowed their heads, then turned away to sit in one of the pews. Annie couldn't drag her eyes away from the long wooden chest. It was as though she were hypnotised by the simple pine box which was all Alex had wanted. The only decoration was a small bunch of flowers with a card Frankie had written, and Harry and Kitty had added their names. Ethel had tried several times to persuade Annie to buy some flowers and sign a card but she'd always answered that she'd been too tired or too upset.

Now, Annie stared at the coffin. Try as she might, she couldn't believe Alex was lying in a wooden box when he'd always been so full of life. Under her veil a tear slowly dripped down her cheek. He was far away from her already.

People began to troop in. So many people Annie had never seen before among the many villagers she knew. Several of them nodded to her, giving half smiles of understanding. So different from how they'd treated her when she and Alex had first moved in together.

"E's not from these parts,' one woman who went to church twice on a Sunday had commented with pursed lips. "E's from Australia. Speaks funny.'

'Fancy him coming here, all this way, to be with our Annie.'

'He's a good doctor, I'll say that for him,' some of them had muttered.

Over time it seemed they'd learned to accept him. And when she'd told them how sick he was, several of the women had been very kind. A pot of soup or a casserole of stew or a whole cake would appear on the doorstep.

Word must have spread, she thought, as she nodded back at them. In fifteen minutes the church was packed. People stood at the back, blocking the doors. It seemed everyone wanted to pay their respects to the esteemed doctor. Her Alex.

The vicar took them through the service but Annie found she couldn't concentrate on the words or the hymns. She tried. Her mouth opened and closed but nothing came out. Maybe her voice was lost forever. All she could think of was Alex alone in a box. Heart racing, she put a hand to her forehead, feeling the cold perspiration under her fingertips. She tried to keep her eyes fixed on the vicar but he looked strange – as though his body was breaking up into little pieces. Her head started to swim but she mustn't faint...her knees...weak...must sit down. And then she felt Frankie's small warm hand slide into hers, pressing it. She looked down at her daughter, her lips forming a grateful smile but Frankie was staring ahead and singing loudly.

After the hymn, to her surprise Johnnie got up and walked over to one of the lecterns. He pulled out a piece of paper and unfolded it, then cleared his throat. Everyone was perfectly quiet.

'I only want to say a few words,' he began. Annie sat up a little straighter. Johnnie knew Alex far better than the vicar. Her brother-in-law cleared his throat again and glanced down at his paper. 'Dr Alexander Townsend left Australia to come to England to find our Annie, who he'd fallen in love with. They had five happy years together, and a lovely daughter, Kitty. He was a fine man and a dedicated doctor. Always had time for everyone, no matter whether they could pay him or not. He wouldn't turn anyone away. Often's the time he's come home from some patient who's short of cash with a sack of potatoes or a couple of live chickens, whether Annie could do with them or not.' He raised his eyes and smiled, and there was a low chuckle from some of the men. 'Besides Kitty, he was a wonderful father to Annie's other children, Frankie and Harry, and me and my wife, Ethel, who many of you know is Annie's sister, feel privileged to have known him. He'll be much missed. But Annie will miss him most of all. So please be kind to her. That's all.' He stepped down and returned to his seat.

Tears that Annie had so desperately tried to hold back flowed down her cheeks. She didn't know whether she was glad or sorry that Johnnie had made the last remark, but several people threw her sympathetic glances.

The service was over. Annie blinked in the sunlight, her stomach heavy with dread. She wondered if her legs would even carry her to the graveyard, but there was Johnnie beside her, holding her arm, and Ethel holding the other with Frankie. The four of them trudged across the patchy grass towards the spot where Alex would be buried. A breeze blew her veil up and she suddenly felt vulnerable, as though the whole world could see her and her misery. Lips tight with grief, she smoothed the veil back into position.

It seemed she stood by the open grave for hours until finally the coffin was let down and the gravediggers shovelled the first layer of earth. Frankie, who was looking pale, gave a strangled scream and twisted her head away, clinging on to her aunt's hand. Annie knew she was supposed to pick up a clod but she couldn't bring herself to perform the action. Dear Johnnie did it for her. When the gravediggers had finished their job the vicar began to sing 'Abide With Me', and the crowd joined in. Annie stood as still as one of the gravestones, the breeze becoming stronger and drying her tears.

People were turning away, some of the women crying into their handkerchiefs.

'It's a sad day and no mistake,' one woman said, patting her arm.

'Thank you, Mrs Draper.'

It became her set reply. She only had to remember to change their names.

'And to my dearest Annie, I leave my entire savings of eight hundred pounds.'

Annie jumped at the solicitor's words. She knew Alex was always worried about the future and wanted her to feel secure, especially as they couldn't marry, but she'd had no idea he had this much in his savings. She'd thought since he'd put Camellia House in her name that there was not much left. It sounded a great deal of money, but if there was anything major to be done on the house in the future it might not be many years before it was all used up.

49

How cruel fate was, Annie thought, when she read a letter from Ferguson only days after Alex was buried.

Letter dated 15th November 1927

Dear Annie,

I have decided to divorce you on the grounds that you have been unfaithful to me and are living with another man.

I am sorry it has come to this but I know it is what you want. I always thought that one day we might make up our differences but perhaps it was not to be. I have Margaret, as you know. I was honest about her from the start and never kept her a secret. Maybe one day she and I will get married, but I am cautious in that respect.

Well, Annie, I am giving you your freedom. I will get the legal side underway but you will have to pay for it as I have very little money. Or ask your doctor to pay as presumably he is the one who is pressing you to take this serious step.

I would be grateful if you would write to me sometimes to let me know about the children.

Yours,

Ferguson Percy Bishop

Annie read the letter with a chilled heart. It was the letter she and Alex had dreamed of receiving years before. The letter that would have meant they could have married. Instead, they'd been forced to live in sin, practically ostracised by half the village; that was, until Kitty was born. Things had then taken a better turn. It seemed everyone loved a baby, and Kitty unwittingly brought out the best in people. Annie smiled at the thought. If she had to do it over again she would have done exactly the same. She wouldn't have sacrificed those precious years she and Alex and the children had spent together for anything or anyone in the world. They were the happiest years of her life, and Alex had given her their precious daughter, Kitty. Kitty, with her dark hair and wide smile, would remind her as long as she lived of Alex.

She screwed up the letter, enjoying the satisfying crunch it made, and threw it in the bin. Then for some reason she retrieved it and squashed it under some letters in the chiffonier drawer, vowing never to answer it.

Life went on from day to day, week to week, month to month. Lady Hamilton asked Annie if she would resume her six days a week, but until Kitty was in school Annie felt it was too much to ask Ethel, especially as she had Eleanor to take care of.

'I'll have to hire another cook,' Lady Hamilton told her, 'though it's going to be difficult finding someone who can cook as well as you, Annie. The one we had from the agency when you were looking after Dr Townsend was hopeless.'

The compliment didn't soften the blow.

'Would you allow me to work five days instead of six?' Annie said. One day wasn't much to ask for but it was better than nothing.

Lady Hamilton looked doubtful. 'Well...until I can replace you, I suppose it's the best solution.'

But Annie knew she was on borrowed time. She'd have to find something which allowed her to be home when the children came out of school. And if she couldn't cook for Lady Hamilton, what then? But things were different for women now, she thought. The

Suffragettes had finally won. All women twenty-one and over had the vote. They were learning shorthand and typewriting, or worked in shops, or were teachers. Some even had their own businesses. An image of Adele floated in front of her and she couldn't help smiling. Adele had been an independent woman following her own destiny before Annie had even heard about the Suffragettes. She made a decision there and then. When her job with Lady Hamilton came to an end she would never go back into service.

February 1930

'Letter for you from America, Mrs Townsend,' the postman said, almost with reverence, as he handed it to her. 'New York postmark.'

Annie glanced at the envelope. After two years' silence, it came as a guilty shock. She'd ignored Ferguson's last letter. He must be losing patience. Well, maybe he knew now what it was like to want to remarry and one person was stopping you. She wondered why he'd left it so long before reminding her he'd had no answer. Slowly, she slit open the envelope, her heart beginning to pound.

Letter dated 22nd November 1929

My dear Annie,

I hope this letter finds you and the children well.

I'm not sure if you get news of what is happening in America, but I am in bad straits. The whole stock market in New York has crashed. Thousands of people immediately lost their jobs. I managed to hold on to mine at the gentlemen's dining club until last week when they closed. Now I have nowhere to go because I was living in a room above the club when Margaret left. At the moment I'm staying with a friend for a short time while his wife is visiting her brother in England.

Margaret wanted children and as I already had two I said I didn't want any more. She was very upset and so she left me. Simple as that. She was a good woman but I never really loved her and I think she knew it. She always said I'd never got over you.

I heard Dr Townsend had passed away. I know the village people said he was a decent man and did his best for you and the children, but now he has gone I am asking you to take me back. I know I haven't always treated you well, but you are the dearest woman I have ever known, and I am, after all, the children's father. I should never have left you, and now I know how it feels. Dearest Annie, can you find it in your heart to forgive me?

I await your reply and hope it will say what I am hoping to hear. You can reach me here: Box No. 3402, New York City, New York.

Yours ever,

Ferguson Percy Bishop

Annie bit her lip. *Did his best for you and the children.* Ferguson really had no inkling of what that meant. Alex had loved her more than life itself, and loved Frankie and Harry as though they were his own flesh and blood. He would have done anything in the world for them. Annie pursed her lips. She reread Ferguson's words: *I should never have left you.* But he *had* left her and the children to get on without him. He'd never been loyal. She recalled once again the horror of finding out Ruby was having his baby. And his face that time when Susan had come to the cottage apologising for only leaving Harry alone for a few minutes. Their expressions had told her everything. And when he'd met Margaret he'd even stopped the children's allowance.

How had he found out about Alex? She knew it couldn't be Ethel, as her sister hadn't had much time for him the minute he'd made up his mind to leave his family and go off to America. Ethel could never understand anyone shirking their responsibilities. So who could possibly have told him?

Her mind whirled. Could it possibly be Ruby? Annie had written that Alex was ill and she was nursing him at home, and when he'd died she'd managed to write a few lines to let her sister know. Yes, Ruby knew Ferguson had gone to America but Annie had never told her his address in New York and Ruby hadn't asked. So that only left Adele. Annie had had a letter of sympathy straight back from Adele, but again, how could her friend have found out his address? And why should she write to him anyway? It didn't make sense.

So who had told Ferguson? The only possible person, after all, was Ethel. Annie determined to ask her at the first opportunity.

She didn't have long to wait. Ethel and Eleanor walked over the very next day.

'I do love your house,' Ethel said, walking towards the window. 'And it's such a perfect garden for the children.'

Annie glanced out of the kitchen window. The garden looked bedraggled. She'd done her best to keep it tidy since Alex died, but he'd been the gardener whenever he had a few spare hours. It was too big for one person to manage. A powerful wind had got up in the night and part of the fence had blown over. The silver birch swayed, some of its branches almost touching the ground, before the wind lifted them up again. It was Eleanor and Kitty's favourite tree – the one they always chose to play under with their dolls, but at this time of the year it wasn't safe.

In her mind's eye she saw the children. Blonde Eleanor and dark-haired Kitty; they were both adorable, but Eleanor had her mother's gentle temperament whereas Kitty was already desperate to break away and show her independence at every opportunity. She needed a father's firm hand. If only...

'I'll put the kettle on.' Annie turned away, tears brimming once again at the thought of Kitty growing up without her father. How proud Alex would have been. And her own dear dad. He would have loved all four of his grandchildren.

'Ethel, I've got something to ask you, and I won't be upset, whatever you answer.'

'What is it, dear?' Ethel breathed out a long sigh as she sank down in one of the easy chairs.

'It's just that I've had a letter from Ferguson and he knows that Alex d-died.' She swallowed.

'How did he find out?'

'That's just it. You didn't tell him, did you?'

'Me?' Ethel looked horrified. 'No, of course not. It isn't any of my business. I'd never have written without telling you. I've never written him a letter anyway, though many's the time I've felt I should – particularly when he stopped sending you any money.'

'I was sure you hadn't.' Annie frowned. 'So who could it have been?'

'I wonder.' Ethel looked thoughtful as she took a sip of tea. 'Have you spoken to Frankie?'

'Frankie?' Annie's eyes widened. 'What about?'

'Writing to Ferguson. After all, he is her father and she knows it. It's the only possible solution.'

'But she's a child. She wouldn't have taken that upon herself – not without my permission, anyway.'

'She's fifteen. Almost a young woman. She'll be leaving school this summer. You just haven't noticed her growing up, with nursing Alex.'

'You're saying she might have been snooping through my private papers?'

'I wouldn't call it snooping.' Ethel shook her head. 'It was probably quite accidental.' She looked up. 'Where did you keep Ferguson's letter?'

'In the chiffonier. I never answered it. To be truthful, I didn't think he deserved an answer.' Annie swallowed. 'And I couldn't face telling him about Alex.'

'Well, it wouldn't have taken much for Frankie to have found the letter,' Ethel said, 'with his return address conveniently on the envelope. She'd be curious to know what had happened to her real father. I would, in the circumstances.'

'She never talks about him.' Annie poured a second cup of tea.

'That doesn't mean she doesn't think about him,' Ethel said firmly. 'You'll have to ask her.'

'It would be awful if I accused her of something and she was innocent.'

'Don't accuse. But don't be upset if she says she wrote to him. You asked her to tell the truth and you'll be pleased she's owned up.'

'I'll speak to her when she comes home from school,' Annie said.

'Children are very inquisitive.' Ethel fiddled with her hair though it was perfectly tidy. 'I'm finding that out every day with Eleanor. And it will be the same with the next one.' She turned and looked at Annie, who suddenly realised what her sister was implying.

'Ethel. Are you—?'

'I am,' Ethel laughed. 'Isn't it exciting?'

'It's the most wonderful news!' Annie jumped up and hugged her sister. 'I've been so wrapped up in myself I haven't even noticed you getting fat.' She forced a laugh as she gently patted Ethel's swollen stomach. 'When is it due?'

'The doctor says early July. A summer baby for a change,' she chuckled, and then became serious. 'Oh, Annie, I'm so happy and I know how sad you've been. Now it's made worse with this letter. I feel terrible for you.'

'Don't,' Annie said firmly. 'I don't want anything to take away your happiness. I'll work things out. Until then, we've got to prepare for the new baby. Johnnie must be so thrilled.'

'He is. He adores Eleanor, but I know he's secretly hoping for a son this time, though he's not breathed a word to me about it.'

'A brother for Eleanor,' Annie said, swallowing hard. 'Yes, that would be perfect.'

'How was school?' Annie asked, when her daughter arrived home that same day.

Frankie flung her coat and scarf on the kitchen chair. Her hat fell to the floor and she bent down to pick it up. 'All right,' she mumbled.

'Frankie, I want to ask you something. And I want the truth.'

Frankie glanced at her mother, her eyes wary. 'What's the matter?'

'Come and sit down.'

Frankie followed her mother into the sitting room and flopped down in Alex's chair. A silence fell between them. Annie decided not to waste any words.

'Have you been writing to your father in America?'

'Once or twice.' Frankie didn't meet her mother's gaze. 'What's for tea?'

'Never mind what's for tea,' Annie snapped. 'Just answer my question.'

'I said I had, once or twice. Am I supposed to feel guilty?'

'Please don't be cheeky, Frankie. I would rather have known, that's all.' Annie paused. 'Did you tell your father that Alex had died?' She studied her daughter's face. It was deliberately blank; the kind of expression that told her nothing.

'No, I haven't written since then.'

'Are you sure you're telling me the truth?'

Frankie's cheeks flared red. 'I told you. I haven't written lately. You're talking to the wrong person, Mum.' Her eyes finally locked with Annie's. 'It's Harry you need to ask.'

'Harry?'

'Yes, Harry. He's the one who's been sneaking around your things. Talk to him. Not me.'

'I didn't mean anything.' Harry looked at her defiantly. 'I just thought he might want to know, that's all.' He made to run out of the kitchen door.

'*Stop!*' Harry practically skidded to a halt. 'What you've done is very wrong. You've meddled in things that don't concern you.'

'Weren't you going to tell him?'

'No, I wasn't,' Annie flashed. 'Not until I was ready.'

'Why not?' Harry's eyes blazed. 'He's my real father, so why can't he know?'

Shocked, Annie stared at her son. 'How long have you known he's your real father?'

'Ages ago.'

Annie bit her lip so hard she tasted blood. She'd wanted to tell Harry herself – when the time was right. But it had never seemed to be the right time.

'Who told you?' she demanded.

Harry stared at the floor.

'I asked you a question, Harry.'

'Frankie,' Harry mumbled.

Oh, Frankie, that was the last thing I wanted you to tell your brother.

'That was not her business to say anything, so I shall be having a word with her, too.'

'Why didn't *you* tell me?' Harry looked up defiantly, his face flushed.

'I would have…when I felt you were old enough to understand.'

'I'm not a baby, Mum, whatever you think.' Harry began tapping his fingers on the arm of the chair, and her heart twisted. 'I'm old enough to know who my own father is and I wanted to let *him* know. And that Da…Alex died.'

'So you thought to go through my private papers?'

'I didn't go looking for any address at the time, if that's what you mean,' Harry said, his eyes suddenly fearful. 'I just wanted some sheets of writing paper.'

'You've got your school exercise book. Why do you need separate paper?'

'If you must know, I'm writing a story, and it's not for homework.'

'I want to forget about this.' Annie's voice was thick with suppressed anger. 'You are never to touch my private papers, or anything else of mine. I'm very cross with you for going behind my back.'

'I hate it here!' Harry shouted as he jumped up and opened the kitchen door. 'I hate school. I want to go to America and stay with my father.'

'You can't. This is your home. Your father can't support you. He doesn't even have anywhere proper to live himself. Can't you understand once and for all that he left us for good?'

As soon as the words slipped from her mouth, Annie wished with all her heart they could be retracted. 'Harry, I—'

Harry, his face crimson with rage, flung her a look of contempt and disappeared, slamming the door behind him.

Annie sank down on one of the kitchen chairs, her eyes wet with tears. *Don't be hard on the child,* she could hear Alex say, his voice as clear as it used to be before he became sick. *Harry's going through a difficult time without a father's guidance.*

What would Harry have thought if she'd told him his father wanted to come home and she hadn't even bothered to reply? Harry would hate her.

She looked about her in bewilderment, then covered her face with her hands and wept.

Oh, Alex, why did you have to die when I need you so?

50

When Harry had left for school the next morning after barely speaking to her, Annie found the day dragged. It had begun to snow, softly at first, covering the garden like fairy cobwebs. Several times she went to the window, and by eleven o'clock she could see the snowflakes were thicker and relentless. She opened the front door to have a proper look at the sky. The cold sliced through her, and when she craned her head up, she saw a dull grey blanket tinged with yellow. Her mother would have said the sky was full of snow. She stepped outside and took a few deep breaths, enjoying the cold prickly sensation in her nostrils, but without a coat she soon escaped back into the warm.

Luckily, Lady Hamilton had not found anyone suitable to cook. There'd been a couple of replacements but neither of them had worked out and Lady Hamilton had called Annie back on both occasions. Annie had been grateful but she was constantly worried someone would come along and she'd be out of a job. But today was her day off. It had been a tiring week. The Hamiltons had had guests for lunch on three consecutive days and Annie's feet felt as though rats were gnawing at them. She decided she would sit and write to Ruby. It seemed a long time since she'd heard from her sister.

Even after all that had happened, she missed her younger sister's irrepressible laugh and quick wit. But what should she say? After several minutes, the ink drying on her pen, she decided not to mention Ferguson wanted to come back to her and the children. It was best that Ruby thought he was still making a life in New York.

She finished her letter but it would take four months or more to get a reply, even if Ruby wrote straight back. Surely there was a letter from her sister already on its way.

She thought to do some ironing next. Although she didn't much feel like it, it would pass the time. The decision about Ferguson was weighing heavily and she knew she'd have no peace until she'd made up her mind what to do. She folded the pile of laundry and cut some bread and cheese for her lunch. After she'd finished without really tasting anything she leaned back in Alex's chair and closed her eyes. She must have dozed because when she opened her eyes and looked at the time it was already three o'clock. She'd go and meet Harry even though he hated it when she was there at the gate.

'I'm old enough to go to school and back on my own,' he frequently told her.

She usually let him but today she was worried about the weather. It was getting worse. She buttoned on her thick winter coat, wound a scarf around her neck and pulled her boots on, all the time feeling a twinge of apprehension. Telling herself not to be so silly, she pulled on her hat, grabbed her gloves and bag and locked the door behind her.

The sky was dark already and it was still snowing. She walked as swiftly as she could down the drive and into the lane, her boots crunching through the un-trodden snow. There was no one about but in the distance she saw two boys who she thought looked about Harry's age, throwing snowballs at one another. When she got nearer she recognised them from Harry's class.

'Have you seen Harry Bishop?' she called.

'He was talking to teacher,' one of them said, chucking another snowball at his friend.

'Did he say he was going straight home?'

'He never said.'

They passed Annie, shouting and laughing and throwing more snowballs.

Several more children hurtled by but there was no sign of Harry. She stood at the school gates with a handful of mothers, who one by one collected a child or two and nodded goodbye. Soon she was the only one left. A trickle of fear ran down her spine. She told herself Harry was still talking to his teacher but that was over half an hour ago. Surely the teacher wouldn't have delayed him in this weather. The wind was getting up and blowing flakes of snow in her face and on her lashes. Blinking, she pulled her scarf over her mouth. Just as she was opening the school gate to find a teacher a voice from behind called out, 'Mrs Bishop?'

Annie spun round. Most of the village people by now had got used to calling her Mrs Townsend. A woman was framed in the doorway of the house with the bright yellow window frames opposite the school. She was gesturing to Annie to come over. How did this woman know her? She was obviously one of the few who refused to use Alex's name. Who disapproved. Annie screwed up her eyes against what was becoming a blizzard.

There was something about the woman that echoed within her. Had she met her at one of the sports days? Or a school concert? No, she'd remember if she had. Even at a distance she could see the woman was very blonde and extraordinarily pretty. She pointed to herself and the woman nodded. Annie walked unsteadily across the icy road, thankful for the heavy boots Alex had bought her.

'I've been looking out for you. Harry's here.'

The woman looked serious and Annie's legs turned to blancmange.

'What's happened?' She could feel anxiety rising in her throat. Oh, why had she let Harry—

'Please come in, Mrs Bishop. I've got him safe and sound. June slipped on the ice and fell over as she was crossing the road. Your Harry grabbed her and pulled her out of the path of a motor car.

He's a real hero. I've just given them both a cup of tea and a slice of Dundee.'

She took Annie's arm in a firm grip and led her inside. Annie noticed the woman had a limp. She stole a glance at her. Yes, even her profile seemed oddly familiar. But before she could rack her brain Harry flew out of one of the rooms.

'Mummy!' He rushed into his mother's arms. 'I knew you'd be worried but Mrs Greenway made me come in and sit down and have some tea. I was just going home.'

'I wouldn't have let him go back on his own in this weather,' Mrs Greenway assured her. 'June would have been all right for half an hour.'

'I'm glad you didn't have to. It's getting worse outside,' Annie said, thinking of the woman limping all that way and how kind she was. 'You're a brave boy, Harry.' She hugged and kissed Harry and for once he didn't struggle. She turned to Mrs Greenway. 'Was June hurt?'

'Not badly. She's in the front room. Come and say hello to her.'

A little girl with a mop of bright red hair was resting on the sofa. She sat up as soon as the two women appeared.

'Look at my arm.' The child held out a thin white arm, the elbow bandaged to twice its size.

'It was a bad graze,' Mrs Greenway said, turning to Annie. 'You sit down, and I'll make a fresh pot of tea. You must have been worried to death when you didn't see Harry with his friends.'

'And my leg.' June tripped off the sofa and hopped over on one leg to show Annie her bruised knee.

'Oh, dear,' Annie said, bending down to look at it. 'You did have a nasty accident.'

'Harry saved me.' June looked at Harry adoringly and he grinned back.

'You've been very kind.' Annie took the cup of tea Mrs Greenway handed her, but her hand trembled and the cup fell on to the carpet. She burst into tears. 'I'm so sorry,' she said, but Mrs Greenway had already rushed to her side, and wrapped her arms around her.

'Don't worry, dear. There's no damage done.'

'But your carpet...let me wipe it up.'

'You sit right there and don't move.'

Mrs Greenway was back in a trice with a cloth. 'Go and take Harry upstairs and show him your room, Junie, there's a good girl,' she gestured with a jerk of her head. Wide eyed, the children disappeared. 'It's all over now, dear,' she soothed, as she blotted up the liquid. 'Your Harry is a son to be proud of.'

'I know,' Annie said, the tears still streaming. 'But you see, I was horrid to him this morning. I should never have let him go off on his own when I was so cross. I wasn't being fair. He thought he was doing the right thing. But it was the worst.'

'Do you want to tell me about it?' Mrs Greenway asked in a soft voice.

Even the voice struck a chord. She was a little too plump for her height and wore her long pale-blonde hair tied back off her face by a black ribbon, enhancing her elfin features. Her eyes, the colour of autumn leaves, were full of concern and sympathy as they held Annie's own. The rosebud mouth, with perfect even teeth, was smiling encouragingly.

'You've been so kind,' Annie repeated, 'and I'm not used to it. Ever since Alex...Alex...'

'Dr Townsend?'

'Yes.' She turned tear-stained eyes to Mrs Greenway. 'How do you know?'

'Bonham might have grown a bit during the last ten years or so, but there's not much goes on that the whole village doesn't know about – sometimes before it even happens,' Mrs Greenway chuckled.

'I suppose so.' Annie hesitated. 'You knew he'd died?'

'It was a shame, him being so young, and such a good doctor.

He was *my* doctor, you know. I went to the funeral but you didn't notice me.'

Annie reddened. That must be where she'd glimpsed her. 'I'm so sorry. I was upset that day and—'

'No need to apologise, my dear. I wish I'd spoken to you but I could see you weren't in any condition.' She patted Annie's arm and offered her some of the fruit cake. Annie shook her head, but not before she noticed the state of Mrs Greenway's hands. Rough, red hands that had been used to hard work.

'The last time I saw you to speak to was a very long time ago,' Mrs Greenway went on. 'You were engaged to be married to one of the footmen from Hatherleigh Hall. A cheeky one at that.'

Annie stared at the woman, goose pimples crawling up her arms.

'Mollie! Of course.' A feeling of shame swept over her. No wonder she hadn't recognised her. An image of the scullery maid scrubbing the pine table at Bonham Place swam in front of her. That girl was slight in frame and health, and she, Annie, had felt sorry for her. And how lucky she was, she'd thought herself at the time, to be engaged to Ferguson, whereas poor Mollie with her leg... Then only a month or so later Gladys had told her the awful news that Mollie had been sacked because she'd got herself in the family way. If Mollie had married the baby's father the child would be about fourteen now.

As though Mollie had read her thoughts, she said, 'I lost the baby and never saw the father again. I loved him but he only wanted a good time. He wasn't there when I needed him. I went back to Mum's and she looked after me when I had the miscarriage.' A shadow crossed Mollie's lovely face.

'But things are better for you now.' Annie bit back a twinge of envy. Mollie was obviously happily married, with a daughter. 'Is your husband—?'

'Gordon died two years ago.' She said it matter-of-factly but her lower lip trembled and her eyes were luminous with tears. 'He wasn't the same man when he came back from the war.'

Impulsively, Annie hugged her. 'I'm so sorry, Mollie. I thought I had my troubles but fate's been very unkind to you.' She gently held Mollie away and looked at her. 'I don't know why I didn't immediately recognise you,' she said. 'You're just as pretty as you always were. It's just that I'm not thinking straight at the moment. But why haven't we bumped into one another before now?'

'I've seen you sometimes in the village, but didn't like to make myself known,' Mollie said, hugging her back. 'I don't go out much. My husband and I chose this house because it was opposite the school and any children we had could walk on their own. I still get tired if I'm on my legs too long.' She looked down at her withered leg which had taken the brunt of the polio and gave Annie a rueful smile.

'What happened after you lost the baby?' Annie said, her heart going out to her. It seemed they had plenty in common.

'I managed to get another job with a much smaller family,' Mollie answered, 'and the cook taught me how to be a professional. I enjoyed it. They were a nice family but they weren't living in the same sort of luxury as the Bonhams. Not that it bothered me. Then the war came and most of the men went to fight. It wasn't the same. I got a job in the grocer's, but it didn't do my leg any good standing on a stone floor all day. I was so lucky meeting Gordon because he was Scottish. He was sent to Norfolk in the war. Anyway, he was a customer. We fell in love and he took me away from all that. But after he died,' her voice shook, 'there's been nobody. It can get quite lonely. But I'm used to it.' She smiled and her face lit up. 'And of course I've got Junie.'

As though on cue, June appeared.

'Mummy, Harry says he'll come and see me tomorrow on his way home from school. Can he come to tea?'

'Of course he can.' Mollie smiled at her daughter. She turned to Annie. 'And I'd like you to come too, Annie.'

'I'd love to, if the snow doesn't get worse.'

June grinned, showing crooked teeth, and ran off.

'But you married the footman from Hatherleigh Hall. What was his name?' Mollie continued as though they'd never been interrupted. 'And went to live in Australia?'

'Ferguson? Yes. We went to Melbourne. But I got homesick and here I am, back in Norfolk.' She bit her lip. 'But Ferguson... we'd only been home a few months and he suddenly announced he was going to New York to live.'

'Someone told me Ferguson Bishop had gone to America but I couldn't believe he'd left you and the children behind. What happened?'

'He said he wanted us all to go, but I didn't want to unsettle the children again. And I'd changed countries once already... I wasn't prepared to do it a second time.'

'And he's still out there?' Mollie said it as though she didn't expect an answer.

'Yes, and he met someone else,' Annie said.

'It's often the case.' Mollie hesitated, looking puzzled. 'So did you meet Dr Townsend in Australia?'

'He was the doctor on the ship we sailed on to Australia. It's a long story. I'll tell you sometime. I admired him straight away. Then he came to England after Ferguson went to America and... we fell in love.'

Mollie nodded as though that was the most probable outcome. 'I saw him a couple of times with my nerves,' she said. 'I thought he was a lovely man. I'd heard some gossip in the village that he was living with someone called Annie, but it was a while before I realised it was you.' She chuckled.

Annie sat quietly, happy to be talking about Alex so naturally, and relieved Mollie hadn't used that horrible term 'living in sin'.

'But there's something else.' Mollie gazed intently at Annie. 'You said you'd upset Harry.'

'Yes,' Annie admitted, chewing her lip. 'Harry wrote to Ferguson and told him Alex had died. So Ferguson thinks he can just come back and pick up the pieces. That's why I was so cross.'

'Good Lord,' Mollie said. 'Isn't life full of complications? But your son doesn't appear to hold any grudge. You saw how he greeted you.'

'I didn't deserve it. I'll tell him how sorry I am.'

'If I were you I would do no such thing.' Mollie's golden-brown eyes focused on her. 'He's all but forgotten it, but when he has time to think he'll realise he mustn't interfere with grown-up affairs. Though I'm sure he did it with the best intentions.'

'I know he did,' Annie said, swallowing the last mouthfuls of tea which had gone cold. 'Oh, Mollie, I can't tell you how happy I am we've found one another. I'd love us to be proper friends. Half the village turned their backs on me when Alex and I moved in together even though a lot of them were his patients. It was only when Kitty was born that they began to talk to me again, and that was mostly about the baby, though I knew they were curious as to where Ferguson was. Well, let them gossip, is what I thought at first. I had all the family I wanted with Alex. But it's so lonely without him.'

Her shoulders slumped and she choked back the tears.

Annie felt Mollie's warm hand on her shoulder and somehow the tiny action comforted her.

'There, there. Don't take on so,' Mollie said. 'Everything will be all right, you'll see. If I can get through it, so can you.'

'Stupid of me,' Annie said, looking up with red-rimmed eyes.

'Cry all you like,' Mollie said. 'You're safe here.'

Annie blew her nose.

'Your sister lives near, doesn't she?' Mollie asked. 'I remember meeting her once at Bonham Place. Harry mentioned Auntie Ethel looks after him sometimes.'

'Yes. She's expecting her second child. And although we're

very close it's still nice to have a friend.' She thought of Adele as she spoke the words. How she'd fought Ferguson for that friendship, until it changed when Ruby swept on the scene. She squashed the seed of bitterness and rose to her feet.

'I'd love to be friends,' Mollie smiled. 'Don't forget you're coming for tea tomorrow. I want to hear the rest of your story.' She set the empty cups and saucers on the tray with a clatter. 'Now let's go and see what those two are up to.'

A week passed and Annie was no closer to seeing a clear path into the future. Did Ferguson suddenly miss his family? Or did he merely see it as a convenience? She wasn't sure whether she cared one way or the other. She'd loved him once, but after the affair with Ruby, he'd broken her trust in him. Yet if it hadn't been for that, she would never have had Harry to help ease the loss of her own little Harry.

And then the miracle. Alex had come to England to find her and she'd fallen in love with him.

A sudden memory tugged at the corners of her mind; the strange feeling she'd had in the hospital having her first baby, that Alex was Frankie's father, not Ferguson. How embarrassed she'd felt because she was a married woman. She'd had to dismiss such ridiculous nonsense. Her lips curved into a smile at the memory, as she tidied her daughter's room. She'd probably loved him ever since then.

Alex had been so hard-working; a wonderful doctor, faithful and reliable, and best of all he loved Frankie and Harry as his own. She knew she shouldn't compare the two men but she couldn't help it. If she took Ferguson back she would feel disloyal to Alex. If she didn't take him back she'd be depriving the children of their natural father. That was what must have been in Harry's mind. That they'd be a family again. He was only a bewildered child and she'd been so angry. She sat on Frankie's bed and closed her eyes in despair.

What about Kitty? Every day she could see Alex in Kitty. The same dark wavy hair and captivating smile. It breaks my heart that she is too young to remember much about her father, Annie thought. She tried to tell her about him every day but if Ferguson came back she wouldn't be able to. Kitty would get confused. And Ferguson didn't even know she had another child. Unless, of course...she bit her lip. Unless...one of the children had told their father about Kitty.

What would you have me do, my darling? she silently asked Alex. But the empty room gave up no answer.

5th March 1930

I asked Ethel for her advice. She's the youngest but she's the wisest. I know I've said it before, but the more I'm with her, the more I know it to be true.

Ethel thinks it would be a mistake. She said he's treated me badly in the past, so what's to stop him doing it again? Well, there's no guarantee, I told her, but if I didn't give him the chance, could I live with myself? She said the decision would have to be mine alone.

The only other person I told was Mollie. She was very doubtful. She doesn't think he'll settle in England after all his travels.

But I keep thinking of Frankie and Harry growing up and getting married and having children of their own. Our grandchildren. Surely I can't deny him the chance to know them. But to have him come back when my heart is breaking for someone I will never see again... Oh, what shall I do? What would be for the best?

I don't suppose I would have heard from him if it hadn't been for the Wall Street crash. He said he has nowhere to go and I doubt he's got any money. Is he just looking for a roof over his head? And someone to look after him now that Margaret has left?

I will write to him tomorrow.

The weeks went by and still she hadn't answered Ferguson's letter. One hour she felt obliged to take him back for the children's sake; the next, her heart dropped to her boots when she thought of all the pain he'd caused her. She wondered if she'd never met Alex whether she would have still felt the same way. Maybe she would have written to Ferguson immediately with relief and happiness that he wanted to come back to her. But if she were honest, she knew he'd killed her love for him long ago.

Every time she imagined Ferguson coming home, walking through the front door of the cottage she and Alex had lived in so joyfully for the few painfully short years, there was such an ache in her belly, such a longing for Alex, that it didn't seem possible she could ever have another man in her house, let alone someone who, by words on a piece of paper, was still her husband.

Letter dated 5th April 1930

Dear Ferguson,

I am sorry things have not turned out well for you.

I have thought a great deal about everything and have come to the conclusion that you and I have been apart too long, and there has been too much between us that can never be repaired. I don't blame you for everything. You wanted excitement and adventure, and although I'm glad now that we went to Australia, all I ever really wanted was for us to be a family together.

I hope you won't be too disappointed with this reply, and I want you to know I always wish the best for you. I am sure that in a few months' time things will look brighter in America. We've been devastated by the crash in England as well. People can't find jobs. There are long queues every day outside the Labour Exchange. One day a poor man begged for some money from me when I was out with Frankie.

You would never be happy in a Norfolk village when you

405

have seen so many different places. You always wanted to travel. I want to stay put. A year or two might go by and then you would leave. I couldn't go through all that again. I've been on my own for getting on two years and am used to it now.

She dipped her pen in the ink, her mouth set in concentration as she tried to think how to finish. In the end she simply wrote:

I will always write to let you know how the children are.
    All the very best,
    Annie

She hesitated. Then carefully added: *Townsend.*

51

Annie got into the habit of visiting Mollie at least once a week before collecting Kitty from Ethel's.

'How do you manage?' Annie asked her one morning, deciding that she knew Mollie well enough by now to ask such a personal question.

'Not too well, really,' came Mollie's answer. 'I get a small widow's pension and I take in some laundry and do a bit of cleaning.'

'Do you mind after being a cook?'

'Needs must,' Mollie sighed. 'The decent cooking jobs require you to live in. You were lucky with Lady Hamilton. And now, with the general state of things, a lot of households can't afford a cook so they're doing their own cooking.'

'This Depression has certainly affected us all,' Annie said. 'I had some bad news yesterday.'

'Oh?'

'Lady Hamilton told me she'd found someone who's willing to work six days. I'm finding it difficult to do five when I don't get home until gone seven. And even then it's not ideal as I have to leave everything ready for Rose to finish. It's a good thing she doesn't do so much entertaining these days else she'd have given me notice long ago.'

'What will you do?' Mollie's eyes were sympathetic.

'I don't know. Cooking's the only thing I've been trained for, but I've made up my mind not to go back into service. As you said once, times are changing. Women want something more than just keeping house and bringing up the children.'

'It's hard to find the right thing when you've got kids.' Mollie nudged the plate of homemade shortcakes nearer to Annie. 'Come on, Annie, have another shortbread. *You* don't have to watch your figure.' Mollie looked down at her own well-covered body and grimaced.

'Maybe half a one,' Annie said. 'They're so delicious. Good enough to sell.'

Good enough to sell.

A sudden image of Melbourne, and the foyer in the Hotel Esplanade, rushed into her head. She remembered how shocked, and yet how full of admiration she'd been when Adele had announced she owned the hotel.

What must it be like to have your own business? she'd thought at the time. So why shouldn't they sell Mollie's cakes? And sandwiches and teas. Alex had left her eight hundred pounds. Her heart began to beat fast. She looked at Mollie.

'Mollie, I've had an idea. Something we could *both* do to earn a living.'

'What's that, love?'

'We'll open a tea room. You could make all the cakes and I'll make soup and sandwiches, and hundreds of cups of tea. It could be especially for ladies. Somewhere for them to go and talk on their own. After all, the men have their working clubs so the women should have their own place to go, too.' The words spilled out in her excitement.

'Oh, Annie, I don't know...' Mollie sounded doubtful. 'You wouldn't get enough customers in Bonham.'

'They wouldn't be just Bonham people,' Annie said, her face alight with excitement. 'It would work so long as we could find premises at a reasonable rent. It needs to be somewhere in the high street that could easily be turned into a tea room.'

'It'll be expensive in the high street,' Mollie said. 'And I've not seen any empty shops lately.'

'Then we must look at any possibility.' Annie's brain began to race with ideas. 'We'd need a kitchen behind and a preparation area. And have a garden so we can set up tables outside. People will come from Bridgewater and Bonham and some of the other villages. I'm sure word would soon get around. It will be something different. Better than gossiping in the butcher's.' She turned to her friend, her eyes sparkling like sapphires. 'So what do you think?'

'I think you should allow the men in as well,' Mollie said. 'Their money is as good as anyone else's, and you'd be banning half the population if you didn't let them in. It wouldn't be sensible in these times.'

'You're right.' Annie looked at her friend. 'But I want to make it really welcoming and attractive, so the ladies feel comfortable and want to stay as long as they like.'

'Sounds perfect,' Mollie said. 'I'd love to put some money in but I don't have any spare from Gordon's pension.' She sounded genuinely disappointed. '*You* could do it,' she added, smiling at Annie with affection. 'You're that determined.'

'Not on my own, I can't.'

'Yes, you can,' Mollie said. Annie opened her mouth to argue but Mollie went on. 'It has to be *your* business, but I'll help. If you think my cakes are good enough, of course.'

'Oh, yes, they're definitely good enough.' Annie reached over and picked up half a buttered scone. 'These are light as feathers. They'll go like...well, like hot cakes.'

The two women laughed.

'What will you call it?' Mollie said.

'Something simple.'

'With Annie in the name. So they know it's you.' Mollie looked across the table at her friend and chuckled. 'What about Annie's Tea Rooms?'

Annie's Tea Rooms. Yes, it had a good ring to it. Then she laughed out loud. Her maiden name was Annie Ring.

Ethel beamed and clapped her hands when Annie told her what she was planning.

'I can make sandwiches at home, or anything else you want,' Ethel said, 'though I don't suppose you'll be set up until after the baby's born.' She patted her stomach tenderly. 'It will be lovely to have something to do which will fit in with the baby.'

Annie pressed her sister's hand with affection. 'I hoped you'd say you'd like to be part of it, even though I know the new baby will keep you busy.' She smiled delightedly. 'Of course I'll pay you the proper rate. And a bit extra.'

'I don't want paying for my time. Just the ingredients.'

Annie held up the flat of her hand. 'Then I shan't let you help,' she said.

'Well, if you put it like that.'

They burst out laughing.

It was harder finding suitable premises than Annie had envisioned. Bonham had a long, winding high street but all the shops had been there ever since Annie could remember. The only possible one was the hardware shop where the owner had recently moved to smaller premises a hundred yards along. He seemed to have taken the only shop available and his old shop was too big and the rent too expensive. On the fourth day, as she trudged up and down the high street wondering if she'd missed something, she began to feel disheartened. Maybe it was a foolish idea and this was a sign that she shouldn't pursue it. But no. She wanted the tea room more than ever. Annie set her mouth in a determined line and turned to go home.

Walking by the post office she suddenly remembered she had a letter for Ruby in her bag. Annie sighed. Her younger sister worried her sick. Ruby rarely wrote and when she did, she never answered Annie's questions, except to say she was doing all right.

'The usual stamp for Australia, Mrs Townsend?' Mr Lincoln enquired.

'Yes, please,' Annie said, handing him the envelope. She glanced idly around and spotted a notice pinned on a door marked Private. WORK IN PROGRESS. PLEASE DO NOT ENTER.

'Are you having your house decorated?' Annie couldn't help asking.

'Just tidying up a couple of rooms,' Mr Lincoln said, as he licked the stamp. 'It used to be a store room for the post office, but we're going to have to rent it out. The post office don't pay its way nowadays.'

'Who's going to take it over?' Annie's heart pounded.

'Oh, I haven't advertised it yet.' Mr Lincoln scratched his beard and looked at her with shrewd eyes. 'Why, d'ya know anyone who might be interested?'

'I do,' Annie smiled. '*I'm* interested.'

'You?' Mr Lincoln's mouth remained open.

'Yes. I'm looking for somewhere to have a tea room. It would be perfect at the back of the post office. Your customers could post their letters and parcels and then walk through to the tea room and put their feet up for a while and have a natter.'

Mr Lincoln gave her a piercing glance, then studied his watch. He seemed to make a decision. Reaching for the blind, he pulled it down firmly so it showed the CLOSED sign, and came out from behind the counter.

'Follow me. See what you think.'

Annie stepped through the door to a good-sized room which appeared to be an extension to the main building, with French windows opening on to the garden. Two men in overalls were decorating the room; one on a ladder painting the ceiling, the other dipping his brush into a tin of cream paint.

'The important thing is, I'll need use of a kitchen,' Annie said, turning to Mr Lincoln, trying to quell the rush of excitement.

'That can easily be arranged.'

Mr Lincoln lit his pipe. He pulled on it a few times and the aroma of tobacco filled Annie's nostrils, reminding her of her father. For the first time since he'd died, her eyes didn't fill with tears. What would he think of her plan? She forced herself to concentrate on what Mr Lincoln was saying. This was important.

'The wife don't do much cooking as she's laid up permanent, so you can use our kitchen,' Mr Lincoln went on. 'Our daughter comes every day with our dinner so we'd only be making our breakfast and a cup of tea here and there. And seeing as you want a tea shop, that shouldn't be no problem.' He chuckled at his little joke.

Her pulse racing, Annie smiled back. It all seemed to be fitting in.

'There's another room through here.' Mr Lincoln shuffled over and opened a door which led to a rather gloomy scullery. 'I could put a big table in here so's you've got somewhere to prepare the trays, an' all. And fix some better lighting. The kitchen's through there,' he gestured, 'if you want to put your head inside.'

The kitchen was small and basic but spotlessly clean. It would do. Oh, yes, it would definitely do. After all, Mollie and Ethel were going to make cakes and sandwiches in their own kitchens, so it left plenty of room to prepare soups and drinks.

'I think it would work,' she told Mr Lincoln, who was watching her with open curiosity. 'May I look at the garden? I was hoping to find somewhere I could put a few tables out in the summer.'

'Good idea,' he said, unbolting the back door.

The garden was disappointingly small, but Annie guessed there was space to set out four or five tables. It was better than nothing. She only hesitated a moment.

'Mr Lincoln,' she took a deep breath, 'I'd really like to rent the rooms. How much are you asking?'

'Well, now, let's see.' He pondered a minute and Annie thought she would go mad with impatience. 'What about ten bob a week?'

It was half what she was prepared to pay. 'Are you sure?'

'Quite sure. Especially if you might have a spot of soup left over for the missus sometimes.'

'She'd be welcome to a bowl anytime...and you, too, of course,' Annie laughed. 'When might the room be ready?'

'I'll have it all ship-shape in three weeks. That suit?'

'It would suit perfectly,' Annie said. 'And may I put up a sign in your front window so people know there's a tea room at the back?'

'You can do that, and you can put one outside at the back so when folk are sitting in the garden they can see it. Remind them to come back,' he grinned. 'But it won't take long before the whole village finds out you're running a tea room, so don't you fear. I'll tell everyone who comes in.'

'Thank you very much, Mr Lincoln.'

'We'll shake hands on it then.' He put out a work-worn, freckled hand and Annie grasped it.

'Afternoon, Mrs Townsend,' the butcher said cheerfully, a fortnight later, as Annie stepped through the door. Her shoes, damp from her walk, picked up the sawdust but she was too excited to notice. 'What can I get you today?'

'Some liver and sausages, please.' Annie smiled.

Now, waiting for Mr White to fill her order she glanced around the shop and noticed how few pieces of meat were displayed in the window. The Depression was lasting longer than people were expecting. Maybe a tea shop was a luxury to most people in Bonham, and if things got worse they might tighten their belts even further. Which would mean no coffees and teas and lunches out. Her business would be ruined before she'd hardly got started. Ribbons of doubt taunted her. Was she really doing the right thing?

The smell of the shop was making her feel sick. She noticed

the blood which had soaked into the white cloth beneath the meat display. A sudden image flashed though her mind of her first night with Ferguson at that awful inn. Her face flushing with embarrassment as though Mr White could read her thoughts, she fumbled in her basket for her purse.

'Two shillings and threepence.' Mr White wrapped the meat and laid it on the counter. His apron, too, was smeared with blood stains. She swallowed hard as she handed him the coins.

'You look after yourself, love,' he called as she went to the door. 'I'll be sure to remind the missus when the tea shop opens.'

'Thank you, Mr White,' she said, as she turned and smiled at him. 'Gentlemen are allowed as well, you know.'

52

Annie opened her eyes, wondering for an instant why today was different. She hadn't slept well except for the last two hours when she'd finally succumbed, just when she'd wanted to be up extra early. Still, the clock only showed five minutes to six, and it was ten minutes fast. She lay there for a full minute, almost happy, as she remembered today was the first day of Annie's Tea Rooms. Whatever would Alex say if he could see her now? She pictured him smiling and giving her words of encouragement among the kisses. Dearest Alex. Maybe he could see her. Maybe he knew how important today of all days would be and was watching over her.

Well, it's no use lying here, she thought, leaping out of bed. There's work to be done.

Frankie had promised to make the children's breakfast and see that Harry had his homework in his school bag. Her daughter had even volunteered to drop Kitty off at Ethel's.

'I want to go to the tea room place,' Kitty said, swinging one leg and then the other backwards and forwards. 'I can help, too.'

'No, darling, not today,' Annie said, looking down at the little girl with affection. 'When Mummy's used to it you can come. But there's so much new for me to learn, I need to give it all my attention. And you've got to go to school.'

'Can I go tomorrow?' Kitty persisted.

'Maybe Saturday when there's no school.'

Mr Lincoln had told her to knock hard on the door so he could let her in early, but he opened the door before her hand was even on the knocker.

'I thought I'd better be around in case you wanted any help,' he said. 'I think one of the tables should be moved closer to the window so's they can see the garden. But I haven't done anything until you give me the say-so.'

'Good idea,' Annie said, smiling at him. She and Mollie had already set up the tables the evening before, so all she had to do was make sure everything was ready in the preparation room for the orders to be filled.

'I got here as soon as I could,' Mollie said breathlessly, just after nine o'clock, as she plonked two large covered baskets on the table. She took off her jacket and hung it on one of the hooks behind the kitchen door. 'Thank goodness Junie can just walk over the road to school. I never realised how handy that would be.'

'I smell cakes,' Annie laughed as she removed one of the cloths and peeped in. 'Mmm. They look good.'

'What would you like me to do?' Mollie scrutinised Annie. 'Are you all right? You look washed out.'

'I had a bad night,' Annie said. 'All the excitement, I expect.' She paused. 'Oh, Mollie, do you think it will be all right? Do you think people will come? Especially the women, which is really what I'm aiming for.'

'As I said, a man's money is as good as a woman's.' Mollie laughed. 'But it will be nice for women to have a place where they can chat while their men are at work.'

They looked around the tea room, checking every detail. There were doilies on the cake stands, ready for Mollie to arrange the cakes, and coffee pots and tea pots set out alongside the row of fine bone china cups and saucers decorated with flowers which Annie had insisted upon. 'I want the ladies to feel spoilt,' she'd explained

416

to Ethel and Mollie when they'd pointed out how much cheaper ordinary white ones would be.

As if on cue, two older women stepped heavily through the door. Annie's heart dropped. Her first customers, Mrs Lewis and Mrs Jones. Why did it have to be them? Her mind flew back to when Ferguson had first left her.

She'd gone into the grocer's one afternoon to buy some flour and heard her name spoken loud and clear.

'That Annie Bishop can't even keep 'er 'usband. 'E's gone to America,' Mrs Jones said triumphantly.

'There's talk they got into debt and the Australian government sent them packing,' said her friend, Mrs Lewis.

'That's the last she'll see of 'im, you mark my words.'

'Seems a shame though, with three young'uns to keep.'

'Good afternoon, Mrs Lewis – Mrs Jones,' Annie had interrupted, pasting a smile on her face.

Both women had swung round, Mrs Lewis's face red with embarrassment.

Now, the two very same women were in her tea room on her first morning, gazing at Annie, hesitating, but seeming to overcome any awkwardness by the enticing smell of coffee and cakes.

'Good morning, dear,' Mrs Jones said with a wide smile, show-ing yellowing, fiercely crossed teeth, her eyes darting over to the counter where the cakes were set out. 'Are we your first customers?'

Annie caught Mollie's eye, beseeching her to take over.

'Would you like the table by the window so you can see the garden?' Mollie said quickly.

'That would suit very well,' said Mrs Jones.

Annie nodded to the women and disappeared into the preparation room.

'Five coffees and one tea, and two egg custards and a whole Bakewell tart cut into slices,' Mollie called from the dividing door. She was smiling from ear to ear.

That must mean we have more customers, Annie thought happily, the two women almost forgotten. She set to work with the order, listening to the sounds of chatter as she set up the trays. Mollie kept her busy for the next hour until she put her head round the door.

'Why not change over, Annie? The customers keep asking for you. It's you they've come to see.'

'More likely for another gossip,' Annie said, but she smiled as she spoke the words. The tea room was going to be a success. She was sure of it. She glanced round to make certain it was neat and tidy before Mollie took over, changed her apron to a white frilly one, and stepped into her tea room. It was buzzing. There were at least a dozen people already drinking and eating. Mrs Jones and Mrs Lewis were still there, their empty cups and plates in front of them, their jaws working hard. Annie bit her lip as she walked over to where a man was reading a newspaper, obviously waiting to be served. She was not going to let the likes of those two women upset her anymore. She had her own business. She was independent. She could cope with anything.

She stood, her pencil poised, her mind still on the two gossips. A spicy smell of cologne filled her nostrils. Oh, it couldn't be. Don't let it be. She could only see the top of the man's head behind his newspaper but she knew. Her hand trembled and her pencil slipped from her fingers on to the wooden floor as she grabbed the edge of his table.

The man put down his paper and bent to pick it up. He handed it to her with a crooked, somewhat flirtatious smile.

'Annie!' His smile evaporated. 'What a surprise.'

She could have walked past him in the street without realising. The change was even more noticeable than two years ago. It wasn't just his coat bursting over his stomach, or the heavy jowl. Or even the grey of his skin. No, she thought, the greatest change was his eyes. The extra fat seemed to be pushing his eyes forward, making them bulge slightly. Eyes that were once the colour of a summer sky were now faded, with puffy folds of skin under them. She shook her head, trying to remember how he used to look. She tried to picture his hair – like ripened corn, she would tell him. The same as Frankie's. Now it was dull and peppered with grey. She took a deep breath.

'Why are you here?' It was an accusation.

'I've come back.'

'No!' The word escaped Annie's lips before she could stop herself. Several heads turned in their direction. Mrs Jones and Mrs Lewis stopped talking and cocked their heads in her direction but Annie was barely aware of them. 'Didn't you get my letter?' she asked in a low tone.

'What letter?' Ferguson sounded puzzled. 'You never answered mine.'

'I wrote to you.'

Ferguson shook his head. 'I never got it. I waited and waited for a reply, and then I thought it must have got lost.' He hesitated. 'I telephoned twice but there was no answer.'

Is he telling the truth?

'How did you know my number?'

'I took it down that time I came to see you,' Ferguson said. 'Thought it might come in handy one day.' He gave his old captivating smile.

Annie was silent.

'What did you say in the letter?' Ferguson didn't sound quite so confident.

'I told you not to come,' Annie said, so softly she wasn't sure he'd heard.

'Annie, you didn't mean it. You couldn't have.' His face drained as she remained silent. Time hung between them and still she hadn't moved. 'Please, Annie.' He smiled again.

She realised whatever she'd written would have made no

difference. The tea room had suddenly gone quiet, as though it, too, were waiting for her reply. Her heart pounded in her throat. She tried to compose herself.

'We need to talk in private,' she hissed.

'Can I come to the house after you finish here?' he said, in a tone almost humble.

She nodded, though she felt like screaming. 'I'll bring you a cup of tea so it doesn't look odd.'

'That's what I came in for,' Ferguson said, looking at her intently. Under his breath he muttered, 'I honestly had no idea you worked here. I wouldn't want to get you into trouble.' He shifted his chair a little as though to get a better view of the room. 'Seems a popular place. Has it been here long?'

She gave him a swift glance. He was serious. *He doesn't realise I'm the owner.*

Annie turned her face so he couldn't see her flush of annoyance, as though he'd somehow caught her out. Maybe it's for the best that he doesn't know I own the tea room, she thought. But her name was as clear as anything in the post office window.

'It opened today,' she told him, her hands shaking so much she had to fold them behind her back.

'Well I never.' The faded blue eyes looked into hers. 'I wondered if I might bump into you. I didn't think it would be here though.' He patted her arm.

'I'll get your tea.'

She wended her way among the tables, trying to ignore the curious glances. She didn't have to turn round to know the customers would be staring at Ferguson, wondering who he was, thinking he looked vaguely familiar, and why the new owner suddenly appeared so nervous. The chatter started up again as Annie went through the door to where Mollie was putting the second kettle on the stove to boil.

'He's come back!' Annie almost choked on the words.

'Who?' Mollie asked. She turned round and saw Annie's face. 'What on earth's the matter? You look as though you've seen a ghost.

'You're not far wrong. It's Ferguson. He's over in the right-hand corner, large as life. I can't believe it.'

'Good Lord,' Mollie said, her eyes wide. 'What are you going to do?'

'What can I do? I have to finish here and then go home. He doesn't have a clue it's my tea room. He thinks I just work here as a waitress.'

'Just be careful, that's all. What you tell him, I mean.'

'I know,' Annie said. She quickly poured a cup of tea, paused, then placed two cherry scones on a plate. Ferguson had always had a good appetite.

'What time will you finish?' Ferguson looked at his watch as she set the cup of tea and scones in front of him.

'It depends,' she said, feeling resentful that he was playing his old tricks. How could she know what time she'd finish?

'Well, approximately.'

'I don't know,' she said. 'It depends upon how busy the afternoon is and how much clearing up we have to do. I'll be home as soon as I can.'

'I'll wait at Ma and Pa's,' Ferguson said. 'I haven't seen them yet.'

There didn't seem any point in warning him his parents were wasting away with broken hearts.

'Yes, you do that. And Ferguson—' Annie bit her lip, 'please don't come before six o'clock.'

53

Before Annie had written the letter telling Ferguson not to come she had gone over and over what Ferguson was asking her.

There had been all kinds of things to consider. Practicalities, for one thing. She hadn't exaggerated about the effect of the Wall Street crash in England. There would be an extra mouth to feed, at least for a while, as she couldn't see Ferguson getting a job that easily when others who had always lived in the area were having such difficulty.

A fortnight ago she'd invited Ethel and Johnnie and Eleanor to supper and given Johnnie the letter from Ferguson to read. Frankie was having tea with one of her school friends and Harry was upstairs in bed with a cold, so at least the older children wouldn't hear what needed to be a private conversation.

'What about Camellia House?' Johnnie had asked, taking off his glasses and putting the letter back into its envelope. 'Ferguson's still your husband. He might be able to claim half as his.'

'Never,' Annie answered. 'It's in my name only.'

'I think you'd better see a solicitor,' Johnnie warned her. 'You need to know if you died before him he couldn't claim it, especially if he was back living in England.'

It hadn't occurred to her that Ferguson could do such a thing. They'd lost all their nest egg in Melbourne through his gambling. She pulled her mouth in a determined line.

'I can't risk him having his hands on the house,' she said.

'It's for the children when I've gone.'

'You can probably have it put in a trust for them,' Johnnie told her. 'I think there are ways. But you should find out where you stand, and what you can do to safeguard the house, whether you have Ferguson back or not.'

'I think Alex would have made sure nothing like that could happen,' Annie said. 'He was always wary of Ferguson's ambitions, even though he'd gone to America.'

'It's not just the house.' Ethel helped Annie to collect the empty plates together. She fastened her eyes on Annie and lowered her voice. 'There's Kitty. How's he going to feel about her?'

Kitty immediately called out, 'Why did Auntie Ethel say my name?'

'We're just talking about grown-up things, darling. But it's time you put Teddy to bed. He's tired and so are you.' Annie looked across the table at her daughter, who was playing with the salt and pepper pots, and humming a tune.

Annie swallowed to dislodge the lump in her throat. Ferguson wouldn't want to bring up another man's child. And if she died, Ethel and Johnnie were godparents to all three children. Then she thought of Harry. Wasn't she already bringing up Ferguson's child? Her heart began to pump so hard it was making her dizzy.

But what made her change her mind a dozen times was that Ferguson was Frankie and Harry's father. And she alone had the power to let him see his children every day, or not. It had taken weeks and months of indecision, until at last she'd made up her mind to leave things as they were. And she'd written to tell him so.

But now he was here without invitation, today of all days, on the opening of her tea room. She had the sudden thought that if it proved successful it was a steady income Ferguson might be able to claim part of. She shook her head in despair. It was all so complicated.

The clock had struck six ten minutes ago. Every nerve in her body was alert for the knock at her door, but when it sounded she almost jumped from her skin.

He was here.

She walked slowly to the door and opened it. There he was, smiling, waiting to be asked in. Her stomach churned as she showed him into the front room. Once again, he took Alex's chair.

She must get it over with.

But as though he suspected she was about to tell him things he would rather not hear, he began to tell her about his impossible life in New York since the Wall Street crash, and even though he'd lived with Margaret he'd never forgotten Annie, his wife.

'Ferguson,' Annie finally managed to interrupt him, 'you need to know a few things about me. I'm not the same person I was when we got married.'

'Of course you're not,' Ferguson smiled. 'None of us are. You only have to look at *me*.' He gave a chuckle. 'But *you* haven't changed at all.'

'I don't mean a physical change.'

'Well, I'm sorry you've had to go back to waitress work,' Ferguson said, 'especially as you're such a good cook. It seems a bit of a waste to me.'

'I'm not just a waitress in the tea room,' she started. 'I'm—'

'Don't tell me you're the manageress?' He threw her a look as though he couldn't believe she might have risen so high. 'Is that what you're saying? Well, didn't I say I always want us to better ourselves?' He laughed. 'And so you have.'

'Yes, you did say that.' *Go on, Annie, tell him.* 'But I'm not the manageress.'

'Ah,' Ferguson leaned back. 'I didn't think so, but—'

'I own the tea room.'

'You *own* it?' Ferguson's tone was one of amazement. 'How can you own it?'

'Quite easily. It's my tea room.'

'I don't believe it.' Ferguson's eyes almost popped from his head. He took out a handkerchief and wiped his forehead. 'Where did you get the money to set it up?'

It was the old Ferguson again, questioning her as he would have about Adele.

'That's not the point.' Annie was annoyed with herself after Mollie had warned her not to say too much. 'The point is I have to make a living and it has to work round the children and their school hours. Ethel helps me.' She paused. 'Do you remember Mollie? The kitchen maid at Bonham Place who'd had polio?'

'Vaguely,' Ferguson said, his brows drawn together.

'Well, she's a widow with a daughter, and she's making most of the cakes for the tea room.'

'How did you come across her?'

'It's a long story.'

'Well, it's wonderful that you have your own business,' Ferguson said, after a few moments. It sounded a little forced, as though he was trying to assimilate all the information and was not quite sure how to respond. 'And if you'll have me back I can help you. I'd be glad to do anything in the tea room. Don't forget, waiting on tables is my speciality.' He chuckled nervously. 'So you only have to ask.'

Here it was. The words she knew he'd say. She gazed at him, her eyes never wavering. She would never be able to make him understand.

'Ferguson,' she said firmly. 'The business is mine. I pay Ethel and Mollie. I'm happy they're working for me. Mollie's become like family. And I'm grateful for your offer, Ferguson, don't think I'm not. But it wouldn't work. I'm independent now. And I want to keep it that way.'

Ferguson heaved himself from the chair. 'Annie, you can't mean that. You're a woman. You need a man to do jobs, to help with the accounts—' He suddenly flushed red. 'Oh, I know you don't think I'm any good with money, but I've changed. I don't gamble

425

anymore. I learned a hard lesson when we had to leave Melbourne. You do believe me, don't you?' He kneeled awkwardly by the side of her chair. 'Annie,' he gazed up at her, his eyes pleading. 'Annie,' he repeated softly, 'please give me another chance.'

'I—'

'You don't trust me, do you?' he said. 'Go on. Tell me the truth.'

'Not really, no, I don't. You've let me down too often. That's why I told you not to come back. You'll try to take over, and I won't have it.'

'I promise I won't. The tea room is yours. Of course it is. I won't interfere. What can I do to make you feel safe?'

Annie looked down at him. He suddenly looked younger, almost as he had when she'd first met him. Her heart ached with the memory.

As though he'd read her mind, he said, 'We loved one another once. I still do. Let me prove it to you.' He caught hold of her hand but she gently pulled it away.

'Ferguson, I can't continue this conversation. I have to go and collect the children from Ethel's.'

'We'll go and see a solicitor. Tell him I have nothing to do with the tea room – financially, that is, though you know I'll always help you if you ask – or,' he looked round the room, 'your house. I'll sign anything you want, if that will make you happy.'

She didn't want to hear any more. It was too new, too much to think about. She needed time. And she'd still not told him about Kitty.

'Would you like to walk to Ethel's with me?' she managed to ask, knowing it couldn't be put off a moment longer. 'The children will have finished their tea by now.'

'I'd like that very much,' he said, smiling at her.

She followed him out to the hall to collect his coat. Ferguson in her house – not Alex. How could she bear it?

She watched as he thrust his arms into the coat sleeves and

buttoned it up, wound a scarf around his neck, and with a quick glance in the hall mirror, straightened his cap.

Her heart contracted. She would never regret her decision to live with Alex as his wife. Her only regret was that they could never marry. But forget him? Not for a moment. Never. And if his face grew dimmer with the passing years...as Alex once said...there was always Kitty.

As she closed the front door behind her she couldn't help smiling at the thought of her precocious daughter. Ferguson stood watching her and smiled back, and she knew he thought she was smiling at him. Well, there was no need to make any decision right away. She would take it a day at a time. Ferguson crooked his arm, and hesitating, but only for a second or two, she stepped nearer to him and took it.

Juliet's Story

Kingston-upon-Thames, July 2005

It's Juliet's chance of a lifetime and however crazy the idea, she's going to grab it with both hands. An ex-client has offered to run Juliet's business to give her the freedom and time to sail to Australia to trace her emigrant grandparents' story back in 1913. But Juliet has a secret buried in her heart that only her late grandmother, Annie, knew.

There's a man Juliet loves more than life itself. And she's determined to find him. Her only clue is that he travelled to Sydney, but that was thirty years ago when she was just sixteen.

But when she boards the *Alexandria* at Tilbury she doesn't count on meeting the enigmatic Jack Delaney, and definitely not falling in love with him. Could his strange behaviour mean he, too, is carrying secrets?

And then an unexpected encounter knocks Juliet off her feet.

One man with eyes she's never forgotten.

Acknowledgements

There are many people who have contributed to *Annie's Story*, but here are the ones who probably had the most impact.

Carole Ann Barnes – my dear sister. She was a great companion and sounding board when we travelled to Australia so I could a) track down our grandparents' whereabouts in Melbourne and Sydney and b) gather material for *Annie's Story*, and Book 2: *Juliet's Story* – both mainly set in Australia. I discovered so many missing fragments from our grandparents' lives, and even found the Hotel Esplanade at St Kilda where Pop worked as head waiter when they first arrived. In 2010 it was a rather shabby pub, but it would have been a gracious Victorian building, only 35 years old, in my grandfather's time.

Jean Potter – my father's cousin and therefore my second cousin. My grandmother and Jean's mother were sisters so Jean knew a family secret which none of us had any idea about. After a bit of pumping she let me in on it. With some adapting it was perfect for one of my plots. This is the sort of thing we novelists adore!

Barry York – I Googled the *Orsova*, the ship my grandparents sailed on, and Barry's name came up. Barry is a historian, journalist and writer, and on his website was a tantalising extract from the diary of Amelia Duckles who, with her husband and young daughter, had made exactly the same journey in 1912 as my grandparents made the following year on the same ship. Barry passed me the name of Amelia Duckles' great-niece, Carol Arnold.

Carol Arnold – a stained-glass artist in Bristol. Carol was equally as excited as I was with the contact and she knocked my socks off when she asked if I would like a copy of her great-aunt's diary of the entire voyage to Australia! I couldn't believe it. It duly arrived in the post a few days later. The writing looked exactly like my grandmother's. What a thrill to read the diary giving me little snippets I could never have unearthed. Talk about trusting strangers, Carol. I am eternally grateful. She and I have since met and spent a wonderful day together in Bristol.

Geoff Brand – an Aussie who has a bookshop called Ulverston Books (they are books which are out of print). He used to watch the *Orsova* come into Railway Pier, Melbourne (from England) when he was a boy in the fifties. I asked if he could come up with some memories and he kindly jotted down lots of helpful details for the novel.

Edwin Stanton – my father-in-law. A razor-sharp mind with a bottomless pit of information on the machinations of people 'above and below stairs', as he worked as a butler in some of the top country houses in Britain, including the spectacular neo-classical mansion, Kedleston Hall. Auberon Waugh wanted to write his biography but Edwin wasn't having it. Discretion was always the key word in those days. Luckily, I was able to complete the first draft of *Annie's Story* before he died three weeks short of 101. Oh, and he gave me permission to use his name for my butler in *Annie's Story*.

Malcolm Davidson – my tutor at Tunbridge Wells Adult Education Centre. He taught scriptwriting which was the only writing course that year so I grabbed it. At the time I was writing short stories and articles but had An Idea for a novel. Malcolm was a great tutor with a wicked dry humour. Turned out he was one of the team writing for the American sit-com, The Golden Girls, in the seventies, which happened to be my favourite comedy. At the end of the course it was Malcolm who encouraged me to write this novel.

The Romantic Novelists' Association – An amazing bevy of romantic writers who encouraged me from the first day I joined. I've made so many lovely friends there.

The Historical Novel Society – I'm a new member but was warmly welcomed at their conference last year. It's an interesting mix of authors and readers from all over the world.

Alison Morton – the best critique writing partner and friend a writer could have. We've known one another for 25 years, but for the first 20 as being entrepreneurs – she with her translation company and me with my estate agency chain. Neither of us had any idea we'd just completed the first draft of our first novel until we had a more personal chat one day. We bravely swapped our babies – I mean, our manuscripts – even though we write in completely different genres. *Annie's Story* is all the better for her incredible eye on the big picture as well as the tiny detail. Her red pen had a ball, and still does! I can't wait to get my own back for her fourth novel in her Roma Nova series! We call it 'brutal love'. Heartfelt thanks, Alison.

And last but not least, Helen Hart and her fantastic team at *SilverWood*, together with their talented designer who (with permission) used a photograph of the actual ship, the *Orsova*, on the beautiful front cover. What a heart-warming surprise.

Lightning Source UK Ltd.
Milton Keynes UK
UKOW04f0612200315

248169UK00002B/45/P